THE BEST OF EDMOND HAMILTON

D1617536

THE BEST OF EDMOND HAMILTON

Edited and with an Introduction by
Leigh Brackett

an imprint of

MANOR

Rockville, Maryland

ISBN: 978-1-60450-489-7

www.PhoenixPick.com

Free Ebooks Every Month. Sign up Now.

Published by Phoenix Pick
an imprint of Arc Manor
P. O. Box 10339
Rockville, MD 20849-0339
www.ArcManor.com

In Memory of Farnsworth Wright

♈

ACKNOWLEDGMENTS

Contents

Fifty Years of Wonder[1]

When it was decided that Ballantine was going to do a *Best of Edmond Hamilton* and that I was going to edit it, Ed allowed as how after nearly thirty years of being married to him I was probably better qualified than most, having *read* more Hamilton stories, and he gave me only one word of advice concerning the introduction I was to write.

"Years ago," he said, "a young reader wrote to me, saying that if he had his way there would be a golden statue of Edmond Hamilton in every city, and that each of those golden statues would be garlanded with roses. I said at the time that that was all I had ever wanted from my readers...not praise, just good honest criticism. And that is all I want from you."

Gazing into the middle distance, he added thoughtfully, "You should also bear in mind that I am going to edit a *Best of You...*"

So, getting briskly to it...

Edmond Hamilton's remarkable career spans half a century, and is still going strong. This says much for his staying power. It says even more for his ability to give the readers what they want in 1976 as well as he did in 1926. The world has changed in five decades, so much so that it is hardly the same planet. Yet Hamilton has managed, not only to keep abreast of the changes, but to stay a couple of jumps ahead of them.

He was a child prodigy, but that does not seem to have affected his boyhood materially. He looks back on it as an active and happy time, full of the normal fun and scrapes and pummellings. Only one thing set him apart from his playmates. He read, everything he could get his hands on,

---

1   Introduction to the original Ballantine edition published in 1977.

and especially anything that was fantastic or science fictional. He was in college at fourteen and out again three years later, leaving his professors to wonder why a kid with a genius IQ didn't do better at his studies. He was just too busy reading, and dreaming.

He had planned to be an electrical engineer. But when the crunch came, he knew what he really wanted to be, what he *had* to be, and that was a writer of fiction—specifically, of science fiction.

His first story, "The Monster-God of Mamurth," appeared in the August 1926 issue of *Weird Tales,* and it's as good a yarn now as it was then, foreshadowing what was to become Hamilton's trademark for many years: the action-adventure story, strong on suspense and atmosphere, spiced with a delight in the alien and the strange.

Having sold that all-important first story, Hamilton sold the next forty without even a request for revision. When the forty-first came back with a polite suggestion that some changes might be in order, he was outraged. But after a few days he managed to swallow his pride and see that there was a good reason for the changes, and he made them—thus crossing the divide that forever separates the gifted amateur from the professional.

You might suppose that Hamilton waxed rich and fat on the proceeds of those forty quick sales, that he indulged himself in Stutz Bearcats and mink-lined polo coats. Far from it. Things are better now, but in those days the going price for a science-fiction story, in the very few and very small magazines that published them, was around thirty dollars, generally on publication, which could be a year or more after acceptance. And even then it was sometimes necessary to catch up with the publisher, knock him down, and sit on him until he signed the check. Science fiction then was written for love, or because of mental imbalance, but not for money.

During the 20s and 30s the "mad scientist" story was very popular, and Hamilton wrote a number of them, notably "The Man Who Evolved," which appeared in the old Gernsback *Wonder Stories* in April of 1931, and "Fessenden's Worlds," in *Weird Tales* for April 1937. The first carries the question of man's future evolution to its logical and quite chilling conclusion; the story is also a fine example of Hamilton's skill in encapsulating an enormous theme into the neat and perfect compass of a short story. The second, a classic which has been translated into almost every language—including Tamil and Tagalog—is a brilliantly cruel little analogue which leaves the reader thinking, and thinking again. Here too the theme is condensed into a rapier point more piercing than is possible with any novel.

But Hamilton was writing other things as well, stories which earned him the nickname of World-Wrecker, or World-Saver. He was an innovator from the first, and let it be said that he did not think small. In a day when science fiction was concerned chiefly with laboratories and test tubes, he wanted the stars. And he got them. His Interstellar Patrol stories set the pattern for the many others that followed later on. He invented the spacesuit. He was the first to take a man *outside* a spaceship, for what we now call a "space walk." He wrote about the "great booming suns of outer space"—and if they don't boom, they by God ought to!—and the readers loved it. Hamilton more than anybody opened up the horizons of science fiction, taking it out beyond Earth, out beyond the solar system, out to the farthest star, and still outward and onward to other galaxies.

"Thundering Worlds" is in this tradition. Style and characterization are less important here than the central idea, which might be summed up as nine planets in search of a sun. High adventure, heroism, and great storytelling.

He was an innovator also in the realm of ideas. A born bibliophile, his reading was not restricted to fiction of any sort, but roved over all the world's treasure of literature, history, and philosophy, and he was not above having Big Thinks, though he seldom waved them at people.

He became irritated with the stereotypical rendering of Earthmen as heroes with a divine right to conquer other planets, which were always inhabited by stereotypical nasty monsters. "A Conquest of Two Worlds," which appeared in Gernsback's *Wonder Stories* in February of 1932, was a landmark story that made a profound impression on its readers. In a remarkably realistic, bitter, and downbeat fashion, it questioned the philosophy of the "Earthman's burden" and the rightness of territorial wars, and it portrayed the aliens as sympathetic victims of aggression rather than the brainless menaces of the "look-out-they're-coming-over-the-rocks" type of thing which was so common in those days. Atom bombs are tossed about here with rather too much abandon, even assuming small tactical weapons; but then, the happy folk of 1932 had never seen an atom bomb and could only guess at what it might do. This is a technicality, and in no way lessens the power of the story.

At about the same time, Hamilton wrote another short novel on another theme, the first landing of a manned spacecraft on Mars. He wrote it for the same reason. He was fed up with the easy assumptions about spaceflight, which had clever geniuses tinkering up spaceships in their back yards and making incredible voyages with no thought at all for any of the actual problems that would be involved. He was convinced that if spaceflight were ever to be achieved, it would be done only through a massive national effort, requiring enormous expenditure of money and manpower, and he did not believe that manned landings on other worlds would be achieved without danger and loss. He wrote a realistic story of how he thought things would be, and every editor in the business turned it down. Too grim, they said; the readers wouldn't accept it. So the story was tucked away in the files and forgotten. But if an old story is any good it never dies, it only gets rewritten, and more of this later on.

A streak of misanthropy shows through occasionally in some of Hamilton's writings. One feels, in his earlier stories, that he really preferred aliens to humans. In "The Accursed Galaxy" he went even farther than that in offering a really startling explanation of the expanding universe. And he might just be right!

So this was the early Hamilton, prodigal of fresh ideas, pounding out stories of crashing suns and thundering worlds, of nebulae bright and dark and unimaginable menaces from outer space. Sense of wonder? Oh, yes. If his body was forced to inhabit a dull mundane world, his mind was free to wander the universe, and he found there the stuff that myths are made of, heroes and demons, superhuman adventures, beauty and terror.

There were smaller myths, lovely fragile things that were almost completely overlooked by the people who called him World-Wrecker and World-Saver. Perhaps it was because he did his lapidary work in the short-story form, so that it lacked the impact of his novels. It is only in comparatively recent years that Hamilton's true literary talent has come to be recognized.

There is a great dichotomy between Hamilton the novelist and Hamilton the short-story writer. Seldom does an author demonstrate such an ability to be two people, and seldom does one possess the technical mastery over two such different forms. Generally speaking, a writer's mind is geared toward one or the other. A novelist seldom excels in the short story. The writer of short stories tends to lose himself in the complexities of the longer form. It's a matter of how the writer *sees* a story when he tells it to himself in the quiet precincts of his mind. Is it one small luminous brilliant point, the single thrust? Or does it spread wide, with many characters and many fascinating avenues that require time and words for exploration? It's a rare writer who can see stories both ways and be equally expert at developing them.

Hamilton seems to manage this without effort. And not only does the form change, but the content. The novels are big and vigorous and splashy, interstellar adventures on a grand scale. The short stories are cerebral, astonishingly human, and, yes, poetic.

"Child of the Winds," which appeared in *Weird Tales* in May of 1936, is sheer fantasy, a beautiful and graceful tale that leaves the reader with a poignant sense of loss even though the love story involved has come to a happy conclusion—or has it?

Two years later, in July of 1938, *Weird Tales* published what many people consider to be the best of all the Hamilton stories of that period, equalled but not surpassed by anything he has done since. "He That Hath Wings" became an instant classic. It is, simply, the story of a child born with wings, and how that affects him in the time of his growing up, and in the time of his maturity when he falls in love and has to choose between a normal Earthly life and the freedom of the skies. Hamilton's ability to think himself inside the skin of another being, to know what it would feel like to be something other than an ordinary mortal, is nowhere more evident than in this unforgettable tale.

Quite different from these two, both in mood and in theme, is "In the World's Dusk," published in *Weird Tales* in 1936. Hamilton sold a great many stories to *Weird Tales*. The magazine, under the brilliant guidance of Farnsworth Wright, offered a unique market, since there were no arbitrary bans against any type of story so long as it fitted into the general editorial policy. Science fiction, fantasy, the supernatural—anything went, and there were no prescribed limits to a writer's imagination. "In the World's Dusk" could be called a science fantasy, but it is chiefly an exercise in mood. The doom-haunted, somber claustrophobia of this one is worthy of Poe.

"The Man Who Returned" is another one that won't leave you with a smile on your lips. Personally, I have always hated this story, and that's why I've included it. A story has to be good to rouse that much feeling in a reader. The trouble with this one is, it's too damned true.

By contrast, Hamilton wrote an occasional humorous story. Two of the best of these were "The Island of Unreason," a gentle satire which is funny, and "Easy Money," which is funnier; an unashamed farce, this one inspired the Pete Manx series which ran for some time in *Thrilling Wonder Stories* in the late 30s.

After the late 30s, of course, came the early 40s, and the war, and the paper shortage, and the end of the Pulp Era. Some of the science-fiction magazines died outright. The survivors were forced to cut back severely, going bimonthly or quarterly and living on their inventories.

Hamilton was not at first greatly worried about the shrinking market. He volunteered for service, was put in 1B because of a sinus condition, and then was called up only to be caught at the last minute by the "over-38" edict. He kept on trying. He even volunteered for the Merchant Marine, but when he learned that the only rating open to him was that of cook, he decided—mercifully, for the health and well-being of merchant sea-men—to go back to writing.

Because of the dearth of science-fiction magazines, it became neces-sary to turn to other fields in order to keep afloat. He became one of the two or three top writers for *Batman* and *Superman* comics, and this took up much of his time and energy for nearly twenty years. During the 40s, however, he turned out the classic "Star-Kings," which did not see the light for several years, until the market opened up again, and a number of shorter stories. Among the best of these are the O. Henry-ish short-short "Exile," a look at a quaint and not unpleasant postatomic Earth called "Day of Judgment," and one of my own favorites, "Alien Earth." This one seems to have been pretty well overlooked, and I don't know why.

It was inspired by a film which featured some stunning time-lapse photography of how plants grow, and the revelation of what actually goes on—these nice pretty innocent green things do in fact wage as fierce and savage a battle for survival as the most toothed-and-clawed predator, lit-erally murdering each other by stabbing and strangulation, but at a rate of speed so slow that we are unable to see it—made a great impression on Hamilton. "Alien Earth" is more than an action-adventure story, it's a fine mood piece that takes us into the heart of that secret jungle and gives us a new perspective on the world we live in.

In the 50s the science-fiction market expanded again—ballooned might be a better word—and there were many new faces and new names and new mastheads in the business. New ideas came with them. It was a time of good growth. And it was the time when Hamilton, with no great urging, brought forth his file of unsold stories (there were remarkably few of them) for his recently acquired wife to look at and perhaps see some-thing worth salvaging.

The one that sprang instantly to the forefront was the story he had done way back in the 30s, that too grim and realistic account of the first manned landing on Mars. It was a great story, and times had changed. So had editorial policies. It only needed to be brought up to date.

But he did more than that. He trimmed it and turned it around for a different point of attack, and came up with "What's It Like Out There?", unquestionably one of the finest science-fiction stories ever done by anyone.

The differences between the original version of the story and the one finally published in *Thrilling Wonder Stories* for December of 1952, were quite striking. The original, told in a rather harsh and clanging style, met the subject head on and battered it. The reader was somehow more aware of the agony of the crashing ships than he was of the men inside them. In the final version, which was considerably shorter, the viewpoint is oblique and restrained, the style quiet but expert, with not a word out of place, and the human emphasis is all-important, touching the heart without ever faltering into sentimentality. The writer had added a new dimension to his talents. His style had matured and his grasp of character had deepened. Mood and introspection had replaced some of the driving action, and his people had acquired a full set of human insides.

Because of this, Hamilton was able to segue easily into the 50s and 60s, when styles of writing and storytelling had changed completely from those of the earlier days. In a time when wide-ranging star-adventures were out of fashion, he continued to write them with eminent success; they had become more literary without becoming dull or pretentious. These were generally novels or novelettes. In the short-story line he wrote much as he had always written; with more polish, perhaps, and with the deeper insights into the affairs of men that had come with years, but with no lessened ability to stir the emotions.

"Requiem," which appeared in *Amazing Stories* in April of 1962, is one of Hamilton's favorites, and one of mine. Again, here is a big theme handled in brief compass, with telling effect.

"The Pro," which he did for Avram Davidson at *The Magazine of Fantasy and Science Fiction* in 1964, has a less cosmic theme than "Requiem," but it is a more universal one: a father-son relationship in a situation that is no longer science fictional, but very real.

The little story "Castaway" was done on assignment. Sam Moskowitz was putting together an anthology about Edgar Allan Poe, and he asked Hamilton for something on that subject, in about three thousand words. Now, this kind of thing—doing a story to order, on a subject chosen by someone else, in a length dictated by someone else—is referred to in some of the loftier circles as "hackwork." And, to be sure, if the writer is indeed a hack, i.e., one who will write anything at all for money, without love, without joy, without pride, it can be. But if the writer is sufficiently skilled in his craft to accept the dictates of length and subject and within those limits to shape a story with love and pride and pleasure, he can turn out a gem like this one. I call this being a professional in the best sense of the word; an artist who has control of his talent, rather than being always subject to its whim.

Many things have happened in the real world since Hamilton began spinning his fantasies in 1926. There have been enormous advances in technology. The two faces of atomic power have been revealed to us, the Savior/Destroyer who haunts us daily with promises of unlimited energy and equally unlimited catastrophe. Our view of the universe has altered. One of Hamilton's early yarns was ruined by the untimely discovery of Pluto. Now we discuss black holes and probe into distant galaxies. Even conservative scientists admit the possibility of intelligent life, other than our own, somewhere in this vast jungle of stars we call the Milky Way, and the mention of spaceflight no longer brings a derisive laugh from the listener.

For Hamilton, it all came true. He sat in the press box at Cape Kennedy and watched Apollo 12 take off in flame and thunder, just as he had written it a hundred times, and there was a thrill to it that no child of the space age will ever quite know. He had predicted, accurately, the year when men would first land on the moon, but he never really believed that it would actually happen while he was still around to see it. Now that it has happened, and the first step into a wider universe has been taken, he profoundly hopes that mankind will not falter and turn back. The future is Out There.

One serious mistake he made—the same mistake that nearly all of us made who were writing in the pre-Sputnik years—was in the assumption that when man did achieve spaceflight he would also have achieved maturity, and there would be a World Government of law and reason, and we would have no more wars. That, unfortunately, has not come true.

Still, mankind has always lived on the narrow edge of doom, and managed to survive somehow. And perhaps the challenge of space will help to solve some of the problems of Earth. One can hope.

And one wonders. If Hamilton were starting his career now, or if spaceflight had been achieved in 1926, would he still have chosen to write science fiction, or would he have entered instead into the reality of his dream and become involved in the space program? If so, he might have given us the Hamilton FTL Drive and sent us to the stars direct.

But he did not have that choice, and so we, as readers, may enjoy the product of a many-faceted mind at work over fifty years of wonder.

As one reader, I'm glad of it.

Leigh Brackett

Lancaster, California, 1976

(PS to EH: I didn't even mention that one story you wrote back around 1927 that was perhaps just a shade less than inspired. Okay?)

The Monster-God of Mamurth

Out of the desert night he came to us, stumbling into our little circle of firelight and collapsing at once. Mitchell and I sprang to our feet with startled exclamations, for men who travel alone and on foot are a strange sight in the deserts of North Africa.

For the first few minutes that we worked over him, I thought he would die at once, but gradually we brought him back to consciousness. While Mitchell held a cup of water to his cracked lips, I looked him over and saw that he was too far gone to live much longer. His clothes were in rags, and his hands and knees literally flayed, from crawling over the sands, I judged. So when he motioned feebly for more water, I gave it to him, knowing that in any case his time was short. Soon he could talk, in a dead, croaking voice.

"I'm alone," he told us, in answer to our first question; "no more out there to look for. What are you two—traders? I thought so. No, I'm an archeologist. A digger-up of the past." His voice broke for a moment. "It's not always good to dig up dead secrets. There are some things the past should be allowed to hide."

He caught the look that passed between Mitchell and me.

"No, I'm not mad," he said. "You will hear, I'll tell you the whole thing. But listen to me, you two," and in his earnestness he raised himself to a sitting position, "keep out of Igidi Desert. Remember that I told you that. I had a warning, too, but I disregarded it. And I went into hell—into hell! But there, I will tell you from the beginning.

"My name—that doesn't matter now. I left Mogador more than a year ago, and came through the foot-hills of the Atlas ranges, striking out into the desert in hopes of finding some of the Carthaginian ruins the North African deserts are known to hold.

"I spent months in the search, traveling among the squalid Arab villages, now near an oasis and now far into the black, untracked desert. And as I went farther into that savage country, I found more and more of the ruins I sought, crumbled remnants of temples and fortresses, relics, almost destroyed, of the age when Carthage meant empire and ruled all of North Africa from her walled city. And then, on the side of a massive block of stone, I found that which turned me toward Igidi.

"It was an inscription in the garbled Phenician of the traders of Carthage, short enough so that I remembered it and can repeat it word for word. It read, literally, as follows:

"Merchants, go not into the city of Mamurth, which lies beyond the mountain pass. For I, San-Drabat of Carthage, entering the city with four companions in the month of Eschmoun, to trade, on the third night of our stay came priests and seized my fellows, I escaping by hiding. My companions they sacrificed to the evil god of the city, who has dwelt there from the beginning of time, and for whom the wise men of Mamurth have built a great temple the like of which is not on Earth elsewhere, where the people of Mamurth worship their god. I escaped from the city and set this warning here that others may not turn their steps to Mamurth and to death.

"Perhaps you can imagine the effect that inscription had on me. It was the last trace of a city unknown to the memory of men, a last floating spar of a civilization sunken in the sea of time. That there could have been such a city at all seemed to me quite probable. What do we know of Carthage even, but a few names? No city, no civilization was ever so completely blotted off the Earth as Carthage, when Roman Scipio ground its temples and palaces into the very dust, and plowed up the ground with salt, and the eagles of conquering Rome flew across a desert where a metropolis had been.

"It was on the outskirts of one of those wretched little Arab villages that I had found the block and its inscription, and I tried to find someone in the village to accompany me, but none would do so. I could plainly see the mountain pass, a mere crack between towering blue cliffs. In reality it was miles and miles away, but the deceptive optical qualities of the desert light made it seem very near. My maps placed that mountain range all right, as a lower branch of the Atlas, and the expanse behind the mountains was marked as 'Igidi Desert,' but that was all I got from them. All that I could reckon on as certain was that it was desert that lay on the other side of the pass, and I must carry enough supplies to meet it.

"But the Arabs knew more! Though I offered what must have been fabulous riches to those poor devils, not one would come with me when I let them know what place I was heading for. None had ever been there, they would not even ride far into the desert in that direction; but all had very definite ideas of the place beyond the mountains as a nest of devils, a haunt of evil Jinns.

"Knowing how firmly superstition is implanted in their kind, I tried no longer to persuade them, and started alone, with two scrawny camels carrying my water and supplies. So for three days I forged across the desert under a broiling sun, and on the morning of the fourth I reached the pass.

"It was only a narrow crevice to begin with, and great boulders were strewn so thickly on its floor that it was a long, hard job getting through. And the cliffs on each side towered to such a height that the space between was a place of shadows and whispers and semi-darkness. It was late in the afternoon when I finally came through, and for a moment I stood motionless; for from that side of the pass the desert sloped down into a vast basin, and at the basin's center, perhaps two miles from where I stood, gleamed the white ruins of Mamurth.

"I remember that I was very calm as I covered the two miles between myself and the ruins. I had taken the existence of the city as a fact, so much so that if the ruins had not been there I should have been vastly more surprised than at finding them.

"From the pass I had seen only a tangled mass of white fragments, but as I drew nearer, some of these began to take outline as crumbling blocks, and walls, and columns. The sand had drifted, too, and the ruins were completely buried in some sections, while nearly all were half covered.

"And then it was that I made a curious discovery. I had stopped to examine the material of the ruins, a smooth, veinless stone, much like an artificial marble or a superfine concrete. And while I looked about me, intent on this, I noticed that on almost every shaft and block, on broken cornice and column, was carved the same symbol—if it was a symbol. It was a rough picture of a queer, outlandish creature, much like an octopus, with a round, almost shapeless body, and several long tentacles or arms branching out from the body, not supple and boneless, like those of an octopus, but seemingly stiff and jointed, like a spider's legs. In fact, the

21

thing might have been intended to represent a spider, I thought, though some of the details were wrong. I speculated for a moment on the profusion of these creatures carved on the ruins all around me, then gave it up as an enigma that was unsolvable.

"And the riddle of the city about me seemed unsolvable also. What could I find in this half-buried mass of stone fragments to throw light on the past? I could not even superficially explore the place, for the scantiness of my supplies and water would not permit a long stay. It was with a discouraged heart that I went back to the camels and, leading them to an open spot in the ruins, made my camp for the night. And when night had fallen, and I sat beside my little fire, the vast, brooding silence of this place of death was awful. There were no laughing human voices, or cries of animals, or even cries of birds or insects. There was nothing but the darkness and silence that crowded around me, flowed down upon me, beat sullenly against the glowing spears of light my little fire threw out.

"As I sat .there musing, I was startled by a slight sound behind me. I turned to see its cause, and then stiffened. As I have mentioned, the space directly around my camp was clear sand, smoothed level by the winds. Well, as I stared at that flat expanse of sand, a hole several inches across suddenly appeared in its surface, yards from where I stood, but clearly visible in the firelight.

"There was nothing whatever to be seen there, not even a shadow, but there it was, one moment the level surface of the sand, the next moment a hole appearing in it, accompanied by a soft, crunching sound. As I stood gazing at it in wonder, that sound was repeated, and simultaneously another hole appeared in the sand's surface, five or six feet nearer to me than the other.

"When I saw that, ice-tipped arrows of fear seemed to shoot through me, and then, yielding to a mad impulse, I snatched a blazing piece of fuel from the fire and hurled it, a comet of red flame, at the place where the holes had appeared. There was a slight sound of scurrying and shuffling, and I felt that whatever thing had made those marks had retreated, if a living thing had made them at all. What it had been, I could not imagine, for there had been absolutely nothing in sight, one track and then another appearing magically in the clear sand, if indeed they were really tracks at all.

"The mystery of the thing haunted me. Even in sleep I found no rest, for evil dreams seemed to flow into my brain from the dead city around me. All the dusty sins of ages past, in the forgotten place, seemed to be focused on me in the dreams I had. Strange shapes walked through them, unearthly as the spawn of a distant star, half seen and vanishing again.

"It was little enough sleep I got that night, but when the sun finally came, with its first golden rays, my fears and oppressions dropped from me like a cloak. No wonder the early peoples were sun-worshippers!

"And with my renewed strength and courage, a new thought struck me. In the inscription I have quoted to you, that long-dead merchant-adventurer had mentioned the great temple of the city and dwelt on its grandeur. Where, then, were its ruins? I wondered. I decided that what time I had would be better spent in investigating the ruins of this temple, which should be prominent, if that ancient Carthaginian had been correct as to its size.

"I ascended a near-by hillock and looked about me in all directions, and though I could not perceive any vast pile of ruins that might have been the temple's, I did see for the first time, far away, two great figures of stone that stood out black against the rosy flame of the sunrise. It was a discovery that filled me with excitement, and I broke camp at once, starting in the direction of those two shapes.

"They were on the very edge of the farther side of the city, and it was noon before I finally stood before them. And now I saw clearly their nature: two great, sitting figures, carved of black stone, all of fifty feet in height, and almost that far apart, facing both toward the city and toward me. They were of human shape and dressed in a queer, scaled armor, but the faces I cannot describe, for they were unhuman. The features were human, well-proportioned, even, but the face, the expression, suggested no kinship whatever with humanity as we know it. Were they carved from life? I wondered. If so, it must have been a strange sort of people who had lived in this city and set up these two statues.

"And now I tore my gaze away from them, and looked around. On each side of those shapes, the remains of what must once have been a mighty wall branched out, a long pile of crumbling ruins. But there had been no wall between the statues, that being evidently the gateway through the barrier. I wondered why the two guardians of the gate had survived, apparently entirely unharmed, while the wall and the city behind me had fallen into ruins. They were of a different material, I could see; but what was that material?

"And now I noticed for the first time the long avenue that began on the other side of the statues and stretched away into the desert for a half-mile or more. The sides of this avenue were two rows of smaller stone figures that ran in parallel lines away from the two colossi. So I started down that avenue, passing between the two great shapes that stood at its head. And as I went between them, I noticed for the first time the inscription graven on the inner side of each.

23

"On the pedestal of each figure, four or five feet from the ground, was a raised tablet of the same material, perhaps a yard square, and covered with strange symbols—characters, no doubt, of a lost language, undecipherable, at least to me. One symbol, though, that was especially prominent in the inscription, was not new to me. It was the carven picture of the spider, or octopus, which I have mentioned that I had found everywhere on the ruins of the city. And here it was scattered thickly among the symbols that made up the inscription. The tablet on the other statue was a replica of the first, and I could learn no more from it. So I started down the avenue, turning over in my mind the riddle of that omnipresent symbol, and then forgetting it, as I observed the things about me.

"That long street was like the avenue of sphinxes at Karnak, down which Pharaoh swung in his litter, borne to his temple on the necks of men. But the statues that made up its sides were not sphinx shaped. They were carved in strange forms, shapes of animals unknown to us, as far removed from anything we can imagine as the beasts of another world. I cannot describe them, any more than you could describe a dragon to a man who had been blind all his life. Yet they were of evil, reptilian shapes; they tore at my nerves as I looked at them.

"Down between the two rows of them I went, until I came to the end of the avenue. Standing there between the last two figures, I could see nothing before me but the yellow sands of the desert, as far as the eye could reach. I was puzzled. What had been the object of all the pains that had been taken, the wall, the two great statues, and this long avenue, if it but led into the desert?

"Gradually I began to see that there was something queer about the part of the desert that lay directly before me. It was *flat*. For an area, seemingly round in shape, that must have covered several acres, the surface of the desert seemed absolutely level. It was as though the sands within that great circle had been packed down with tremendous force, leaving not even the littlest ridge of dune on its surface. Beyond this flat area, and all around it, the desert was broken up by small hills and valleys, and traversed by whirling sand-clouds, but nothing stirred on the flat surface of the circle.

"Interested at once, I strode forward to the edge of the circle, only a few yards away. I had just reached that edge when an invisible hand seemed to strike me a great blow on the face and chest, knocking me backward in the sand.

"It was minutes before I advanced again, but I did advance, for all my curiosity was now aroused. I crawled toward the circle's edge, holding my pistol before me, pushing slowly forward.

"When the automatic in my outstretched hand reached the line of the circle, it struck against something hard, and I could push it no farther. It was exactly as if it had struck against the side of a wall, but no wall or anything else was to be seen. Reaching out my hand, I touched the same hard barrier, and in a moment I was on my feet.

"For I knew now that it was solid matter I had run into, not force. When I thrust out my hands, the edge of the circle was as far as they would go, for there they met a smooth wall, totally invisible, yet at the same time quite material. And the phenomenon was one which even I could partly understand. Somehow, in the dead past, the scientists of the city behind me, the 'wise men' mentioned in the inscription, had discovered the secret of making solid matter invisible, and had applied it to the work that I was now examining. Such a thing was far from impossible. Even our own scientists can make matter partly invisible, with the X-ray. Evidently these people had known the whole process, a secret that had been lost in the succeeding ages, like the secret of hard gold, and malleable glass, and others that we find mentioned in ancient writings. Yet I wondered how they had done this, so that, ages after those who had built the thing were wind-driven dust, it remained as invisible as ever.

"I stood back and threw pebbles into the air, toward the circle. No matter how high I threw them, when they reached the line of the circle's edge they rebounded with a clicking sound; so I knew that the wall must tower to a great height above me. I was on fire to get inside the wall, and examine the place from the inside, but how to do it? There must be an entrance, but where? And I suddenly remembered the two guardian statues at the head of the great avenue, with their carven tablets, and wondered what connection they had with this place.

"Suddenly the strangeness of the whole thing struck me like a blow. The great, unseen wall before me, the circle of sand, flat and unchanging, and myself, standing there and wondering, wondering. A voice from out the dead city behind me seemed to sound in my heart, bidding me to turn and flee, to get away. I remembered the warning of the inscription, 'Go not to Mamurth.' And as I thought of the inscription, I had no doubt that this was the great temple described by San-Drabat. Surely he was right: the like of it was not on Earth elsewhere.

"But I would not go, I could not go, until I had examined the wall from the inside. Calmly reasoning the matter, I decided that the logical place for the gateway through the wall would be at the end of the avenue, so that those who came down the street could pass directly through the wall.

And my reasoning was good, for it was at that spot that I found the entrance: an opening in the barrier, several yards wide, and running higher than I could reach, how high I had no means of telling.

"I felt my way through the gate, and stepped at once upon a floor of hard material, not as smooth as the wall's surface, but equally invisible. Inside the entrance lay a corridor of equal width, leading into the center of the circle, and I felt my way forward.

"I must have made a strange picture, had there been any there to observe it. For while I knew that all around me were the towering, invisible walls, and I knew not what else, yet all my eyes could see was the great flat circle of sand beneath me, carpeted with the afternoon sunshine. Only, I seemed to be walking a foot above the ground, in thin air. That was the thickness of the floor beneath me, and it was the weight of this great floor, I knew, that held the circle of sand under it forever flat and unchanging.

"I walked slowly down the passageway, with hands outstretched before me, and had gone but a short distance when I brought up against another smooth wall that lay directly across the corridor, seemingly making it a blind alley. But I was not discouraged now, for I knew that there must be a door somewhere, and began to feel around me in search of it.

"I found the door. In groping about the sides of the corridor my hands encountered a smoothly rounded knob set in the wall, and as I laid my hand on this, the door opened. There was a sighing, as of a little wind, and when I again felt my way forward, the wall that had lain across the passageway was gone, and I was free to go forward. But I dared not go through at once. I went back to the knob on the wall, and found that no amount of pressing or twisting of it would close the door that had opened. Some subtle mechanism within the knob had operated, that needed only a touch of the hand to work it, and the whole end of the corridor had moved out of the way, sliding up in grooves, I think, like a portcullis, though of this I am not sure.

"But the door was safely opened, and I passed through it. Moving about, like a blind man in a strange place, I found that I was in a vast inner court, the walls of which sloped away in a great curve. When I discovered this, I came back to the spot where the corridor opened into the court, and then walked straight out into the court itself.

"It was steps that I encountered: the first broad steps of what was evidently a staircase of titanic proportions. And I went up, slowly, carefully, feeling before me every foot of the way. It was only the feel of the staircase under me that gave reality to it, for as far as I could see, I was simply climbing up into empty space. It was weird beyond telling.

"Up and up I went, until I was all of a hundred feet above the ground, and then the staircase narrowed, the sides drew together. A few more steps, and I came out on a flat floor again, which, after some groping about, I found to be a broad landing, with high, railed edges. I crawled across this landing on hands and knees, and then struck against another wall, and in it, another door. I went through this too, still crawling, and though everything about me was still invisible, I sensed that I was no longer in the open air, but in a great room.

"I stopped short, and then, as I crouched on the floor, I felt a sudden prescience of evil, of some malignant, menacing entity that was native here. Nothing I could see, or hear, but strong upon my brain beat the thought of something infinitely ancient, infinitely evil, that was a part of this place. Was it a consciousness, I wonder, of the horror that had filled the place in ages long dead? Whatever caused it, I could go no farther in the face of the terror that possessed me; so I drew back and walked to the edge of the landing, leaning over its high, invisible railing and surveying the scene below.

"The setting sun hung like a great ball of red-hot iron in the western sky, and in its lurid rays the two great statues cast long shadows on the yellow sands. Not far away, my two camels, hobbled, moved restlessly about. To all appearances I was standing on thin air, a hundred feet or more above the ground, but in my mind's eye I had a picture of the great courts and corridors below me, through which I had felt my way.

"As I mused there in the red light, it was clear to me that this was the great temple of the city. What a sight it must have been, in the time of the city's life! I could imagine the long procession of priests and people, in somber and gorgeous robes, coming out from the city, between the great statues and down the long avenue, dragging with them, perhaps, an unhappy prisoner to sacrifice to their god in this, his temple.

"The sun was now dipping beneath the horizon, and I turned to go, but before ever I moved, I became rigid and my heart seemed to stand still. For on the farther edge of the clear stretch of sand that lay beneath the temple and the city, a hole suddenly appeared in the sand, springing into being on the desert's face exactly like the one I had seen at my campfire the night before. I watched, as fascinated as by the eyes of a snake. And before my eyes, another and another appeared, not in a straight line, but in a zigzag fashion. Two such holes would be punched down on one side, then two more on the other side, then one in the middle, making a series

27

of tracks, perhaps two yards in width from side to side, and advancing straight toward the temple and myself. And I could see nothing!

"It was like—the comparison suddenly struck me—like the tracks a many-legged insect might make in the sand, only magnified to unheard-of proportions. And with that thought, the truth rushed on me, for I remembered the spider carved on the ruins and on the statues, and I knew now what it had signified to the dwellers in the city. What was it the inscription had said? 'The evil god of the city, who has dwelt there from the beginning of time.' And as I saw those tracks advancing toward me, I knew that the city's ancient evil god still dwelt here, and that I was in his temple, alone and unarmed.

"What strange creatures might there not have been in the dawn of time? And this one, this gigantic monster in a spider's form—had not those who built the city found it here when they came, and, in awe, taken it as the city's god, and built for it the mighty temple in which I now stood? And they, who had the wisdom and art to make this vast fane invisible, not to be seen by human eyes, had they done the same to their god, and made of him almost a true god, invisible, powerful, undying? Undying! Almost it must have been, to survive the ages, as it had done. Yet I knew that even some kinds of parrots live for centuries, and what could I know of this monstrous relic of dead ages? And when the city died and crumbled, and the victims were no longer brought to its lair in the temple, did it not live, as I thought, by ranging the desert? No wonder the Arabs had feared the country in this direction! It would be death for anything that came even within view of such a horror, that could clutch and spring and chase, and yet remain always unseen. And was it death for me?

"Such were some of the thoughts that pounded through my brain, as I watched death approach, with those steadily advancing tracks in the sand. And now the paralysis of terror that had gripped me was broken, and I ran down the great staircase, and into the court. I could think of no place in that great hall where I might hide. Imagine hiding in a place where all is invisible! But I must go some place, and finally I dashed past the foot of the great staircase until I reached a wall directly under the landing on which I had stood, and against this I crouched, praying that the deepening shadows of dusk might hide me from the gaze of the creature whose lair this was.

"I knew instantly when the thing entered the gate through which I too had come. Pad, pad, pad—that was the soft, cushioned sound of its passage. I heard the feet stop for a moment by the opened door at the end of the corridor. Perhaps it was in surprise that the door was open, I thought, for how could I know how great or little intelligence lay in that unseen creature's brain? Then, pad, pad—across the court it came, and I heard the soft sound of its passing as it ascended the staircase. Had I not been afraid to breathe, I would have almost screamed with relief.

"Yet still fear held me, and I remained crouched against the wall while the thing went up the great stairs. Imagine that scene! All around me was absolutely nothing visible, nothing but the great flat circle of sand that lay a foot below me; yet I saw the place with my mind's eye, and knew of the walls and courts that lay about me, and the thing above me, in fear of which I was crouching there in the gathering darkness.

"The sound of feet above me had ceased, and I judged that the thing had gone into the great room above, which I had feared to enter. Now, if ever, was the time to make my escape in the darkness; so I rose, with infinite carefulness, and softly walked across the court to the door that led into the corridor. But when I had walked only half of the distance, as I thought, I crashed squarely into another invisible wall across my path, and fell backward, the metal handle of the sheath-knife at my belt striking the flooring with a loud clang. God help me, I had misjudged the position of the door, and had walked straight into the wall, instead!

"I lay there, motionless, with cold fear flooding every part of my being. Then, pad, pad—the soft steps of the thing across the landing, and then silence for a moment. Could it see me from the landing? I wondered. Could it? For a moment, hope warmed me, as no sound came, but the next instant I knew that death had me by the throat, for pad, pad—down the stairs it came.

"With that sound my last vestige of self-control fled and I scrambled to my feet and made another mad dash in the direction of the door. Crash!—into another wall I went, and rose to my feet trembling. There was no sound of footsteps now, and as quietly as I could, I walked into the great court still farther, as I thought, for all my ideas of direction were hopelessly confused. God, what a weird game it was we played there on that darkened circle of sand!

"No sound whatever came from the thing that hunted me, and my hope flickered up again. And with a dreadful irony, it was at that exact moment that I walked straight into the thing. My outstretched hand touched and grasped what must have been one of its limbs, thick and cold and hairy, which was instantly torn from my grasp and then seized me again, while another and another clutched me also. The thing had stood quite still, leaving me to walk directly into its grasp—the drama of the spider and the fly!

"A moment only it held me, for that cold grasp filled me with such deep shuddering abhorrence that I wrenched myself loose and fled madly across the court, stumbling again on the first step of the great staircase. I raced up the stairs, and even as I ran I heard the thing in pursuit.

"Up I went, and across the landing, and grasped the edge of the railing, for I meant to throw myself down from there, to a clean death on the floor below. But under my hands, the top of the railing moved, one of the great blocks that evidently made up its top was loosened and rocked toward me. In a flash I grasped the great block and staggered across the landing with it in my arms, to the head of the staircase. Two men could hardly have lifted it, I think, yet I did more, in a sudden access of mad strength; for as I heard that monster coming swiftly up the great stairs, I raised the block, invisible as ever, above my head, and sent it crashing down the staircase upon the place where I thought the thing was at that moment.

"For an instant after the crash there was silence, and then a low humming sound began, that waxed into a loud droning. And at the same time, at a spot half-way down the staircase where the block had crashed, a thin, purple liquid seemed to well out of the empty air, giving form to a few of the invisible steps as it flowed over them, and outlining, too, the block I had thrown, and a great hairy limb that lay crushed beneath it, and from which the fluid that was the monster's blood was oozing. I had not killed the thing, but had chained it down with the block that held it prisoner.

"There was a thrashing sound on the staircase, and the purple stream ran more freely, and by the outline of its splashes, I saw, dimly, the monstrous god that had been known in Mamurth in ages past. It was like a giant spider, with angled limbs that were yards long, and a hairy, repellent body. Even as I stood there, I wondered that the thing, invisible as it was, was yet visible by the life-blood in it, when that blood was spilled. Yet so it was, nor can I even suggest a reason. But one glimpse I got of its half-visible, purple-splashed outline, and then, hugging the farther side of the stairs, I descended. When I passed the thing, the intolerable odor of a crushed insect almost smothered me, and the monster itself made frantic efforts to loosen itself and spring at me. But it could not, and I got safely down, shuddering and hardly able to walk.

"Straight across the great court I went, and ran shakily through the corridor, and down the long avenue, and out between the two great statues. The moonlight shone on them, and the tablets of inscriptions stood out clearly on the sides of the statues, with their strange symbols and carved spider forms. But I knew now what their message was!

"It was well that my camels had wandered into the ruins, for such was the fear that struck through me that I would never have returned for them had they lingered by the invisible wall. All that night I rode to the north, and when morning came I did not stop, but still pushed north. And as I went through the mountain pass, one camel stumbled and fell, and in falling burst open all my water supplies that were lashed on its back.

"No water at all was left, but I still held north, killing the other camel by my constant speed, and then staggered on, afoot. On hands and knees I crawled forward, when my legs gave out, always north, away from that temple of evil and its evil god. And tonight, I had been crawling, how many miles I do not know, and I saw your fire. And that is all."

He lay back exhausted, and Mitchell and I looked at each other's faces in the firelight. Then, rising, Mitchell strode to the edge of our camp and looked for a long time at the moonlit desert, which lay toward the south. What his thoughts were, I do not know. I was nursing my own, as I watched the man who lay beside our fire.

It was early the next morning that he died, muttering about great walls around him. We wrapped his body securely, and bearing it with us held our way across the desert.

In Algiers we cabled to the friends whose address we found in his moneybelt, and arranged to ship the body to them, for such had been his only request. Later they wrote that he had been buried in the little churchyard of the New England village that had been his childhood home. I do not think that his sleep there will be troubled by dreams of that place of evil which he fled. I pray that it will not.

Often and often have Mitchell and I discussed the thing, over lonely campfires and in the inns of the seaport towns. Did he kill the invisible monster he spoke of, and is it lying now, a withered remnant, under the block on the great staircase? Or did it gnaw its way loose; does it still roam the desert and make its lair in the vast, ancient temple, as unseen as itself?

Or, different still, was the man simply crazed by the heat and thirst of the desert, and his tale but the product of a maddened mind? I do not think that this is so. I think that he told truth, yet I do not know. Nor shall I ever know, for never, Mitchell and I have decided, shall we be the ones to venture into the place of hell on Earth where that ancient god of evil may still be living, amid the invisible courts and towers, beyond the unseen wall.

The Man Who Evolved

There were three of us in Pollard's house on that night that I try vainly to forget. Dr. John Pollard himself, Hugh Dutton and I, Arthur Wright—we were the three. Pollard met that night a fate whose horror none could dream; Dutton has since that night inhabited a state institution reserved for the insane, and I alone am left to tell what happened.

It was on Pollard's invitation that Dutton and I went up to his isolated cottage. We three had been friends and roommates at the New York Technical University. Our friendship was perhaps a little unusual, for Pollard was a number of years older than Dutton and myself and was different in temperament, being rather quieter by nature. He had followed an intensive course of biological studies, too, instead of the ordinary engineering courses Dutton and I had taken.

As Dutton and I drove northward along the Hudson on that afternoon, we found ourselves reviewing what we knew of Pollard's career. We had known of his taking his master's and doctor's degrees, and had heard of his work under Braun, the Vienna biologist whose theories had stirred up such turmoil. We had heard casually, too, that afterwards he had come back to plunge himself in private research at the country-house beside the Hudson he had inherited. But since then we had had no word from him and had been somewhat surprised to receive his telegrams inviting us to spend the weekend with him.

It was drawing into early-summer twilight when Dutton and I reached a small riverside village and were directed to Pollard's place, a mile or so beyond. We found it easily enough, a splendid old pegged-frame house that for a hundred-odd years had squatted on a low hill above the river. Its outbuildings were clustered around the big house like the chicks about some protecting hen.

Pollard himself came out to greet us. "Why, you boys have grown up!" was his first exclamation. "Here I've remembered you as Hughie and Art, the campus trouble-raisers, and you look as though you belong to business clubs and talk everlastingly about sales-resistance!"

"That's the sobering effect of commercial life," Dutton explained, grinning. "It hasn't touched you, you old oyster—you look the same as you did five years ago."

He did, too, his lanky figure and slow smile and curiously thoughtful eyes having changed not a jot. Yet Pollard's bearing seemed to show some rather more than usual excitement and I commented on it.

"If I seem a little excited it's because this is a great day for me," he answered.

"Well, you *are* in luck to get two fine fellows like Dutton and me to trail up to this hermitage of yours," I began, but he shook his head smilingly.

"I don't refer to that, Art, though I'm mighty glad you've come. As for my hermitage, as you call it, don't say a word against it. I've been able to do work here I could never have done amid the distractions of a city laboratory."

His eyes were alight. "If you two knew what—but there, you'll hear it soon enough. Let's get inside—I suppose you're hungry?"

"Hungry—not I," I assured him. "I might devour half a steer or some trifle like that, but I have really no appetite for anything else today."

"Same here," Dutton said. "I just pick at my food lately. Give me a few dozen sandwiches and a bucket of coffee and I consider it a full meal."

"Well, we'll see what we can do to tempt your delicate appetites," said Pollard, as we went inside.

We found his big house comfortable enough, with long, low-ceilinged rooms and broad windows looking riverward. After putting our bags in a bedroom, and while his housekeeper and cook prepared dinner, Pollard escorted us on a tour of inspection of the place. We were most interested in his laboratory.

It was a small wing he had added to the house, of frame construction outside to harmonize with the rest of the building, but inside offering a gleaming vista of white-tiled walls and polished instruments. A big cube-like structure of transparent metal surmounted by a huge metal cylinder resembling a monster vacuum tube took up the room's center, and he showed us in an adjoining stone-floored room the dynamos and motors of his private power-plant.

Night had fallen by the time we finished dinner, the meal having been prolonged by our reminiscences. The housekeeper and cook had gone, Pollard explaining that the servants did not sleep in the place. We sat smoking for a while in his living-room, Dutton looking appreciatively around at our comfortable surroundings.

"Your hermitage doesn't seem half-bad, Pollard," he commented. "I wouldn't mind this easy life for a while myself."

"Easy life?" repeated Pollard. "That's all you know about it, Hugh. The fact is that I've never worked so hard in my life as I've done up here in the last two years."

"What in the world have you been working at?" I asked. "Something so unholy you've had to keep it hidden here?"

A MAD SCHEME

Pollard chuckled. "That's what they think down in the village. They know I'm a biologist and have a laboratory here, so it's a foregone conclusion with them that I'm doing vivisection of a specially dreadful nature. That's why the servants won't stay here at night."

"As a matter of fact," he added, "if they knew down in the village what I've really been working on they'd be ten times as fearful as they are now."

"Are you trying to play the mysterious great scientist for our benefit?" Dutton demanded. "If you are you're wasting time—I know you, stranger, so take off that mask."

"That's right," I told him. "If you're trying to get our curiosity worked up you'll find we can scram you as neatly as we could five years ago."

"Which scramming generally ended in black eyes for both of you," he retorted. "But I've no intention of working up your curiosity—as a matter of fact I asked you up here to see what I've been doing and help me finish it."

"Help you?" echoed Dutton. "What can we help you do—dissect worms? Some week-end, I can see right now!"

"There's more to this than dissecting worms," Pollard said. He leaned back and smoked for a little time in silence before he spoke again.

"Do you two have any knowledge at all of evolution?" he asked.

"I know that it's a fighting word in some states," I answered, "and that when you say it you've got to smile, damn you."

He smiled himself. "I suppose you're aware of the fact, however, that all life on this Earth began as simple uni-cellular protoplasm, and by successive evolutionary mutations or changes developed into its present forms and is still slowly developing?"

"We know that much—just because we're not biologists you needn't think we're totally ignorant of biology," Dutton said.

"Shut up, Dutton," I warned. "What's evolution got to do with your work up here, Pollard?"

"It *is* my work up here," Pollard answered.

He bent forward. "I'll try to make this clear to you from the start. You know, or say you know, the main steps of evolutionary development. Life began on this Earth as simple protoplasm, a jelly-like mass from which developed small protoplasmic organisms. From these developed in turn sea-creatures, land-lizards, mammals, by successive mutations. This infinitely slow evolutionary process has reached its highest point so far in the mammal man, and is still going on with the same slowness.

"This much is certain biological knowledge, but two great questions concerning this process of evolution have remained hitherto unanswered. First, what is the cause of evolutionary change, the cause of these slow, steady mutations into higher forms? Second, what is the future course of man's evolution going to be, what will be the forms into which in the future man will evolve, and where will his evolution stop? Those two questions biology has so far been unable to answer."

Pollard was silent a moment and then said quietly, "I have found the answer to one of those questions, and am going to find the answer to the other tonight."

We stared at him. "Are you trying to spoof us?" I asked finally.

"I'm absolutely serious, Arthur. I have actually solved the first of those problems, have found the cause of evolution."

"What is it, then?" burst out of Dutton.

"What it has been thought by some biologists for years to be," Pollard answered. "The cosmic rays."

"The cosmic rays?" I echoed. "The vibrations from space that Millikan discovered?"

"Yes, the cosmic rays, the shortest wavelength and most highly penetrating of all vibratory forces. It has been known that they beat unceasingly upon the Earth from outer space, cast forth by the huge generators of the stars, and it has also been known that they must have some great effect in one way or another upon the life of the Earth."

"I have proved that they do have such an effect, and that that effect is what we call evolution! For it is the cosmic rays, beating upon every living organism on Earth, that cause the profound changes in the structure of those organisms which we call mutations. Those changes are slow indeed, but it is due to them that through the ages life has been raised from the first protoplasm to man, and is still being raised higher."

"Good Lord, you can't be serious on this, Pollard!" Dutton protested.

"I am so serious that I am going to stake my life on my discovery tonight," Pollard answered, quietly.

We were startled. "What do you mean?"

"I mean that I have found in the cosmic rays the cause of evolution, the answer to the first question, and that tonight by means of them I am going to answer the second question and find out what the future evolutionary development of man will be!"

"But how could you possibly—"

Pollard interrupted. "Easily enough. I have been able in the last months to do something no physicist has been able to do, to concentrate the cosmic rays and yet remove from them their harmful properties. You saw the cylinder over the metal cube in my laboratory? That cylinder literally gathers in from an immense distance the cosmic rays that strike this part of the Earth, and reflects them down inside the cube.

"Now suppose those concentrated cosmic rays, millions of times stronger than the ordinary cosmic rays that strike one spot on Earth, fall upon a man standing inside the cube. What will be the result? It is the cosmic rays that cause evolutionary change, and you heard me say that they are still changing all life on Earth, still changing man, but so slowly as to be unnoticeable. But what about the man under those terrifically intensified rays? He will be changed millions of times faster than ordinarily, will go forward in hours or minutes through the evolutionary mutations that all mankind will go forward through in eons to come!"

"And you propose to try that experiment?" I cried.

"I propose to try it on myself," said Pollard gravely, "and to find out for myself the evolutionary changes that await humankind."

"Why, it's insane!" Dutton exclaimed.

Pollard smiled. "The old cry," he commented. "Never an attempt has been made yet to tamper with nature's laws, but that cry has been raised."

"But Dutton's right!" I cried. "Pollard, you've worked here alone too long—you've let your mind become warped—"

"You are trying to tell me that I have become a little mad," he said. "No, I am sane—perhaps wonderfully sane, in trying this."

His expression changed, his eyes brooding. "Can't you two see what this may mean to humanity? As we are to the apes, so must the men of the future be to us. If we could use this method of mine to take all mankind forward through millions of years of evolutionary development at one stride, wouldn't it be sane to do so?"

My mind was whirling. "Good heavens, the whole thing is so crazy," I protested. "To accelerate the evolution of the human race? It seems somehow a thing forbidden."

"It's a thing glorious if it can be done," he returned, "and I know that it can be done. But first one must go ahead, must travel on through stage after stage of man's future development to find out to which stage it would be most desirable for all mankind to be transferred. I know there is such an age."

"And you asked us up here to take part in that?"

"Just that. I mean to enter the cube and let the concentrated rays whirl me forward along the paths of evolution, but I must have someone to turn the rays on and off at the right moments."

"It's all incredible!" Dutton exclaimed. "Pollard, if this is a joke it's gone far enough for me."

For answer Pollard rose. "We will go to the laboratory now," he said simply. "I am eager to get started."

I cannot remember following Pollard and Dutton to the laboratory, my thoughts were spinning so at the time. It was not until we stood before the great cube from which the huge metal cylinder towered that I was aware of the reality of it all.

Pollard had gone into the dynamo-room and as Dutton and I stared wordlessly at the great cube and cylinder, at the retorts and flasks of acids and strange equipment about us, we heard the hum of motor-generators. Pollard came back to the switchboard supported in a steel frame beside the cube, and as he closed a switch there came a crackling and the cylinder glowed with white light.

Pollard pointed to it and the big quartz-like disk in the cubical chamber's ceiling, from which the white force-shafts shot downward.

"The cylinder is now gathering cosmic rays from an immense area of space," he said, "and those concentrated rays are falling through that disk into the cube's interior. To cut off the rays it is necessary only to open this switch." He reached to open the switch, the light died.

THE MAN WHO EVOLVED

Quickly, while we stared, he removed his clothing, donning in place of it a loose white running suit.

"I will want to observe the changes of my own body as much as possible," he exclaimed. "Now, I will stand inside the cube and you will turn on the rays and let them play upon me for fifteen minutes. Roughly, that should represent a period of some fifty million years of future evolutionary change. At the end of fifteen minutes you will turn the rays off and we will be able to observe what changes they have caused. We will then resume the process, going forward by fifteen-minute or rather fifty-million-year periods."

"But where will it stop—where will we quit the process?" Dutton asked.

Pollard shrugged. "We'll stop where evolution stops, that is, where the rays no longer affect me. You know, biologists have often wondered what the last change or final development of man will be, the last mutation. Well, we are going to see tonight what it will be."

He stepped toward the cube and then paused, went to a desk and brought from it a sealed envelope he handed to me.

"This is just in case something happens to me of a fatal nature," he said. "It contains an attestation signed by myself that you two are in no way responsible for what I am undertaking."

"Pollard, give up this unholy business!" I cried, clutching his arm. "It's not too late, and this whole thing seems ghastly to me!"

"I'm afraid it is too late," he smiled. "If I backed out now I'd be ashamed to look in a mirror hereafter. And no explorer was ever more eager than I am to start down the path of man's future evolution!"

He stepped up into the cube, standing directly beneath the disk in its ceiling. He motioned imperatively, and like an automaton I closed the door and then threw the switch.

The cylinder broke again into glowing white light, and as the shafts of glowing white force shot down from the disk in the cube's ceiling upon Pollard, we glimpsed his whole body writhing as though beneath a terrifically concentrated electrical force. The shaft of glowing emanations almost hid him from our view. I knew that the cosmic rays in themselves were invisible but guessed that the light of the cylinder and shaft was in some way a transformation of part of the rays into visible light.

Dutton and I stared with beating hearts into the cubical chamber, having but fleeting glimpses of Pollard's form. My watch was in one hand, the other hand on the switch. The fifteen minutes that followed seemed to me to pass with the slowness of fifteen eternities. Neither of us spoke and the only sounds were the hum of the generators and the crackling of the cylinder that from the far spaces was gathering and concentrating the rays of evolution.

At last the watch's hand marked the quarter-hour and I snapped off the switch, the light of the cylinder and inside the cube dying. Exclamations burst from us both.

Pollard stood inside the cube, staggering as though still dazed by the impact of the experience, but he was not the Pollard who had entered the chamber! He was transfigured, godlike! His body had literally expanded into a great figure of such physical power and beauty as we had not imagined could exist! He was many inches taller and broader, his skin a clear pink, every limb and muscle molded as though by some master sculptor.

The greatest change, though, was in his face. Pollard's homely, good-humored features were gone, replaced by a face whose perfectly-cut features held the stamp of immense intellectual power that shone almost overpoweringly from the clear dark eyes. It was not Pollard who stood before us, I told myself, but a being as far above us as the most advanced man of today is above the troglodyte!

He was stepping out of the cube and his voice reached our ears, clear and bell-like, triumphant.

"You see? It worked as I knew it would work! I'm fifty million years ahead of the rest of humanity in evolutionary development!"

"Pollard!" My lips moved with difficulty. "Pollard, this is terrible—this change—"

His radiant eyes flashed. "Terrible? It's wonderful! Do you two realize what I now am, can you realize it? This body of mine is the kind of body all men will have in fifty million years, and the brain inside it is a brain fifty million years ahead of yours in development!"

He swept his hand about. "Why, all this laboratory and former work of mine seems infinitely petty, childish, to me! The problems that I worked on for years I could solve now in minutes. I could do more for mankind now than all the men now living could do together!"

"Then you're going to stop at this stage?" Dutton cried eagerly. "You're not going further with this?"

"Of course I am! If fifty million years' development makes this much change in man, what will a hundred million years, two hundred million make? I'm going to find that out."

I grasped his hand. "Pollard, listen to me! Your experiment has succeeded, has fulfilled your wildest dreams. Stop it now! Think what you can accomplish, man! I know your ambition has always been to be one of humanity's great benefactors—by stopping here you can be the greatest! You can be a living proof to mankind of what your process can make it, and with that proof before it all humanity will be eager to become the same as you!"

He freed himself from my grasp. "No, Arthur—I have gone part of the way into humanity's future and I'm going on."

He stepped back into the chamber, while Dutton and I stared help-lessly. It seemed half a dream, the laboratory, the cubical chamber, the godlike figure inside that was and still was not Pollard.

"Turn on the rays, and let them play for fifteen minutes more," he was directing. "It will project me ahead another fifty million years."

His eyes and voice were imperative, and I glanced at my watch, and snicked over the switch. Again the cylinder broke into light, again the shaft of force shot down into the cube to hide Pollard's splendid figure.

Dutton and I waited with feverish intensity in the next minutes. Pollard was standing still beneath the broad shaft of force, and so was hidden in it from our eyes. What would its lifting disclose? Would he have changed still more, into some giant form, or would he be the same, having already reached humanity's highest possible development?

When I shut off the mechanism at the end of the appointed period, Dutton and I received a shock. For again Pollard had changed!

He was no longer the radiant, physically perfect figure of the first metamorphosis. His body instead seemed to have grown thin and shriv-elled, the outlines of bones visible through its flesh. His body, indeed, seemed to have lost half its bulk and many inches of stature and breadth, but these were compensated for by the change in his head.

For the head supported by this weak body was an immense, bulg-ing balloon that measured fully eighteen inches from brow to back! It was almost entirely hairless, its great mass balanced precariously upon his slender shoulders and neck. And his face too was changed greatly, the eyes larger and the mouth smaller, the ears seeming smaller also. The great bulging forehead dominated the face.

Could this be Pollard? His voice sounded thin and weak to our ears.

"You are surprised to see me this time? Well, you see a man a hundred million years ahead of you in development. And I must confess that you appear to me as two brutish, hairy cave-men would appear to you."

"But Pollard, this is awful!" Dutton cried. "This change is more terrible than the first...if you had only stopped at the first..."

The eyes of the shrivelled, huge-headed figure in the cube fired with anger. "Stop at that first stage? I'm glad now that I didn't! The man I was fifteen minutes ago...fifty million years ago in development...seems now to me to have been half-animal! What was his big animal-like body beside my immense brain?"

"You say that because in this change you're getting away from all human emotions and sentiments!" I burst. "Pollard, do you realize what you're doing? You're changing out of human semblance!"

"I realize it perfectly," he snapped, "and I see nothing to be deplored in the fact. It means that in a hundred million years man will be developing in brain-capacity and will care nothing for the development of body. To you two crude beings, of what is to me the past, this seems terrible; but to me it is desirable and natural. Turn on the rays again!"

"Don't do it, Art!" cried Dutton. "This madness has gone far enough!"

Pollard's great eyes surveyed us with cold menace. "You will turn on the rays," his thin voice ordered deliberately. "If you do not, it will be but the work of a moment for me to annihilate both of you and go on with this alone."

"You'd kill us?" I said dumbfoundedly. "We two, two of your best friends?"

His narrow mouth seemed to sneer. "Friends? I am millions of years past such irrational emotions as friendship. The only emotion you awaken in me is a contempt for your crudity. Turn on the rays!"

THE BRAIN MONSTER

His eyes blazed as he snapped the last order, and as though propelled by a force outside myself, I closed the switch. The shaft of glowing force again hid him from our view.

Of our thoughts during the following quarter-hour I can say nothing, for both Dutton and I were so rigid with awe and horror as to make our minds chaotic. I shall never forget, though, that first moment after the time had passed and I had again switched off the mechanism.

The change had continued, and Pollard—I could not call him that in my own mind—stood in the cube-chamber as a shape the sight of which stunned our minds.

He had become simply a great head! A huge hairless head fully a yard in diameter, supported on tiny legs, the arms having dwindled to mere hands that projected just below the head! The eyes were enormous, saucerlike, but the ears were mere pin-holes at either side of the head, the nose and mouth being similar holes below the eyes!

He was stepping out of the chamber on his ridiculously little limbs, and as Dutton and I reeled back in unreasoning horror, his voice came to us as an almost inaudible piping. And it held pride!

"You tried to keep me from going on, and you see what I have become? To such as you, no doubt, I seem terrible, yet you two and all like you seem as low to me as the worms that crawl!"

"Good God, Pollard, you've made yourself a monster!" The words burst from me without thought.

His enormous eyes turned on me. "You call me Pollard, yet I am no more the Pollard you knew, and who entered that chamber first, than you are the ape of millions of years ago from whom you sprang! And all mankind is like you two! Well, they will all learn the powers of one who is a hundred and fifty million years in advance of them!"

"What do you mean?" Dutton exclaimed.

"I mean that with the colossal brain I have I will master without a struggle this man-swarming planet, and make it a huge laboratory in which to pursue the experiments that please me."

"But Pollard—remember why you started this!" I cried. "To go ahead and chart the path of future evolution for humanity—to benefit humanity and not to rule it!"

The great head's enormous eyes did not change. "I remember that the creature Pollard that I was until tonight had such foolish ambitions, yes. It would stir mirth now, if I could feel such an emotion. To benefit humanity? Do you men dream of benefitting the animals you rule over? I would no sooner think of working for the benefit of you humans!

"Do you two yet realize that I am so far ahead of you in brain power now as you are ahead of the beasts that perish? Look at this..."

He had climbed onto a chair beside one of the laboratory tables, was reaching among the retorts and apparatus there. Swiftly he poured several compounds into a lead mortar, added others, poured upon the mixed contents another mixture made as swiftly.

There was a puff of intense green smoke from the mortar instantly, and then the great head—I can only call him that—turned the mortar upside down. A lump of shining mottled metal fell out and we gasped as we recognized the yellow sheen of pure gold, made in a moment, apparently, by a mixture of common compounds!

"You see?" the grotesque figure was asking. "What is the transformation of elements to a mind like mine? You two cannot even realize the scope of my intelligence!

"I can destroy all life on this Earth from this room, if I desire. I can construct a telescope that will allow me to look on the planets of the farthest galaxies! I can send my mind forth to make contact with other minds without the slightest material connection. And you think it terrible that I should rule your race! I will not rule them, I will *own* them and this planet as you might own a farm and animals!"

"You couldn't!" I cried. "Pollard, if there is anything of Pollard left in you, give up that thought! We'll kill you ourselves before we'll let you start a monstrous rule of men!"

"We will—by God, we will!" Dutton cried, his face twitching.

We had started desperately forward toward the great head but stopped suddenly in our tracks as his great eyes met ours. I found myself walking backward to where I had stood, walking back and Dutton with me, like two automatons.

"So you two would try to kill me?" queried the head that had been Pollard. "Why, I could direct you without a word to kill yourselves and you'd do so in an instant! What chance has your puny will and brain against mine? And what chance will all the force of men have against me when a glance from me will make them puppets of my will?"

A desperate inspiration flashed through my brain. "Pollard, wait!" I exclaimed. "You were going on with the process, with the rays! If you stop here you'll not know what changes lie beyond your present form!"

He seemed to consider. "That is true," he admitted, "and though it seems impossible to me that by going on I can attain to greater intelligence than I now have, I want to find out for certain."

"Then you'll go under the rays for another fifteen minutes?" I asked quickly.

"I will," he answered, "but lest you harbor any foolish ideas, you may know that even inside the chamber I will be able to read your thoughts and can kill both of you before you can make a move to harm me."

He stepped up into the chamber again, and as I reached for the switch, Dutton trembling beside me, we glimpsed for a moment the huge head before the down-smiting white force hid it from our sight.

The minutes of this period seemed dragging even more slowly than before. It seemed hours before I reached at last to snap off the rays. We gazed into the chamber, shaking.

At first glance the great head inside seemed unchanged, but then we saw that it had changed, and greatly. Instead of being a skin-covered head with at least rudimentary arms and legs, it was now a great gray head-like

THE BEST OF EDMOND HAMILTON

shape of even greater size, supported by two gray muscular tentacles. The surface of this gray head-thing was wrinkled and folded, and its only features were two eyes as small as our own.

"Oh my God!" quaked Dutton. "He's changing from a head into a brain—he's losing all human appearance!"

Into our minds came a thought from the gray head-thing before us, a thought as clear as though spoken. "You have guessed it, for even my former head-body is disappearing, all atrophying except the brain. I am become a walking, seeing brain. As I am so all of your race will be in two hundred million years, gradually losing more and more of their atrophied bodies and developing more and more their great brains."

His eyes seemed to read us. "You need not fear now the things I threatened in my last stage of development. My mind, grown infinitely greater, would no more now want to rule you men and your little planet than you would want to rule an anthill and its inhabitants! My mind, gone fifty million years further ahead in development, can soar out now to vistas of power and knowledge unimagined by me in that last stage, and unimaginable to you."

"Great God, Pollard!" I cried. "What have you become?"

"Pollard?" Dutton was laughing hysterically. "You call that thing Pollard? Why, we had dinner with Pollard three hours ago—he was a human being, and not a thing like this!"

"I have become what all men will become in time," the thing's thought answered me. "I have gone this far along the road of man's future evolution, and am going on to the end of that road, am going to attain the development that the last mutation possible will give me!"

"Turn on the rays," his thought continued. "I think that I must be approaching now the last possible mutation."

I snapped over the switch again and the white shaft of the concentrated rays veiled from us the great gray shape. I felt my own mind giving beneath the strain of horror of the last hour, and Dutton was still half-hysterical.

The humming and crackling of the great apparatus seemed thunderous to my ears as the minutes passed. With every nerve keyed to highest tension, I threw open the switch at last. The rays ceased, and the figure in the chamber was again revealed.

Dutton began to laugh shrilly, and then abruptly was sobbing. I do not know whether I was doing the same, though I have a dim memory of mouthing incoherent things as my eyes took in the shape in the chamber.

It was a great brain! A gray limp mass four feet across, it lay in the chamber, its surface ridged and wrinkled by innumerable fine convolutions. It had no features or limbs of any kind in its gray mass. It was simply a huge brain whose only visible sign of life was its slow, twitching movement.

From it thoughts beat strongly into our own horror-weighted brains.

"You see me now, a great brain only, just as all men will be far in the future. Yes, you might have known, I might have known, when I was like you, that this would be the course of human evolution, that the brain that alone gives man dominance would develop and the body that hampers that brain would atrophy until he would have developed into pure brain as I now am!

"I have no features, no senses that I could describe to you, yet I can realize the universe infinitely better than you can with your elementary senses. I am aware of planes of existence you cannot imagine. I can feed myself with pure energy without the need of a cumbersome body, to transform it, and I can move and act, despite my lack of limbs, by means and with a speed and power utterly beyond your comprehension.

"If you still have fear of the threats I made two stages back against your world and race, banish them! I am pure intelligence now and as such, though I can no more feel the emotions of love or friendship, neither can I feel those of ambition or pride. The only emotion, if such it is, that remains to me still is intellectual curiosity, and this desire for truth that has burned in man since his apehood will thus be the last of all desires to leave him!"

THE LAST MUTATION

"A brain—a great brain!" Dutton was saying dazedly. "Here in Pollard's laboratory—but where's Pollard? He was here, too..."

"Then all men will some day be as you are now?" I cried.

"Yes," came the answering thought, "in two hundred and fifty million years man as you know him and as you are will be no more, and after passing all the stages through which I have passed through tonight, the human race will have developed into great brains inhabiting not only your solar system, no doubt, but the systems of other stars!"

"And that's the end of man's evolutionary road? That is the highest point that he will reach?"

"No, I think he will change still from those great brains into still a higher form," the brain answered—the brain that three hours before had been Pollard!—"and I am going to find out now what that higher form will be. For I think this will be the last mutation of all and that with it I will reach the end of man's evolutionary path, the last and highest form into which he can develop!

"You will turn on the rays now," the brain's order continued, "and in fifteen minutes we will know what that last and highest form is."

My hand was on the switch but Dutton had staggered to me, was clutching my arm. "Don't, Arthur!" he was exclaiming thickly. "We've seen horrors enough—let's not see the last—get out of here..."

"I can't!" I cried. "Oh God, I want to stop but I can't now—I want to see the end myself—I've got to see..."

"Turn on the rays!" came the brain's thought-order again.

"The end of the road—the last mutation," I panted. "We've got to see—to see—" I drove the switch home.

The rays flashed down again to hide the great gray brain in the cube. Dutton's eyes were staring fixedly, he was clinging to me.

The minutes passed! Each tick of the watch in my hand was the mighty note of a great tolling bell in my ears.

An inability to move seemed gripping me. The hand of my watch was approaching the minute for which I waited, yet I could not raise my hand toward the switch!

Then as the hand reached the appointed minute I broke from my immobility and in a sheer frenzy of sudden strength pulled open the switch, rushed forward with Dutton to the cube's very edge!

The great gray brain that had been inside it was gone. There lay on the cube's floor instead of it a quite shapeless mass of clear, jelly-like matter. It was quite motionless save for a slight quivering. My shaking hand went forth to touch it, and then it was that I screamed, such a scream as all the tortures of hell's crudest fiends could not have wrung from a human throat.

The mass inside the cube was a mass of simple *protoplasm!* This then was the end of man's evolution-road, the highest form to which time would bring him, the last mutation of all! The road of man's evolution was a circular one, returning to its beginning!

From the Earth's bosom had risen the first crude organisms. Then sea-creature and land-creature and mammal and ape to man; and from man it would rise in the future through all the forms we had seen that night. There would be super-men, bodiless heads, pure brains; only to be changed by the last mutation of all into the protoplasm from which first it had sprung!

46

I do not know now exactly what followed. I know that I rushed upon that quivering, quiescent mass, calling Pollard's name madly and shouting things I am glad I cannot remember. I know that Dutton was shouting too, with insane laughter, and that as he struck with lunatic howls and fury about the laboratory the crash of breaking glass and the hiss of escaping gases was in my ears. And then from those mingling acids bright flames were leaping and spreading, sudden fires that alone, I think now, saved my own sanity.

For I can remember dragging the insanely laughing Dutton from the room, from the house, into the cool darkness of the night. I remember the chill of dew-wet grass against my hands and face as the flames from Pollard's house soared higher. And I remember that as I saw Dutton's crazy laughter by that crimson light, I knew that he would laugh thus until he died.

*
**

So ends my narrative of the end that came to Pollard and Pollard's house. It is, as I said in beginning, a narrative that I only can tell now, for Dutton has never spoken a sane word since. In the institution where he now is, they think his condition the result of shock from the fire, just as Pollard was believed to have perished in that fire. I have never until now told the truth.

But I am telling it now, hoping that it will in some way lessen the horror it has left with me. For there could be no horror greater than that we saw in Pollard's house that night. I have brooded upon it. With my mind's eyes I have followed that tremendous cycle of change, that purposeless, eon-long climb of life up from simple protoplasm through myriads of forms and lives of ceaseless pain and struggle, only to end in simple protoplasm again.

Will that cycle of evolutionary change be repeated over and over again upon this and other worlds, ceaselessly, purposelessly, until there is no more universe for it to go on in? Is this colossal cycle of life's changes as inevitable and necessary as the cycle that in space makes of the nebulae myriad suns, and of the suns dark-stars, and of the dark-stars colliding with one another nebulae again?

Or is this evolutionary cycle we saw a cycle in appearance only, is there some change that we cannot understand, above and beyond it? I do not know which of these possibilities is truth, but I do know that the first of them haunts me. It would haunt the world if the world believed my story. Perhaps I should be thankful as I write to know that I will not be believed.

A Conquest of Two Worlds

Jimmy Crane, Mart Halkett and Hall Burnham were students together in a New York technical school in the spring when Gillen's flight changed the world. Crane, Halkett and Burnham had been an inseparable trio since boyhood. They had fought youthful foes together, had wrestled together with their lessons, and now read together, as an amazed world was reading, of Ross Gillen's stupendous exploit.

Gillen, the stubby, shy and spectacled Arizona scientist, burst the thing on the world like a bombshell. For sixteen years he had worked on the problem of atomic power. When he finally solved that problem and found himself able to extract almost unlimited power from small amounts of matter, by breaking down its atoms with a simple projector of electrical forces of terrific voltage, Gillen called in a helper, Anson Drake. With Drake he constructed an atom-blast mechanism that would shoot forth as a rocket stream, exploded atoms of immeasurable force, a tremendous means of propulsion.

For Gillen meant to conquer space. Through that momentous winter when Crane, Halkett and Burnham had not a thought beyond their school problems and school sports, Gillen and Drake were constructing a rocket that would use the atom-blast mechanism for propulsion and could carry one man and the necessary supplies of air, food and water. There was installed in the ship a radio transmitter they had devised, which made use of a carrier-beam to send radio impulses through the Earth's Heaviside Layer from outer space. When all was ready Ross Gillen got calmly into the rocket and roared out into space to eternal glory.

Crane, Halkett and Burnham read as tensely as everyone else on Earth the reports that came back from Gillen's radio. He swung sunward first and reported Venus a landless water-covered ball, and Mercury a mass of molten rock. Landing was impossible on either. Then Gillen headed outward in a broad curve for Mars and on a memorable day reported to Earth a landing on that planet.

Mars had thin but breathable air, Gillen reported. It was an arid world of red deserts with oases of gray vegetation wherever there were underground springs or water-courses. There were Martians of some intelligence moving in nomadic groups from oasis to oasis. They were man-like beings with stilt-like legs and arms, with huge bulging chests and bulbous heads covered with light fur. Gillen said the Martian groups or tribes fought some among themselves with spears and like weapons, but that they welcomed him as a friend. He reported signs of large mineral and chemical deposits before he left Mars.

Gillen's radio signals became ever weaker as his rocket moved through space toward Jupiter. He managed a safe landing on that giant planet and found it without oceans, warm and steamy and clad from pole to pole with forests of great fern growths. A strange fauna inhabited these forests and the highest forms of life. The Jovians, as Gillen called them, were erect-walking creatures with big, soft hairless bodies and with thick arms and legs ending in flippers instead of hands or feet. Their heads were small and round, with large dark eyes. They lived peacefully in large communities in the fern forests, on fruits and roots. They had few weapons and were of child-like friendliness. Gillen stayed several days with them before leaving Jupiter.

Gillen said only that Jupiter's greater gravitation and heavy wet atmosphere had made him ill and that he was heading back to Earth. Saturn, Uranus, Neptune and Pluto were, of course, hopelessly cold and uninhabitable.

Crane, Halkett and Burnham were part of a world that was mad with excitement as Gillen swung back through space toward Earth. And when at last Gillen's rocket roared in through Earth's atmosphere and landed, it smashed, and they found Gillen inside it crumpled and dead, but with a smile on his lips.

To Halkett, Crane and Burnham, Gillen was the supreme hero as he was to all Earth. Overnight, Gillen's flight, the fact of interplanetary travel, changed everything. The new planets open to Earthmen brought new and tremendous problems. Even as Anson Drake, Gillen's helper, was supervising construction of ten rockets for a second expedition, the world's governments were meeting and deciding that a terrific war between nations for the rich territories of Mars and Jupiter could only be avoided by formation of one government for the other planets. The Interplanetary Council thus came into being and one of its first acts was to make Drake's expedition its official exploring party.

Drake's expedition became the goal of all the adventure-minded young men of Earth. Jimmy Crane, Mart Halkett and Hall Burnham were among these, but they had what most of the adventurous had not, technical education and skill. The harassed Drake took the three on: and when Drake's ten rockets sailed out with the commission of the Interplanetary Council to explore Mars' mineral and other resources, to establish bases for future exploration on Mars and if possible on Jupiter, Crane, Halkett and Burnham were together in Rocket 8.

Drake's expedition proved a classic in disaster. Two of his ten rockets perished in mid-space in a meteor swarm. Many of the men in the other rockets were struck down by the malign combination of the weightlessness, the unsoftened ultra-violet rays, and the terrific glare and gloom of mid-space. This space-sickness had put about a half of Drake's men out of usefulness, Halkett and Burnham among them, when his eight rockets swung in to land near the Martian equator.

One of Drake's rockets smashed completely in landing, and three others suffered minor damages. They had landed near one of the oases of vegetation, and Drake directed the establishment of a camp. The thin cold Martian air helped bring his space-sick men back to normal, but others were being smitten at the same time by what came to be known later as Martian fever. This seized on Hall Burnham among others, though Halkett and Crane never had it. The fever came as the result of the entirely strange conditions in which the Earthmen found themselves.

Drake's men were in a world in which nothing could be measured by terrestrial standards. The reduced gravitation made their slightest movements give grotesquely disproportionate results. But the thin air made even the slightest effort tire them quickly. The sun's heat was enough by day to give moderate warmth, but the nights in Drake's camp were freezing. Halkett, Crane and Burnham marveled at the splendor of those bitter nights, the stars superb in frosty brilliance, the two Martian moons casting ever-changing shadows.

Then, too, there were the Martians. The first contact of Drake's party with them was amicable enough. The big furry man-like beings, strange looking to the Earthmen with their huge expanded chests and stilt-like limbs, emerged from the vegetation oases to greet Drake's men as friends. News of Gillen's visit had traveled over part of Mars, at least, for these Martians had heard of it.

Drake welcomed the Martians and ordered his men to fraternize with them, for he hoped to learn much from them concerning the planet's resources. He was beginning to see that his expedition was far too small for even the sketchiest exploration of the planet. So Martians and Earthmen mixed and mingled in the little camp at the oasis' edge. Some of the men learned the rudiments of the Martians' speech—Mart Halkett was one of these—and got from them a little information concerning location of mineral deposits. Although most of it was undependable, still Drake felt he was learning something.

But the whole state of affairs changed when one of Drake's men foolishly told some Martians that Drake's expedition was but the forerunner of many others from Earth, and that the Interplanetary Council would direct the destinies of all the planets. It must have been a shock to the Martians, primitive as they were, to find that they were considered subjects of this new government. They withdrew at once from the Earthmen's camp. Drake radioed to Earth that they were acting queerly and that he feared an attack.

Yet when the attack came three days later the Earthmen brought it on themselves. When one of Drake's guards wantonly slew a Martian, the natives rushed the camp. Drake had hastily made ready atom-blast mechanisms for defense and the attacking Martians were almost annihilated by the invisible but terrific fire of disintegrated atoms. Crouching behind their rude dirtworks, the Earthmen, even those staggering from Martian fever, turned the roaring blasts this way and that to mow down the onrushing mobs of furry, big-chested stilt-limbed Martians. Halkett, Crane and Burnham did their part in that one-sided fight.

The Martians had learned their lesson and attacked no more but hemmed in the camp and systematically trailed and killed anyone venturing from it. More of Drake's men were going down with Martian fever and several died. Exploration was out of the question and Drake's position became insupportable. He reported as much and the Interplanetary Council ordered his return to Earth.

Drake foolishly sent four of his rockets, with Halkett and his friends in one, back to Earth in advance. The other three and their crews, including himself, delayed to repair the damage done in landing. The Martians rushed them in force that night, and Drake and all his men perished in what must have been a terrific battle.

Halkett, Crane and Burnham got back to Earth with the four advance rockets some time after Drake's last broken-off radio-messages had told his fate. They found Earth, which welcomed them as heroes, wrathful at the slaying of their commander and comrades by the Martians. The information Drake had sent back regarding Mars' rich chemical and metallic deposits added greed to the earth-people's anger.

Announcement was made immediately by the Interplanetary Council that another force would be sent back to Mars, one better equipped to face Martian conditions and powerful enough to resist any Martian attack. It was evident that the Martians would resist all explorations and must be subdued before a systematic survey of the planet could be made. Once that was done, Mars would become a base for the exploration of Jupiter.

Rockets to the number of a hundred were under construction, embodying all the lessons Drake's disastrous expedition had learned. Instruments, to give warning of meteor swarms by means of magnetic fields projected ahead, were devised. Walls and window ports were constructed to soften the terrific ultra-violet vibrations of free space. Special recoil harnesses were produced to minimize the terrible shocks of starting and landing. These would reduce space-sickness, and Martian fever was to be combatted by special oxygenation treatment to be given periodically to all engaged in this new venture.

Weapons were not forgotten—the atom-blast weapons were improved in power and range, and new atomic bombs that burst with unprecedented violence were being turned out. And while crews were being enlisted and trained for this rocket fleet, the Army of the Interplanetary Council was organized. Most of the survivors of Drake's disastrous expedition joined one department or another of the new force. Crane, Halkett and Burnham had joined at once, and because their Martian experience made them valuable they were commissioned lieutenants in the new army.

Halkett commented on that. "I don't know why we should be going back there to kill those poor furry devils," he told Crane and Burnham. "After all, they're fighting for their world."

"We wouldn't hurt them if they'd be reasonable and not attack us, would we?" Crane demanded. "We're only trying to make of Mars something besides a great useless desert."

"But the Martians seem to be satisfied with it as a desert," Halkett persisted. "What right have we, really, to change it or exploit its resources against their wishes?"

"Halk, if you talk like that people'll think you're pro-Martian," said Crane worriedly. "Don't you know that the Martians will never use those chemical and metal deposits until the end of time, and that Earth needs them badly?"

"Not to speak of the fact that we'll give the Martians a better government than they ever had before," Burnham said. "They've always been fighting among themselves and the Council will stop that."

"I suppose that's so," Halkett admitted. "But just the same, I'm not keen on slaughtering any more of them with the atom-blasts as we did with Drake."

"There'll be nothing like that," Crane told him. "The Martians will see we're too strong and won't start anything."

Crane proved a poor prophet. For when the expedition, commanded by that Richard Weathering who had been Drake's second in command, reached Mars in its hundred rockets, trouble started. There was never a chance to try peaceful methods—fighting with the Martians began almost immediately.

It was evident that since Drake's expedition the Martians had anticipated further parties and had made some preparation. They had combined groups into several large forces and had devised some crude chemical weapons not unlike the ancient Greek fire. With these they rushed Weathering's rockets on the equatorial plateau where they had landed. But Weathering had already brought order out of the confusion of landing and was ready for them.

His first act on landing was to have his men bring the rockets together and throw up dirtworks around them. Both of these tasks were enormously simplified by the lesser gravitation of the planet. He had then set up batteries of atom-blasts at strategic locations behind his works, Jimmy Crane commanding one of these and Halkett another. These opened on the Martians as soon as they came into range. The furry masses, unable to use their rather ineffective chemical weapons, were forced to fall back with some thousands dead. They immediately tried to hem in the Earthmen as they had done with the Drake expedition.

Weathering did not permit this. He knew that the Martians' source of existence was the gray vegetation of the oases. This vegetation was mostly a sage shrub which bore pod-like fruits about the time the polar snow-caps reappeared. Weathering sent parties forth, Lieutenant Jimmy Crane heading one, to devastate the oases for a hundred miles around the Earth-post.

They carried out orders though the Martians in those cases made fierce resistance, and there were mad combats of brown-clad Earthmen and furry Martians in brilliant sunlight of day or black, freezing night. But Crane's and the other parties went stubbornly ahead, destroying the vegetation with atom-blasts. And in the end, with the vegetation that yielded their food-supply destroyed, the Martians in that hundred-mile circle had to retire across the red desert to other oases.

Weathering then split his forces into three divisions using his rockets to transport two of these divisions to points equidistant around Mars' equator. At each point a post like Weathering's own was established, with dirt-works in a square around it and atom-blast batteries mounted. Jimmy Crane, who had shown aptitude thus far in Martian campaigning, was made commander of one of these posts and a Lieutenant Lanson commander of the other. Halkett and Burnham stayed in Weathering's own post.

Eighty of the ninety-seven rockets that had landed safely, Weathering now sent back to Earth for more men and supplies. Word came from Earth that fifty new rockets had been constructed and were on their way with men and materials. Weathering distributed them equally among his three posts when they came and sent them also back to Earth for more. Crane and Lanson, under his orders, had devastated the oases around their posts to drive the Martians back from them.

CHAPTER TWO

THE CONQUEST OF MARS

Weathering's men were becoming acclimated to Martian conditions. The oxygenation treatments eliminated most of the Martian fever, and as the Earthmen's muscles attuned themselves gradually to the new gravitation their movements became more sure. It is worthy of note that some of those first venturers who went back from Mars to Earth after a year on the red planet were stricken by a sort of Earth-sickness due to Earth's different conditions.

As reinforcements came in, Weathering continued to distribute them among the three posts of Crane and Lanson and himself. He wanted to establish the three forts firmly before an overwhelming Martian attack swept them out of existence. There were signs that that could be expected from the Martians.

The Martian attacks were growing fiercer. The Martians could see plainly enough the course Weathering was following, and that each week brought more rockets from Earth with more men, more supplies and more atom-blasts and atomic bombs. They determined upon a concerted attack to wipe out the Earthmen's three forts before they became too strong.

The attack broke against the three forts, so widely separated, at the same time. It did not catch Weathering and Crane and Lanson by surprise—their atom-blasts were ready. But even so, the Martian attack was almost irresistible in sheer weight. From far across the reddish desert surged the furry Martian masses toward the three little forts, coming on despite the atom-blasts that took toll of them by tens of thousands.

Weathering's post and that of Crane withstood the attack by only the utmost endeavor. Halkett had charge of one of the atom-blast batteries at Weathering's fort, on the side that the Martians attacked most determinedly. It was Halkett's battery that wrought the deadliest destruction amid the furry hordes.

The third post, that of Lanson, fell. The Martians got inside with their chemical weapons despite the atom-blasts and bombs of the Earthmen. Lanson and his garrison were massacred to the last man by the Martians. Only one of the three rockets stationed at Lanson's post escaped, a little before the fort fell, and got to Weathering with the news.

Weathering acted at once, despite his own precarious situation. He assembled sixteen rockets from his fort and Crane's, loaded them with men and weapons, and sent them under the command of Mart Halkett to reestablish the third fort. They did so, taking the Martians there by surprise, and managed to hold the place in the face of the Martian attacks that followed.

There followed a lull in the fighting, with Weathering, Crane and Halkett holding grimly on in the three forts. The Martians had lost tremendous numbers without dislodging the Earthmen, and were in no mood for further attacks in force. Yet they did not retire but continued to encircle the forts.

But steadily the Earthmen's strength grew as more rockets came in. Earth was aflame over the situation, cheering Weathering as the upholder of terrestrial honor. The gallant fight of Earth's lonely outposts there amid the Martian hordes had appealed to the popular imagination and there were insistent demands that the Interplanetary Council use all its powers to reinforce them.

It meant to do so. It sent Weathering a message stating as much, advancing him from colonel to general, promoting Jimmy Crane to colonel, and Halkett and Burnham and a number of others to captaincies. The enlistment bureaus of the Council on Earth could not handle the flood of recruits.

Rockets were now pouring from the factories in a steadily increasing stream. Atomic weapons were also being produced in quantity and every few days saw rockets laden with supplies and men taking off for Mars. Many perished still in the dangers of the void but most arrived safely. Weathering continued to distribute the men and supplies they brought among his three posts.

When the three forts were strong enough to be impregnable to any Martian attack, Weathering began the establishment of new posts. He proceeded methodically to dot Mars with small but strong forts, each covering a certain portion of the planet's surface. Hall Burnham was made commander of one of the first of these, Crane and Halkett retaining command of their posts.

Within a year Weathering had a network of fifty forts stretched over Mars' surface from the north polar snow-cap to the southern one. He had in them strong garrisons of bronzed Earthmen thoroughly acclimated to the Martian gravitation and atmosphere, and well-seasoned in fighting with the stilt-limbed Martians. By then Halkett and Burnham were commanding two of the fifty forts, while Jimmy Crane was now Weathering's second in command. The two worked together distributing, according to their plan, among the fifty posts, the streams of men and materials arriving from Earth.

With the next melting of the polar snow-caps, Weathering was ready to begin the final subjugation of Mars. From a circle of six of his forts he sent out strong forces to attack and drive together the Martians in that circular territory. This was the plan evolved by Weathering and Crane, to concentrate forces upon one section of the planet at a time, using the forts around that section as bases, mopping up the Martians in that section thoroughly and then proceeding to another.

Crane had charge of the first operation and it worked perfectly. The Interplanetary Council had directed Weathering to offer the Martians peace if they promised to obey the Government's authority. But Crane's men had no chance even to make the offer, so utterly fierce was the Martian resistance.

The Martians had never expected what happened. The furry, stilt-limbed men had ceased their attacks on the Earthmen's forts some time before, save for occasional raids, and had retired to take up existence in the vegetation oases remoter from the forts. There they had lived as they had for ages, moving in nomadic fashion through the oases gathering the fruits upon which they subsisted, digging as ages of experience had made them skillful in doing for the underground springs. Now the Earthmen were attacking them! The Martians rose madly to the fight.

But Crane's forces were strongly armed and with atom-blasts and atom bombs against their crude weapons the Martians had no chance. Those in that section were mostly killed in the fighting and the few remaining were herded into prison camps. Crane went on under Weathering's order to another section and repeated the maneuver. Halkett's fort was one of the posts around that section, but Halkett and Crane had small opportunity of seeing each other in the midst of the grim business of rounding up the Martians. With that section subdued like the first, the forces of Crane concentrated on another.

Within another year Weathering could send word back to the Council that the plan had succeeded and that except for a few remote wastes near the snow-caps, Mars was entirely subjugated. In that year approximately three-fourths of the Martian race had perished, for in almost every case their forces had resisted to the last. Those who remained could constitute no danger to the Earthmen's system of forts. The Council flashed Weathering congratulations and gave Crane command of the expedition then fitting out at Earth for the exploration of Jupiter.

Crane went back to Earth to take charge of it, first taking warm leave of Mart Halkett and Hall Burnham at the posts they commanded. Crane spent a half year on Earth preparing his expedition of two hundred rockets to meet conditions on Jupiter. For Jupiter presented a greater problem to Earth explorers than had Mars, and biologists and chemists had been working to overcome the obstacles.

The greatest difficulty, Crane saw, was Jupiter's gravitation, almost twice that of Earth despite the swift-spinning planet's counteracting centrifugal force. Gillen's visit to Jupiter on his epochal flight had been terminated by sickness brought on by that greater gravitation and the heavy damp atmosphere. Crane's men must be strengthened to withstand these influences.

Earth's scientists solved the problem to some extent by devising rigid metallic clothing not unlike armor which would support the interior human structure against Jupiter's pull. Crane's men were also administered compounds devised by the biochemists for the rapid building of bone to strengthen the skeleton structure, while respirators which absorbed a percentage of the water vapor in air would solve for Crane's men the problem of the heavy wet atmosphere.

So equipped, Crane's expedition sailed in its two hundred rockets for Jupiter, choosing a time when the asteroid zone between Earth and Jupiter was comparatively clear. Even so, sixteen of the two hundred rockets never reached their destination. The others landed safely in the fern forests of the southern half of Jupiter, and Crane began there establishment of the first Earth-post.

He found himself with troubles enough. For though the metal armor and other protections safeguarded the Earthmen fairly effectively from the greater gravitation, they found it still difficult to make the simplest motions. It took weeks for Crane's men, against the drag of the Jovian gravity, to clear the fern forest around them and turn up dirtworks of the oozy black Jovian soil.

Sickness was rife among them, for the respirators did not work as well as the safeguards against gravitation. The heavy wet air worked havoc with the Earthmen's lungs and the so-called Jovian croup became soon as well-known and much more feared than Martian fever. Men toiling in the thin sunlight were stricken by it. Crane's forces were decimated by it. The fern forests, too, held weird forms of life that proved a problem, some of them disk-shaped things of flesh that enveloped anything living in their bodies and ingested it directly. There were also strange huge worm-like things existing in the oozy soil, and others stranger still. Crane's men had to work with atom-blasts constantly ready to repel these strange predatory forms of life.

Out of fern forests, too, came to watch the Earthmen hosts of the big, soft-bodied creatures Gillen had called the Jovians. These had bodies eight feet high and six feet around, like big cylinders of hairless brown flesh supported on thick flipper-like limbs, with similar flipper-like arms. Their small round heads had dark mild eyes and mouths from which came their deep bass speech. Crane found they were perhaps as intelligent as the Martians but were rather more peaceful, their only weapons spears with which they fought off the things in the fern forests that attacked them.

They were quite friendly toward the Earthmen and watched their operations with child-like interest. Crane intended to avoid Drake's mistake and not clash with the Jovians in any way while his men toiled to establish first one post and then others over southern Jupiter. He reported to the Council that he would only operate in South Jupiter for the time being. And while Earth followed Crane's work on South Jupiter with intense interest, a host of changes were occurring on Mars.

Mart Halkett, still commanding his equatorial Martian post, saw a new kind of migration now going on from Earth to Mars. Hitherto the rockets had carried hardly anything but the reinforcements of the Council and their supplies. But now Halkett saw crowds of civilians pouring into the newly subjugated planet. They were magnates, speculators, engineers, mechanics, for the Council was now granting concessions in the great Martian mineral and chemical deposits.

Halkett saw those forts nearest the deposits, including his own, grow rapidly into raw mine towns packed with Earthmen of all kinds. Martian fever had been completely conquered by Earth's scientists and some of these crude new towns contained thousands of Earthmen. There could be seen among them occasional stilt-limbed, huge-chested Martians moving about as though bewildered by the activity about them, but most of the remaining Martians were on certain oases set aside for them as reservations. Refining and extracting plants were set up as mining operations grew, and Halkett saw the rocket fleets that arrived with men and machinery going back to Earth laden with metals and chemicals.

Halkett went up to Burnham's post in northern Mars sick at heart. He told Burnham he had secured a transfer to Jupiter to serve there in Jimmy Crane's expanding system of forts.

"I can't stand this any longer, Burn," he said. "I mean what we've done to this world—the Martians, its people, almost wiped out and those left treated the way they are."

Burnham looked keenly at him. "You're taking it too hard, Halkett," he said. "It's been a tough time, I admit, but that's all over now the Martians are conquered."

"Conquered—wiped out, I say again," Halkett said bitterly. "Burnham, I dream about it sometimes—those waves of furry stilt-men coming on and on toward certain death, and my atom-blasts mowing them down like grass."

"They had to be conquered," Burnham argued. "Isn't it worth it? Look at all this planet's resources thrown open to real use now instead of lying unused."

"Thrown open to a lot of speculators and financiers to extract a profit from," Halkett amended. "The Martians are killed off and we do the dirty work of killing them and all for what? So this bunch swarming into Mars now can enrich themselves."

"That's too narrow a view," Burnham told him. "It's inevitable that there'll be certain evils in the course of an expansion like this."

"Why expand, then?" asked Halkett. "Why not stay on our own planet and leave these poor devils of Martians and Jovians keep theirs?"

Burnham shook his head. "Expansion is as inevitable as a full tank overflowing into an empty one. Anyway, Halk, the fighting's over here now so why go on to Jupiter?"

"Because I feel like a murderer haunting the scene of his crime," Halkett told him. "When I see some of these degraded Martians hanging around our towns, begging for food and getting cuffed and kicked out of the way by Earthmen, I want to get out of here to I don't care where."

Halkett went on to Jupiter. He found by then Crane had established a dozen posts over the southern half of the vast planet, following Weathering's Martian system. Jovian croup was giving Crane more trouble than anything else and the dreaded disease was often fatal, the death list sometimes appalling while the Earth scientists worked frantically to control the disease. They finally succeeded in evolving a serum which was an effective preventive. Halkett was inoculated with this immediately on reaching Jupiter.

Halkett found that Crane was, despite the difficulties, strengthening his system of posts as reinforcements arrived constantly from Earth. He had been successful in avoiding trouble with the Jovians so far—the strange forms of life that came out from the steamy fern forests to attack the Earthmen were of more concern than the numberless but peaceful hosts of the Jovians.

Crane commented on the Jovians to Halkett the night after the latter's arrival. The two had been outside the post and Halkett had met the Jovians for the first time, the big, soft-eyed flipper-men clustering around him like interested children. Now he and Crane sat in Crane's lamplit office, whose windows looked out across the post to the mighty wall of the surrounding fern forest. Halkett could hear the calls and screams of the forest's various weird tenants, and could see its steamy mists rising into the light of the two moons then in the sky, Callisto and Europa.

"These Jovians aren't a bad bunch, Halk," Colonel Jimmy Crane told his friend. "They seem too mild to give us any real trouble, though God knows how many millions of them there are."

He was enthusiastic about Jupiter's possibilities. "I tell you, this is the planet of the future. Stick a seed in the ground and in a week you've a tree—this planet will be supporting trillions of humans some day when Earth and Mars are overcrowded."

"Where will the Jovians be when that day arrives?" Halkett asked him. Crane looked at him.

"Still holding to that viewpoint? Halkett, we have to let some things take care of themselves. Be sure we'll not harm the Jovians if they don't try harming us."

"Well, we may be able to get along with them," Halkett said thoughtfully. "They seem rather more peaceful than the Martians."

CHAPTER THREE

JUPITER NEXT!

But trouble came soon after Halkett's arrival, with the Jovians. Crane had been engaged in strengthening his dozen posts scattered over the southern half of Jupiter. He had not tried to establish any forts in North Jupiter, realizing the insufficiency of his resources, for even the dozen on the huge planet's southern half were separated by tremendous distances. Rocket communication between them was fairly quick but Crane preferred to strengthen the twelve forts before establishing more.

Then came the trouble. It began as on Mars—a bad-tempered Earthman at one of the forts beat a flipper-man for some reason and in a brawl that ensued one Earthman and five Jovians were killed. Word must have spread somehow in the fern forests for the Jovians retired from the forts of the Earthmen. Jimmy Crane cursed in private but acted, punishing the Earthmen concerned and sending Halkett to the Jovian communities to patch up matters.

Halkett had learned the Jovian language and proved a good ambassador for he was sympathetic with the flipper-men. He did his best to fulfill his mission but could not succeed. The flipper-men told Halkett that they had no hard feelings but would prefer to avoid the Earthmen lest further trouble develop.

Halkett went back with this word and Crane realized that trouble was ahead. He flashed word back to the Interplanetary Council and it ordered him to hold all his posts and await reinforcements from Earth and Mars. Weathering would send on most of the Martian divisions of the Council's Army as rapidly as possible.

Soon after the arrival of the first reinforcements the storm broke. The Jovians had come to see, despite Halkett's attempt at reassurance, what Crane's expanding system of posts would mean in time. They went to Crane asking from him a promise that no more Earthmen would come to Jupiter. Crane curtly refused to make such a promise. Even so the flipper-men might have remained inactive had not by some inconceivable brutality an atom-blast been turned upon their envoys as they left the fort.

Crane's summary execution of the men responsible for the action could not mend matters.

For the Jovians, aroused at last, rose upon the Earthmen. Over all South Jupiter they poured out of the fern forests in incalculable masses upon the forts of the Earthmen. They had not even the crude chemical weapons the Martians had used, their only arms spears and great maces, but there were tens of thousands of them to every Earthman. Crane set himself grimly to hold his dozen posts against the floods of the flipper-men.

He had given Halkett command of one of the posts on the other side of South Jupiter. Halkett gripped himself and used all his experience to hold the post. He fought as all of Crane's twelve posts were fighting, to hold back the endless Jovian masses. The atom-blasts scythed them down, the atomic bombs burst in terrific destruction among them, but the Jovians came on to the attack with a sort of mild but resolute determination.

Crane now was fighting to maintain Earth's hold upon South Jupiter until reinforcements could come. He sent brief reports back to the Earth. The Council appreciated the situation, commandeered all rockets for the sole purpose of transporting their legions and weapons to South Jupiter. Only skeleton garrisons were left in the Martian posts. Yet it seemed that by sheer numbers the Jovians would overwhelm the Earthmen.

One of Crane's twelve posts they did indeed take. A strange sidelight on the nature of the Jovians is that after losing hundreds of thousands in the long attack on the fort, they contented themselves with razing it to the ground when they had captured it and holding the Earthmen in it prisoners. There was no massacre as had been the case on Mars. Crane, however, managed with the coming of further reinforcements to reestablish the fort.

The tide was turning in the Earthmen's favor. Every day brought in new rockets of men and supplies to Crane and the flipper-men could not face the atom-blasts and bombs forever, even with their incalculable numbers. Their attacks died away as the twelve forts grew stronger and they retired into the great forests. Any parties venturing from the forts they fell upon. It was the same situation as on Mars three years before, and Crane dealt with it in the same way. Halkett was one of his own aides now, and so too was Hall Burnham who had come on from Mars with the reinforcements.

Crane held his hand until he had strengthened his twelve posts beyond danger of attack, then established at gradual intervals no less than ninety more posts in a network around South Jupiter. He was going to proceed on Weathering's Martian plan, subjugating the planet section by section, except that Crane was operating only in South Jupiter and leaving the northern half of the great planet quite untouched. Patiently he established and strengthened his hundred-odd posts.

When his network of strong forts around South Jupiter was complete, Crane went ahead to conquer it section by section as he had planned. It was a herculean undertaking for the Earthmen. Their greatest obstacle was not the Jovians themselves, who could offer no effective resistance to the atom-blasts and bombs of Crane's men, but the terrible Jovian gravity that made each movement an effort, that required them to wear the metal body-support armor and made their movements still more difficult.

Yet in section after section the divisions of Crane's mobile forces, Halkett and Burnham among their commanders, crashed through the steamy fern forests with atom-blasts and drove the Jovians slowly but resistlessly until they were hemmed in and brought to action. There were fights of terrific fury in the green twilight of the huge damp forests, for few of the Jovians surrendered, the great majority fighting with immovable resolution until the atom-blasts and bombs slew them.

Crane's grip upon South Jupiter tightened with each section subjugated by the superhuman endeavors of his men. He flashed word to the Interplanetary Council that his plan was following schedule. He was conquering sections in such a way as to cut off from each other by subjugated territories the larger Jovian masses. Then in the midst of this tremendous task occurred an astonishing incident, one that made Earth first incredulous and then wrathful. Halkett became a traitor.

The first reports of Halkett's treachery that got back to Earth were confused and contradictory. Later ones stated that Captain Halkett was under guard in one of the South Jupiter posts. He had been the cause of the hard-fought subjugation campaign in one of the sections failing, and of a large Jovian force escaping. That was all that was known certainly at first.

Then came details. Three forces under Halkett and Burnham and an officer named James had been operating against the Jovians in that section. Halkett commanded a heavy atom-blast battery and Burnham and James had been driving the Jovian forces toward it. For a score of the short Jovian days and nights the men of Burnham and James had pushed the Jovians in the desired direction, toiling against the relentless gravitation's drag, through the endless fern forests they had to cut through and against the weird beasts they dislodged from those forests. They had without question done their part against the Jovians.

But Halkett had not. He had deliberately ordered his men not to fire on the Jovians and the flipper-men had escaped past him. Earth could hardly credit the news. There came from soldiers and civilians alike a swift demand for Halkett's punishment. The Council ordered Crane to send Halkett home for court-martial.

Crane told Halkett that in the guardhouse on South Jupiter, and told him much more for he was half-crazed with the thing.

"Halk, how could you have done it?" he kept saying. "I've got to send you back now and God knows what a court-martial will do to you with feeling against you so strong on Earth."

"Don't worry about it, Crane," said Halkett steadily. "I did as I wanted and I'm willing to take my medicine."

"But why did you do it?" Crane demanded for the hundredth time. "Halkett, if you'll only plead that you didn't know the Jovians were coming through—that it was some kind of blunder—"

Hall Burnham seconded him. "A blunder on your part would lose you your commission but you'd escape a sentence," he told Halkett. "Surely it was partly that, at least."

Halkett shook his head. "It wasn't. I can't explain just what it was, why I did it—but if you'd have seen those Jovians coming through the forest there, weary, terrorized, hunted onward for days yet somehow unresentful—I *couldn't* turn the atom-blasts loose on them!"

Crane made a gesture. "Halkett, I understand what you felt but even so, you shouldn't have done it. I'd go back with you to Earth for the trial but I can't leave here now."

"It's all right, Jimmy," Halkett told him. "I'm willing to take what comes."

Halkett departed for Earth under guard in one of the next detachment of rockets, while Crane and Burnham and the rest went on with the subjugation of South Jupiter. During the voyage the rocket's officers were careful to show Halkett consideration but no man of them spoke a word to him except when necessary. Feeling in the army against its first traitor was intense.

When Halkett reached Earth after that strange voyage from Jupiter, the heads of the Council ordered an immediate court-martial. It took place in the great Army building. Halkett's trial occupied four days and during those days the building was surrounded by crowds waiting to hear his fate.

Popular indignation at Halkett ran high, and many cries for his summary execution were being voiced. People contrasted the gallant struggles of Crane and the rest to hold South Jupiter for humanity with this treachery on the part of a trusted officer. Halkett might have been lynched if he had been less well guarded.

Inside the great building Halkett stood up and heard his conduct judged. The officers who heard the case gave him a fair trial. His counsel argued ably concerning Halkett's previous gallant record, the possibility of temporary aberrations and the like. Halkett might have escaped but for his own testimony a little later.

"I was quite in command of all my faculties when I ordered the atom-batteries not to fire," he said quietly.

"Did you realize, Captain Halkett," asked the presiding officer crisply, "that in so doing you were betraying your sworn oath?"

Halkett said that he had realized. "Then what reason can you give for your deliberate breach of trust?"

Halkett hesitated. "I can't give any reason that you'd understand," he said.

Then he burst out with sudden white passion—"Why shouldn't I have done it? After all, Jupiter belonged to the Jovians, didn't it? What were we there but invaders, interlopers? How could I order those hunted flipper-men destroyed when all they were trying to do was to keep their own world?"

His counsel made frantic signals to him but Halkett was beyond restraint. "What right have we Earth races on Mars or Jupiter either? What right had we to wipe out almost all the Martians as we did, and to repeat it now on Jupiter? Because their planet has resources, the Jovians have to be killed!"

That outburst removed any chance of Halkett's acquittal. The presiding officer read gravely the sentence of ten years in military prison.

"It is only consideration of your former record on Mars and South Jupiter and the fact that you were one of Drake's historic party," he stated, "that keeps this court from giving you a life-sentence or even the extreme penalty."

Halkett took the verdict without any show of emotion and was led back to his cell. Burnham, who had come in from Jupiter in time for the trial's end, went to see him before he was taken to the military prison. Halkett shook hands with him in silence—the two had nothing to say.

With Halkett in prison the world's wrath was appeased. His name was stricken off all the records of the Council's Army. Burnham went back to Jupiter. Halkett spent his days in the shops of the military prison, helping manufacture atom-blasts and bombs and other army supplies. He stood imprisonment quietly.

Crane had moved heaven and earth to get Halkett acquitted but had found his influence useless. Burnham came back and told him how Halkett had taken the verdict. For a long time these two sat silent, perhaps thinking of three thrilled youngsters in technical school who had followed Gillen's flight and rushed to join Drake.

Crane went grimly on with the business of subduing South Jupiter. In the excited activity of that campaign the world forgot Halkett quickly. Crane's plan was working with the precision of a machine, section after section of the great planet being subjugated. Over all South Jupiter those Jovians not yet attacked were moving up into the planet's northern half as yet unvisited by the Earthmen's forces.

In four Earth years South Jupiter was under Earth control. It was gripped tightly by Crane's system of forts, most of its forests had been destroyed by atom-blasts, and as towns grew slowly around the forts great grain-planting projects were getting under way. There were some reservations of Jovians, but the greater part of the Jovians not slain during the subjugation were in North Jupiter. There the fern forests still stretched untouched from the equator to the northern pole, the same as when Gillen first had seen them. But now Crane was looking north toward them.

Jimmy Crane was now General James Crane, thirty-one years old and with gray showing at his temples from nine years of strenuous campaigning on Mars and Jupiter. He had been back to Earth twice from Jupiter, once with Burnham who was now a colonel, and both times had tried to see Halkett but had been prevented by strict regulations. Halkett had for four years now worked quietly on in the prison shops making atom-blasts, bombs and rocket parts.

Crane and the Council laid plans for the subjugation of North Jupiter. It was to be done peacefully if possible—the Jovians were to be offered great fern forest reservations and other inducements. But peacefully or not, the planet had to come under control. Crane, who knew the Jovians, began assembling forces on South Jupiter, even as he sent Burnham into North Jupiter to offer the Jovians the Government's terms.

Burnham failed absolutely, as Crane and almost everyone else had expected, to win the Jovians to peaceful settlement. The flipper-men had no faith at all in the Earthmen's promises, and no desire to live on reservations. Crane flashed word of that to the Council, which authorized him to proceed by force. A great preparation began on Earth and on South Jupiter.

In the midst of his preparations Crane learned that Halkett had been released, his sentence halved for good behavior. He tried to locate Halkett through agents but no one knew where Halkett had gone on leaving prison. Crane was doing the work of two men in the great preparations for the North Jupiter campaign, and could not for the time institute any search for his former comrade.

CHAPTER FOUR
THE RENEGADE

Rocket fleets arrived ceaselessly, pouring men and materials into South Jupiter from Earth and Mars. The recruiting offices on Earth were working night and day. Crane took the men they sent and mixed them with his veterans, drilled them, trained them in Jovian fighting, made disciplined armies of them. He concentrated men and materials at the equatorial posts.

For Crane was going to follow a different plan in North Jupiter. Instead of establishing a network of posts as on Mars and South Jupiter, he was going to encircle Jupiter with a thin band of Earth forces and then push that band northward toward the pole. His circle, Crane saw, would grow smaller and stronger the farther north it pushed, and would drive the Jovians in North Jupiter onward until those not slain were hemmed in in the warm north polar region.

It took two years of preparation before Crane deemed his forces sufficient. Neither he nor Burnham had in that time heard anything of Halkett, nor had any one else. Burnham thought that Halkett must be dead. But both had other things enough to think of when Crane began the long-planned campaign. With his forces encircling the equator of the planet, he ordered an advance. The band around the planet began to crawl north.

Fighting with the flipper-men began in days. The Jovians by that time knew better than to charge atom-blasts or expose themselves to the barrage of atomic bombs. They tried a kind of guerrilla fighting which was not ineffective in the dense fern forests. But Crane's forces simply blasted the forests out of the way as they advanced, and the Jovians had either to flee or be slain.

Crane moved his headquarters north behind his band of forces. He directed the band's northward movement by radio, sending reinforcements in rockets to whatever part that was held back by fiercer resistance. Crane chose to advance slowly and avoid undue losses. There was no haste—the Jovians were being pushed ever northward by the contracting circle. Within a half-year Earth heard that its forces had advanced half the distance between Jupiter's equator and northern pole.

Then came to Earth surprising news of a check to Crane's advance. His band had been flung back with heavy losses by the Jovians at a half-dozen places around the planet! Incredibly, it had been done by Jovians armed with atom-blasts and atomic bombs! They had prepared a circle of rude trenches and earthworks at strategic locations around the planet and had inflicted terrible damage on Crane's band of men when it advanced to that circle!

Earth was aflame instantly with apprehensive excitement. Until then it had taken Crane's final success as certain—the Council had even granted future concessions to the North Jupiter territories. How had the primitive Jovians come to use the atomic weapons? From Crane, who had hastily halted the advance of his circle, came the answer. The Jovians were being led by a renegade Earthman who for the past two years had been training them in the production and use of the atom-blasts and bombs. And this renegade was Mart Halkett!

Halkett had been recognized unmistakably by some of Crane's officers during the attack on the Jovian works, had been seen directing the Jovian defense. Halkett! The man who seven years before had played the traitor and who now had become renegade, leading the flipper-men against his own race! It was evident that on his release from prison Halkett had got to South Jupiter in some rocket and then had made his way into North Jupiter and used his technical skill and prison factory experience to set the Jovians making atom-blasts and atomic bombs and digging defenses for the coming struggle.

Halkett became immediately the supreme malefactor to the Earth peoples. On Earth and on Mars and on South Jupiter men flamed with rage at his name. A thousand deaths were advocated for Halkett if ever he were captured. Crane and Burnham and the rest of the Council Army's men appeared even greater in heroism against the black background of this renegade's treachery. A fierce desire to crush the Jovians and execute Halkett swept Earthmen everywhere.

"You will enter into no treatments whatever with the Jovians' renegade leader," flashed the Council to Crane. "Proceed with the North Jupiter campaign according to your own judgment."

Crane read the message. He and Burnham had been stunned by the news about Halkett and Crane for a time would not believe it. "It can't be Halkett," he had said over and over. "I tell you he wouldn't fight against the Council—against us."

"It's beyond doubt," Burnham told him. "Halkett was recognized by men who knew him well there with the Jovians. And you know what his views have always been on the Jovians."

"Yes, but to become a renegade against his own race! I tell you, Burn, Halkett could never have done that!"

Yet by the time the Council's message reached him, even Crane was convinced that Halkett was the renegade Jovian leader. He called his officers. "We will begin the advance again tomorrow," he said grimly. "Radio all headquarters to make ready."

The advance started again, this time not calmly as before but in deadly earnest. The band of Earth forces crawled forward until it met again the line of Jovian defenses. Crane had flung all his forces forward in that attack against Halkett's line, and the battle was terrific. But this time the Earthmen were attacking, and the Jovians fighting from cover.

The Jovian atom-blasts and bombs, though comparatively few in number and inefficiently handled, yet did terrific execution among the advancing Earthmen. Halkett's line held all around the planet though the Earthmen attacked like mad beings. Crane at last gave the order to withdraw. Earth was appalled by the casualty lists that were sent home. But though Crane was checked he was not stopped.

He let Halkett's Jovians alone until enough reinforcements had come in to make up his losses. Then he started the attack again, but this time not in a steady wave but in a series of punches. Great spearheads of men and atom weapons were thrust at Halkett's line in a dozen different places. Crane's plan was to shatter the Jovian defenses by repeated concentrated thrusts until it had to withdraw.

Halkett fought fiercely to hold that line. His communications were poor though it was known he had trained some of the Jovians in radio and was directing their fight all round the planet. He had no rockets and could not parry Crane's smashing thrusts by rushing reinforcements to the points attacked. He foresaw inevitable retreat and had the Jovians prepare other lines of defenses farther north toward the pole. The flipper-men followed him with absolute faith.

Soon Halkett was forced to withdraw the Jovians to the next of these hastily prepared defense lines. Crane made no attempt to pursue the

Jovians but spread his forces again into a band and advanced northward, destroying forests and mopping up stray groups of Jovians. When his band reached Halkett's new line Crane did not attack but began again his strategy of punching at the line.

The battle-lines on the Jupiter globes by which Earth's people followed the struggle crept steadily northward toward the pole in the following year. Ever Halkett's Jovians were forced to retreat to new defenses and ever after them came Crane and Burnham and the hosts of the Council's Army, contracting upon them in a steadily diminishing circle. They would ultimately press the Jovians together near the pole and Halkett fought to prevent that.

It was in some ways a strange situation. The three inseparable friends of boyhood and youth become men and fighting the war of races there on North Jupiter, one of them renegade to an alien race and the other two advancing always with their forces on him. No one could accuse Crane of letting his former friendship affect him, in the face of his grim determination. He pushed Halkett's line unrelentingly northward.

And as Halkett's line, the defenses of the Jovians, reached the warm polar regions, Halkett's own military genius flamed. He commanded the Jovians in a way which, despite the meagerness of their atomic weapons, held Crane's forces to the slowest advance. The once-mild flipper-men fought like demons under his leadership. Crane, of all men, appreciated Halkett's supreme generalship in those grim days on North Jupiter. But he punched grimly on, and Halkett's circular line grew smaller and smaller as the Jovians retreated.

It was the retreat of a race—the weary hosts of the Jovians ever backing northward through the steamy fern forests that had been theirs for untold time, throwing up new dirtworks and digging new trenches always at Halkett's command, using every sort of ambush device Halkett could think of to hold back the Earthmen. The fern forests resounded with the roar of atom-blasts and crash of atom bombs, strange things flopping this way and that in the green depths to escape the battle, the Jovians all round the planet fighting bitterly now for existence.

And ever after them Crane's men, the metal-armored hosts of Earthmen struggling against every obstacle of heat and gravitation and illness. For days they would toil through the giant ferns without meeting resistance and then would come upon the new line Halkett had massed the Jovians upon. And then again the blasts would be roaring in death from Jovians and Earthmen as the Earthmen attacked. And ever despite their desperate resistance the Jovians were pushed back northward, toward the pole.

Reconnoitering rockets brought word to Crane that Halkett had established a refugee camp near the pole that held several millions of the Jovians and that he was collecting atom-blasts and bombs there and digging works around it. Crane sought to cut this base out of Halkett's circle but Halkett saw the maneuver and occupied the place with most of his remaining forces. To do so he had to abandon his circular line of defense except for some smaller bases. So at last the circle of Halkett's line around North Jupiter was gone, and the Jovians held only those fortified bases.

Earth flamed with gladness as Crane went systematically about the work of reducing these bases. He sent Burnham with a force of Earthmen large enough to hold Halkett and his Jovians inside the main base, while he reduced the smaller ones. There was bloody fighting before he took them. Those Jovians, miserably few in number, who survived in them, were sent to temporary prison-camps pending their removal to the reservations established. Then with that done, Crane came with all his forces and joined Burnham in front of the last Jovian base in which sat Halkett and his battered remaining Jovians, fighters and refugees.

Crane surprised Burnham and his officers by stating he would treat with Halkett for surrender, though the Council had ordered otherwise.

He sent in a messenger summoning Halkett to surrender and avoid further bloodshed, promising the Jovians would be sent to reservations and pointing out the futility of resistance.

Halkett's reply was calm. "There will be no surrender unless the Jovians are given their rights as natives and owners of this planet. Nothing the Jovians endure now can be worse than what they've already gone through."

Crane read the answer to Burnham, his bronzed lined face set. "Halkett and the Jovians mean it," he said. "They'll resist to the last and we'll have to attack."

Burnham leaned to him. "Crane, tell me," he said, "are you trying to save the Jovians in there or Halkett?"

Crane looked at him, heartsickness on his face. "Burn, it's not Halkett. Better for him if he died in an attack rather than to be taken back to Earth and executed. But those Jovians—I'm tired of killing them."

Burnham nodded thoughtfully. "But what are you going to do? Order the attack tomorrow? The men are impatient to start it."

Crane thought, then surprised him. "Burn, you and I are going in to see Halkett and try to get him to take these terms. He won't come out but we can go in safely enough."

"But the Council—" Burnham began. Crane waved him impatiently aside. "I'm conducting this campaign and not the Council. I say we're going in."

He sent a message through the works to Halkett, and Halkett replied that he would be glad to confer with General Crane and Colonel Burnham regarding terms, but anticipated no change of mind. Crane ordered all hostilities suspended and at sunset he and Burnham went with two Jovians and a white flag toward the Jovian defenses. The misty red sun was sinking behind the horizon, so distant from the huge planet, when they reached the Jovian works.

The two flipper-men blindfolded them before taking them through the dirtworks and entrenchments, no doubt at Halkett's order, and took off the bandages when they were inside. Crane and Burnham saw before them the great enclosure that held the innumerable masses of the Jovian refugees. There was no shelter for most but at some sheds small portions of fruit and makeshift vegetable foods were being rationed out to some of them. The crowds of flipper-men, bulky strange figures in the dying light, looked mildly at Crane and Burnham as they were led through the great enclosure.

As they followed their guides Crane saw for himself the battered Jovian forces he had pushed north for so long, with their crudely made atom-blasts and bombs, many standing guard round the inner works. Here and there in the enclosure were large dumps of atomic bombs, protected by shelters. Near one of these was a small hut toward which the two Jovians led them.

Halkett and three Jovians came out of the hut as Crane and Burnham approached. Halkett and his aides waited for them and the two Earthmen went on toward them, with the slow laborious steps against the gravity-drag that were second nature to Earthmen on Jupiter now. It was a strange meeting. The three had not met together since they had parted on South Jupiter eight years before.

Halkett wore an old suit of the metal body-strengthening armor and had a bandage round his lower left arm. His face was bronzed, and was lined and worn-looking, but his eyes were calm. He was a contrast to Crane and Burnham, trim in their metal body-protection with on it the insignia of the Council Army that Halkett once had worn.

Halkett did not offer to shake hands with them, but waited. Crane's first words were confused and stiffly formal. He mentioned the terms.

"We can't accept them," Halkett told him calmly. "We've fought against them from the first and these Jovians would rather die than go to your Jovian reservations."

"But what else can you do?" asked Crane. "You know as well as I do that I've enough forces to take this place and that we'll do it if you don't give in."

"I know," said Halkett, "but the Jovians wouldn't do it if I told them to, and I'm not going to tell them. Besides, I've a way out for these Jovians."

"A way out?" Burnham said. "There's no way out with your works completely surrounded."

One of the Jovians beside Halkett said something to him in his odd bass voice. Halkett replied to him patiently, almost gently. Crane was watching him. Halkett turned back to him.

"Be reasonable, Halkett," Crane urged. "You can't save the Jovians and there'll be just that many more of them killed in the attack."

"Do a few more Jovians killed now make any difference?" Halkett asked. "After all those killed on South and North Jupiter?"

He looked beyond them, thoughtful. "I wonder if Gillen foresaw any of this that's happened on Mars and Jupiter when he made his flight? What would Gillen think, I wonder, if he came back and saw all this that he started?"

They were silent for a little while. The short Jovian day was over and with the sunset's fading, twilight was upon them. Callisto and Io were at the zenith and Ganymede was climbing eastward, the three moons shedding a pale light over the great enclosure. Dimly they disclosed the masses of dark flipper-forms about Crane and Burnham and Halkett.

Burnham and Crane could hear with Halkett the occasional bass voices of the Jovians that were the only sounds. Most of them were silent and did not move about, huddling in masses for the night. By the inner works the Jovian fighters still stood calmly, big, dark motionless shapes seen strangely through the dim-lit darkness.

Crane spoke with an effort. "Then that's your last word on the terms, Halkett?"

Halkett nodded. "It's not mine, but that of the Jovians themselves."

Crane's restraint broke momentarily. "Halkett, why did you do it? Why did you become renegade to your own race, no matter what happened? Why have you made us hunt you north this way, fighting against you and with a duty to kill you?"

"I'm not sorry, Crane," said Halkett. "I've come to love these Jovians—so mild and child-like, so trustful to anyone friendly. It just seemed that somebody ought to stand up for them and give them at least a chance to fight. I don't care what you call me."

"Hell, let's get a rocket and the three of us will head for somewhere else together!" cried the Jimmy Crane of ten years before. "Some other planet—we'll make out without this damned Jupiter and Earth and everyone on them! How did we three ever get into this, against each other, trying to kill each other?"

Halkett smiled, grasped Crane's hand then. "Jimmy!" he said. "You and Burn and I, back with Drake's expedition, three kids—you remember? But we can't change things now, and none of us are to blame, perhaps no one at all is really to blame, for what's happened."

Jimmy Crane with an effort became General James Crane. "Goodbye, Halkett," he said. "I'm sorry you can't accept the terms. Come on, Burnham."

Burnham tried to speak, his face working, but Halkett only smiled and shook his hand. He turned and went with Crane and the two Jovian guides, to the inner edge of the enclosure's defenses.

They saw Halkett standing with his three Jovian aides where they had left him. He was not looking after them. One of the Jovians was saying something and Crane and Burnham could see momentarily in the dim light Halkett's tanned, worn face as he turned to listen.

Crane and Burnham got back to their own camp and Crane called his officers. "We'll not delay attack until tomorrow but will start in two hours," he said. "They'll not expect an attack so soon."

Halkett must have expected it, though, for when the Earth-forces moved upon the Jovian works from all sides they were met by every atom-blast of the Jovians. Europa had climbed into the sky by then and Jupiter's moons looked down on the terrific assault. Blasts roared deafeningly and the thundering detonation of atomic bombs followed each other ceaselessly as the hosts of Earthmen clambered into the Jovian works.

The Jovians beat back the attack. Crane concentrated forces in an attack on the enclosure's west side. He sent his rockets overhead to add to his barrage of atom bombs and managed to make a breach in the western defenses. Halkett, though, flung all his Jovians to close these openings and Crane's forces were beaten back from it after terrible losses on both sides.

Dawn was breaking after the brief night as Crane ordered the third attack, one from all sides again with the heaviest forces on the western side. This time Halkett could not concentrate his forces to hold the western breach. The ground heaved with the roar of bombs and blasts as the Earthmen struggled in with high-pitched yells and with hand blasts spitting.

They poured into the breach despite the mad resistance of the remaining Jovian fighters, while on the eastern side the Earth hosts also were penetrating the Jovian works. Then, as Crane and Burnham watched from the camp outside, they saw with the rising of the sun the sudden end.

The whole interior of the great circular Jovian enclosure went skyward in a terrific series of explosions that wiped out not only all of Halkett's Jovian followers and massed refugees but most of the Jovians and many of the Earthmen fighting in the surrounding works. There was left only a huge crater.

"The dumps of atom bombs there in the enclosure!" cried Burnham. "A blast must have reached them and set them off!"

Crane nodded, his face strange. "Yes, a blast and in Halkett's hand. He set them off to wipe out his Jovians rather than see them sent to the reservations."

"My God!" Burnham cried. "That was Halkett's way out for the Jovians, then—old Halkett—"

Crane looked stonily at him. "Didn't you see that that was what he meant all the time to do? Give orders to round up those last Jovians in the works and bring them in.

"Then send this message back to Earth. 'Last Jovian base taken and renegade Jovian leader Halkett dead. Jupiter under complete control. Accept my resignation from Council Army. Crane.'"

The Island of Unreason

The director of city 72, North American Division 16, looked up enquiringly from his desk at his assistant.

"The next case is Allan Mann, Serial Number 2473R6," said the First Assistant Director. "The charge is breach of reason."

"The prisoner is ready?" asked the Director, and when his subordinate nodded he ordered, "Send him in."

The First Assistant Director went out and re-entered in a moment, followed by two guards who had the prisoner between them. He was a young man dressed in the regulation sleeveless white shirt and white shorts, with the blue square of the Mechanical Department on his shoulder.

He looked a little uncertainly around the big office, at the keyboards of the big calculating and predicting machines, at the televisor disks through which could be seen cities half around the world, and at the broad windows that looked out across the huge cubical metal buildings of City 72.

The Director read from a sheet on his desk. "Allan Mann, Serial Number 2473R6, was apprehended two days ago on a charge of breach of reason.

"The specific charge is that Allan Mann, who had been working two years on development of a new atomic motor, refused to turn over his work to Michael Russ, Serial Number 1877R6, when ordered to do so by a superior. He could give no reasonable cause for his refusal but stated only that he had developed the new motor for two years and wanted to finish it himself. As this was a plain breach of reason, officers were called."

The Director looked up at the prisoner. "Have you any defense, Allan Mann?"

The young man flushed. "No, sir, I have not. I wish only to say that I realize now I was wrong."

"Why did you rebel against your superior's order? Did he not tell you that Michael Russ was better fitted than you to finish development of your motor?"

"He did, yes," Allan Mann answered. "But I had worked on the motor so long I wanted very much to finish it myself, even though it took longer—I realize it was unreasonable of me—"

The Director laid down the sheet and bent earnestly forward. "You are right, Allan Mann, it was unreasonable of you. It was a breach of reason and as such, it was a blow at the very foundation of our modern world-civilization!"

He raised a lean finger in emphasis. "What is it, Allan Mann, that has built up the present world-state out of a mass of warring nations? What has eliminated conflict, fear, poverty, hardship from the world? What but reason?

"Reason has raised man from the beast-like level he formerly occupied to his present status. Why, in the old days of unreason the very ground on which this city now stands was occupied by a city called New York where men struggled and strove with each other blindly and without cooperation and with infinite waste and toil.

"All that has been changed by reason. The old emotions which twisted and warped men's minds have been overruled and we listen now only to the calm dictates of reason. Reason has brought us up from the barbarism of the twentieth century and to commit a breach of reason has become a serious crime. For it is a crime that aims directly at the demolition of our world-order."

Beneath the Director's calm statement, Allan Mann wilted. "I realize that that is so, sir," he said. "It is my hope that my breach of reason will be regarded only as a temporary aberration."

"I do so regard it," the Director said. "I am sure that by now you realize the wrongness of unreasonable conduct.

"But," he continued, "this explanation of your act does not excuse it. The fact remains that you have committed a breach of reason and that you must be corrected in the way specified by law."

"What is this way of correction?" asked Allan Mann.

The Director considered him. "You are not the first one to commit a breach of reason, Allan Mann. In the past more than one person has let irrational emotions sway him. These atavistic returns to unreason are becoming rarer, but they still occur.

"Long ago we devised a plan for the correction of these *unreasonables,* as we call them. We do not punish them, of course, for to inflict punishment on anyone for wrong-doing would be itself unreasonable. We try instead to cure them. We send them to what we call the Island of Unreason.

"That is a small island a few hundred miles out at sea from this coast. There are taken all the unreasonables and there they are left. There is no form of government on the island and only unreasonables live there. They are not given any of the comforts of life which human reason has devised but instead must live there as best they may in primitive fashion.

"If they fight or attack each other, it is nothing to us. If they steal from each other, we care not. For living like that, in a place where there is no rule of reason, they soon come to see what society would be like without reason. They see and never forget and most of them when their sentence is finished and they are brought back are only too glad for the rest of their lives to live in reasonable fashion. Though a few incorrigible unreasonables must stay on the island all their lives.

"It is to this island that all guilty of breach of reason must be sent. And so as provided by law, I must sentence you to go there."

"To the Island of Unreason?" Allan Mann said, dismay plain on his face. "But for how long?"

"We never tell those sent there how long their sentence is to be," the Director told him. "We want them to feel that they have a lifetime ahead of them on the island and this brings the lesson further home to them. When your sentence is finished, the guard-flier that takes you there will go there to bring you back."

He stood up. "Have you any complaint to make against this sentence?"

Allan Mann was silent, then spoke in subdued voice. "No, sir, it is but reasonable that I be corrected according to custom."

The Director smiled. "I am glad to see that you are already recovering. When your sentence has expired I hope to see you completely cured."

The guard-flier split the air like a slim metal torpedo as it hurtled eastward over the gray ocean. Long minutes before the coastline had faded from sight behind, and now beneath the noonday sun there extended to the horizons only the gray wastes of the empty ocean.

Allan Mann regarded it from the flier's window with deepening dismay. Reared in the great cities like every other member of civilized humanity, he had an inborn dislike of this solitude. He sought to evade it temporarily by conversing with the two guards who, with a pilot, were the flier's other occupants. But Allan found that they disliked to talk much to unreasonables.

"It'll be in sight in a few minutes," one of them said in answer to his question. "Soon enough for you, I guess."

"Where do you land me there?" Allan asked. "There's some kind of city there?"

"A city on the Island of Unreason?" The guard shook his head. "Of course not. Those unreasonables couldn't cooperate long enough on anything to build any kind of a city."

"But there's some sort of a place for us to live, isn't there?" asked Allan Mann anxiously.

"No place but what you find for yourself," said the guard unsympathetically. "Some of the unreasonables do have a kind of village of huts but some of them just run wild."

"But even those must sleep and eat *somewhere*," insisted Allan with all the firm faith of his kind in the omnipresence of bed and food and hygienic amusements provided by a paternal government.

"They sleep in the best places they can find, I suppose," said the guard. "They eat fruits and berries and kill small animals and eat them—"

"Eat animals?" Allan Mann, of the world's fiftieth generation of vegetarians, was so shocked by the revolting thought that he sat silent until the pilot droned over his shoulder, "Island ahead!"

He looked anxiously down with the guards as the flier circled and came back and dropped in a spiral toward the island.

It was not a large island, just an oblong bit of land that lay on the great ocean like a sleeping sea-monster. Dense green forest covered its low hills and shallow ravines and extended down to the shelving sandy beaches.

To Allan Mann it looked savage, wild, forbidding.

He could see smoke rising in several thin curls from the island's western end but this evidence of man's presence repelled rather than reassured him. Those smokes came from crude fires where men were perhaps scorching and eating the flesh of lately-living things—

The guard-flier dipped lower, shot along the beach and came to rest with its vertical air-jets spuming up sand.

"Out with you," said the chief guard as he opened the door. "Can stay here but a moment."

Allan Mann, stepping down onto the hot sand, clung to the flier's door as a last link to civilization. "You'll come back for me when my sentence is up?" he cried. "You'll know where to find me?"

"We'll find you if you're on the island but don't worry about that— maybe your sentence was life," grinned the chief guard. "If it wasn't, we'll get you unless some unreasonable has killed you."

"Killed me?" said Allan, aghast. "Do you mean to say that they kill each other?"

"They do, and with pleasure," said the guard. "Better get off this beach before you're seen. Remember, you're not living with reasonable people now!"

With the slam of its door the guard-flier's jets roared and it shot up-ward. Allan Mann watched stupefiedly as it rose, circled in the sunshine like a gleaming gull, and then headed back westward. Sickly, he watched it vanish, westward toward the land where people were reasonable and life went safely and smoothly without the dangers that threatened him here.

With a start Allan Mann realized that he was increasing his danger by remaining out on the open beach where he might easily be seen by anyone in the woods. He could not yet conceive why any of the unreasonables might want to kill him but he feared the worst. Allan Mann started on a run up the beach toward the woods.

His feet slipped in the hot sands and though Allan was physically per-fect like all other citizens of the modern world, he found progress difficult. Each moment he expected to see a horde of yelling unreasonables appear along the beach. He quite forgot that he was a condemned unreasonable himself, and saw himself as a lone representative of civilization marooned on this savage island.

He reached the woods and plumped down behind a bush, panting for breath and looking this way and that. The forest was very hot and silent, a place of green gloom pillared by bars of golden sunlight that struck down through chinks in the leafy canopy above. Allan heard birds chittering around him.

He considered his predicament. He must live on this island for an unguessable length of time. It might be a month, a year, even many years. He saw now how true was the fact that the prisoner's ignorance of his sentence's length made it all the more felt. Why, he might, as the guard had said, have to spend all his life on the island!

He tried to tell himself that this was improbable and that his sentence could not be so severe. But no matter what its length, he must prepare to live here. The essentials were shelter and food, and escape from the other unreasonables. He decided that he would first find some secluded spot for a shelter, construct one, and then try to find berries or fruits such as the guard had mentioned. Meat was not to be thought of without revulsion.

Cautiously Allan Mann got to his feet and looked about. The green forest seemed still and peaceful but he peopled it with myriad dangers. From behind every bush menacing eyes might be spying on him. Nevertheless, he must win to a more hidden spot and so he started in through the woods, determining to keep away from the island's western end where he had seen the smokes.

Allan Mann had gone but a dozen fearful steps when he stopped short, whirled. Through the brush someone was crashing toward him.

His panic-stricken mind had not the time to think of flight before the running figure emerged from the brush beside him, then at sight of him recoiled.

It was a girl clad in a stained, ragged tunic. Her limbs showed brown below its tattered hem, her black hair was cut very short, and as she threw herself back from him in alarm a short spear in her right hand flashed up ready to dart toward him.

Had he made a move toward her the spear would have been driven at him; but he stood as quivering and startled as she. Gradually as they confronted each other, the fact that he was harmless became apparent to the girl and some of the terror left her eyes.

Yet with her gaze still upon him she backed cautiously away until just behind her were some dense bushes. With a quick escape thus assured her, she surveyed him.

"You're new?" she said. "I saw the flier come."

"New?" said Allan mystified.

"New to the island, I mean," she said quickly. "They just left you, didn't they?"

Allan nodded. He was still trembling slightly. "Yes, they just left me. It was breach of reason—"

"Of course," she said. "That's what we're all here for, we unreasonables. Those old fogies of directors send someone here every few days or so."

At this heretical description of the executives of the reasonable world, Allan Mann stared. "Why shouldn't they send them?" he demanded. "It's only fair they should correct unreasonables."

Her bright black eyes widened. "*You* don't talk like an unreasonable," she accused.

"I should hope not," he returned. "I committed a breach of reason but I realize it and I'm sorry I did it."

"Oh," she said, and seemed disappointed. "What's your name? Mine's Lita."

"Mine is Allan Mann. My serial number—" He stopped.

CHAPTER TWO
FIRST STRUGGLES

A bird had called loudly back in the woods and the sound had seemed to recall something to the girl and bring fear back into her eyes.

"We'd better get out of here," she said quickly. "Hara will be along here after me—he was chasing me."

"Chasing you?" Allan remembered with a cold feeling the guard's warning. "Who is Hara?"

"Hara's boss of the island—he's a lifer they just brought a few weeks ago but he's beaten all the strongest men here."

"You mean that they *fight* here to see who is to be the leader?" Allan asked incredulously. Lita nodded.

"Of course they do. This isn't back in civilization where the best mind ranks highest, you know. And Hara's after me."

"He wants to kill you?"

"Of course not! He wants me for his woman and I won't consent. I never will, either." The black eyes flashed.

Allan Mann felt that he had strayed into some mystifying new world. "His woman?" he said with knitted brows.

Lita nodded impatiently. "When people here mate there's no Eugenic Board to assign them to each other so they simply fight for mates.

"Hara has been after me and I won't have him. He got angry today and said he'd make me but I fled the village and when he and some of the others started after me I was—*listen!*"

Lita stopped with the tense command and Allan, listening with her, heard from somewhere in the woods distant trampling and crashing, a hoarse voice calling and others answering.

"They're coming!" Lita cried. "Come on, quick!"

"But they can't—" Allan started vainly to say, and then was cut off as he found himself running with the girl through the woods.

Branches tore at his shorts and briars pricked his legs savagely as they forced through the brush. Lita led inward toward the island's center and Allan struggled to keep beside her.

His muscles were in the pink of condition but he now found that running from danger through a forest was oddly different from running beneath the sunlamps of one of the great city gymnasiums. There was a tightness across his chest, a cold at his spine, as he heard the hoarse voices behind.

Lita looked back, her face white through its brown, as she and Allan ran. Allan Mann told himself that there was no reason why he should follow this girl into trouble. Before he could formulate the thought further they emerged into a small clearing just as from one side of it there crashed another man.

A bull-like roar of triumph went up and Allan Mann saw that the man was a barrel-bodied, stocky individual with flaming red hair on his head and chest, his hard face alight. He grasped Lita's arm as the girl swiftly shrank back beside Allan.

"Hara!" she panted, trying in vain to break free.

"Ran away, eh?" he said savagely, and then his eyes took in Allan Mann. "And with this white-faced sheep!

"Well, we'll see whether he's good enough to take a girl away from Hara!" he added. "You've no spear or club so we'll make it fists!"

He tossed his own club and spear to the ground and advanced with balled fists on Allan, "What do you mean?" asked Allan dazedly.

"Fight, of course!" bellowed Hara. "You wanted this girl and you can fight me for her!"

Allan Mann thought swiftly. Against this brutal fighter he would have small chance—now, if ever, he must use the reason that is man's advantage over the brute. "But I don't want her!" he said. "I don't want to fight for her!"

Hara stopped in sheer surprise and Allan saw Lita's dark eyes stare at him. "Don't want to fight?" cried the other. "Then run, rat!" And as he snarled that in contempt he turned to grasp the girl.

As he turned Allan stooped swiftly, scooped up his heavy club and slammed it against the back of Hara's neck. The red-head went down like a sack of meal.

"Come on!" cried Allan tensely to Lita. "Before he comes to we can get away—quick!"

They rushed in to the brush. Soon they heard the calling voices become suddenly noisy, then die away. They stopped, panting.

"That was brain-work," said Allan Mann exultantly. "He won't come to for an hour."

Lita looked scornfully at him. "That wasn't fair fighting," she accused.

Allan Mann was aghast. "Fair fighting?" he repeated. "But surely when you wanted to get away from him—you didn't expect me to fight him with my fists—"

"It wasn't fair," she repeated. "You hit him when he wasn't looking and that's cowardly."

If Allan Mann had not been super-civilized he would have sworn.

"But what's wrong about it?" he asked bewilderedly. "Surely it's only reasonable for me to use cunning against his strength?"

"We don't care much on this island about being reasonable—you ought to know that," she told him. "But we do believe in fighting fair."

"In that case you can get away from him the next time yourself," he said furiously. "You unreasonables—"

A thought struck him. "How did you come to be sent to this island anyway?"

Lita smiled. "I'm a lifer. So are Hara and most of the others at the village."

"A lifer? What did you do to get a life-sentence in this horrible place?"

"Well, six months ago the Eugenic Board in my city assigned me a mate. I refused to have him. The Board had me charged with breach of reason and when I persisted in my refusal I was sentenced here for life."

"No wonder," breathed Allan Mann. "To refuse the mate the Board assigned—I never heard of such a thing! Why did you do it?"

"I didn't like the way he looked at me," said Lita, as though that explained everything.

Allan Mann shook his head helplessly. He could not understand the thought-processes of these unreasonables.

"We'd better get on into the island," Lita was saying. "Hara will come to in a little while and he will be very angry with you and will want to catch you."

At that thought Allan's blood ran cold. He could picture the big Hara in bull-like rage and the thought of himself in the grip of those hairy hands was terrifying. He stood up with Lita and looked apprehensively around.

"Which way?" he asked in a whisper.

She nodded toward the island's center. "The woods in there will be best. We'll have to avoid the village."

They started through the woods. Lita went first, her spear ready at all times. Allan followed, and after a few minutes he picked up a heavy section of hard wood that would make an effective club at need. He held the weapon awkwardly as they went on.

They were penetrating into deeper woods, and it was all a strange world to Allan. He knew forests only as seen from a flier, green masses that lay between the great cities. Now he was down in one, part of it. The birds and insects, the small animals in the brush, all of these were new to him. More than once Lita had to caution him as he made a noise in stepping on dry sticks. The girl went as quietly through the woods as a cat.

They climbed a slope and went over its ridge. On the ridge Lita halted to point out to him the clearing at the island's west end that held the village, a score or more of solid log cabins. Smoke curled from their chimneys and Allan Mann saw men standing about and children playing in the sunlit clearing. He was deeply interested by this village. But Lita led onward.

The woods about them were now so dense that Allan felt more safe. He had acquired a certain confidence of step. Then he was suddenly startled out of it. As a rabbit dashed by under their feet, bolting for cover, Lita's short spear flashed like a streak of light. The rabbit rolled over and over and then lay still.

The girl ran and picked it up, turned and held up the furry thing with her face exultant. It would be their supper, she told him. Allan stared at her incredulously. He felt as revolted by her act as his ancestors of generations before would have been by a murder. He tried not to show Lita how he regarded her.

When they reached a tiny gully deep in the woods, Lita stopped. The sun was sinking and already darkness was invading the forest. They would spend the night there, Lita told him, and she began construction of two tiny branch-shelters.

Under her orders Allan tore branches from the trees and stacked them. More than once she had to correct him and he felt ridiculously incompetent. When they had finished, before them stood two fairly tight little huts. Allan, looking at these shelters that had been brought out of nothing, for the first time felt a certain respect for the girl.

He watched her, as slowly with stone and steel she took from a pouch at her belt, she constructed a fire. He found the business of eliciting and nursing the sparks intensely engrossing. Soon she had a tiny little blaze, too small to show smoke above the darkening woods or to be seen for far.

She calmly cleaned the rabbit then. Allan watched her in entranced horror. When she had finished she began to roast it.

She offered him a red bit on a stick, to roast for himself. "I can't eat that!" he said sickly.

Lita looked at him, then smiled. "I was the same way when I came to the island," she said. "All of us are but we get to like it."

"Like eating the flesh of another living creature?" Allan said. "I'll never like that."

"You will when you're hungry enough," she said calmly, and went on roasting the rest of the rabbit.

Allan, watching her eat the browned meat, became aware that he was already very hungry. He had not eaten since that morning.

He contrasted that morning meal in the Nutrition Dispensary, with its automatic service and mushy predigested foods, with this place.

It was too dark for him to look for berries. He sat watching the girl eat. The smell of the scorched flesh, which at first he had found revolting, did not now seem so bad.

"Go ahead, eat it," Lita told him, handing him one of the roasted bits. "No matter how bad it is, it's only reasonable to eat anything that will keep you living, isn't it?"

CHAPTER THREE
A WORLD OF TURMOIL

Allan's face cleared and he nodded troubledly. It certainly was only reasonable to eat what was at hand in necessity. "I don't think I can do it, though," he said, eyeing the browned bit.

He bit gingerly into it. At the thought that he had in his mouth the flesh of another once-living creature, his stomach almost revolted. But with an effort he swallowed the bit.

It was hot and did not seem unpleasant. There were certain juices—quite unlike the foods of the Nutrition Dispensary, he thought. He reached doubtfully for another piece.

From behind her lashes with a secret smile Lita watched him eat another piece and then another of the rabbit. His jaws ached with the unaccustomed labor of chewing but his stomach sent up messages of gladness. He did not stop until all of the rabbit was gone and then he went back to some of the bones he had already discarded and polished them off more thoroughly.

He looked up at last, greasy of hands, to meet Lita's enigmatic expression. Allan flushed.

"It was only reasonable to eat all of it, since it had to be eaten," he defended.

"Did you like it?" she said.

"What has liking got to do with the nutritive qualities of food?" he countered. Lita laughed.

They put out the fire and retired to the two huts. Lita kept her spear but he retained his club. She showed him how to close up his hut once he was inside.

For a time Allan Mann lay awake in the darkness on the branch-bed she had built. It was very uncomfortable, he found.

He could not but contrast it with his neat bed back in the dormitory that was his home in City 72. How long would it be before he was again in it, he wondered. How long—

Allan sat up, rubbing his eyes, to find bright sunlight filtering through the interstices of his leafy shelter. He had slept on the branches after all, and soundly. Yet he felt stiff and sore as he got to his feet and went out.

It was still early morning though the sunlight was bright. The other hut was empty and Lita was not anywhere in sight.

Allan felt a sudden sense of alarm. Had anything happened to his companion?

He was about to risk calling aloud when bushes rustled behind him and as he spun about she emerged from them. Her hands were full of bright red little berries.

"Breakfast," she smiled at him. "It's all there is."

They ate them. "What are we going to do now?" asked Allan.

Lita's brows knit. "I don't dare to go back to the village yet for Hara might be there. Neither can you go now after what you did."

"I don't want to go there," Allan protested quickly. He had no desire to face any more unreasonables like the one he had met.

"We'd better keep moving on into the island," she said. "We can live for a while in the woods, anyway."

They started on, the girl with her spear and Allan bringing his rude club.

The soreness and stiffness quickly left Allan's muscles as they moved on. He found a certain pleasure in this tramp through the sun-dappled woods.

They heard no sign of pursuit and relaxed their cautiousness of progress a little. It was a mistake, as Allan Mann found when something struck him a numbing blow on the left arm and he spun to find two ragged men charging fiercely from a clump of brush.

One of them had flung his club to stun Allan. The other now rushed forward with bludgeon upraised to do what his companion had failed to do. There was no possible chance to flee or to use strategy and with the blind desperate terror of a cornered animal Allan Mann struck wildly out with his own club at the onrushing attacker.

He knocked the club spinning from the other's hand by his first wild blow. He heard Lita cry out but he was now gone amuck with terror, was showering crazy blows upon his opponent. Then Allan became suddenly aware that the other was no longer standing before him but lay stunned at his feet. The second man was running to pick up his club.

Lita's spear flashed at the running man and missed. But as the man bent for his weapon Allan swung his club in a mighty blow.

It missed the stooping man by a foot but the terrific swing seemed to unnerve him for he abandoned his weapon and took to his heels, running back into the woods.

"Hara!" he yelled hoarsely as he ran. "Hara, here they are—!"

Lita ran to the side of the panting Allan. "You're not hurt?" she cried. "You beat them both—it was wonderful!"

But Allan Mann's sudden insanity had left him and he felt only terror. "He'll bring Hara and the rest here!" he cried. "We've got to flee—"

The girl picked up her spear and they hastened on into the forest. They heard other calling voices behind them now.

"You needn't be so afraid when you can fight like that!" Lita exclaimed as they hurried on, but Allan shook his head.

"I didn't know what I was doing! This terrible place with its fighting and turmoil and craziness—It's even got me acting as unreasonably as the others! If I ever get away from here—"

The calling voices were louder and closer behind them as the two ran on. There seemed a dozen or more of them.

Allan thought he could distinguish the bull-like voice of Hara. At the thought of that red-haired giant his body went taut.

He and the girl stumbled down still another wooded slope and emerged suddenly onto an open beach, the blue sea beyond it.

"They've driven us clear to the eastern end of the island!" Allan cried. "We can't go any further and we can't hope to slip back through them!"

Lita halted, seemed to make a sudden decision. "Yes, you can get back through them!" she told him. "I'll stay out here on the beach and they'll rush out toward me when they see me. It'll give you a chance to get back through the woods!"

"But I can't go like that and leave you here for Hara to capture!" said Allan in dismay.

"Why not? It wouldn't be reasonable for you to stay here and meet Hara, would it? You know what he would do to you!"

Allan shook his head troubled. "No, that wouldn't be reasonable for it wouldn't do you any good. But even though it's unreasonable I don't like to go—"

"Go and go quickly!" Lita urged, pushing him back toward the dense woods. "They'll be here in a moment!"

Allan Mann stepped reluctantly toward the woods, entered the concealing brush. He stopped, looked back to where Lita stood on the beach. He could now hear a tramping of brush as the pursuers approached.

He felt somehow that there was a defect in his reasoning, something wrong. Yet search as he might he could find nothing unreasonable in his conduct. He had never seen this girl before the preceding day, she was a life-term unreasonable, and altogether it would be completely irrational for him to imperil himself further with the atavistic Hara for her sake. This was indisputable, yet—

A big form crashed through the brush close beside the hiding Allan and a triumphant bellow went up from Hara as he emerged onto the beach and saw Lita. Before she could turn on him Hara had grasped her arm, tossed her spear aside. The next instant all of Allan's faculty of reason was forgotten as with a crazy red tide of fury running through his veins he leapt out onto the beach.

"Let her go!" he yelled and charged on Hara with uplifted club.

The red-haired giant spun about, released the girl and as Allan swung in a mad blow struck out with his own club, shattering Allan's weapon with stunning force and knocking him back onto the sand.

"So it's you!" gritted Hara. He dropped his own club, clenched his huge fists. "All right, get up and take what's coming to you this time!"

Allan felt as though some resistless outside force was bringing him to his feet and hurling him toward Hara.

He saw the hard, scowling face through a red mist and then it shifted and as his clenched hand suddenly hurt him he was aware that he had struck Hara a stinging blow in the face.

Hara roared, swung furiously. Allan felt a dazing impact and then was aware that he was scrambling up again from the sand and that something warm was running over his cheek.

He flung in upon Hara and this time raised both clenched hands and hammered with them at the redhead's face.

Something hard hit his chest with stunning force, and the world, the beach, the blue sea and sky rocked wildly.

His vision cleared momentarily and he saw Hara's raging face and flailing fists, glimpsed beyond him other ragged men who were yelling as they watched, and then again the feel of hot sand on his back made him aware that he was on the ground and made him struggle up and forward.

He jabbed blindly with his fists into the red haze in which Hara's face seemed dancing. There was something running in his eyes that kept him from seeing well but it seemed to him that Hara's face was bloody.

Something colliding with his head forced him to his knees but he swayed up and struck again with both fists. Now Hara's eyes held astonishment as much as anger. He was backing away as Allan swung crazily.

Allan felt his strength fast running away, hunched himself and then drove forward both fists waist-high with all the weight of his body behind them. He felt smashing blows on mouth and ear as he struck, but in the next instant heard a gasp and glimpsed Hara with face gray toppling over on his side.

Then Allan was conscious of the bright sand of the beach running up to meet his face. There were men yelling and Lita's voice crying something.

He was aware of Lita's arms supporting him, her hands wiping something from his face—her hands—

Her hands became suddenly big and rough. He opened his eyes and it was not Lita at all but a white-clad guard who stood over him.

Allan stared beyond him and saw not beach and sea but the metal-walled interior of a small flier. He could see the back of a pilot sitting in the nose of the craft and could hear the roar of air outside.

"Conscious at last, eh?" said the guard. "You've been out for half an hour."

"But where—how——" Allan struggled to say.

"You don't remember?" the guard said. "I'm not surprised—you were just passing out when we got there. You see, your sentence on the island was only one day. We came to get you and found you'd apparently been having trouble with one of the other unreasonables, but we picked you up and started back. We're almost back to City 72 now."

Allan Mann sat up, utterly dismayed. "But Lita! Where's Lita?"

The guard stared. "You mean the girl unreasonable who was there? Why, she's still there, of course. She's a lifer. She made quite a fuss when we dropped down and got you."

"But I don't want to leave Lita there!" cried Allan. "I tell you, I don't want to leave her!"

"Don't want to leave her?" repeated the astonished guard. "Listen, you're being unreasonable again. If you keep it up you'll get another sentence to the island and it'll be more than a day!"

Allan looked keenly at him. "You mean that if I'm unreasonable enough they'd send me back to the island—for life?"

"They sure would!" the guard declared. "You're mighty lucky to get off with one day there this time."

Allan Mann did not answer nor did he speak again until their destination was reached and he faced the Director once more.

The Director looked at his bruised face and smiled. "Well, it seems that even one day on the island has taught you what it is to live without reason," he said.

"Yes, if s taught me that," Allan answered.

"I am glad of that," the Director told him. "You realize now that my only motive in sending you there was to cure you of unreasonable tendencies."

Allan nodded quietly. "It would be about the most unreasonable thing possible for me to resent your efforts to cure and help me, wouldn't it?"

The Director smiled complacently. "Yes, my boy, that would certainly be the height of unreason."

"I thought it would," said Allan Mann in the same quiet voice.

His fist came back—

The guards were wholly unsympathetic as their flier sped with Allan Mann for a second time toward the island.

"It's your own fault you got a life-sentence on the island," the chief guard said. "Whoever heard of anyone doing such a crazy thing as knocking down a Director?"

But Allan, unlistening, was gazing eagerly ahead. "There it is!" he bawled joyfully. "There's the island!"

"And you're glad to get back?" The chief guard gave up in disgust. "Of all the unreasonables we ever carried, you're the worst."

The flier sank down through the warm afternoon sunlight and poised again above the sandy beach.

Allan leapt out and started up the beach. He did not hear what the guard shouted as the flier rose and departed.

Nor did he look after it as it vanished this time. He pressed along the beach and then through the woods toward the island's western end.

He came into the clearing where was the village of cabins. There were people in the clearing and one of them saw Allan Mann, ran toward him with a glad cry. It was a girl—it was Lita!

They met and somehow Allan found it natural to be holding her in the curve of his arm as she clung to him.

"They took you away this morning!" she was crying. "I thought you'd never come back—"

"I've come back to stay," Allan told her. "I'm a lifer now, too." He said it almost proudly.

"You a lifer?" Rapidly he told her what he had done.

"I didn't want to stay back there. I like it better here!" he finished.

"So you're back, are you?" It was Hara's bull-voice that sounded close beside them and Allan spun with a snarl on his lips.

But Hara was grinning across all his battered face as he came forward and extended his hand to Allan. "I'm glad that you're back! You're the first man ever to knock me out and I like you!"

Allan stared dazedly. "But you surely don't like me because I did that? It's not reasonable—"

A chorus of laughs from the men and women gathered around cut him short. "Remember that you're living on the Island of Unreason, lad!" cried Hara.

"But Lita?" exclaimed Allan. "You can't have her—you—"

"Calm yourself," advised Hara with a grin. He beckoned and a pert blond girl came out of the others to him. "Look what was left by a flier while you were gone, and with a life-sentence too. I forgot all about Lita when I saw her, didn't I, darling?"

"You'd better," she advised him and then smiled at Allan. "We're getting married this evening."

"Married?" he repeated, and Hara nodded.

"Sure, by the old ceremonies like we use here. We've a religious preacher here that was sent here because religion's unreasonable too, and he performs them."

Allan Mann turned to the girl in his arm, a great new idea dawning across his brain. "Then Lita, you and I—"

That evening after the double marriage had been performed and those in the village were engaged in noisy and completely irrational merrymaking, Allan and Lita sat with Hara and his bride on a bluff at the island's western end, looking toward the last glow of sunset's red embers in the darkening sky.

"Some day," said Hara, "when there's a lot more of us unreasonables we'll go back there and take the world and make it all unreasonable and inefficient and human again."

"Some day—" Allan murmured.

Thundering Worlds

S tanding with Hurg of Venus at the window, I pointed up at a number of dark, long shapes sinking out of the gray sky. "There come our fellow Council-members," I said.

Hurg nodded. "Yes, Lonnat—that first ship looks like that of Tolarg of Pluto, and the next two are those of Murdat of Uranus and Zintnor of Mars."

"And the last one is that of Runnal of Earth," I added. "Well, the solar system's peoples will soon know how we of the Council decide on the plan, whether it's accepted or rejected."

"Most of them are praying it will be accepted," Hurg said. "If it were not for Wald of Jupiter and your enemy, Tolarg of Pluto, I would be sure it would be accepted, but as it is—"

He lapsed into thoughtful silence and I too was silent with my thoughts as we gazed out of the window. The panorama that stretched before us was enough to make any man think.

We were gazing across the city of dome-shaped metal buildings that completely covered the planet Mercury. Many flyers, torpedo-shaped craft propelled by atomic blasts, swarmed over the city, rising from or descending into the heat-locks at the tops of the buildings. In the snow-sheathed streets between the buildings no people at all were to be seen. Long ago Mercury had grown too cold for life in the open.

Mercury cold? Mercury, the innermost of the sun's nine planets, that had once been heated to furnace-temperatures by the blazing sun? That had been many ages before, though, when the sun was hot and yellow and in the full tide of its middle-life. It was not such a sun that hung in the gray heavens over Mercury now. No, the sun above us was a huge sullen blood-red disk, a darkening crimson sun which gave forth little heat and light. It was a sun that was dying!

Yes, our sun was dying! It no longer cast out a flood of heat and light on its nine planets, and the others were even icier and colder than this one of Mercury. Long ago in the past, men had journeyed out from the planet of their origin, the world Earth, to the sun's other worlds. They had colonized all the nine planets from Mercury to Pluto, until each held a great human population. Their interplanetary ships filled the ways between the worlds, and the whole system was ruled by a Council of Nine in which each member represented the planet of which he was the head.

This stable civilization of man in the solar system had lasted for ages upon ages. It had seemed that nothing could ever threaten it. But it was threatened at last and by a most awful menace. The sun was cooling! It was changing from yellow to red, following the course that every sun follows, and as it cooled, its planets became colder and colder. Their peoples were forced to live in cities of artificially heated dome-buildings, and move about in enclosed, warmed flyers. And still the sun cooled until men saw that in the near future it would become completely dead and dark, and that life upon its worlds would then be impossible in the awful cold.

The Council of Nine considered this situation. Julud of Saturn, ranking member of the Council and as such its chairman, called on the scientists of the solar system to suggest a way to save humanity. Many plans were proposed, and finally one plan, a stupendous one, was put forward as the one way by which humanity's continued life could be assured. It was verified in every detail by the scientists. Now we of the Council were going to vote on whether or not the plan should be followed, and I, Lonnat of Mercury, meant to cast my world's vote in favor of it. So did my friend Hurg of Venus and most of the other members, but one or two of the nine were doubtful.

Hurg was looking up now at the enormous dull-red sun that swung overhead. In the gray sky around it shone the bright points of the nearer stars, now visible by day.

"We've got the one real answer to that dying sun," I said, "if all the Council's members will see it!"

"They must!" Hurg exclaimed. "In this crisis we've got to forget our individual worlds and think only of the whole nine!"

"I fear we won't do that while Tolarg and Wald are of us," I said. "But enough—here come the others now."

They were coming down into the round, metal-walled Council chamber in which we two were. These other members of the Council were clad like Hurg and me in sleeveless tunics and knee-length shorts, each wearing on his shoulder the insignia of his planet, the arrow of Mars or square of Uranus, and so on.

Julud of Saturn and Runnal of Earth were the first to reach our side. Julud, our chairman, was a thin, white-haired old man with a noble face. Runnal of Earth was tall and forceful, and in his gray eyes shone the audacious humor characteristic of his world's people.

"So Hurg is here before the rest of us," smiled Julud as we greeted them. "I was detained on Saturn by the final rechecking our Saturnian scientists were giving the details of the plan."

"They checked all right?" I asked, and Julud nodded.

"Yes, our scientists repeated their decision that the plan was perfectly practicable."

"So did the scientists of Earth," Runnal told us.

Zintnor of Mars and Wald of Jupiter had joined us, and the big Wald shook his head. "Our Jovian scientists say the same," he said, "but nevertheless I hesitate to risk my world on what is, after all, only a theoretical scheme."

"Why not risk it?" Zintnor asked him curtly. "All of us will be risking our planets too."

"Yes, but as representative of the largest planet—" Wald was saying ponderously, when Hurg nudged me.

"Here comes your friend, Lonnat—Tolarg of Pluto."

Tolarg strode into our group almost insolently, with Murdat of Uranus and Noll of Neptune by his side. He saw me, and his black eyes and saturnine face became mocking in expression.

"Well, Lonnat," he greeted me, "here we all are on your toy planet Mercury once more, though it seems hardly big enough to hold all nine of us."

I was about to retort when Runnal of Earth intervened. "It is hardly the size of a planet that measures its importance, Tolarg," he said calmly. "My own Earth is not large," he added proudly, "but I think no planet in the solar system has been of more importance."

"I meant no offense," said Tolarg, his mocking smile belying his words. "In fact, I really rather like Mercury—it reminds me of the satellites of our outer planets."

I controlled my temper and kept silent by an effort, though I could see Murdat of Uranus and Noll of Neptune smiling.

"It seems to me," said Julud of Saturn, "that since we are all here, the sooner we open our meeting the better."

Zintnor agreed impatiently. "I didn't come all the way in from Mars to hear these stale jests of Tolarg's," he said, and got a black look from the Plutonian in return as we took our seats.

Julud of Saturn faced us from the dais of the chairman, a sheaf of papers in his hand. He spoke calmly to us.

"There is no need for me to rehearse what has brought us here today," he said. "We must make today the gravest decision that the human race has ever been called on to make.

"Our sun is dying. Our nine worlds' peoples are menaced by awful and increasing cold, and unless something is done soon their inhabitants will perish. We cannot hope to revive our dying sun. Its doom is already close at hand. But out in space there lie other suns, other stars, many of them young and hot with life. If our nine worlds revolved around one of those hotter, younger suns, we could look forward to new ages of life for our race.

"It has been proposed, therefore, that we cause our nine worlds to leave our dying sun and voyage across space to one of those other suns! That our nine planets be torn loose from our sun and steered out into space like nine great ships in quest of a new sun among the countless suns of the universe! That we carry out a colossal migration of worlds through the vast interstellar spaces!

"This stupendous plan to voyage out from our sun into space on our nine worlds has a sound scientific basis. Our worlds can be propelled in space under their own power just as our space-ships are. Our ships, as you know, are moved through the void by atom-blasts that fire backward and thus by their reaction hurl the ship forward. It is possible to apply this principle on a vast scale to our planets, to fit our worlds with colossal atom-blasts which will fire backward with unthinkable power and push our worlds forward in space!

"Our worlds would be so fitted with atom-blasts that they could move at will in space, could turn in any desired direction. They would become in effect vast ships, and just as a ship has its controls centered, so would our worlds' propulsion-blasts have their controls concentrated so that one man could guide each world, at will.

"The plan is that our worlds should by this means tear loose from the sun's hold and voyage out into space in a great column or chain. The worlds with moons would take their satellites with them, of course. The nine planets would head toward the nearest sun, which is the yellow star Nugat. It would only take months to reach Nugat, as our sun is much nearer to other stars than it was in ages past.

"If Nugat proved satisfactory as a sun for our worlds, they would be guided into orbits around it. If it was not satisfactory they would go on to the next nearest suns, to Antol or Mithak or Walaz or Vira or others. They would voyage on through the starry spaces until they found a sun satisfactory to them, and when they found it they would halt there and become planets of that sun!

"During the voyage through sunless space our worlds would receive no heat or light, of course. But during that time our peoples could live in their dome-cities by means of artificial heat and light. And though in the intense cold of space our worlds' atmospheres would freeze, preparation to assure an artificial air-supply could be made. There would be hardships during the great voyage, but it should not prove disastrous.

"This is the plan on which we are to vote today. Every detail of it has been checked many times by the scientists of our worlds and pronounced practicable. If we decide in favor of it, work will begin at once on the fitting of our worlds with the propulsion-blasts. If we decide against it another plan will have to be found. Do any of you wish to be enlightened further on any detail of it before we make our decision?"

As Julud paused, Murdat of Uranus rose to his feet, his face anxious.

"I would like to understand more fully the procedure by which our planets will leave the sun and move through space," he said.

"I too," said Noll of Neptune. "In what order will our worlds start?"

Julud consulted the papers in his hand. "According to the plan," he said, "Pluto, our outermost world, will start first. It will be followed by Neptune, then by Uranus, and the other planets will follow in order with Mercury last. This is so that the outer planets will be gone and out of the way when the inner planets cross their orbits on the way out. It will remove all chances of collisions.

"On their way through space, the nine planets will proceed in a long column in the same order, with Pluto first and Mercury last. When they find a satisfactory sun they will take up orbits around it in relatively the same position as their present orbits around this sun."

Tolarg of Pluto rose. "Why take this little worldlet of Mercury along with us? We could take its people on one of the other planets and thus not have to be bothered with it."

"You can't abandon Mercury, no matter how small it is! It's as important as Pluto or any other world!" I cried.

"Lonnat is right!" Hurg of Venus seconded me. "Mercury had cities on it when Pluto was just a ball of ice!"

"That will do," Julud said peremptorily to us. "Tolarg, your suggestion is out of order. Neither Mercury nor any other world will be left behind when and if we start."

"But what about Jupiter?" Wald asked anxiously. "It is all very well for you to move your worlds, but Jupiter is bigger than all of them and will be a different matter. It'll be more risky."

Julud shook his head. "Wald, if the calculations of our scientists are followed, Jupiter can be guided through space as surely as the other worlds. You take no more risk with your world than the rest of us with ours."

There was a pause, and then Julud addressed himself to all of us. There was a tremor in his voice that he could not quite prevent.

"If no one has further questions to ask, the time has come for our decision on this proposal. The nine worlds wait to hear that decision, so now think well before you make it. If you vote against this plan, then we cling to our dying sun that our race has always known; and though with its dying, death will overtake all on our worlds, it may be that our science can spin out existence for us for a longer time than we now think.

"If you vote for the plan, you enter our worlds on a great risk; for risk there will be despite all the calculations of our scientists. You enter our worlds on a colossal adventure, the tremendous voyage of nine planets out into the starry spaces. That voyage will mean either death soon for our worlds or a new life, a new sun to warm and light them, a boundless future again open to our race. You have heard the plan—now vote against or for it!"

With the words Julud of Saturn raised his right hand, showing himself voting in favor of the plan. The hands of Hurg and Zintnor and myself shot up almost at the same moment. More slowly and thoughtfully Runnal of Earth and Noll of Neptune raised theirs.

Murdat of Uranus had his hand up now to record his world for the plan, and there remained only Tolarg of Pluto and Wald of Jupiter. And Tolarg was calmly raising his hand—only Wald was left now!

We waited tensely. One vote would defeat the plan, and from the first Jupiter had been strongest against it. Then a roar ripped from us as at last Wald slowly, gravely, raised his hand. Shouting, we were on our feet.

Julud bent forward solemnly. "We have decided," he said, "and now we have staked man and man's nine worlds irrevocably on the issue. As soon as we can make ready, then, our planets will start out into space on their mighty voyage in quest of a new sun!"

2

Tolarg of Pluto was visible in one section of my televisor screen, speaking from the control-tower on Pluto. "All ready," the Plutonian reported. "In five minutes we start."

Julud's anxious face appeared on another section of the screen. "You will be certain to start at the calculated moment, Tolarg? It is vital that our worlds move out in the calculated order."

"Do not fear," Tolarg answered confidently. Then he must have caught sight of me in a section of his own screen, for he waved mockingly to me. "Farewell, Lonnat. Don't forget to bring your baby planet after the rest of us."

He laughed and those around him laughed. I wanted to make a retort into the televisor, but restrained myself.

I stood in the circular, many-windowed room at the top of the Mercury control-tower. On each planet had been built a tower in which were concentrated the controls of the atom-blasts that would propel that planet through space. And now each one of us nine of the Council, from Tolarg out on Pluto to me here on Mercury, were ready with our scientist-assistants in our control-towers, since the time had come for the start of our planets into space.

Around me in the room were the banks of shining levers that controlled Mercury's propulsion-blasts. Also in the room were the myriad instruments necessary to guide our world in its flight through space, the great telescopic and spectroscopic instruments and other astronomical equipment. Also there was a great televisor whose screen was divided into eight sections, each one of which gave me vision into the control-tower of one of the other planets.

In the various sections of it I could see Tolarg in the Pluto control-tower, his assistants standing at the controls ready to start the planet; Noll and Murdat in the towers of Neptune and Uranus, ready to follow with their worlds; Julud anxiously waiting for Tolarg's start; Wald of Jupiter waiting with troubled brow for his mighty world's take-off; Zintnor of Mars and Runnal of Earth impatiently watching from their planets' towers; and Hurg smiling at me from the control-tower on Venus. By this means we could communicate freely with one another during our worlds' flight, as well as using our ships to go from one world to another in mid-flight.

In the Pluto tower, Tolarg was watching the time-dial. In minutes more Pluto would hurtle out into the void away from the sun, starting the great migration of our nine worlds. A tenseness was upon us all as we watched for the moment, a tenseness born of the suspense of the past months of preparations. For the months that had passed since we of the Council of Nine had voted to follow the great plan had been ones of feverish preparation.

Every world had to be fitted with the huge atom-blasts that would propel it in space, and also had to be made ready so that its people could live during the voyage through the sunless void. The greatest labor had been the fitting of the atom-blasts. This was a task so titanic that only by devoting almost all the energies of our planets' peoples to it were we able to complete it in so short a time.

Huge pits miles across and many miles deep were sunk in each planet at three points around its equator. These pits were metal-lined and thus were in fact stupendous tubes sunk in the planet. At the bottom of them was the apparatus for exploding the matter there, blowing its atoms into streams of electrons and protons that shot out of the huge tubes with inconceivable force. This tremendous force would be enough to propel the planet in the opposite direction. By using the suitable one of the three huge blasts, the world could be propelled in any desired course.

It was necessary, of course, that each planet should have its propulsion-blasts controlled from a single spot. So the control-towers had been built, one on each of the nine worlds, and fitted with all necessary aids for the navigation of our worlds on their tremendous voyage. Each one of us was to have charge of his planet's guidance, with a corps of scientists to assist him and relieve him at the controls and chart the path to be followed through space.

Besides these preparations it was needful to make the nine worlds ready so that their peoples could exist during the voyage. This was a simpler task, for though it would be terribly cold and dark on the worlds once we had launched out from our sun, our peoples were already more or less used to cold and absence of light. In their cities of heated domes they could exist, and arrangements had been made to supply air to the buildings, as it was foreseen that the cold would be so intense that our worlds' atmospheres would freeze.

So now all these preparations were finished and the great moment had come when Pluto, first of our nine planets, was to start forth on this awful voyage.

I looked from the televisor to the time-dial beside it, which almost indicated the prearranged time at which Pluto was to start. In the televisor I could see Hurg and all the others watching intently.

Then one of the scientists in the Pluto control-tower spoke a single word to Tolarg, at the controls. "Time!"

Tolarg rapidly depressed six levers, and the tower on Pluto quivered violently. "We're off!" he exclaimed.

I turned quickly to one of the telescopes in my own tower, gazed through it at Pluto. The planet was a little brown ball out there at the solar system's edge. And now from that little ball tiny jets of fire seemed darting backward in steady succession. They were the great atom-blasts of Pluto, firing regularly backward. And as they fired, the little planet was beginning slowly to leave its accustomed orbit and move away from the sun, out into the great void where burned the hosts of distant stars.

I was awed despite myself. There was something so tremendous about this starting out of the planet into space under its own power. Watching in the telescope I could see it moving farther and farther off its orbit, booming out into the infinite with every atom-blast at its rear firing as Tolarg calmly steered it on. And far out there in space shone the yellow star that was to be our first goal, the yellow sun Nugat. Faster and faster Pluto was moving toward it and was already well out from our sun and its other eight worlds.

"Neptune's next," came Julud's voice from the televisor. "All ready, Noll?"

"We are ready to go in two minutes," Noll of Neptune answered quietly.

Julud nodded. "Be sure not to follow Pluto too closely, so there'll be no danger of your moon colliding with it."

Noll nodded quietly. The rest of us watched, and then as the two minutes passed I went again to the telescope.

When the moment had come, I saw the little fire-jets shooting back from Neptune's little green sphere also. And rapidly at mounting speed Neptune too was moving out from its orbit, heading after Pluto. As I watched, I saw that Neptune's moon, Triton, was moving out with its parent-planet, still circling around it as it sailed out from its orbit.

This was a relief to all of us, especially to those of us whose planets had moons, for there had been a little doubt as to whether the satellites would follow their worlds. But Triton clung to Neptune as it launched outward after Pluto. And now Pluto and Neptune, one behind the other, were moving out toward the distant yellow star of Nugat.

It was Uranus' turn next. Murdat waited until Pluto and Neptune were even farther out before he started his planet after them. Uranus was a splendid sight as it started, a pale-green planet with a family of four moons that continued to circle it steadily as it moved away. Murdat headed his world directly after Neptune, so that the chain of two worlds had by now become one of three.

Then it was the turn of Saturn, the planet of our chairman Julud. It had been necessary to fit the huge atom-blasts on Saturn in special positions because of that planet's vast rings. Now when Julud drove his planet out after the other three, double-blasts of fire shot back from it. Only slowly did this, the second largest of the sun's worlds, get under way. Saturn was a magnificent sight as with its encircling rings and ten thronging moons it thundered out after Pluto and Neptune and Uranus.

Four planets were now well under way, moving in a chain through the void with Pluto first and Saturn last. And now had come the most risky moment of the entire start, the start of Jupiter. Jupiter, the monarch of the solar system, was so colossal in size that it required immense forces to move it at all, and for that reason its people had always been nervous about this mighty undertaking.

We watched tensely as Wald started his giant world. Terrific streams of fire shot back from the planet's mighty mass as its atom-blasts were turned on. It seemed not to change position at all. Not so easily was great Jupiter to be torn from the sun! Again and again the blasts fired, until at last, slowly and ponderously, the great world and its nine moons began veering outward from its orbit.

The blasts continued to fire, time after time, until Jupiter was moving out at a speed equal to the other four worlds that had started, and following them in space. We all breathed more easily at that. For the four planets that were left were comparatively small and there should be no trouble in getting them under way now that the huger outer planets had started.

Zintnor's world, Mars, was next. The fiery Martian chafed impatiently until it was time to start, and then his red world and its two tiny moons shot outward with tremendous speed as he opened his back-blasts with all their power. The little red ball of Mars sped out into space after Jupiter's mighty white globe, looking like a belated satellite trying to catch up with its parent-planet, a comparison that would have aroused Zintnor's wrath.

Pluto, Neptune, Uranus, Saturn, Jupiter and Mars under way—and Earth next. Already Runnal of Earth was starting his planet after the others. And now, as his world and its single moon started out after Mars and the others, something tightened in the throats of all of us who watched; something strange that we felt at seeing Earth leaving the Sun.

Earth, the parent-world of our human race, had always had a special place in our hearts. Even those of us whose ancestors for a thousand generations back have been born on Pluto or Saturn or one of the other worlds, feel somehow when we visit Earth for the first time that we are getting home. The green planet with its beautiful moon is more than just one of the nine worlds, and so it was with more than ordinary emotion that we now watched it go.

Now only Venus and my own world of Mercury were left, and the time was at hand for Venus to start.

"Good-bye, Lonnat," said Hurg from the televisor-screen. "Here goes my world too!"

"And then mine the last," I said smilingly. "The tail end of the procession, so to speak."

"Well, that's the proper place for the littlest world, isn't it?" Hurg grinned.

In the telescope then I saw the great back-blasts of fire from Hurg's cloudy planet. Venus too was starting. I watched as it sped on after the others, out away from the sun after the great chain of worlds that was now marching steadily into the void, with Pluto in the lead. Venus took its place at the end of that chain, and moved on with it.

And now Mercury alone was left of all the sun's worlds. Little Mercury, held close to the dying sun as though it were loth to let this, the last of its children, leave it. As I walked to the great bank of control-levers, ready to send my planet out after the others, I felt strangely lonely, oppressed.

I held the levers in my hand as the time-dial's hands crept onward. About me my assistants were ready at other levers and instruments. The awful responsibility of my position, the power that was mine to guide a whole world through space at will, weighed upon me. With an effort I remained calm. Then as the time-dial indicated the moment, I threw down the levers.

Instantly the control-tower, the whole planet, was shaken by a shuddering convulsion and there came to our ears the tremendous roar of the atom-blasts firing back from our world. The starry heavens seemed to jerk and quiver as Mercury lurched forward under the impetus of the back-blasts. And as it moved faster I threw down other levers, fired the side-blasts that drove us outward from our orbit. Tensely I watched, firing blast after blast as I guided Mercury out after the chain of other worlds.

Mercury lurched and swayed as I steered the planet outward. Ahead moved the column of the eight other planets, eight mighty worlds thundering through the void toward the distant yellow star, with Pluto leading and the other worlds with their families of moons solemnly following. And as Mercury moved after them with increasing speed, the light faded on its surface and its atmosphere began to freeze and fall in great flakes. I looked back at the sun we were leaving.

There it spun, the crimson sun, old, waning, dying. Planetless now, the nine worlds that long ago had been born from it leaving it. And as Mercury left it last of all, the significance of it struck home to my heart. We were leaving the sun where mankind and its world had come into existence, the sun that for millions of generations had been *the* sun, the sun beneath which man had grown great.

I flung back my hand wordlessly toward that diminishing, dying star. I wanted to speak to it as though to a dying, conscious parent whom we were leaving, but I could only make that gesture. And in that gesture, as my world sped out after the other worlds into the great void with its atmosphere freezing and falling, man bade farewell to his sun forever.

3

Julud of Saturn spoke to me from my televisor-screen. "Tolarg reports that Pluto is within ten billion miles of the sun Nugat, Lonnat!" he told me.

"That's good!" I exclaimed. "We won't be much longer reaching it, then."

Hurg of Venus spoke from another section of the televisor. "As for me, I don't care how soon we reach it. I'm getting pretty tired of this journey and I don't care who knows it."

Julud smiled. "We'll all be glad when it ends, I think. And if Nugat proves a satisfactory sun, as we think it will, the journey will end here. Our scientists report that this sun is a young and hot one, which promises well. They also say it has two planets and some strange radiation-lines in its spectrum."

"You're going to send ships ahead to investigate the sun before our worlds reach it, aren't you?" I asked, and Julud nodded.

"Yes, when we get a little closer a scouting force of ships will go ahead and see what the sun and its worlds are like."

He and Hurg disappeared from the televisor, and I turned from it to stare out the control-tower's window. About me in the tower were some of my scientist-assistants, who never ceased their watch over our instruments as we guided Mercury through the void after the other planets. Outside the tower stretched Mercury's surface, its countless dome-buildings now covered by a blanket of frozen air and lying in unchanging darkness relieved only by the light of the stars.

Ahead of our speeding world, against those stars, I could make out the vague light-points of the other eight worlds whose columns we were following through space. Their formation was the same as when we had started months before, with great Pluto thundering in the van under the guidance of Tolarg. I wondered how the self-confident Plutonian liked the task of leading the nine worlds on their march through the void. Far behind us burned the red star that was the sun we had left months before.

And ahead there shone the sun toward which we were moving, the yellow star Nugat. It had grown steadily in brightness as we approached it, and now we were so near that it presented a visible disk, a small yellow sun in seeming. It gleamed now like a great yellow star of hope, for we all hoped that we could halt our journey here.

Our hopes grew in the next days as we drew even closer to Nugat. It was growing in visible size and seemed in every way suitable as a sun for our nine worlds. It had two planets of its own, but we could easily allow for them in guiding our world into orbits around it. Also the strange radiation from it mentioned by Julud continued to puzzle our scientists, but we gave little attention to it.

When we were within six billion miles of Nugat, Julud called me again on the televisor.

"You will command a scouting expedition to go ahead and explore the sun, Lonnat," he told me. "Take a hundred ships."

"Why not give me the task?" asked Tolarg from Pluto on the televisor. "I'm nearer to Nugat than Lonnat is, and it would save time."

"It is my order," Julud said calmly. "You will start at once, Lonnat."

As I turned to go I caught sight of Hurg's rueful face in another section of the televisor. "Cheer up, Hurg," I told him. "When I get back I'll tell you all about it."

"The only reason they send you is because it doesn't matter what happens to your puny little planet," Hurg retorted, and then we both laughed.

I gave my scientist-assistants instructions on maintaining Mercury on its course during my absence. Then our hundred ships tore up from Mercury and started forward.

Our ships could, of course, move much faster in space than our worlds were moving. So, flying ahead at top speed, we soon passed Venus, then Earth, Mars, Jupiter and all the others one by one. To save time we went close past the column of worlds, cutting in between them and their circling moons and speeding ahead until we were past Pluto and shooting ahead toward the yellow sun Nugat.

Our speed was so great that we were soon far ahead of our nine moving worlds. On we shot, until the blazing yellow disk of Nugat had become a huge sphere of golden fire in the heavens before us. We headed toward its two planets, that spun close together off to one side of the sun, and as I felt the flood of blistering heat and dazzling light that poured upon us I saw in it a wonderful sun for our worlds.

I felt also at the same time a strange tingling through all my body, one that became steadily stronger and more disconcerting, but did not pay much attention to the phenomenon at the time, so engrossed was I with our task. We were close to one of the two planets now, and were descending rapidly toward its surface, when from one of the scientists in my ship who were training their astronomical instruments upon Nugat came a cry.

"This sun is giving off radiations unlike anything our own sun ever produced!" he cried. "Do you feel anything strange?"

"A sort of tingling," I said. "What is it?"

"It's radio-active radiation—rays that crumble and disintegrate matter!" he cried. "This sun must have a great mass of gaseous radio-active matter in it and is pouring out waves that are deadly to all life!"

"But there's life on the world below us!" cried someone else. "Look—those things!"

We were still dropping low toward the planet we had been approaching and could now see its surface. It was a world of nightmare, a radio-active planet! Its whole mass shone dimly with white light, and it was evident that this radio-active world, child of a radium sun, was itself constantly giving off deadly radiation. A planet upon which no conceivable living thing could exist!

Yet there was life upon it! It was such life as we would never have deemed possible had we not seen it. The living things we saw below were things of shining matter whose bodies were glowing and disintegrating and changing even as they moved about! They were radio-active creatures of this deadly world!

We glimpsed swarms of them, moving to and fro amid buildings and streets that were themselves built of glowing, disintegrating matter. We even saw, some distance off from their weird city, the glowing waves of a great radium sea or ocean whose whole liquid mass must have been composed of radio-active elements.

Then one of my pilots cried, "Look, our ship is beginning to glow and disintegrate too! And the others!"

I stared, amazed. Our ship was glowing dimly with a waxing white light, and small fragments were breaking from it here and there. And the other ships too were shining.

"Quick, out of here!" I shouted. "It's death for us to stay near this sun longer."

"And death for our nine worlds too if they come closer to this sun!" another cried. "We must get back to them, they must be turned aside!"

Our ships whirled upward. The tingling in our bodies had now become a wrenching that seemed tearing the atoms of our tissues apart. As we shot outward from the radio-active sun and its shining pair of worlds I thought that we were about to perish. But as we drew away from Nugat and out of the stronger zone of its deadly radiation, our ships ceased to glow and the worst of the sickness left us. We headed back at top speed toward our oncoming nine worlds.

In brief words there I reported to Julud the danger of approaching closer to the radium sun. Promptly Julud gave orders for all our worlds to turn aside from it at once so that we would pass it at a safe distance. By the time I got back to the control-tower on Mercury, Pluto was already turning aside at the head of our column and the other worlds following its lead. I shifted Mercury's course to follow them.

We headed past Nugat and toward the next nearest sun, the yellow star Antol. As we passed Nugat we all watched anxiously, but we were at a distance that kept us out of the stronger of its deadly radiations. Even so, passing it was a risky business, for its pull upon us was great. Julud and Wald in particular had an anxious time with Saturn and Jupiter and had to fire continually side-blasts toward Nugat to keep the great sun from pulling their worlds out of their course.

But at last we were all past and the devil-sun that would have destroyed all life on our worlds was dropping behind. Antol now was our goal, and this meant that our months of voyaging through space must be repeated before we could reach that sun. And if Antol, like Nugat, proved unsatisfactory as a sun for us, we must go on from it to some of the other nearer stars, to Mithak or Walaz or Vira or other suns beyond. It was a discouraging prospect, for we had hoped that our voyage of worlds would end at Nugat.

On and on in the next months, steadily forward through the starry spaces forged our travelling worlds. Nugat contracted again to a yellow star behind us, and again the sunless void was about us, again we kept ceaseless watch as we drove our worlds through the great emptiness. Still in the van led dark Pluto; still after it came the other planets one by one; still my own little world of Mercury followed last of all in this mighty voyage.

Our hopes rose once more, as after months of this tremendous journeying the yellow sun Antol grew in size and brightness ahead. Julud announced that according to our astronomers Antol was in its late youth and that it had four planets. It had in its spectrum none of the mysterious radiations we had found so deadly at Nugat, and though our astronomers said that there were some peculiarities in its physical makeup, they saw no reason why it should not be the sun we sought.

So our hopes again grew as we drew near to Antol. When within twelve billion miles of it, our scientists found that its four worlds were apparently habitable. They had found also that Antol's physical makeup was of an odd type apparently rare among suns, but repeated that the yellow sun should prove a sufficient source of heat and light for our worlds. When within eight billion miles of it, Julud announced that on the next day he would send another scouting force ahead to investigate Antol and its worlds, as we had done at Nugat.

But that night, though night and day were the same unchanging dusk as respects light, there came a sudden alarm from Tolarg of Pluto.

"Pluto is being attacked by strange spherical ships in immense numbers!" Tolarg cried. "They outnumber us and are trying to destroy us!"

"Saturn has just been attacked also!" Julud exclaimed. "Are any other planets assailed?"

"Yes, Neptune has been descended upon by floods of spheres!" Noll cried. "They are fighting over this control-tower with our ships!"

"And Uranus too!" came Murdat's shout. "They seem to be coming from ahead."

"They must be creatures of Antol's worlds!" Julud cried. "Creatures who have come to meet us and are attacking our first four worlds!"

4

"Every ship in the last five worlds come to our aid at once!" Julud commanded. "These creatures must be repelled before they overpower us!"

"Keep Mercury in its course after the other worlds," I cried to my scientist-assistants. "I'm going ahead with our ships."

In minutes every space-ship that we of Mercury possessed was darting up from our world and tearing ahead through space. I was in the foremost ship, and as we flew on our crews made ready the ship's weapons, atom-blasts that shot forth highly concentrated streams of atomic force that had great range and enormous destructive power.

As our ships shot past Venus we were joined by the ships of that world, with Hurg at their head. Already the ships of Earth and Mars and Jupiter were on their way forward with Runnal and Zintnor and Wald leading them. We were all heading for the four first worlds of our moving column, Pluto and Neptune and Uranus and Saturn, since it was these that had been so suddenly and terribly attacked.

The ships of Jupiter and Mars and Earth went on to aid the first three planets, leaving the forces of Hurg and myself to succor Saturn. We tore in toward the ringed planet, over twenty thousand ships strong, and darted down to take part in the wild and awful battle that was raging all around Saturn.

The scene over Saturn's surface was appalling. Space seemed filled with darting spheres, black metal balls of greater size than any of our ships. They were raining disks of white flame upon the dome-city that covered Saturn, and as the flame-disks fell they annihilated whatever they touched. Saturnian ships were battling the black spheres above the planet, using their atomic fire-blasts against the flame-disks of the spheres.

The Saturnians were badly outnumbered and were being overwhelmed as we appeared. Without hesitation our ships dived down into the wild struggle. Hurg and his Venerian craft were a little below my own, and I saw them crash into the battle and flash their fire-blasts right and left upon the swarming spheres. Then we too were in the thick of the fight, and space about us seemed choked with hurtling spheres and ships, with atomic fire-flashes and destroying flame-disks.

As calmly as I was able, I gave orders to our craft as Mercurian, Venerian and Saturnian ships struggled with the spheres. I had a thousand kaleidoscopic glimpses of death dealt and averted. Two spheres loosed flame-disks at us, and our ship darted between them and drove fire-blasts to either side to destroy the spheres. A Venerian ship rammed a sphere and both exploded in flame. A Saturnian recklessly attacked three spheres and was annihilated by a half-dozen flame-disks.

The battle went on. Through the windows of the darting spheres I had momentary sight now and then of the creatures attacking us, black, formless things whose bodies seemed liquid! The fight now was raging out from the surface of Saturn. We were close to Saturn's rings, those mighty belts of whirling meteors that girdled the planet. Around and between the spinning rings and the planet's ten thronging moons our mad battle with the invaders went on. Ships and spheres blundered into death in the rings or crashed against the moons.

The scene was stupendous: the nine great worlds still thundering on in a column toward the glaring sun of Antol ahead; the creatures that had come from that sun's worlds attacking us in their spheres with the flame-disks; and we of three worlds struggling with them there amid the whirling rings and moons of Saturn, with death above and death below and the cold stars watching our mad fight.

The Antolians gave back! Their spheres had been halved in number by our fierce attack and they fled abruptly in the direction of Uranus.

"On to Uranus and Neptune and Pluto!" came Julud's cry from the televisors. "We must repel them there too!"

Our ships rushed on toward Uranus, the next world in the column. A fight still was raging around its moons, but as we attacked the Antolians there they fled ahead.

Now all our ships, with those of Uranus too, sped on toward Neptune and Pluto. We found Neptune already deserted by the invaders, but when we reached Pluto found that world in bad straits. Hosts of the spheres were overwhelming and destroying the Plutonian ships.

"Here's our chance to show Tolarg how we of the inner planets can fight!" came Hurg's yell from my televisor as we shot into the battle.

If the battle at Saturn had been fierce, the one at Pluto was terrific. The Antolians were in far greater numbers and seemed fiercely resolved to capture at least this one planet. They had concentrated their forces there now, and the fight that followed our reaching them was of the maddest kind.

Ships of every one of our nine worlds, Venerians and Mercurians and Earthmen, Jovians and Saturnians, ships with the square of Uranus or the oval of Neptune or the black bar of Pluto on them, dashed against the Antolian spheres in that tremendous battle. It seemed impossible that any ship could continue to exist in that hell of flying flame-disks and dancing atom-blasts. Wrecked spheres and ships rained in ruin upon the surface of Pluto.

But the Antolians could not stand the terrific onslaught we men of the nine worlds made upon them. They gave back into space from Pluto, then turned and dashed back toward their sun. From those in our ships came wild cheers as we saw them flee toward Antol. Then while our fleets continued to guard our advancing worlds, we nine of the Council descended at Julud's command to meet in the Pluto control-tower.

"That attack nearly captured four of our worlds," Julud exclaimed. "They would have done so had it not been for the aid of the inner planets."

"Yes, they of Mercury and Venus and the rest came in time," Tolarg conceded. "But why did these Antolians attack us? Why did they want to capture those four planets?"

"Some of the Antolians were captured," Runnal said. "We could question one telepathically and find out their reason."

"We'll do it," Julud said. "Have one of them brought in."

One of the Antolian prisoners was soon brought before us. The creature was utterly grotesque looking. It was like the others we had glimpsed, a liquid creature whose body was simply a pool of thick, viscous black liquid. In this floated two eyes, and it could extend arms and limbs at will from its viscous mass. It was utterly unlike anything we had ever seen.

"It looks intelligent enough to receive and project thought," Julud said.

He projected a thought at the thing. "You are one of the inhabitants of the four worlds of Antol—the yellow sun ahead?"

"Yes," came the thing's thought-answer. "Our race is a mighty one and covers with its numbers all of those four worlds."

"Why did you attack our planets?"

"We saw them coming through space and wished to capture four of them, so that we could leave our sun in them," the Antolian answered.

"Leave your sun?" Julud repeated. "Why do you want to do that? Doesn't Antol give your worlds sufficient warmth and light?"

"It does," the Antolian replied, "but it is about to become a nova."

Cries burst from us. Antol about to become a nova! That meant that the sun would explode, expanding out to far greater size with inconceivable speed and destroying planets or anything else near to it!

"So that's why you want to leave it?" Hurg asked.

"Yes, for when it becomes a nova, which it will do very soon, it will destroy our worlds. We thought if we captured four of your travelling worlds we could move on them to another sun."

Julud looked at us. "We must not stop at Antol but go on toward another sun, then," he said.

It was so decided and we returned to our own planets. Then Pluto veered aside and after it our other planets until all were veering away from Antol. We had decided to head toward the next nearest sun, the orange sun Mithak, which lay not a great distance from Antol. As we drew away from Antol we expected another attack by the Antolians, but it did not come. We headed steadily on toward Mithak.

Looking back, we could see from disturbances in its physical appearance that the sun Antol was very near the point of explosion into a nova. Then not long after we left it, the explosion came. From a large yellow star behind us, Antol expanded suddenly into a terrific, dazzling sphere of light! It had burst into a sun hundreds of times larger than it had formerly been!

I looked to see the little light-flashes that would mark the destruction of its four planets in its fires, but saw nothing of the sort. Then I suddenly looked more intently. There against the fiery brilliance of Antol's fiery new sphere were four dark little points, coming on in a little column after us! They were the four worlds of Antol!

"The four Antolian worlds!" I cried into the televisor. "They're coming after us—they escaped their sun's explosion!"

"Impossible!" Julud cried. "How could they move their worlds away from their sun?"

"In the-same way we moved our worlds!" I cried. "They've imitated us and fitted atom-blasts on their worlds—they're following us and will dispute possession with our worlds of any sun we reach!"

5

"Mithak a disappointment too, now that we've reached it! And the four Antolian worlds still following us! How long are our planets to continue this quest?"

It was Wald of Jupiter speaking in my televisor, and I heard Murdat answer from Uranus. "We can't go on indefinitely like this," he said. "Our peoples can't exist much longer on this terrible journey."

"I feared it would be so," said Wald. "Nugat unsuitable, Antol unsuitable, and now Mithak unsuitable—one sun after another we've reached and still we have to go on. Are our worlds to go on vainly searching space for a sun for themselves until all life on them is dead? Better to have stayed at our old sun, where at least we could have lived a little longer."

"Why this discouragement?" I demanded. "It's true that Mithak is impossible as a sun for us, but there are still Walaz and Vira beyond. One of them may be the sun we seek!"

"I say the same, Lonnat!" exclaimed Hurg of Venus.

But there came Tolarg's mocking voice from Pluto. "It's all right for you, Lonnat, your planet doesn't amount to much if it is lost."

"And what about those four Antolian worlds following us?" Murdat asked. "If we do find a suitable sun they'll try to take it from us and will make terrible enemies."

Julud intervened. "As to the Antolian worlds, they may stop at another sun than the one we settle at, and in any case we'll take things one at a time. It is true that Mithak is impossible as a sun for us, but there still lie Walaz and Vira beyond. One of them may be the sun we seek."

We stared silently for a time toward the sun Mithak. Since leaving Antol our nine worlds had marched steadily on toward Mithak, hoping that the orange sun would prove satisfactory and that our great voyage would end at it. But our hope had ended now that we had almost reached Mithak. For we found that it was surrounded by numberless vast belts and zones of whirling meteors, the only satellites the sun had, a tremendous storm of stone ceaselessly circling it

To venture our nine worlds into that terrific zone of meteors would be to destroy them almost at once, to turn them into semi-molten condition by the impact of the thousands of great meteoric masses that would strike them in minutes. No, Mithak was not the sun at which our weary worlds could rest. We must go on, to Walaz or Vira. And so worn by the hardships of the voyage through sunless space on our frozen worlds were our peoples that we might not even be able to reach those suns.

Nevertheless, go on we must, as it was impossible to turn back. So at Julud's order, Tolarg turned Pluto away from Mithak and toward Walaz. Walaz was a yellowish-red sun that shone in the heavens as a variable star, regularly increasing and decreasing its brilliance. One by one we turned our worlds after Pluto until all our chain was moving in the direction of Walaz.

I looked back into space along the way we had come. There I could see by means of our telescopes the four little light-points that were the four worlds of the Antolians, marching on after us, following us. They seemed moving even faster than our worlds, no doubt because they had been fitted with more atom-blasts than ours. Somberly I looked back at them. Even if we did find a sun for our nine worlds, those pursuing planets would seek to share it with us, and we had seen enough of the liquid-bodied

Antolians to know that they would make terrible foes and might be able to wrest our own worlds from us.

So our nine worlds moved on toward Walaz, with the Antolians' planets behind and our fate ahead. On a day when we had almost reached Walaz, we looked back and saw that by then the four Antolian worlds had reached Mithak. We watched to see if they would stop at that sun, but they came on past it and after us. No more than we would they destroy their worlds in that cosmic stone-storm around Mithak.

Walaz loomed ahead of us. And almost the last of our resolution fled when we saw its nature. It was a variable star; that we had known. We saw now the reason. Walaz had a dark companion, a dead star as large as itself. The dead star and the yellow-red sun revolved around each other and so the dark one regularly eclipsed the bright one. It meant that this sun was no haven for our planets either. For if our planets circled these two companions, the dark one would constantly be cutting off by its regular eclipses the warmth and light of the bright one. We must go on still farther.

Julud again gave the order and our planets turned from Walaz and headed toward Vira. Vira, the blue-white sun that shone brightly in the distance, was now our last hope. For beyond it there were no suns for a vast distance. If for any reason Vira was unsuitable, then we were doomed. It might even be that our peoples could not continue existence until Vira was reached, so numbed and weakened were they by the intense cold and darkness of sunless space.

We drove our planets forward toward Vira at the highest possible speed. Forgotten now were the Antolian worlds pursuing us, forgotten everything but the blue-white sun ahead. Our worlds lurched and bucked as we fired blast after blast, urged them on at greater and greater speed. What we found Vira to be would mean life or death for us, and hungrily, tensely, we watched the sun as we sped on toward it.

Behind us at speed even greater than ours, the four Antolian worlds came steadily on our track. They were now drawing near to the sun Walaz. Walaz should be suitable, we thought, for the four Antolian worlds and they would stop there. In any case, we were not thinking now of them but of the sun ahead. Steadily now we were drawing nearer to Vira.

What a cosmic trail we had blazed across the void in our stupendous voyage! Since leaving our own sun, our worlds had touched at four others: at the deadly radioactive sun of Nugat; at Antol, on the brink of explosion, where we had fought its creatures; at Mithak with its awful zones of whirling meteors; and at Walaz with its huge dead companion. And now our worlds were racing on toward a fifth sun at which their fate would be decided, with four worlds of alien beings thundering through the void behind us.

Vira grew larger, larger, as we drew closer. Then when within ten billion miles of it, Hurg of Venus went ahead with a scouting force of ships.

Tensely we waited for Hurg's report, the news that meant life or death. When he returned he gave it at once to us.

"Vira seems entirely satisfactory!" Hurg cried. "It has no harmful radiations or surrounding meteors, and it has no planets! It is a young sun that will warm our worlds for ages!"

"We've won, then!" cried Zintnor of Mars. "We've found a sun at last!"

Julud's face gleamed in the televisor. "Make ready all of you to turn your worlds in around this sun. Tolarg, when we draw nearer you will turn Pluto first into an orbit of four billion miles radius, and Neptune and Uranus and the others will follow in successively closer orbits."

"All ready here on Pluto," Tolarg reported. "But what about those four Antolian worlds following us?"

"They'll not come on to Vira when they see us already settled here— they'll stop at the sun Walaz," said Julud. "The thing for us to do now is to bring our planets safely into orbits around Vira."

An utter tenseness held us as our worlds moved closer to Vira. The great blue-white sun was a stupendous sight, an awesome ball of fire pouring out light and heat that already warmed our nearing worlds.

As we came closer to the sun our tenseness increased. This was the most critical part of the whole vast voyage, we knew. If we made a misstep in bringing our planets into orbits around this sun it would mean that some or all of them would crash into the sun and be destroyed. Every movement of our worlds must be calculated with nicety so that they would follow a safe path in around the sun.

Our column of worlds drew nearer to Vira, passing the sun on one side. Then when a little past it, Pluto turned in around the sun. We saw the planet's side-blasts fire rapidly as Tolarg turned his world, and rapidly Pluto curved in and as it felt the full force of Vira's attraction took up a circular orbit around the sun. Almost at the same time Neptune also turned, taking up an orbit not far inside that of Pluto's.

Rapidly our other planets followed. Murdat and Julud swung Uranus and Saturn without difficulty into correct orbits. But when Wald turned Jupiter it seemed for a moment that disaster lay ahead. Wald had underestimated the force needed to turn his huge planet and had to fire his side-blasts frantically to get it into the proper path. Even so, Jupiter's outer moons barely grazed past Saturn as the great world curved inward.

Mars and Earth followed, cutting in smoothly across the paths of the other planets and taking up orbits closer to the great sun. Hurg was already swinging Venus in inside the path of Earth. And then it was my turn. It was a ticklish job for me to take Mercury in to its orbit, for I had to take my world closer to the glaring blue sun than any of the others. But I manipulated side-blasts and back-blasts until Mercury had glided in and was moving smoothly in an orbit comparatively close to the sun Vira.

A cheer broke from all of us as we saw that on Mercury and on all our worlds the frozen-air blanket was melting into vapor, as our atmospheres thawed. And the snows that had long covered our worlds now were melting too, even those on Pluto and the outer planets. For from great Vira a tremendous outpouring of warmth and light bathed our worlds such as they had not known for many ages.

But into our exultation broke suddenly a sharp cry from Runnal of Earth. In the televisor his face was tense.

"Look back!" he cried. "The four Antolian worlds are passing the sun Walaz! They're coming on to Vira!"

We stared, our triumph frozen. In the telescopes the four Antolian planets were plainly visible, passing Walaz and moving on with mounting speed toward us.

"We must do something!" Hurg cried. "If those Antolian worlds reach this sun and take up orbits around it, it means endless war with them, war that may result in our destruction!"

"We cannot stop them from coming on," Julud said sadly. "I had hoped they would stop their worlds at Walaz, but they are coming on."

"If there were only some way to stop them before they get here!" Runnal exclaimed.

An idea seared across my brain. "There *is* a way of stopping them!" I cried. "I can stop them with my world, with Mercury!

"Don't you understand?" I said. "All of Mercury's inhabitants can be transferred to other of our worlds and then I'll take Mercury out and crash it head-on into those four oncoming worlds!"

"Good, and I'll go with you, Lonnat!" cried Hurg.

"And I too!" said Tolarg, eyes gleaming.

Immediately Julud ordered the transfer of Mercury's people to other worlds as I requested. All our worlds' ships swarmed to Mercury and engaged in transporting Mercury's people to the other planets.

It was so tremendous a task that by the time Tolarg and Hurg and I with my assistants in the control-tower were the only people left on Mercury, the four oncoming worlds of the Antolians had almost reached Vira.

Quickly I opened up Mercury's propulsion-blasts and sent the little planet hurtling out from Vira, back along the way we had come toward the four nearing worlds. Tensely I and Tolarg and Hurg held it toward them. Outside the control-tower were our waiting ships.

Toward each other, booming through space with immense speed, thundered Mercury and the four oncoming worlds. The Antolian worlds loomed larger and larger before us. Then they veered to one side.

"They're veering! They're trying to escape the collision!" cried Hurg.

"It'll do them no good!" I exclaimed. I swung Mercury aside in the same direction to meet them.

Again the column of four planets veered as they rushed closer, seeking desperately to escape the oncoming doom. Again I swung Mercury to meet them. Then the foremost of the oncoming Antolian worlds loomed immense in the heavens before our rushing planet.

"They're going to crash!" I cried. *"Up and away before they meet!"*

"Up and away!" yelled Tolarg and Hurg as we threw ourselves from the control-tower into the ships.

Our ships darted up like lightning. The rushing globe of Mercury was almost to the oncoming sphere of the first Antolian world. And then as we shot away from them into space, they met!

There was no sound in the soundless void, but there was a blinding, dazing glare of light that darkened even the great sun behind us for the moment, and then the two worlds became glowing red, molten, blazing with doom! A wave of force struck through space that rocked our fleeing ships.

And behind the first Antolian world the other three of the column came on and crashed into that glowing mass! One by one they crashed and were destroyed; and then the four worlds were one white-hot mass that veered off into space at right-angles to Vira and away from it. The four colliding worlds had become a new small sun!

I stared after that receding, dazzling mass. There were tears in my eyes as I watched it move away, with the remains of Mercury in it. Mercury, my world, that I had piloted across the great void through the suns only to hurl it at the last into doom.

Hurg was grasping my arm excitedly. "We've won, Lonnat!" he cried. "The Antolians and their worlds destroyed, and Vira ours now for our eight remaining worlds!"

Tolarg held out his hand to me, all mockery gone from his face now. "What you said was right, Lonnat," he said. "It's not the size of a planet that measures its importance. Yours has saved us all."

Slowly I smiled as I grasped his hand. "And you wanted to leave it behind when we started our voyage!" I said. "Well, at last our voyage is ended."

Hurg shook his head, gestured widely from Vira out toward the universe's thronging stars. "Ended for a time only. When Vira dies as our old sun died, we can go on in our worlds to another sun. Sun after sun we can hold, and man and man's power shall not end until the universe itself has ended!"

The Man Who Returned

John Woodford in his first moments of returning consciousness was not aware that he was lying in his coffin. He had only a dull knowledge that he lay in utter darkness and that there was a close, heavy quality in the air he breathed. He felt very weak and had only a dim curiosity as to where he was and how he had come there.

He knew that he was not lying in his bedroom at home, for the darkness there was never so complete as this. Home? That memory brought others to John Woodford's dulled brain and he recalled his wife now, and his son. He remembered too that he had been ill at home, very ill. And that was all that he could remember.

What was this place to which he had been brought? Why was the darkness so complete and the silence so unbroken, and why was there no one near him? He was a sick man, and they should have given him better care than this. He lay with a dull irritation at this treatment growing in his mind.

Then he became aware that breathing was beginning to hurt his lungs, that the air seemed warm and foul. Why did not someone open a window? His irritation grew to such a point that it spurred his muscles into action. He put out his right hand to reach for a bell or a light-button.

His hand moved slowly only a few inches to the side and then was stopped by an unyielding barrier. His fingers feebly examined it. It seemed a solid wall of wood or metal faced with smooth satin. It extended all along his right side, and when he weakly moved his other arm he found a similar wall on that side too.

His irritation gave way to mystification. Why in the world had they put him, a sick man, into this narrow place? Why, his shoulders rubbed against the sides on either side. He would soon know the reason for it, he told himself. He raised up to give utterance to a call that would bring those in attendance on him.

To his utter amazement his head bumped against a similar silk-lined wall directly above his face. He raised his arms in the darkness and discovered with growing astonishment that this wall or ceiling extended above him from head to foot, like those on either side. He lay upon a similar silk-padded surface. Why in the name of all that was holy had they put him into a silk-lined box like this?

Woodford's brain was puzzling this when a minor irritation made itself felt. His collar was hurting him. It was a high, stiff collar and it was pressing into the flesh of his neck. But this again was mystery—that he should be wearing a stiff collar. Why had they dressed a sick man in formal clothes and put him into this box?

Suddenly John Woodford shrieked, and the echoes of his scream reverberated around his ears like hideous, demoniac laughter. He suddenly knew the answer to it all. He was not a sick man any more at all. He was a dead man! Or at least they had thought him dead and had put him into this coffin and closed it down! He was buried alive!

The fears of his lifetime had come true; his secret, dark forebodings were hideously realized. From earliest childhood he had feared this very horror, for he had known himself subject to cataleptic sleeps hardly to be distinguished from death. He had had nightmares of premature burial. Even after the proneness to the cataleptic condition seemed to have left him, his fears had clung to him.

He had never told his wife or son of his fears, but they had persisted. They had inspired him to exact a promise that he would not be embalmed when buried, and would be interred in his private vault instead of in the Earth. He had thought that in case he were not really dead these provisions might save his life, but now he realized that they only laid him open to the horrible fate he had dreaded. He knew with terrible certainty that he lay now in his coffin in the stone vault in the quiet cemetery. His screams could not be heard outside the vault, probably not even outside the coffin. As long as he had lain in cataleptic sleep he had not breathed, but now that he was awake and breathing, the air in the coffin was rapidly being exhausted and he was doomed to perish of suffocation.

John Woodford went temporarily mad. He screamed with fear-choked throat, and as he shrieked he clawed with hands and feet at the unyielding satin-covered surfaces around and above him. He beat upward as best he could upon the coffin's lid with his clenched fists, but the heavy fastenings held firm.

He yelled until his throat was too swollen to give utterance to further sound. He clawed at the top until he broke his nails against the metal behind the silk padding. He raised his head and beat against the top with it until he fell back half-stunned.

He lay exhausted for moments, unable to make further efforts. In his brain marched a hideous pageant of horrors. The air seemed much closer and hotter now, seemed to burn his lungs with each breath he inhaled. With sudden return of his frenzy he shrieked and shrieked again.

This would not do. He was in a horrible situation but he must do the best he could not to give way to the horror. He had not many minutes left and he must use them in the most rational way possible to try to escape his terrible prison.

With this resolution a little calm came to him and he began to test his powers of movement. He clenched his fists again and hammered upward. But this did no good. His arms were jammed so close against his body by the coffin's narrowness that he could not strike a strong blow, nor had he any leverage to push strongly upward.

What about his feet? Feverishly he tried them, but found his kicks upward even less powerful. He thought of hunching up his knees and thus bursting up the lid, but found that he could not raise his knees high enough, and that when he pressed upward with them against the lid his feet simply slid away on the smooth silk of the coffin's bottom.

Now the breaths he drew seared his lungs and nostrils and his brain seemed on fire. He knew his strength was waning and that before long he would lose consciousness. He must do whatever he could swiftly. He felt the soft silk about him and the dreadful irony of it came home to him— he had been placed so lovingly in this death-trap!

He tried to turn on his side, for he thought now that he might use his shoulders to heave up against the lid. But turning was not easy in the cramped coffin and had to be accomplished by a myriad little hitching movements, an infinitely slow and painful process.

John Woodford hitched and squirmed desperately until he lay on his left side. He found then that his right shoulder touched the lid above. He braced his left shoulder on the coffin's bottom and heaved upward with all his strength. There was no result: the lid seemed as immovable as ever.

He heaved again, despair fast filling his heart. He knew that very soon he would give way and shriek and claw. There was already a ringing in his ears. He had not many minutes left. With the utter frenzy of despair he heaved upward again with his shoulder.

This time there was a grating sound of something giving above. The sound was like the wild peal of thousands of bells of hope to John Woodford's ears. He heaved quickly again and again at the lid. Paying no attention to the bruising of his shoulder, he pressed upward with every ounce of his strength.

There was another grating sound, then a snap of metal fastenings breaking, and as he shoved upward with convulsive effort the heavy metal lid swung up and over and struck the stone wall with a deep clang. A flood of cold air struck him. He struggled up over the coffin's side, dropped a few feet to a stone floor, and lay in a huddled mass.

It was minutes before he had mastered himself and summoned enough strength to stand up. He stood inside a little vault that held no coffin but his own. Its interior was in darkness save for a dim shaft of starlight that came through a tiny window high up in one wall.

John Woodford stumbled to the vault's heavy iron doors and fumbled at their lock. He had an uncontrollable horror of this place that had almost been the scene of his perishing. The coffin there on the shelf with its lid leaning against the stone wall seemed gaping for him with its dark, cavernous mouth.

He worked frantically at the lock. What if he were not able to escape from the vault? But the heavy lock was easily manipulated on the inside, he found. He managed to turn its tumbler and shoot its bar and then the heavy iron doors swung open. John Woodford stepped eagerly out into the night.

He stopped on the vault's threshold, closing the doors behind him and then looking forth with inexpressible emotions. The cemetery lay in the starlight before him as a dim, ghostly city of looming monuments and vaults. Little sheets of ice glinted here and there in the dim light, and the air was biting in its cold. Outside the cemetery's low wall blinked the lights of the surrounding city.

Woodford started eagerly across the cemetery, unheeding of the cold. Somewhere across the lights of the city was his home, his wife, and somewhere his son—thinking him dead, mourning him. How glad they would be when he came back to them, alive! His heart expanded as he pictured their amazement and their joy at his return.

He came to the low stone wall of the cemetery and clambered quickly over it. It was apparently well after midnight, for the cars and pedestrians in sight in this suburban section were few.

Woodford hurried along the street. He passed people who looked at him in surprise, and only after some time did he realize the oddness of his appearance. A middle-aged man clad in a formal suit and lacking hat and overcoat was an odd person to meet on a suburban street on a winter midnight.

But he paid small attention to their stares. He did turn up the collar of his frock coat to keep out the cold. But he hardly felt the frigid air in the emotions that filled him. He wanted to get home, to get back to Helen, to witness her stupefaction and dawning joy when she saw him returned from the dead, living.

A street-car came clanging along and John Woodford stepped quickly out to board it, but almost as quickly stepped back. He had mechanically thrust his hand into his pocket and found it quite empty. That was to be expected, of course. They didn't put money in a dead man's clothes. No matter, he would soon be there on foot.

As he reached the section in which his home was located, he glanced in a store-window in passing and saw on a tear-sheet calendar a big black date that made him gasp. It was a date ten days later than the one he last remembered. He had been buried in the vault for more than a week!

More than a week in that coffin! It seemed incredible, terrible. But that did not matter now, he told himself. It would only make the joy of his wife and son the greater when they found he was alive. To Woodford himself it seemed as though he were returning from a journey rather than from the dead.

Returned from the dead! As he hastened along the tree-bordered street on which his home was located, he almost laughed aloud as he thought of how amazed some of his friends would be when they met him. They would think him a ghost or a walking corpse, would perhaps shrink in terror from him at first.

But that thought brought another: he must not walk in on Helen too abruptly. The husband she had buried ten days ago must not appear too suddenly or the shock might easily kill her. He must contrive somehow to soften the shock of his appearance, must make sure that he did not startle her too much.

With this resolve in mind, when he reached his big house set well back from the street, Woodford turned aside through the grounds instead of approaching the front entrance. He saw windows lighted in the library of the house and he went toward them. He would see who was there, would try to break the news of his return gently to Helen.

He silently climbed onto the terrace outside the library windows and approached the tall casements. He peered in.

Through the silken curtains inside he could clearly see the room's soft-lit interior, cozy with the shelves of his books and with the lamps and fireplace.

Helen, his wife, sat on a sofa with her back partly toward the window. Beside her sat a man that Woodford recognized as one of their closest friends, Curtis Dawes.

Sight of Dawes gave Woodford an idea. He would get Dawes outside in some way and have him break the news of his return to Helen. His heart was pounding at sight of his wife.

Then Curtis Dawes spoke, his words dimly audible to Woodford outside the window, "Happy, Helen?" he was asking.

"*So* happy, dear," she answered, turning toward him.

Out in the darkness Woodford stared in perplexed wonder. How could she be happy when she thought her husband dead and buried?

He heard Curtis Dawes speaking again. "It was a long time," the man was saying. "Those years that I waited, Helen."

She laid her hand tenderly on his. "I know, and you never said a word. I respected so your loyalty to John."

She looked into the fire musingly. "John was a good husband, Curt. He really loved me and I never let him guess that I didn't love him, that it was you, his friend, I loved. But when he died I couldn't feel grief. I felt regret for his sake, of course, but underneath it was the consciousness that at last you and I were free to love each other."

Dawes' arm went tenderly around her shoulder. "Darling, you don't regret that I talked you into marrying me right away? You don't care that people may be talking about us?"

"I don't care for anything but you," she told him. "John was dead, young Jack has his own home and wife, and there was no reason in the world why we should not marry. I'm glad that we did."

In the darkness outside the window a stunned, dazed John Woodford saw her lift an illumined face toward the man's.

"I'm proud to be your wife at last, dear, no matter what anyone may say about us," he heard.

Woodford drew slowly back from the window. He paused in the darkness under the trees, his mind shaken, torn.

So *this* was his homecoming from the tomb? This was the joy he had anticipated in Helen when he returned?

It couldn't be the truth! His ears had deceived him—Helen could not be the wife of Curtis Dawes! Yet part of his mind told him remorselessly that it was true.

He had always sensed that Helen's feeling for him was not as strong as his for her. But that she had loved Dawes he had never dreamed. Yet now he remembered Dawes' frequent visits, the odd silences between him and Helen. He remembered a thousand trifles that spoke of the love which these two had cherished for each other.

What was he, John Woodford, to do? Walk in upon them and tell them that they had been premature in counting him dead, that he had come back to claim his position in life and his wife again?

He couldn't do it! If Helen during those years had wavered in the least in her loyalty to him, he would have had less compunction. But in the face of those years of silent, uncomplaining life with him, he couldn't now reappear to her and blast her new-found happiness and blacken her name.

Woodford laughed a little, bitterly. He was then to be an Enoch Arden from the tomb. A strange role, surely, yet it was the only one open to him.

What was he to do? He couldn't let Helen know now that he was alive, couldn't return to the home that had been his. Yet he must go somewhere. Where?

With a sudden leap of the heart he thought of Jack, his son. He could at least go to Jack, let his son know that he was living. Jack at least would be overjoyed to see him, and would keep the fact of his return secret from his mother.

John Woodford, with that thought rekindling a little his numbed feelings, started back through the trees toward the street. Where he had approached the house but minutes before with eager steps, he stole away now like a thief fearful of being observed.

He reached the street and started across the blocks toward the cottage of his son. Few were abroad, for the cold seemed increasing and it was well past midnight. Woodford mechanically rubbed his stiffened hands as he hurried along.

He came to his son's neat little white cottage, and felt relief as he saw lights from its lower windows also. He had feared that no one would be up. He crossed the frozen lawn to the lighted windows, intent on seeing if Jack were there and if he were alone.

He peered in, as he had done at his own home. Jack was sitting at a little desk and his young wife was perched on the arm of his chair and was listening as he explained something to her from a sheet of writing on the desk.

John Woodford, pressing his face against the cold window-pane, could hear Jack's words.

"You see, Dorothy, we can just make it by adding our savings to Dad's insurance money," Jack was saying.

"Oh, Jack!" cried Dorothy happily. "And it's what you've wanted so long, a little business of your own!"

Jack nodded. "It won't be very big to start with, but I'll make it grow, all right. This is the chance I've been hoping for and I'm sure going to make the most of it.

"Of course," he said, his face sobering a little, "it's too bad about Dad going like that. But seeing that he *did* die, the insurance money solves our problems of getting started. Now you take the overhead—" he said, and began unreeling a string of figures to the intent Dorothy.

John Woodford drew slowly back from the window. He felt more dazed and bewildered than ever. He had forgotten the insurance he had carried, which he had intended to give Jack his start. But of course, he saw now, it had been paid over when he was believed dead.

He was not dead, but living. Yet if he let Jack know that, it meant the end of his son's long-desired opportunity. Jack would have to return the insurance money to the company, wrecking his dreamed-of chance. How could he let him know, then?

He, John Woodford, had already decided that he must remain dead to his wife and therefore to the world. He might as well remain so to his son, also. It was for the best. John Woodford melted away from the cottage into the darkness.

When he reached the street he stood in indecision. A freezing wind had begun to blow, and he felt very cold without an overcoat. Mechanically he turned his coat-collar closer around his neck.

He tried to think what he must do. Neither Helen nor Jack must know that he was living, and that meant that no one in the city must know. He must get out of the town to some other place, take up life under some other name.

But he would need help, money, to do that. Where was he to get them? Barred as he was from calling on his wife or son, to whom could he turn for help without letting his return become generally known?

Howard Norse! The name came at once to Woodford's lips. Norse had been his employer, head of the firm where Woodford had held a position for many years. Woodford had been one of his oldest employees. Howard Norse would help him to get a position somewhere else, and would keep his reappearance secret.

He knew where Norse's residence was, several miles out in the country. But he couldn't walk that far, and he had no taxi or trolley fare. He would have to telephone Norse.

Woodford walked back toward the city's central section, head bent against the piercing cold wind. He succeeded in finding an all-night lunchroom whose proprietor allowed him to use the telephone. With cold-stiffened fingers he dialed Norse's number.

Howard Norse's sleepy voice soon came over the wire. "Mr. Norse, this is Woodford—John Woodford," he said quickly.

There was an incredulous exclamation from Howard Norse. "You're crazy! John Woodford's been dead and buried for a couple of weeks!"

"No, I tell you it's John Woodford!" insisted Woodford. "I'm not dead at all, I'm as living as you are! If you'll come into town for me you'll see for yourself."

"I'm not likely to drive to town at two in the morning to look at a maniac," Norse replied acidly. "Whatever your game is, you're wasting your time on me."

"But you've got to help me!" Woodford cried. "I've got to have money, a chance to get out of the city without anyone knowing. I gave your firm my services for years and now you've got to give me help!"

"Listen to me, whoever you are," snapped Norse over the wire. "I was bothered long enough with John Woodford when he was living—he was so inefficient we'd have kicked him out long ago if we hadn't been sorry for him. But now that he's dead, you needn't think you can bother me in his name. Good-night!"

The receiver clicked in Woodford's unbelieving ear.

He stared at the instrument. So *that* was what they had really thought of him at the firm—there where he had always thought himself one of the most highly valued of employees!

But there must be someone upon whom he could call for help; someone he could convince that John Woodford was still living; someone who would be glad to think that he might be living.

What about Willis Grann? Grann had been his closest friend next to Curtis Dawes. He had lent money more than once to Woodford in the past, and certainly should be willing to do so now.

Hastily Woodford called Grann's number. This time he was more careful in his approach, when he heard the other's voice.

"Willis, I've got something to tell you that may sound incredible, but you've got to believe, do you hear?" he said.

"Who is this and what in the world are you talking about?" demanded Grann's startled voice.

"Willis, this is John Woodford. Do you hear, John Woodford! Everyone thinks I'm dead but I'm not, and I've got to see you."

"What?" cried the other's voice over the telephone. "Why, you must be drunk. I saw Woodford lying in his coffin myself, so I know he's dead."

"I tell you, it's not so, I'm not dead!" Woodford almost screamed. "I've got to get some money, though, to get away from here and you must lend it to me! You always lent it to me before, and I need it now worse than ever I did. I've got to get away!"

"So that's it!" said Willis Grann. "Because I used to help Woodford out you think you can get money from me by just calling me up and pretending that you're he. Why, Woodford himself was the biggest pest in the world with his constant borrowings. I felt almost relieved when he died. And now you try to make me believe that he's come back from the dead to pester me again!"

"But he never died—I'm John Woodford really—" Woodford protested vainly.

"Sorry, old top," returned Grann's mocking voice. "Next time pick a living person to impersonate, not a dead one."

He hung up. John Woodford slowly replaced the receiver and made his way out to the street.

The wind was blowing harder and now was bringing with it clouds of fine snow that stung against his face like sand. He shivered as he stumbled along the streets of dark shops, his body freezing as his mind was frozen.

There was no one from whom he could get help, he saw. His paramount necessity was still to get out of the city, and to do that he must rely on himself.

The icy blasts of the snow-laden wind penetrated through his thin coat. His hands were shaking with the cold.

A sign caught Woodford's eye, the illuminated beacon of a relief lodging-house. At once he made his way toward it. He could at least sleep there tonight, get started from the city in the morning.

The shabby men dozing inside in chairs looked queerly at him as he entered. So did the young clerk to whom he made his way.

"I'd—I'd like to stay here tonight," he said to the clerk.

The clerk stared. "Are you trying to kid me?"

Woodford shook his head. "No, I'm penniless and it's cold outside. I've got to stay somewhere."

The clerk smiled disdainfully. "Listen, fellow, no one with duds like yours is that hard up. Scram before I call a cop."

Woodford looked down at his clothes, his frock coat and stiff white shirt and gleaming patent-leather shoes, and understood.

He said desperately to the clerk, "But these clothes don't mean anything. I tell you, I haven't a penny!"

"Will you beat it before I have you thrown out of here?" the clerk demanded.

Woodford backed toward the door. He went outside again into the cold. The wind had increased and more snow was falling. The front of Woodford's coat was soon covered with it as he pushed along.

It came to him as a queer joke that the splendor of his funeral clothes should keep him from getting help now. He couldn't even beg a passer-by for a dime. Who would give to a panhandler in formal clothes?

Woodford felt his body quivering and his teeth chattering from sheer cold. If he could only get out of the blast of the icy wind! His eyes sought desperately along the street for a hallway where he might shelter himself.

He found a deep doorway and crouched down inside it, out of the wind and driving snow. But hardly had he done so when a heavy step paused in front of him and a nightstick rapped his feet smartly. An authoritative voice ordered him to get up and go home.

Woodford did not try to explain to the policeman that he was not a drunken citizen fallen by the way. He got wearily to his feet and moved on along the street, unable to see more than a few feet ahead for the whirl of snow.

The snow on which he was walking penetrated the thin shoes he wore, and his feet were soon even colder than the rest of his body. He walked with slow, dragging steps, head bent against the storm of white.

He was dully aware that the dark shops beside him had given way to a low stone wall. With a sudden start he recognized it as the wall of the cemetery which he had left but hours before, the cemetery containing the vault from which he had escaped.

The vault! Why hadn't he thought of it before? he asked himself. The vault would be a shelter from the freezing wind and snow. He could stay there for the night without anyone objecting.

He paused, feeling for a moment a little renewal of his former terrors. Did he dare go back into that place from which he had struggled to escape? Then an extra-strong blast of icy air struck him and decided him—the vault would be shelter and that was what his frozen body craved more than anything else.

Stiffly he climbed over the low stone wall and made his way through the cemetery's whitened monuments and vaults toward the one from which he had escaped. The driving snow covered his tracks almost as he made them, as he trudged toward the vault.

He reached it and tried its iron doors anxiously. Suppose he had locked them when he left! But to his relief they swung open, and he entered and shut them. It was dark inside, but he was out of the wind and snow now and his numbed body felt a little relief.

Woodford sat down in the corner of the vault. It was a shelter for the night, at least. It seemed rather ironic that he had had to come back here for shelter, but it was something to be thankful for that he had even this. In the morning, when the storm was over, he could leave without anyone seeing and get out of the city.

He sat listening to the wind and snow shriek outside. The stone floor of the vault was very cold, so cold that he felt his limbs stiffening and cramping, and finally he stood up unsteadily and paced to and fro in the vault, chafing his arms and hands.

It he had only a blanket, or even a heavy coat, to lie upon! He'd freeze there upon the stone floor. Then as he turned in his pacing he bumped into the coffin on the shelf and a new idea was born in his mind.

The coffin! Why, the interior of it was lined deep with silk and satin padding. It would be warm in the coffin. He could sleep in it far better than on the cold stone floor. But did he dare to reenter it?

Again Woodford felt faintly the former terrors he had experienced when he had awakened in it. But they meant nothing, he told himself. He would not be fastened in, this time, and his frozen flesh yearned for the warmth of the coffin's lining.

Slowly, carefully, he climbed up and lowered himself into the coffin and stretched out. The silk and padding he sank into had a grateful warmth. He lowered his head upon the soft little pillow with a sigh of relief. This was better.

He experienced an almost luxurious comfort now; but after he had lain for a little while he felt that the top of his body was still cold, where the cold air came into the open coffin's top. That cold air entering kept him from being completely warm. If the lid above him were just closed to keep out the cold air—

He reached up and got the edge of the heavy metal lid, then let it down upon himself. He was completely in the dark, now, inside the closed coffin. But he was warm, too, for the lid kept out the cold air. And he was getting warmer all the time, as his body warmed up the interior.

Yes, it was far more comfortable with the lid closed. An even warmth now pervaded his whole being, and the air inside the coffin was still, getting warmer and thicker. He felt a little drowsy now, as he breathed that warm air, felt luxuriously sleepy as he lay on the soft silk.

It was getting a little harder to breathe, somehow, as the air became thicker. He ought really to raise the coffin lid and let in some fresh air. But it was so warm now, and the air outside was so cold, and he was more and more sleepy.

Something dim and receding in his fading consciousness told him that he was on the way to suffocation. But what if he was? was his sleepy thought. He was better off in here than back in the world outside. He had been a fool ever to fight so hard before to get out of his warm, comfortable coffin, to get back to that outside world.

No, it was better like this, the darkness and the warmth and the sleep that advanced. Nobody would ever know that he had awakened at all, that he had been away from here at all. Everything would be just as before— just as before. And with that comforting assurance, John Woodford was swept farther and farther down the dark stream of unconsciousness from which this time there would be no returning.

The Accursed Galaxy

A thin, tearing sound like the ripping of thousands of sheets of paper grew with lightning speed to a vibrant roar that brought Garry Adams to his feet in a jump.

He leaped to the door of his cabin and as he flung it open, he saw a sword of white fire cleave the night vertically and heard an abrupt ear-shattering crash from the distant darkness.

Then all was dark and still again, but down in the dimly starlit valley he could see clouds of smoke slowly rising.

"Good heavens, a meteorite!" Garry exclaimed. "And it's fallen right into my lap."

His eyes suddenly lighted. "Will this make a story! Reporter Sole Witness of Meteor's Fall—"

He grabbed a flashlight from the shelf by the door and the next minute was hurrying down the rude path that twisted from his hilltop cabin down the wooded slope to the valley.

Garry Adams was for fifty weeks of each year a reporter on one of the more sensational New York dailies. But two weeks each summer he spent in this lonely cabin in the northern Adirondacks and washed the taste of slayings, scandals and corruption out of his mind.

"Hope there's something left of it," he muttered as he tripped over a root in the dark. "It would rate a three-column picture."

Stopping for a moment at a place where the rude path emerged from the trees, he scanned the darkness of the valley. He spotted the place where faint wisps of smoke were still rising and plunged unhesitatingly in that direction through the woods.

Briers tore Garry's trousers and scratched his hands, and boughs whipped and stung his face as he struggled ahead. He dropped the flashlight once and had a hard time getting it. But before long he heard a crackle of small flames and smelled smoke. He emerged a few minutes later into a hundred-foot circle crushed flat by the impact of the meteorite.

Brush and grass, set afire by the heat of impact, were burning feebly, several places around the edge of this circle, and smoke got into Garry's eyes. He stood blinking, then saw the meteorite.

It was not an ordinary meteorite at all. He saw that at the first glance, even though the thing was half buried in the soft earth which it had flung up around itself. It was a glowing polyhedron ten feet in diameter, its surface a multitude of small flat facets, perfectly geometrical in shape. An artificial polyhedron that had fallen from outer space.

Garry Adams stared, and as he stared the visioned news headings in his mind expanded into black headlines.

"Meteorite Proves Shot from Space! Reporter Finds Shell from Space that Contains—"

What *did* the thing contain? Garry took a step toward it, cautiously because of the heat the white glow of it betokened. To his surprise, he found that the polyhedron was not hot at all. The ground under his feet was hot from the impact but the faceted thing before him was not. Its glow, whatever it was, was not of heat.

Garry stared, his black brows concentrated into a frown beneath which his brain worked excitedly. It must be, he argued, a thing made by intelligent beings, somewhere out in space.

It could hardly contain living beings, for they could not have survived its fall. But there might be books, machines, models—

Garry came to a sudden decision. This story was too big for him to handle alone. He knew the man he needed here. He turned around and struggled back through the woods to the path, then followed it, not back up to the cabin but on down the valley until it joined a narrow, rude dirt road.

An hour of walking on this brought him to a somewhat better dirt road, and an hour more on this brought him, tired but still vibrant with excitement, into a dark, sleeping little village.

Garry pounded on the door of the general store until a querulous, sleepy storekeeper came down in his nightshirt and let him in. He made straight for the telephone.

"I want to call a Dr. Peters, Dr. Ferdinand Peters of Manhattan University Observatory, in New York," he said to the operator. "And keep ringing until you get him."

Ten minutes later the astronomer's sleepy, irritated voice greeted his ears. "Well, who's this?"

"It's Garry Adams, doctor," Garry said rapidly. "You remember, the reporter who wrote up your solar researches last month?"

"I remember that your story contained no less than thirty errors," Dr. Peters answered acidly. "What in the devil do you want at this time of night?"

Garry talked steadily for five minutes, and when he had finished there was so long a silence that he shouted into the transmitter, "Did you hear me? Are you there?"

"Of course I'm here—don't yell so loud," retorted the astronomer's voice. "I was just considering." He began to speak rapidly. "Adams, I'm coming up to that village of yours on the dot, by plane if possible. You wait there for me and we'll go out and look at the thing together. If you're telling me the truth, you've got a story that will make you famous forever. If you're hoaxing me, I'll flay you alive if I have to chase you around the world to do it."

"Don't let anyone else know about it, whatever you do," cautioned Garry. "I don't want any other paper to get it."

"All right, all right," said the scientist. "A lot of difference it makes to me whether any of your filthy rags get it."

Four hours later Garry Adams saw a plane buzzing earthward through the dawn mists east of the village. He waited, and in another half hour the astronomer tramped into the place.

Dr. Peters saw Garry and came straight toward him. Peters' keen, spectacled black eyes and ascetic, shaven face wore an expression in which were mixed doubt and repressed excitement.

Characteristically, he wasted no time in greetings or preliminaries. "You're sure the thing is a geometrical polyhedron? Not just a natural meteorite with some resemblance to that shape?" he queried.

"Wait till you see it for yourself," Garry told him. "I've rented a car that will take us almost there."

"Drive out to my plane first," the doctor ordered. "I've brought some equipment that may prove useful."

134

The equipment consisted of bars, tools and wrenches of fine steel and a complete oxy-acetylene torch outfit, with the necessary tanks. They stowed it into the back of the car and then bumped and rattled over the uncertain mountain roads until they reached the beginning of the path.

When Dr. Peters emerged with the reporter into the clearing where lay the half-buried, glowing polyhedron, he stared at it for some moments in silence.

"Well?" asked Garry impatiently.

"It's not a natural meteorite, that's sure."

"But what is it?" Garry exclaimed. "A projectile from another world? What's in it?"

"We'll know that when we've opened it," Peters answered coolly. "The first thing is to dig away the dirt so that we can examine it."

Despite the astronomer's calmness, Adams saw a glitter in his eyes as they lugged the heavy equipment from the automobile to the clearing. And the driving energy with which Dr. Peters worked was further index of the intensity of his interest.

They started at once digging away the earth around the thing. Two hours of hard work did it, and the whole polyhedron stood naked before them, still glowing whitely in the morning sunlight. The scientist then made minute examination of the substance of the glowing thing. He shook his head.

"It's not like any terrestrial substance ever heard of. Is there any sign of a door or opening?"

"Not a trace of one," Garry answered, then added suddenly, "but here's something on one of the facets, a sort of diagram."

Dr. Peters hurried quickly to his side. The reporter pointed to what he had discovered, a curious and complex sign graven deep on a facet half-way up the side of the polyhedron.

The diagram represented a small, spiral-shaped swarm of densely crowded dots. A little out from this central swarm were other little swarms of graven dots, mostly spiral shaped also. Above this curious diagram was a row of grotesque, interlinked symbols.

"By heaven, it's writing of some sort, an inscription!" Garry cried. "I wish we had a photographer here."

"And a pretty girl to sit with her knees crossed and give the picture sex-appeal," Peters observed caustically." You can think of your dirty sheet in the presence of—this."

His eyes were brilliant with controlled excitement. "The symbols, we can't guess what they mean, of course. Undoubtedly they tell something about this thing's contents. But the diagram—"

"What do you think the diagram means?" Garry asked excitedly as the astronomer paused.

"Well, those swarms of dots seem intended to represent galaxies of stars," Peters said slowly. "The central one, no doubt, symbolizes our own galaxy, which has just such a spiral shape, and the other swarms stand for the other galaxies of the cosmos.

"But they're too close to ours, those others—too close. If they were actually that close when this thing was made, it means that the thing was made back when the universe first started to expand!"

He shook off his abstracted ponderings and turned briskly toward the pile of tools and equipment.

"Come on, Adams, we'll try to open it up on the side opposite the inscription. If the bars won't do it, the torch will."

Two hours later, Garry and Dr. Peters, exhausted, sweating and baffled, stood back and gazed at each other in wordless futility. All of their efforts to open the mysterious polyhedron had utterly failed.

Their sharpest tools made not the slightest scratch on the glowing walls. The oxy-acetylene torch had not the least bit more effect, its flame not even seeming to heat the substance. And even a variety of acids which Dr. Peters had brought with him had no effect.

"Whatever it is," Garry panted, "I'll say it's the hardest and most intractable matter I ever heard of."

The astronomer nodded slowly. "If it is matter at all," he said.

Garry stared. "If it is matter? Why, we can see the thing's matter; it's solid and real as we are."

"It's solid and real," Peters agreed, "but that does not prove that it is matter. Adams, I think that it is force of some kind, crystallized in some superhuman and unknown way into a solid-seeming polyhedron. Frozen force!

"And I don't think we'll ever open it with ordinary tools. They would work with ordinary matter, but not with this thing."

The reporter looked perplexedly from him to the glowing mystery. "Frozen force? Then what are we going to do?"

Peters shook his head. "The thing's beyond me. There isn't a way in the world that I can think of to—"

He stopped suddenly. Garry, looking up sharply at the interruption in his words, saw that an odd listening expression had fallen upon the scientist's face.

It was at the same time an expression of surprise, as though some part of his mind were surprised at something another part told it.

Dr. Peters spoke in a moment, and with the same surprise in his voice.

"Why, what am I talking about? Of course we can open the thing. A way just occurred to me—. The thing is made of crystallized force. Well, all we need to do is to de-crystallize that force, to melt it away by the application of other forces."

"But surely it's beyond your scientific knowledge how to do a thing like that!" the reporter said.

"Not at all; I can do it easily but I'll need more equipment," the scientist said.

He fished an envelope and pencil from his pocket and hastily jotted down a list of items. "We'll go into the village and I'll telephone New York to have these things rushed up."

Garry waited in the village store while the astronomer read his list into the telephone. By the time this was done and they returned to the clearing in the valley woods, darkness had fallen.

The polyhedron was glowing weirdly in the night, a shimmering, faceted enigma. Garry had to tear his companion away from his fascinated inspection. He finally did so and they climbed to the cabin and cooked and ate a sketchy supper.

The two sat after supper and tried to play cards by the light of the kerosene lamp. Both men were silent except for the occasional monosyllables of the game. They made error after error, until at last Garry Adams flung the cards down.

"What's the use of this? We're both too wrought up over that darned thing down there to give a thought to anything else. We might as well admit that we're dying with curiosity. Where did the thing come from and what's in it? What do those symbols on it mean, and that diagram you said represented the galaxies? I can't get it all out of my head."

Peters nodded thoughtfully. "Such a thing doesn't come to Earth every day. I doubt if such a thing has ever come to Earth before."

He sat staring into the soft flame of the lamp, his eyes abstracted and his ascetic face frowning in intense interest and disturbed perplexity.

Garry remembered something. "You said when we looked at that queer diagram on it that it might mean the polyhedron was made when the universe first started expanding. What the devil did you mean by that? *Is* the universe expanding?"

"Of course it is. I thought everyone was aware of the fact," Dr. Peters said irritably.

Then he smiled suddenly. "But I keep forgetting, since I associate almost always with fellow scientists, how completely ignorant most people are of the universe in which they live."

"Thanks for the compliment," Garry said. "Suppose you enlighten my ignorance a little on this point."

"Well," said the other, "you know what a galaxy is?"

"A swarm of stars like our sun, isn't it—a whole lot of them?"

"Yes, our sun is only one of billions of stars gathered together in a great swarm which we call our galaxy. We know that the swarm has a roughly spiral shape and that as it floats in space the whole spiral swarm is rotating on its center.

"Now, there are other galaxies in space besides our own, other great swarms of stars. It is estimated, indeed, that their number runs into billions and each of them, of course, contains billions of stars. But—and this has seemed to astronomers a curious thing—our own galaxy is definitely larger than any of the others.

"Those other galaxies lie at enormous distances from our own. The nearest is more than a million light years away and the others are much farther. And all of them are moving through space, each star cloud sweeping through the void.

"We astronomers have been able to ascertain the speed and direction of their movements. When a star, or a swarm of stars, is moving in the line of sight of the observer, the movement has a definite effect upon its spectrum. If the swarm is moving away from the observer, the lines in its spectrum will shift toward the red end of the spectrum. The faster it is moving away, the greater will be the shift toward the red.

"Using this method, Hubble, Humason, Slipher and other astronomers have measured the speed and direction of movement of the other galaxies. They have found an amazing thing, a thing that has created a tremendous sensation in astronomical circles. They have found that those other galaxies are all running away from our own!

"It is not just a few of them that are moving away from our own but all of them. In every side, every galaxy in the cosmos is hurtling away from our own galaxy! And they are doing so at speeds as high as fifteen thousand miles a second, which is almost a tenth the speed of light itself.

"At first astronomers could not believe their own observations. It seemed incredible that all other galaxies should be fleeing from our own, and for a time it was thought that certain of the nearer ones were not receding. But that has been seen to be an observational error and we now accept the incredible fact that all other galaxies are flying away from our own.

"What does that mean? It means that there must once have been a time when all those outward-speeding galaxies were gathered with our own into a single giant supergalaxy that contained all the stars in the universe. By calculating back from their present speeds and distances, we find that that time was about two billion years ago.

"Then something made that supergalaxy suddenly break up, and all its outer portions went flying off into space in all directions. The portions that flew off are the galaxies that are still flying away from us. Our own is without doubt the center or core of the original supergalaxy.

"What caused that break-up of the gigantic supergalaxy? That we do not know, though many theories have been advanced. Sir Arthur Eddington believes that the break-up was caused by some unknown principle of repulsion in matter which he calls the cosmical constant. Others have suggested that space itself started expanding, an even more incredible explanation. Whatever the cause, we know that that supergalaxy did break up and that all the other galaxies formed by its break-up are flying away from our own at tremendous speeds."

Garry Adams had listened intently to Dr. Peters as the astronomer spoke in quick, nervous fashion.

His own lean, newly tanned face was serious in the glow of the lamp. "It seems strange, at that," he commented. "A cosmos in which all the other galaxies are fleeing from us. But that diagram on the side of the polyhedron—you said that indicated the thing was made when the expansion first started?"

"Yes." Peters nodded. "You see, that diagram was made by intelligent or superintelligent beings, for they knew our own galaxy is spiral shaped and so depicted it.

"But they depicted the other galaxies as almost touching our own. In other words, that diagram must have been made when the giant supergalaxy first started breaking up, when the other galaxies first started running away from our own. That was some two billion years ago, as I said. Two thousand million years. So you see, if the polyhedron was actually made that long ago it—"

"I see enough to feel that I'm going crazy with speculation," Garry Adams said, getting to his feet. "I'm going to bed, whether I'm able to sleep or not."

Dr. Peters shrugged. "I suppose we might as well. The equipment I sent for won't be out until morning."

Garry Adams lay thinking in the darkness after he had retired to the upper of the two bunks in the cabin. What was this visitant from outer space and what would they find in it when they opened it?

His wonderings merged into sleep mists out of which he suddenly awoke to find the cabin bright with morning sunshine. He woke the scientist and after a hasty breakfast they hurried down to the point on the dirt road where Dr. Peters had directed the ordered equipment to be brought.

They had waited there but a half hour when the sleek high-speed truck came humming along the narrow road. Its driver halted it at sight of them, and they helped him unload the equipment it carried. Then he drove back the way he had come.

Garry Adams surveyed the pile of equipment dubiously. It looked too simple to him, consisting only of a dozen or so sealed containers of chemicals, some large copper and glass containers, a pile of copper strips and wiring, and some slender ebonite rods.

He turned to Dr. Peters, who was also gazing at the pile.

"This sure looks like a lot of junk to me," the reporter said. "How are you going to use this stuff to de-crystallize the frozen force of the polyhedron?"

Dr. Peters turned to him a blank, bewildered stare. "I don't know," he answered slowly.

"You don't know?" Garry echoed. "Why, what do you mean? Yesterday there at the polyhedron you said it was quite clear to you how to do it. You must have known, to order all this stuff."

The astronomer seemed even more bewildered. "Garry, I remember that I did know how then, when I jotted down the list of these things. But I don't now. I haven't the slightest idea of how they could be used on the polyhedron."

Garry dropped his arms, stared unbelievingly at his companion.

He started to say something, but as he saw the other's evident mental distress he checked himself.

"Well, we'll take the stuff over to the polyhedron now," he said calmly. "Maybe by that time you'll remember the plan you've forgotten."

"But I've never before forgotten anything in this way," Peters said dazedly as he helped pick up the mass of things. "It's simply beyond my understanding."

They emerged into the crushed clearing where the enigmatic polyhedron still glowed and shimmered. As they set down their burdens beside the thing, Peters burst suddenly into a laugh.

"Why, of course I know how to use this stuff on the polyhedron. It's simple enough."

Garry stared at him again. "You've remembered?"

"Of course," the scientist answered confidently. "Hand me that biggest box marked barium oxide, and two of those containers. We'll soon have the polyhedron open."

The reporter, his jaw hanging in surprise, watched Peters start confidently to work with the supplies. Chemicals foamed together in the containers as rapidly as he mixed them.

He worked swiftly, smoothly, without asking any aid of the reporter. He had an utter efficiency and utter confidence, so dissimilar to his attitude of a few minutes before, that an incredible idea was born and grew in Garry Adams' mind.

He said suddenly to Peters. "Doctor, you know completely what you're doing now?"

Peters looked up impatiently. "Of course I do," he replied sharply. "Doesn't it look like it?"

"Will you do something for me?" asked Garry. "Will you come back with me to the road where we unloaded the supplies?"

"Why in the world do that?" demanded the scientist. "I want to get this finished."

"Never mind; I'm not asking for fun but because it's important," Garry said. "Come on, will you?"

"Oh, damn such foolishness, but I'll go," the scientist said, dropping his work. "It'll lose us half an hour."

Fuming over this, he tramped back with Garry to the dirt road, a half mile from the polyhedron.

"Now what do you want to show me?" he snapped, looking around. "I only want to ask you something," Garry said. "Do you still know how to open the polyhedron?"

Dr. Peters' expression showed pure anger. "Why, you time-wasting young fool! Of course I—"

He stopped suddenly, and abruptly panic fell on his face, blind terror of the unknown.

"But I don't!" he cried. "I did there a few minutes ago but now I don't even know just what I was doing there!"

"I thought so," said Garry Adams, and though his voice was level there was a sudden chill along his spine. "When you're at the polyhedron, you know well enough how to go about a process that is completely beyond present-day human science.

"But as soon as you go some distance away from the polyhedron, you know no more about it than any other scientist would. Do you see what it means?"

Peters' face showed astounded comprehension. "You think that something—something about that polyhedron, is putting into my mind the way to get it open?"

His eyes widened. "It seems incredible, yet at that it may be true. Neither I nor any other scientist of Earth would know how to melt frozen force. Yet when I'm there at the polyhedron I *do* know how to do it!"

Their eyes met. "If something wants that open," Garry said slowly, "it's something inside the polyhedron. Something that can't open it from the inside, but is getting you to do so from the outside."

For a space of seconds they stood in the warm morning sunlight looking at each other. The woods around them gave off a smell of warm leaves, a sleepy hum of insects. When the reporter spoke again, his voice was unconsciously lower than it had been.

"We'll go back," he said. "We'll go back, and if you know how again when we're at the thing, we'll know that we're right."

They walked silently, hesitatingly, back toward the polyhedron. Though he said nothing, the hair rose on Garry Adams' neck as they entered the clearing and approached the glowing thing.

They went closer until they stood again beside the thing. Then Peters suddenly turned a white face toward the reporter.

"You were right, Garry!" he said. "Now that I'm back here beside the thing, I suddenly know how to open it!

"Something inside must be telling me, as you said. Something that ages ago was locked up in this and that wants—freedom."

A sudden alien terror fell upon them both, chilling them like a gelid breath from the unknown. With a common impulse of panic they turned hastily.

"Let's get away from it!" Garry cried. "For Heaven's sake, let's get out of here!"

Four steps only they ran when a thought sounded in Garry's brain, clear and loud.

"Wait!"

The word, the pleading request, was as strong in his mind as though his ears had heard it.

Peters looked at him with wide eyes as they unconsciously stopped.

"I heard it, too," he whispered.

"Wait, do not go!" came the rapid thought message into their minds. "Hear me at least, let me at least explain to you, before you flee!"

"Let's go while we can!" Garry cried to the scientist. "Peters, whatever's in that thing, whatever is talking to our minds, isn't human, isn't of Earth. It came from outside space, from ages ago. Let's get away from it!"

But Dr. Peters was looking fascinatedly back at the polyhedron. His face was twisted by conflicting emotions.

"Garry, I'm going to stay and listen to it," he said suddenly. "I've got to find out what I can about it—if you were a scientist you'd understand! You go on and get away; there's no reason for your staying. But I'm going back."

Garry stared at him, then grinned crookedly though he was still a little white beneath his tan. He said, "Just as a scientist is ridden by his passion, doctor, so is a reporter by his. I'm going back with you. But for Heaven's sake don't touch that equipment; don't try to open the polyhedron, until we at least have some idea as to what kind of thing is inside!"

Dr. Peters nodded wordlessly and then slowly they moved back to the glowing polyhedron, feeling as though the ordinary sunlit noonday world had suddenly become unreal. When they neared the polyhedron, the thoughts from within it beat more strongly into their minds.

"I sense that you have stayed. Come closer to the polyhedron—it is only by immense mental effort that I can force my thoughts through this insulating shell of force at all."

Numbly they stepped closer until they were at the very side of the faceted, glowing thing.

"Remember," Garry whispered hoarsely to the scientist, "no matter what it tells us, what it promises, don't open it yet!"

The scientist nodded unsteadily. "I'm as afraid of opening it as you are."

The thought messages came clearer into their brains now from the polyhedron.

"I am a prisoner in this shell of frozen force, as you have guessed. For a time almost longer than you can comprehend, I have been prisoned in it. My prison has at last been cast on your world, wherever that may be. I want your help now and I sense that you are too afraid to help me. If I disclose to you who I am and how I came to be here, you will not then be so afraid. That is why I wish now to tell you these things."

Garry Adams felt as though he stood in a strange dream as the thoughts from the polyhedron beat into his brain.

"Not in mere thought messages will I tell you what I wish to tell, but visually by thought pictures that you can understand better. I do not know the capacity of your mental systems for reception of such pictures, but I will try to make them clear.

"Do not try to think about what you see but merely allow your brains to remain in receptive condition. You will see what I wish you to see and will understand at least partially because my thoughts will accompany the visual impressions."

Garry felt sudden panic as the world seemed suddenly to vanish from around him. Dr. Peters, the polyhedron, the whole noonday sunlit scene, disappeared in an instant. Instead of standing in the sunlight, Garry seemed now to himself to be hanging suspended in the black vault of the cosmos—a lightless, airless void.

Everywhere about him was only that empty blackness, save below him. Below him, far, far below, there floated a colossal cloud of stars shaped like a flattened globe. Its stars could be counted only by the millions of millions.

Garry knew that he looked on the universe as it was two billion years ago. He knew that this below him was the giant supergalaxy in which were all the stars in the cosmos. Now he seemed to rocket down toward the mighty swarm with the swiftness of thought, and now he saw that the worlds of its swarming suns were inhabited.

Their inhabitants were volitient beings of force, each one like a tall, disk-crowned pillar of blue-brilliant light. They were immortal; they needed no nourishment; they passed through space and matter at will. They were the only volitient beings in the whole supergalaxy and its inert matter was almost entirely at their command.

Now Garry's viewpoint shifted to a world near the center of the supergalaxy. There he saw a single force creature who was engaged in a new experiment upon matter. He was seeking to build new forms of it, combining and re-combining atoms in infinite permutations.

Suddenly he came upon a combination of atoms that gave strange results. The matter so formed moved of its own accord. It was able to receive a stimulus and to remember it and act upon it. It was able also to assimilate other matter into itself, and so to grow.

The force creature experimenter was fascinated by this strange disease of matter. He tried it on a larger scale and the diseased matter spread out and assimilated more and more ordinary matter. He named this disease of matter by a name that reproduced itself in Garry's mind as "life."

This strange disease of life escaped from the experimenter's laboratory and began to spread over all that planet. Everywhere it spread, it infected other matter. The experimenter tried to extirpate it but the infection was too widely spread. At last he and his fellows abandoned that diseased world.

But the disease got loose from that world to other worlds. Spores of it, driven by the push of light beams to other suns and planets, spread out in every direction. The life disease was adaptable, took different forms on different worlds, but always it grew and propagated, infected more and more matter.

The force creatures assembled their forces to wipe out this loathsome infection but could not. While they stamped it out on one world, it spread on two others. Always, too, some hidden spore escaped them. Soon nearly all the worlds of the central portion of the supergalaxy were leprous with the life plague.

Garry saw the force creatures make a last great attempt to stamp out this pathology infecting their universe. The attempt failed; the plague continued its resistless spread. The force creatures then saw that it would spread until it had infected all the worlds in the supergalaxy.

They determined to prevent this at all costs. They resolved to break up the supergalaxy, to detach the uninfected outer parts of it from the diseased central portion. It would be a stupendous task but the force creatures were not daunted by it.

Their plan entailed giving to the supergalaxy a rotatory movement of great speed. This they accomplished by generating tremendous waves of continuous force through the ether, waves so directed that gradually they started the supergalaxy rotating on its center.

Faster and faster the giant star swarm turned as time went on. The life disease was still spreading at its center but now the force creatures had hope. They continued their work until the supergalaxy was turning so fast that it could no longer hold together against its own centrifugal force. It broke up like a bursting flywheel.

Garry saw that break-up, as though from high above. He saw the colossal, spinning star cloud disintegrating, swarm after swarm of stars breaking from it and flying away through space. Countless numbers of these smaller new galaxies broke from the parent supergalaxy until at last only the inmost core of the supergalaxy was left.

It was still rotating, and still had the spiral form caused by its rotation. On it now the life plague had spread to nearly every world. The last swarm of clean, uninfected stars had broken away from it and was flying away like the others.

But as this last swarm departed, there took place a ceremony and a punishment. The force creatures had passed judgment upon that one of their number whose experiments had loosed the life plague upon them and had made necessary this great break-up.

They decreed that he should remain forever in this diseased galaxy that all the others were leaving. They imprisoned him in a shell of frozen force so constructed that never could he open it from within. They set that polyhedronal shell floating in the diseased galaxy they left behind.

Garry Adams saw that glowing polyhedron floating in aimless orbits in the galaxy, as the years passed in millions. The other galaxies sped farther and farther away from this infected one in which the life disease now covered every possible world. Only this one force creature remained here, prisoned eternally in the polyhedron.

Garry dimly saw the polyhedron, in its endless orbit through, the suns, chance to strike upon a world. He saw—

He saw only mists, gray mists. The vision was passing and suddenly Garry was aware that he stood in hot sunlight. He stood by the glowing polyhedron, dazed, rapt.

And Dr. Peters, dazed and rapt, too, was working mechanically on something beside him, a triangular thing of copper and ebonite pointed at the polyhedron.

Garry understood instantly and cried out in horror as he leaped toward the astronomer. "Peters, *don't!*"

Peters, only partly awakened, looked dazedly down at the thing which his hands were busy finishing.

"Smash it!" Garry yelled. "The thing inside the polyhedron kept us occupied with that vision so it could keep you working unconsciously to set it free. Don't—oh, Lord!"

For as Garry yelled, the dazed scientist's hands had clicked together the last parts of the copper and ebonite triangle, and from its apex leaped a yellow beam that smote the glowing polyhedron.

The yellow flash spread instantly over the faceted, glowing bulk, and as Garry and the waking Peters stared petrifiedly, they saw the polyhedron dissolving in that saffron flare.

The faceted sides of frozen force melted and vanished in a moment. Up out of the dissolved prison cage burst and towered the Thing that had been in it.

A forty-foot pillar of blazing, blue light, crowned by a disk of light, it loomed supernally splendid in sudden darkness, for with its bursting forth the noonday sunlight had snapped out like turned-off electricity. It swirled and spun in awful, alien glory as Peters and Garry cried out and threw their hands before their blinded eyes.

From the brilliant pillar there beat into their minds a colossal wave of exultation, triumph beyond triumph, joy vaster than any human joy. It was the mighty paean of the Thing, that went out from it not in sound but in thought.

It had been prisoned, cut away from the wide universe, for age after slow-crawling age, and now at last it was free and rejoicing in its freedom. In unbearable madness of cosmic rapture it loomed in the noonday darkness.

Then it flashed up into the heavens like a giant lightning bolt of blue. And as it did so, Garry's darkening brain failed and he staggered into unconsciousness.

He opened his eyes to bright noonday sunlight, which was streaming through the window beside him. He was lying in the cabin and the day was again brilliant outside, and somewhere nearby a metallic voice was speaking.

He recognized that the voice was coming from his own little battery radio. Garry lay unmoving, unremembering for the moment, as the excited voice hurried on.

"—far out as we can make out, the area affected extended from Montreal as far south as Scranton, and from Buffalo in the West to some miles in the Atlantic beyond Boston, in the East.

"It lasted less than two minutes, and in the whole area was a complete blotting out of the sun's light and heat in that time. Also, practically all electrical machinery ceased to function and the telegraph and telephone lines went completely dead.

"People living in certain Adirondack and Northwest Vermont sections have reported also some physical effects. They consisted of a sudden sensation of extreme joy, coincident with the darkness, and followed by brief unconsciousness.

"No one yet knows the cause of this amazing phenomenon though it may be due to a freak of solar forces. Scientists are now being consulted on the matter, and as soon as they—"

Garry Adams by this time was struggling weakly up to a sitting position in the bunk, clutching at its post.

"Peters!" he called over the metallic voice of the radio. "Peters—"

"I'm here," said the astronomer, coming across the cabin.

The scientist's face was pale and his movements a little unsteady, but he, too, was unhurt.

"I came back to consciousness a little sooner than you did and carried you up here," he said.

"That—that Thing caused all the darkness and other things I've just been hearing of?" Garry cried.

Dr. Peters nodded. "It was a creature of force, force so terrific that its bursting forth here damped the heat and light radiations of the sun, the electrical currents of machines, even the electro-nervous impulses of our brains."

"And it's gone; it's really gone?" the reporter cried.

"It's gone after its fellows, out into the void of intergalactic space after the galaxies that are receding from our own," said Dr. Peters solemnly.

"We know now why all the galaxies in the cosmos are fleeing from our own, know that ours is held an accursed galaxy, leprous with the disease of life. But I don't think we'll ever tell the world."

Garry Adams shook his head weakly. "We won't tell; no. And I think we'll try to forget it ourselves. I think we'll try."

In the World's Dusk

The city Zor reared its somber towers and minarets of black marble into the ruddy sunset, a great mass of climbing spires circumvallated by a high black wall. Twelve gates of massive brass opened in that wall, and outside it there lay the white salt desert that now covered the whole of Earth. A cruel, glaring plain that stretched eye-achingly to the horizons, its monotony was broken by no hill or valley or sea. Long ago the last seas had dried up and disappeared, and long ago the ages of geological gradation had smoothed mountain and hill and valley into a featureless blank.

As the sun sank lower, it struck a shaft of red light across the city Zor into a great hall in the topmost spire. The crimson rays cut through the shadowy gloom of the dim, huge room and bathed the sitting figure of Galos Gann.

Brooding in the ruddy glow, Galos Gann looked out across the desert to the sinking sun, and said, "It is another day. The end comes soon."

Chin in hand he brooded, and the sun sank, and the shadows in the great hall deepened and darkened about him. Out in the dusking sky blossomed the stars, and they peered down through the portico like taunting white eyes at him. And it seemed to him that he heard their thin, silvery star-voices cry mockingly across the sky to each other, "The end comes soon to the race of Galos Gann."

For Galos Gann was the last man of all men. Sitting alone in his darksome hall high in somber Zor, he knew that nowhere around the desert globe did there move another human shape nor echo another human voice. He was that one about whom during anticipatory ages a fearful, foreboding fascination had clung—the final survivor. He tasted a loneliness no other man had ever known, for it was his to brood upon all the marching millions of men who had gone before him and who were now no more. He could look back across the millioned millions of years to the tumultuous youth of Earth in whose warm seas had spawned the first protoplasmic life which, under the potent influences of cosmic radiation, had evolved through more and more complex animal forms into the culminating form of man. He could mark how man had risen through primeval savagery to world civilization that had finally given men mighty powers and had lengthened their life-span to centuries. And he could mark too how the grim, grinding mechanism of natural forces had in the end brought doom to the fair cities of that golden age.

Steadily, silently, inexorably, through the ages the hydrosphere or water envelope of Earth had slowly dwindled, due to the loss of its particles into space from molecular dispersion. The seas had dried up as the millions of years had passed, and salt deserts had crept across the world. And men had seen the end close at hand for their race, and because they saw it they ceased to bring forth children.

They were weary of the endless, hopeless struggle, and they would not listen to the pleadings of Galos Gann, their greatest scientist, who alone among them yearned to keep the dying race alive. And so in their weariness the last generation of them had passed away, and in the world was left no living man but the unyielding Galos Gann.

In his dark hall high in Zor, Galos Gann sat huddled in his robes brooding upon these things, his withered face and black, living eyes unchanging. Then at last he stood erect. He strode with his robes swirling about him onto the balcony outside, and in the darkness he looked up at the mocking white eyes of the stars.

He said, "You think that you look down on the last of men, that all the glories of my race are a story that is told and ended, but you are wrong. I am Galos Gann, the greatest man of all the men that have lived on Earth. And it is my unconquerable will that my race shall not die but shall live on to greater glories."

The white stars were silent, wheeling with cynical imperturbability over the deserts beyond night-shrouded Zor.

And Galos Gann raised his hand toward Rigel and Canopus and Achernar in a gesture pregnant with defiance and menace.

"Somewhere and somehow I will find means to keep the race of man living on!" he cried to them. "Yes, and the day will come when our seed will yoke you and all your worlds in submissive harness to man!"

Then Galos Gann, filled with that determination, came to a great resolve and went to his laboratories and procured certain instruments and cryptic mechanisms. Holding them inside his robes, he went down from the tower and walked through the dark streets of the city Zor.

Very small and alone he seemed as he wended through the dim starlight and glooming shadows of the mighty city's ways, yet proudly he stalked; for unconquerable defiance to fate flamed in his heart and vitalized his brain with unshakable resolve.

He came to the low, squat structure that he sought, and its door opened with a sighing sound as he approached. He entered, and there in a small dark room was a stair down which he went. The coils of that spiral stair dropped into a great subterranean hall of black marble illuminated by a feeble blue light that had no visible source.

When Galos Gann stepped at last on its tessellated tile floor, he stood looking along the oblong hall. Upon its far-stretching walls were a hundred high square panels that bore in painted pictures the story of mankind. The first of those panels showed the primal protoplasmic life from which man had descended, and the last of the panels displayed this very subterranean chamber. For in crypts set into the floor of this hall there lay the dead people of the city Zor who had been the last generation of mankind. There was one last empty crypt that waited for Galos Gann when he should lie down in it to die, and since this was the last chapter of mankind's story, it had been pictured in the last panel.

But Galos Gann disregarded the painted walls and strode along the hall, opening the crypts in the floor one after another. He worked on until at last before him lay the scores of dead men and women, their bodies perfectly preserved so that they seemed sleeping.

Galos Gann said to them, "It is my thought that even you who are not now living can mayhap be used to keep mankind from perishing. It seems an ill thing to disturb you in the peace of death. But nowhere else save in death can I find those I must have to perpetuate mankind."

Then Galos Gann began to work upon the bodies of the dead, summoning up from his mighty resolution superhuman scientific powers which even he had hitherto never possessed.

By supreme chemical achievement he synthesized new blood with which he filled the wasted veins of the bodies. And by powerful electric stimulants and glandular injections he set their hearts to beating convulsively, and then regularly. And as their hearts pumped the new blood through their bodies to their perfectly preserved brains, the dead regained slow consciousness and staggered upright and looked dazedly at one another and at the watching Galos Gann.

Galos Gann felt a mighty pride and exultation as he looked at these strong men and fair women whom he had brought back from death. He said to them:

"I have recalled you to life because I have resolved that our race shall not come to an end and be forgotten of the universe. It is my determination that mankind shall continue, and through you I shall effect this."

The jaws of one of the staring men moved stiffly and from between them came the rusty accents of a voice long unused.

"What madness of yours is this, Galos Gann? You have given us the semblance of life but we are still dead, and how can we who are dead prolong the life of man?"

"You move and speak, therefore you are living," insisted Galos Gann. "You shall mate together and bring forth sons, and they shall be the progenitors of new peoples."

The dead man said hollowly, "You strive against the inevitable like a child breaking his hands against a door of marble. It is the law of the universe that everything which exists must come some day to an end. Planets wither and die and fall back into their parent suns, and suns strike one against the other and are transformed into nebulae, and the nebulae last not but in turn condense into other suns and worlds that in their own turn must die.

"How shall you hope amid this universal law of death to keep the race of man forever living? We have lived a fair life for many million million years, we have struggled and won and lost, have laughed in the sunlight and dreamed under the stars, have played our part in the mighty drama of eternity. Now it is time we pass to our appointed end."

As the dead man finished speaking, a hollow, low whisper of assent went up from all the other staring dead.

"Aye," they said, "It is time the tired sons of men rested in the blessed sleep of death."

But the brow of Galos Gann was dark with resolve, and his eyes flashed and his form stiffened with unchangeable will.

"Your words avail you nothing," he told the dead. "Despite your icy counsels of surrender, I am determined that man shall live on to challenge the blind laws of the cosmos. Therefore you shall obey me, for well you know that with my powers and science I can force you to my will. You are not dead now but living, and you shall re-people the city Zor."

Galos Gann with these words walked to the spiral stair and started up its winding way. And helplessly, dully submissive, the dead men and women followed him up the stair, walking stiffly with a confused, heavy trampling up the steps.

A strange spectacle it was when Galos Gann led his silent host out into the starlit streets of the city. And by day and by night thereafter was Zor a weird sight, peopled again by those who once had peopled it before they died. For Galos Gann decreed that they should live in the same buildings in which they had lived before. And those that had been husbands and wives before should be husbands and wives now, and in all things they should dwell as they had before their deaths.

So all day beneath the hot sun the dead went to and fro in Zor and pretended that they were truly living. They walked stiffly in the streets and gave one another greeting in their grating, rusty voices, and those that had had trades in old time followed those trades now, so that the cheery sounds of work and life rang in the city.

By night they thronged into the great theater of the city and sat in stiff immobility while those who had been dancers and singers performed with heavy clumsiness on the stage. And the dead audience applauded, and laughed, and their laughter was a strange sound.

And at night when the stars peered curiously down at Zor, those of them who had been young men and maidens walked apart and with stiff and uncouth gestures made pantomime of love, and spoke words of love to one another. And they wedded one another, for that was the decree of Galos Gann.

In his high tower, Galos Gann watched as moon after moon was born and waxed and died. Great hope was his as the months passed one by one in the dead-tenanted city.

He said to himself, "These are not wholly living—something there was that my powers could not bring back from death. But even such as they are, they will serve to give mankind a new start in the universe."

The slow months passed and at last to one of the dead couples living in the city, a child was born. High flared the hopes of Galos Gann when he heard, and great was his excitement as he hastened through the city to see. But when he saw the child, he felt his heart grow cold. For this infant was like the parents of whom it was born, it was not wholly living. It moved and saw and uttered sounds, but its movements and cries were stiff and strange, and its eyes had death behind them.

Not wholly yet did Galos Gann give up hope in his great plan. He waited for another child to be born, but the next child too was the same.

Then indeed did his faith and hope perish. He called the dead citizens of Zor together and spoke to them. He said:

"Why do you not bring forth wholly living children, seeing that you yourselves are now living? Do you do this but to thwart me?"

Out of the gaunt-eyed throng a dead man answered him.

"Death cannot bring forth life any more than light can be born of darkness. Despite your words we know that we are dead, and we can give birth only to death. Now be convinced of the futility of your mad scheme and allow us to return to the peace of death, and let the race of man come peacefully to its destined end."

Galos Gann told them darkly, "Return then to the nothingness you crave, since you cannot serve my purpose. But know that not now and not ever shall I relinquish my purpose to perpetuate the race."

The dead answered him not, but turning their backs upon him moved in a silent, trampling throng through the streets of the city toward that low, squat building which they knew.

They passed without any word down the spiral stair to the blue-lit chamber of the crypts, and there each lay down once more in the crypt that was his. And the two women who had given birth lay down with their strange, dead little infants at their breasts. Then each drew over his crypt the stone lid that had covered it, until all were covered once more. And again there was solemn silence in the pictured burial-chamber of Zor.

Up in his high tower Galos Gann had watched them go, and there for two days and nights he brooded over the again-silent city.

He said to himself, "It seems my hope was vain and that in truth humanity dies with me, since those who were dead cannot be the progenitors of future men. For where in all the world are there any living men and women such as alone will serve my ends?"

This he said, and then of a sudden a thought struck him that was like a dazzling and perilous lightning-flash across the brooding darkness of his mind. His brain well nigh reeled at the audacity of the thing it had suddenly conceived; yet such was the desperation of his purpose that he seized quakingly upon even this unearthly expedient.

He muttered to himself, "There are no living men and women in the world *today*. But what of the trillions of men and women who have existed on Earth in the past? Those trillions are separated from me by the abyss of time. Yet if I could somehow reach across that abyss, I could draw many living people out of the past into dead Zor."

The brain of Galos Gann fired to that staggering thought. And he, the greatest scientist Earth had ever possessed, began that night the audacious attempt to draw across the gulf of ages living men and women who would father a new race.

Day after day, as the sun blazed on silent Zor, and night after night as the majestic stars wheeled above it, the withered scientist toiled in his laboratories. And gradually there grew up the great cylindrical mechanism of brass and quartz that was to pierce time.

At last the mighty mechanism was finished and Galos Gann prepared to begin his unthinkably daring attempt. Despite the inflexibility of his resolve, his soul quaked within him as he laid hand upon the switches that controlled the great machine. For well he knew that in attempting to thrust an arm across the awful gulf of time he was so outraging and rending the inmost frame of the cosmos that vast cataclysm might well result. Yet Galos Gann, driven by his unshaken determination, closed the switches with a trembling hand.

There came a crash of cosmic thunder and a hissing of blinding white force that filled the cylinder, and all the dead city Zor rocked strangely on its foundations as though shaken by a mighty wind.

Galos Gann was aware that the titanic forces he had loosed were tearing through space and time itself inside that cylinder, and riving the hitherto inviolate dimensions of the universe. The white force flamed and the thunder crashed and the city rocked until at last he convulsively opened the switches again. Then the glare and rumbling and rocking died, and as Galos Gann stared into the cylinder he cried in shrill triumph:

"I have succeeded! The brain of Galos Gann has triumphed over time and fate!"

For there in the cylinder stood a living man and woman who wore the grotesque cloth garments of ages before.

He opened the door of the cylinder and the man and woman came out with slow steps. Galos Gann told them exultantly:

"I have brought you across time to be the fountainhead of a new generation. Be not afraid! You are but the first of very many people I shall bring out of the past in the same way."

The man and woman looked at Galos Gann, and suddenly they laughed. Their laughter was not of mirth but was a maniac shrieking. Wildly, insanely, the man and woman laughed. And Galos Gann saw that they were both utterly mad.

Then he understood. By dint of superhuman science he had contrived to bring their living bodies across the gulf of ages unharmed, but in so doing he had destroyed their minds. Not any science beneath the sun could draw their minds over the abyss of time without wrecking them, for the mind is not of matter and does not obey the laws of matter. Yet Galos Gann was so possessed of his mighty plan that he refused to relinquish it.

"I will bring more across time," he told himself, "and surely some of them will come through with minds unharmed."

So again and again in the nights and days that followed, he operated the great mechanism and with its potent grasp snatched many scores of men and women out of their proper time and brought them across the millenniums to Zor. But always, though he brought their bodies through unharmed, he could not bring their minds; so that it was only mad men and women who came from the cylinder, out of every age and land.

These mad people dwelt in Zor in a most frightful fashion, roaming its streets so that no corner of the city was beyond the sound of their insane shrieking. They ascended the somber towers and raved and gibbered from them at the dead city and at the barren desert beyond it. It seemed that even the insensate city grew fearful of the crazed horde whom it housed, for the city of the mad was more awful than had been the city of the dead.

Finally Galos Gann ceased to draw men and women out of the past, for he saw that never could he hope to bring them through sane. For a time he strove to replace the minds of these crazed people which had been destroyed. But he saw that that too was beyond the power of any material science.

Then in that shrieking city of madness which was the last city on Earth, Galos Gann grew afraid that he too was going mad. He felt a desire to scream with the others through the dark streets.

So in sick disgust and fear he went forth and destroyed those mad people down to the last one, giving them the release of death. And Zor again knew silence as the last man solitary walked its ways.

Finally there came a day when Galos Gann walked onto his balcony and looked fixedly out over the white and barren desert.

He said, "I sought to bring new men out of death, and then out of time, but neither from death nor time it seems can come those to prolong the race. How can I hope to produce men in a little moment of time when it required millioned millions of years for the forces of nature to produce them? So I shall produce the new race in the way that the old was produced. I shall change the face of Earth so that new life may spring from it as it did long ago, and in time that life will evolve once more into men."

Animated by that colossal resolve, Galos Gann, the last and mightiest scientist of Earth, began an awesome task that would hitherto have never even been dreamed of by any man.

He first assembled all the forces of which his race had had knowledge, and many of which he himself had discovered. And he devised even mightier forces such as even a god might fear to unchain too lightly.

Then Galos Gann loosed his powers and began to bore a shaft down into the solid lithosphere of the Earth. Down through sandstone and granite and gneiss he bored until he had passed down through the rock crust and was deep in the mighty core of nickel-iron which is the heart of the planet.

In that iron core he constructed a great chamber which he fitted with the equipment and the mechanisms that he would require for the task ahead of him. And when everything he needed was in that deep chamber, he retired down to it and then collapsed and closed the shaft that led up to the surface.

Then Galos Gann began to shake the Earth. From his deep chamber in the iron core he loosed small impulses of force at exact intervals. And the period of rhythm of these impulses was timed with perfect accuracy to the period of rhythm of the Earth.

At first the little impulses had no effect upon the vast globe of the planet. But little by little their effect accumulated and grew stronger, until finally the whole rocky crust of the lithosphere was shaking violently.

These stresses and strains produced immense pressures and heats within the rocks, melting much of them into lava. And this molten lava burst upward in fiery masses all around the globe, as it had done when the Earth was in its first youth.

Galos Gann in his deep-buried chamber watched through his instruments and saw the changes taking place upon the surface of the Earth. He saw the upthrust masses of molten magma give off their imprisoned gases, and observed those gases combining to form a new hydrosphere of water-vapor clouds around the planet.

The Earth was passing through the same changes it had passed through long ago. As its molten surface began to cool, rain began to fall from the clouds and gathered upon the torn surface of the world in new seas.

Galos Gann watched tensely with his far-seeing, marvelous instruments, and saw complex compounds being built up along the shores of the warm seas, from carbon and hydrogen and oxygen and other elements.

And beneath the photosynthetic action of the sunlight these organic compounds combined into the first beginnings of primal protoplasmic life.

Galos Gann said then to himself, "The new cycle of Earth's life is started. The sun's radiation calls forth life from the inorganic elements as it did ages ago in the past. That life must evolve upward under the same conditions in the same way, and in time men will evolve from it and will again people the Earth."

He calculated the ages that it would take for a new human race to evolve upon the face of Earth. Then he took a carefully measured quantity of a subtle drug which he had prepared, one which suspended indefinitely every vital function of the human body and yet permitted it to remain living in a deathless sleep. He lay down upon his couch in the buried chamber inside the Earth.

"I will sleep now in suspended animation until the new race of man has evolved," said Galos Gann. "When I awake, Earth will again be crowded with the victorious and undying race of men, and I can go forth and look upon them and then die in peace, knowing that man lives."

So saying, he folded his arms upon his breast, and the drug took its effect upon him, and he slept.

And it seemed to him that no sooner had his eyes closed and his consciousness darkened, than he was awaking again, for in sleep an eternity and a moment are the same.

For a little, Galos Gann could not indeed believe that he had slept through the ages for which his drug had been calculated. But his chronometers that measured time by the transmutation of uranium showed him that indeed he had lain sleeping for many million millions of years.

Then he knew that he had come to the moment of his triumph. For in those slow millenniums must have evolved the new race of men that must now people the surface of the Earth above him.

His hands shook as he prepared to blast a new shaft up to the surface from his chamber.

"Death is not far from me," said Galos Gann, "but first these eyes shall look on the new race which I have created to perpetuate the old."

His forces pierced a shaft up through the rocky crust of the lithosphere to the surface, and borne by his powers Galos Gann rose up that shaft and emerged onto the face of Earth into the sunlight.

He stood and looked about him. He was in the midst of a white salt desert that stretched monotonously to the horizons in all directions, and that had nowhere any hill or valley to break its blank expanse.

A queer chill came upon the heart of Galos Gann as he stood in the glaring sunlight of the lonely desert.

"Can it be," he asked himself, "that the forces of nature have dried and worn the Earth just as they did long ago? Even so, somewhere on Earth must be the new races of men that time has evolved."

He looked in one direction after another and finally he saw on one horizon the distant spires of a city. His heart gladdened at that sight and he moved toward that city with quick and eager expectation. But when he came close to the city, he was troubled anew. For it was a city of black marble towers and minarets belted by a high black wall, and in many ways it was very like the city Zor that long ago had perished.

He came to one of its open gates and passed into the city. And like a man in a dream he walked through the streets, turning his head this way and that. For this city was as empty of life as ancient Zor had been. Not in any of its courts or ways did there move one human shape, nor echo one human voice. And now a fatal foreboding and knowledge came upon Galos Gann, and led him into the highest tower and up to a dim and dusky hall at the tower's top.

There at the end of the hall sat huddled in his robes a withered, shrunken man who seemed very near to death.

Galos Gann spoke to him in a strange voice and said, "Who are you, and where are the others of the races of men?"

The other raised his swaying head, and peering blindly at Galos Gann he answered, "There are no others, for I am the last survivor of all the race of man.

"Millioned millions of years ago our life began in the protoplasm of the world's warm seas, and developed through many forms into man, and the civilization and power, of man grew great.

"But the seas dried up, and as Earth withered, our race withered and died also, until I alone am left in this dead city. And my own death is upon me."

With these words, the shrunken, swaying man fell forward, and sighed once, and lay dead upon the floor.

And Galos Gann, the last man, looked across his body at the sinking sun.

Child of the Winds

B rent was drawn by the strong lure of gold to that legended tableland in innermost Turkistan called the Plateau of the Winds. There was an old rumor that lodes of unparalleled richness existed on that unvisited and almost unknown plateau.

Brent knew the place was supposed to lie more than a hundred miles west of the little village Yurgan, so he went to Yurgan and tried to hire camels and drivers with which to cross the desert. There he learned that it was not going to be easy to reach the plateau.

One man he found, a young Turki named Dasan An, who had traveled just enough as the servant of other white men to make him contemptuous of his fellow-villagers. He affected white-man's clothes, spoke execrable English, and talked to Brent as though they were the only two civilized people in the place.

"Very afraid these ignorant people will not go with us as drivers," he told Brent confidentially. "They too afraid of the Plateau of the Winds."

"What is there there for them to be afraid of?" Brent demanded, and Dasan An smiled in superior fashion.

"They very ignorant people, sir. They afraid of the winds—they say that the Plateau of the Winds is the winds' sacred place and that the winds kill all people who try to go there. You see, they think winds are living things, not just air but alive. They say winds not bother men anywhere else but kill any men who go to their sacred plateau, so they not go there."

"Offer them more money," Brent told him irritably. "Tell them I'll give them double pay."

Dasan An held colloquy for a little with his swart-skinned fellows and then turned back to Brent. The cocksure contempt on his face deepened.

"They not go, sir. They say double money no use to a man after the winds kill him."

Brent swore. For a little time he pondered and then he made his resolution and turned back to Dasan An.

"Very well, we'll go without them," he informed him. "We can each ride a camel and lead one, and four camels will carry all the water and supplies we'll need."

"You mean we go just ourselves without anybody else drivers?" asked the Turki, his confidence a little dashed.

"That's what I mean," Brent said, and added, "Why not? You're not afraid of the winds too, are you?"

The Turki laughed noisily. "You are pleased make joke. Dasan An is not ignorant villager like these. I have been servant of white men and have been to Tehran."

"All right; see to getting the camels," Brent told him. "We'll start as soon as the outfit's ready."

That was in two days. In the already brassy glare of the rising sun they rode out of Yurgan with their stalking, sneering camels and pointed due west into the white wastes of salt desert.

Four days later the great, horizon-stretching wall of the Plateau of the Winds rose dimly in the distance ahead of them. That night they camped under it, a steep wall of brown rock a thousand feet high, extending north and south for many miles. And that night they heard winds blowing up there on the plateau.

The looked up into the darkness toward the plateau as they heard the distant tumult.

"Winds blowing very strong up there," said Dasan An, and Brent nodded.

"No doubt this plateau is the center of air-currents that meet and form constant winds, and that would explain why your people think it a sacred place where the winds gather."

"Listen to them blowing up there!" he added. "I'm glad we're not up there tonight."

For the winds they heard up on the plateau were strong. Their distant bellowing, shouting tumult came down through the night to Brent like a hubbub of great voices calling to each other, good-humored, rollicking shouts of jovially brawling wind-giants.

They heard winds of all kinds in that moving uproar high on the plateau: winds that trumpeted and others that wailed and others that shrieked, winds so small that their passage was a whisper and winds so great that they roared; as though winds of all kinds had gathered there and were racing, rollicking, rushing together across the plateau. And as Brent and Dasan An listened they heard over the frolicking wind-voices a different sound. It was a high, silvery whistling, shrill and stabbing and joyous. It was almost the whistle of a screaming wind, yet there was a strange qualitative difference. It rose, fell, rose again and fell again, and as it ceased the wild wind-chorus stormed louder.

They listened until the uproar of winds had receded northward, died out of hearing. Then all was very still.

"Plenty windy up there, all right," Brent repeated, breaking the silence. "I hope it's not that bad tomorrow."

"Maybe better to wait until not so much wind before we try to climb plateau?" Dasan An suggested quickly.

"Nonsense, we're not going to let a little wind hold us back," Brent told him. "The sooner we get up onto the plateau, the better."

"That quite right, quite right," the Turki agreed hastily. "We not ignorant people to be afraid of winds."

Next morning they found a zigzag path up the plateau's side less than a mile from their camp, and started the climb. As they dragged the camels up from ledge to ledge, Brent saw that his companion looked constantly up toward the nearing rim.

It was late afternoon by the time they scaled the last ledge and stood panting on the rim. The Plateau of the Winds lay before them, a brown, barren plain. Miles in toward its center rose two tall pinnacles of rock, but all the rest was level, dusty, bare.

There were no winds blowing where they stood. The only visible sign of winds was a few thousand feet across the plateau where a group of little winds were moving, visible by the sand-whirls they raised from the plain, whisking and scurrying this way and that.

"There ought to be water at those rock-pinnacles," said Brent, gazing against the sun. "We could use it."

But Dasan An was staring at the distant sand-whirls. "See—small winds. Let us hope they not come near."

Brent turned and stared. "What, those little gusts? Why, they couldn't harm us."

"I hope they not come near," the Turki repeated, looking toward them.

"Come on, we'll try to get to those pinnacles before dark," Brent told him.

They started, Dasan An still keeping an eye upon the distant little sand-whirls as he tugged his unwilling lead-camel onward.

Brent was gazing at the rock-pinnacles ahead and wondering what chance they had of finding the legended lodes, even if they located water, when he heard Dasan An cry out suddenly in fear.

"The little winds! They come!"

He turned and saw that in fact the sand-whirls raised by the little winds were now gliding toward them. They looked like little sand-genii as they came on, and it struck him as odd that they should move so in a group. But he frowned when he turned back to his follower.

"Come along, Dasan," he said angrily. "Those winds are not big enough to bother us."

"They come!—they come!" babbled the Turki, almost incoherent with fear.

With a muttered curse Brent started back to shake some sense into him, and just then the little winds reached them. His eyes were filled for a moment with the sand they raised and he had to stop, temporarily blinded. As he stood rubbing his eyes he could feel and hear the little winds blowing all around and through them, whisking and darting about for all the world as though examining the party.

Then suddenly the little winds changed. The little whispering sounds they made became suddenly louder, angry. They pushed men and camels toward the plateau's rim!

Brent called through the flying sand of the miniature tempest for Dasan An to hold his camels. It was all they could do to hold the animals as the raging little gusts strove vainly to push them back.

The miniature wind-storm stopped as suddenly as it had begun. The little winds turned and raced back across the plateau toward the rock-pinnacles, a group of sand-whirls swiftly gliding.

Dasan An emitted a quavering, broken cry. "They have seen us! They have seen we are on the plateau and have gone to summon the great winds to come and kill us!"

"Great winds, nonsense!" Brent told him. "It was just a little flurry of gusts and now it's gone. Do you mean to tell me you're as superstitious as the villagers?"

But this appeal to Dasan An's vanity was in vain, for all his superior skepticism was gone in the panic that now filled him.

"It is not superstition—the winds *are* living, though I denied it!" he wailed. "They have seen us and know now we are here and unless we go back we shall die."

"Forget that stuff and get the packs fixed on those camels of yours," Brent ordered authoritatively. "Then we'll get going again and—"

He stopped. For he was looking at Dasan An's face and as he spoke he saw it changing terribly. It became a swart mask of frozen fear, naked and awful. His eyes bulged with terror as he stared west.

Brent turned and looked, and felt a chill close round his heart. The whole western heavens had grown suddenly dark with clouds of sand lifted by great winds. A rapidly rising moaning filled the air.

He dropped his camel-ropes and leaped toward a near-by depression in the rocks, yelling to Dasan An.

"Get into here with me!" he yelled. "We can't hold the camels—let them go!"

"The winds!" he heard the Turki cry thinly. "The great winds come!"

Then as Brent threw himself into that little hollow he heard no more for the terrific roar of the advancing winds. He saw the camels bolt madly, squealing in terror. He saw Dasan An, staring at the oncoming sand-clouds like a man fascinated by the face of death, prostrate himself like a worshipper. Then to Brent it was as though hell had been suddenly dumped upon them, a hell of wind instead of flame. He lost almost all power to distinguish sensations as the great winds thundered down on them.

He saw Dasan An picked up by the winds and whirled down onto the rock plain. And again the winds lifted and smashed the Turki downward, and again, till his body was mere red pulp.

He glimpsed the camels grasped by the mighty winds and brushed off the rim of the plateau. Then he felt the winds tearing at his own body and heard in his ears their terrible bellowing. It was a thunder of titanic rage, a wrathfulness beyond anything human, a colossal anger bent on rooting him out and beating him into a pulp.

Clawed by those awful winds, Brent clung insensately to his little shelter, digging his fingers into the rock. He felt himself being pulled forth, and the mad bellowing was louder. The winds plucked him farther out of his shelter. He heard over their thunder a shrill, stabbing whistling as he was torn completely loose. The winds started to lift him bodily into the air.

He heard in that second the silver whistling stab swiftly, urgently. The winds dropped him again upon the rock.

Half-conscious only, Brent raised his head to see that the great winds' sand-clouds had withdrawn a little from him. Running toward him through the wild winds was a girl. A girl from whom came the silver whistling! A slim, bronzed girl clad in a flying white garment, bronzed legs and arms bare, her dull-gold hair flying backward like flame as she ran.

She was running toward him through the winds with a swiftness that made her seem a thing of air herself. He saw a face dynamically beautiful, gray-green eyes wide with emotion, fixed on himself. He heard the unearthly whistling stab again from this girl's lips and thought he heard the thunder of winds lessen still further. Then he heard and saw nothing as unconsciousness claimed him.

Brent had no immediate memory of what had happened, when he awoke. He knew only that he lay in darkness on something soft and warm. He tried to remember where he was, and rapidly did remember. He remembered the climb onto the plateau, the winds that had battered Dasan An to death, that had seemed about to kill him also when they had suddenly lessened.

And just as the winds had lessened a girl had appeared, a girl with gray-green eyes who whistled silver-shrilly! Had that girl been real? And where was he now?

Brent sat up, and discovered he had been lying on some soft skin rugs. He looked about him in the dark.

Gradually he made out that he was in a rocky chamber or natural cavern of considerable size. Fruits of different kinds and flowers and skins lay about, and a spring gleamed in the corner. At one end of the cavern a round aperture opened on a sky of thick stars.

Bewildered, he got to his feet and walked out of that opening. Out there in the starlight he saw that the cavern in which he had lain was in a towering pinnacle of weathered rock, and that another pinnacle was close by. But how had he come to these pinnacles?

Before him in the dim starlight stretched a ghost-like plain, the Plateau of the Winds. Out there not a hundred yards from him moved a slender figure in a brief white garment, running, darting, dancing—the girl he had seen as consciousness left him.

The girl was yet unaware of him. She was running and darting to and fro with incredible swiftness. And a half-dozen little winds were blowing around her, whisking little sand-whirls to the eye. Dart and twist as she might, the sand-whirls darted more swiftly after her. The sound of the little winds was a gay whistling whisper as they danced. And from the girl's lips came joyous whistling.

Suddenly she saw Brent. She stopped dead, looking toward him, then came slowly to him. He saw again in the starlight that dynamic beauty of her face. Her eyes looked into his, intently. They were wide eyes, clean and clear as wind-washed skies, clear beyond anything he had ever seen on earth, and in them flickering a wild pulse of freedom.

Around both him and the girl now whirled and whisked the little winds, the dancing sand-whirls. Brent felt them tugging at his coat, exploring his garments, ruffling his hair, like mischievous children darting around two adults.

He stared at the girl, and then his amazement forced him into speech.

"By heaven, you're white!" he exclaimed. "Whatever you're doing here or however you got here, you're a white girl!"

The girl listened fascinatedly, on her face an oddly eager remembering expression. When she spoke, her voice had in it the high, silvery quality of that stabbing whistling.

"Girl?" she repeated, tentatively. Then she pointed a finger at her own breast. "Girl—Lora," she said.

"Your name's Lora?" Brent cried. "Then you must be English. I'm Brent—Dick Brent."

"Brent?" she repeated. Her clear brow was wrinkled in thought, her eyes shining with troubled excitement. "English?"

He caught her arm. He forgot all else in his excitement at finding this white girl on this lonely, unvisited plateau. How had she come here and how long had she stayed here? How had she lived here?

To Brent's rapid, excited questions she answered first only with a puzzled frown. Suddenly speech spilled hesitantly, jerkily from her in that sweet, high voice.

"Almost—I had forgotten—to talk!" she told him. "Until you came I had forgotten—men—people—"

"Forgotten them?" Brent said. "Then how long have you lived here alone?"

"Since—since—" Words seemed lacking to her and she held her hand waist-high from the ground. "Since I was so."

"You mean you've been here since you were a little girl?" Brent said incredulously.

Her head bobbed. She seemed struggling for long-forgotten words with which to express herself.

"My father and other men came here long ago, and I was with them. They hunted something. Gold? I do not know now."

"But what happened to your father and the others?" Brent wanted to know.

Her answer was simple, matter of fact. "The winds killed them. The winds have told me that they have killed many men who tried to come here."

Brent stared at her, staggered by her words. Yet strangely, too, something in him had expected those words, had sensed a strangeness in this girl that made her words seem ordinary coming from her, even though what she said was impossibly fantastic.

"The winds told you?" he said. "You talk as though the winds are living things."

Lora's eyes widened in wonder. "But of course they are," she said, staring at him in surprise.

Brent's denial was forceful. "That's nonsense! Winds are not living—they're just air!"

"Of course they are, but they are living air," Lora told him. "They move in the unliving air just as we living people move on the unliving earth, and like us some of them are great and some small, some strong and some weak. Their life is not our kind of life, but they are living and they know things. Do you think if they were not living they would answer me when I call them like this?"

Lora pursed her lips suddenly, and silver whistling notes stabbed up into the darkness from her tilted face. Then down from the upper night smote winds, loud, wild, trumpeting their strength. They seemed to circle the girl, blow round her and tug and push her and roar about her. The whisking little winds scattered as these strong gusts smote and whirled. A tumult of noisy winds whirled round the girl where a moment before had been almost a calm. Brent heard Lora laugh into the shouting gusts, heard her whistling stab again, and saw the strong winds whip away and upward as suddenly as they had come.

"Now do you believe that the winds are living?" she cried with a silvery laugh.

"Of course I don't believe it," Brent told her. "That was just a little wind-flurry such as must be common here all the time. It hardly proves that the winds are anything but winds."

Lora stamped her foot angrily. "It is not so! I will call them again and show you—"

But Brent caught her arm as she raised her face. "No, don't—I'll believe they're living if you want me to. I'm not interested in the winds, but in you. How have you lived up here a dozen years or more on this barren plateau? How was it possible for you to live as a child, if your father and the others were killed?"

The girl's anger fled as quickly as it had come, and she took Brent's hand, led him into the dim cavern. She pointed to the soft skins, the fruits and the dark-gleaming spring in the cavern's corner.

"It is simple. I sleep on those, and there is what I eat and drink."

"But where can you get fresh fruits here?" Brent asked incredulously.

"I don't get them—the winds bring them to me, all I need," she answered simply.

Brent stared, and her nostrils quivered again in sudden anger. "You do not believe!"

"Of course I believe you," Brent said hastily. "After all, winds do pick up things of all kinds and carry them long distances. But how comes it that you were left living when your father and the others were killed?"

Before answering, Lora took his hand in her own soft little hand and drew him down to sit by her side on the skins. Her face was intent, in the dim light from the opening, and a little frown was on her forehead. Brent watched her fascinatedly, the only sound the distant, ceaseless murmur of the winds.

Her voice was slow, still struggling for words. "Not much can I remember now of that time," she said. "My father and another white man I remember, and dark men that led big animals, on one of which I rode. And I remember the hard climb up onto this plateau. Then the great winds, coming across the plateau in their wrath and smiting all of us. I remember my father and the other men being hurled over the plateau's edge by the winds. I remember the cries of the falling men and the roaring of the winds.

"The winds picked me up too, lifted me into the air. But they did not kill me at once, perhaps because I was so small. They played with me! They tossed me through the air from one wind to another! They shouted with laughter, their anger forgotten, as they played with me. Then one wind took me from the others, a wind that was different from the rest. It was strong but was gentler, softer. It took me here to the rock-pinnacles and set me down. I cried for a long while and then slept, and when I woke that different wind was there again.

"It petted me, caressed me, touched and reassured me, so that I forgot my grief. It left, and after a time it came back with fruits and tanned skins and other things it put down before me. I knew it from all the other winds and I thought of it as the mother-wind, because it cared for me.

"I talked to the mother-wind and I thought it heard me. I was not afraid any longer, for I knew the winds would not hurt me. The other great winds came and picked me up and would have played with me again, but the mother-wind took me from them and would not let them have me.

"In time the winds all came to know me and to be accustomed to me. They brought me food and fruits and things they picked up in distant places where men lived. I came to know one wind from another, and to know the great and mighty winds and the smaller, weaker ones, and the little winds that were smallest of all.

"I listened to the sounds the winds made to one another and to me, and I learned to whistle sounds much like those, to speak to them. And though they could not hear as we hear, I knew somehow that they sensed my whistling, and answered it, and so I became able to talk with them.

"And winds from over all the earth have talked to me, and I to them. For somehow this plateau is a gathering-spot of all the winds, and from all over earth they come here and go again, coming and going high above the earth where men cannot know of them. Here they mix and meet and play, and here I have talked with winds from all the world.

"But many of the great winds stay here almost all the time, and among them is the mother-wind. Never since I came here has the mother-wind gone for long. It is the mother-wind that I love best of all the winds, yet all of them I love."

Brent had listened, rapt in a fascination beyond reason, but now he was forced to voice his incredulity as Lora stopped.

"But girl, this is fantastic, impossible! Winds are not living—you have lived so long with only the winds for company that you have come to think them so. How could a wind talk or hear? How could a wind speak to you and understand you?"

Lora shook her head. "That I do not know, but they do speak and they do hear. They understand my whistling and I understand their sounds. All things I ask they will do for me, or bring to me. Did I not stop them from killing you when they were about to slay you as they did your companion and your animals?"

Brent stared at her. "You mean that you think that wind-storm stopped because you told the winds to stop?"

Lora nodded. "Of course. When I saw you I whistled for them to let you go, and they did so, though they were very unwilling, still wrathful with you. They helped me bring you here to the pinnacles, though they did not want to do that either."

He shook his head. "I can understand your believing all this," he said, half to himself. "No doubt there are always winds up on this high plateau, and no doubt it was a freak of currents that saved you when the winds annihilated your father's party. It's natural enough you should personify the winds that have been your only companions here, too, and fancy that you could talk to them and they to you. But when it comes to telling me that—"

Brent broke off suddenly, aware of an abrupt weakness. He swayed a little and Lora darted quickly to her feet.

"But you are still tired, weak," she said. "I had forgotten that you must be so."

She took some of the tanned skins and made a soft little couch across the cavern from her own.

"Sleep now," she said simply, and when Brent lay down, she lay down as simply upon her own skin-couch.

Weak and sore from the battering of the winds, Brent drifted almost at once into sleep, the distant wind-voices outside in his ears. He woke the next morning to find the cavern gold-bright with sunlight slanting through the opening, and wondered where he was until he heard outside a gay, silvery whistling. He sprang instantly to his feet and went outside, to find Lora standing whistling near by.

She saw him emerge and cried, "Brent, she has come to me already this morning! The mother-wind!"

"What?" said Brent incredulously.

"See, it is she!" Lora exclaimed, her face bright with happiness. "I have been telling her about you—"

Brent saw that a wind was in fact blowing around the girl, gently ruffling her hair, the sound of it a soft, crooning note.

Lora whistled briefly, the silver-shrill notes tumbling over one another. The wind paused in its caressing of her and moved toward Brent.

Brent felt unreasoning panic as that wind touched him. He wanted to run but told himself it was only a wind, only a moving mass of air. He stood there while it touched him softly, as though examining him, investigating him.

Then its touch changed and was no longer investigatory but caressing. He felt its touch against his cheek like the airiest of airy fingers, warm breath on his hair like that of a loving parent. Its strong, crooning note in his ears was infinitely reassuring, calming. His heart expanded in strange warmth.

That warm, strong wind circled him and Lora for a few moments longer, then with a final ruffling of the girl's hair left them. Brent saw it moving westward across the plain, raising the dust a little. He felt strangely content, like a child that has been petted, pacified.

"She liked you, Brent!" Lora was saying. "I could tell that the mother-wind liked you."

Brent told himself that he would have to fall in with the girl's strange fancy. It would do no harm.

"I'm glad she did," he said. And he *did* feel glad, though he told himself it was wholly an unreasoning gladness.

"Always the mother-wind stays near the plateau, near me," Lora confided as they walked across the rock plain. "Many other winds stay here too, but most come and go from the far places. Even little ones like those."

She pointed as she spoke toward a chaotic little group of small sand-whirls dancing about not far away. As she pointed, the little wind-whirls changed direction, suddenly glided toward the girl and the man; came, Brent told himself, like children who had suddenly sighted a beloved person.

The girl laughed, threw out her arms as though welcoming the little winds. They whisked and whirled merrily, gleefully, around girl and man, combating, conflicting, a flurry of quick gusts.

It was senseless, Brent told himself, to let himself be affected by the girl's fancies. Yet he found himself against his reason thinking of these little winds as living, playing, even as she did.

Swiftly as they had come, the little winds whipped away, chasing one another across the plain.

Lora laughed. "They are but very small winds, those, yet I love them almost the most."

Brent asked, "Lora, have you never wanted to leave this plateau? To find other people?"

She turned the clear gaze of her gray-green eyes on him; "Why should I want people when I have the winds?"

"But surely you don't want to live here on this plateau always, even with the winds?"

She shook her head as though explaining something obvious. "But I couldn't leave the winds!"

Her soft, bronzed arms suddenly circled Brent's neck and she looked up into his face like a pleading, affectionate child.

"I want to stay here, and now that you have come I want you to stay here with me. You will, Brent?"

Brent's arms tightened involuntarily around her and he drew a long breath as he answered.

"I'll stay," he said, "for a little while, at least."

Brent stayed. He told himself that it was but for a short time, that in a few days he would cure the girl of her fancies about the winds and that she would leave with him. But he could not change Lora's ideas regarding the winds. And Brent, against his will, against every conscious thought of his reason, found himself insensibly coming to share her viewpoint.

He found himself thinking of the winds as living things, and not just moving air. He found himself distinguishing one wind from another, just as he might one person from another. The great, strong winds that boomed solemn and majestic, the smaller, wilder winds that roared in and away, the little winds that whisked and played on the plateau—he could not keep from thinking of them as one might think of living people.

And there was that strong, gentle wind that Lora called the mother-wind. Every morning when he and Lora emerged from the cavern the mother-wind was there to greet and touch them. And every morning they found there fruits and things that Lora said the winds had brought.

Brent's reason told him that it was not impossible in this high place of strange wind-currents for freak currents constantly to bring objects a long distance and drop them. But reason alone could not combat the strange influence that the girl's belief had upon Brent.

From early morning until late night there were always winds about Lora, it seemed, even more than elsewhere on that plateau of winds. Whether or not they were living as she believed, the girl truly lived with the winds as companions, Brent saw.

And soon it seemed to him that no companions could be more wonderful, more swift and beautiful, than these that blew round all the round world, that roared and whistled and sang with life infinitely above the life of all poor things that grubbed on earth.

They were companions that could be wilder than any else in the world, as when they thundered across the plateau in tremendous wind-charges, Brent and Lora running with them and the girl's sweet whistling stabbing.

They could be playful, as when the strong gusts darted and jerked around the laughing two until they ran to the cavern for shelter. But only the mother-wind among them could be tender with that warm tenderness Brent felt each time that wind blew round him.

To Brent the world he had left came to seem unreal, and he had almost forgotten the quest that had brought him to the plateau. All that was real to him now was Lora and the plateau and the companioning winds. All, until one night sudden awakening came to Brent.

That night when he and Lora entered the cavern something made him take her suddenly into his arms and kiss her. She resisted for a moment, then suddenly returned his kiss. Brent's face was set with abrupt resolve when they separated.

"Lora, we're going to leave here!" he exclaimed. "I love you and we're going back together to the world, our world."

Lora's eyes were shining, but troubled. "But the winds?"

"You'll leave them for me, now?" Brent pressed her.

She hesitated. Brent heard the bursting uproar of rollicking winds outside and held his breath. Then she came closer into his arms.

"Brent, I'll go with you!" she cried. "Wherever you wish!"

But a few moments later the trouble came again into her clear face.

"But the winds," she repeated. "I am afraid, somehow, that they will not let me go."

Brent laughed. He had shaken off the influence of the plateau completely, now.

"After all, they're only winds," he said, and then added to reassure her, "Why should they stop you when you say they love you?"

She said slowly, "That is why I fear that they will not wish to let me go."

Brent busied himself in making skin bottles to hold water and fruit. Two mornings later he and Lora started.

Before they left the pinnacles the wind she called the mother-wind blew round her for minutes while she whistled.

Her clear eyes were near to tears as she turned to Brent. "I was telling the mother-wind—good-bye," she said.

"Tell her good-bye for me, too," said Brent, laughing, and seriously Lora whistled quick silvery notes.

The strong, soft wind touched Brent, blew over him, and at that airy, loving touch he felt suddenly a little ashamed of his flippancy.

He and Lora started eastward across the plateau. Little winds frisked and played around them, and now and then some of the greater winds came down from the upper air to whirl around them. But not now did Lora whistle greetings to any of them.

But when they neared the plateau's rim, the winds changed. Their sounds had now a puzzled, anxious note, it seemed to Brent's slightly strained nerves. He told himself it was well they were getting away from a place that so easily bred such fancies.

The winds began to push them back from the rim with increasing force as they neared it. Lora turned a white face to Brent.

"They do not want me to go farther, Brent," she said.

He took her hand in his. "We're not going to stop just for winds," he said. "Come on."

But the winds now were blowing them back more and more strongly from the plateau's rim. And more winds seemed gathering, their voices becoming a shouting tumult.

Though Brent and Lora bent their heads and pushed forward with all their strength, the winds forced them back, not violently but strongly, determinedly. Their tumult grew angrier.

"Brent, it is as I said, they will not let me go!" cried Lora over the wind-roar. "If we go farther they will kill you for taking me!"

"It's just freak winds—there are always strange winds at the edge of a height like this!" he shouted back.

"We must go back—before they kill you!" she repeated, clinging to him, her face taut with concern.

Brent slowly assented. "All right, we'll go back for this time."

They started back toward the pinnacles. Slowly the winds' angry tumult subsided around them.

Again they whirled playfully around the girl, but Lora did not heed them. And her face still was white when she and he reached the cavern.

"They would have killed you for trying to take me away, Brent!" she said. "We dare not try again."

"We'll try again," said Brent, his chin setting hard. "A bunch of winds can't scare me."

But when he saw the girl's face he added quickly, "We'll try it when it's not so windy there by the rim."

Her face became thoughtful. "If we went at night when the winds are playing elsewhere on the plateau, they would not see us go."

Brent reflected. "It certainly should be less windy there at night," he said, to himself. Then he added quickly to Lora, "We'll try it tonight!"

That night they waited in the cavern after darkness fell, and did not go out, though they heard the winds moving and shouting all around the rock-pinnacles. At last they heard the great wind-tumult move off across the plateau.

They went out then, and found all still outside. In trumpeting, frolicking tumult the winds were receding northward, the sound of them coming back dimly. Brent and Lora at once started eastward across the plateau.

They met no wind now as they crossed it. The distant wind-uproar they still heard as they started down the plateau's side, but when they reached the desert plain below and headed east, it faded.

Morning found them many miles from the plateau, which had dwindled to a thin brown line on the horizon behind them. All around them stretched the white wastes of the salt desert, flat and dead.

"No winds bothering us now!" Brent said. "I knew we'd be all right once we got off that wind-swept plateau."

Lora looked back. "I fear that they will follow when they miss us," she said. "And they can follow swiftly!"

Brent shook his head. "They're only winds. Now that you're away from that plateau you'll come to see that."

She said nothing, but he marked that ever and again she turned to look back as they forged east that day.

That afternoon she uttered a little cry and pointed back to where great clouds of sand moved on the desert, like towering genii of the wastes.

"They have followed, Brent!" she cried. "They search for us!"

Brent looked, and felt a strange chill; yet he kept his voice steady. "It's only some sand-clouds, Lora. We must keep on going."

They went on, but now Brent too turned each few minutes to look back at those monstrous clouds of blown sand that moved here and there across the desert behind them.

The sand-clouds seemed searching all the desert as they advanced, indeed; yet even so they came closer and closer to the hastening pair. There were scores of those towering sand-giants, scores of great winds advancing across the desert.

Soon they could hear the distant roaring of those mighty winds. And then Lora stopped.

"Brent, we must hide!" she cried. "It is our only chance—to find some place of hiding until the great winds are gone."

"But it's senseless to hide from winds," he exclaimed. "They're not hunting us—it's only your fancy."

"I know they hunt us and that they will kill you if they find us," she said swiftly. "We must—"

She stopped suddenly, uttered a little despairing cry and pointed.

"It is too late! They have found us!"

She was pointing at a little whirl of lifted sand moving over the desert close beside them, nearing them.

That little wind stopped, whirled round as though in maddest excitement, then darted back toward the distant huge sand-genii.

"They have found us!" Lora repeated. "Brent, I want to die too if you are killed!"

"We're neither of us going to be killed!" Brent told her. "Come on."

They hastened forward, running now. The distant wind-roar behind them became louder, louder, yet they did not look back. Their feet slipped in the sand as they ran. Louder still swelled the yellowing roar, and now the desert about them seemed darkened swiftly.

Lora fell, and Brent stooped to help her up.

"It is useless!" she sobbed over the oncoming thunder. "We cannot outrun them. They come, Brent! But if you die I die also!"

With one arm around the girl, Brent stared westward like a pigmy fascinated by giants about to destroy him. Across the desert toward them thundered a colossal host of winds, mighty sand-clouds from which came an ear-dazing bellowing, wrathful, raging. There were scores of them, and there were many scores of smaller sand-clouds, great winds and small, charging down together on the two tiny humans.

Lora broke suddenly from Brent's arm and ran forward toward the charging wind-host, whistling wildly, frantically. The winds picked her up and whirled her aside like a toy, setting her down far to the right, holding her safe there.

Brent saw and knew one instant's thankfulness that the girl was safe. Then the raging winds reached him.

He felt himself whirled high, high, into the air as though by colossal hands. In his ears was a thunderous bellowing of stupendous, elemental anger, and over it he heard Lora's distant scream.

He was poised high for an instant, then whirled down with awful force toward the hard desert. He closed his eyes before the annihilating shock.

There was no shock! Out of the grasp of the thundering winds that held him he was suddenly snatched and whirled aside by another wind—a strong, warm wind that set Brent down beside Lora, then held man and girl as they clung together—a wind that he recognized, the wind that Lora had called the mother-wind!

Came a terrific roaring from the other winds, a heart-checking outburst of wild wind-fury. They charged thunderously forward, sought to tear Brent and Lora from the grasp of the mother-wind.

It seemed an inferno of raging gusts, a hell of cyclonic attack, but still that strong, soft wind held firmly man and girl. A wild conflict of combating winds. But soon that conflict subsided. The great winds' raging died, their thunder lessened. They began to move away, blowing toward the west.

And as they blew, their strong wind-voices were loud, but not in wrath now. It seemed that they uttered a great chorus of sorrow. A mighty sadness of farewell.

Still around Brent and Lora moved one wind, strong, soft, warm, touching them as they clung together, caressing them. They felt that light touch as of airy fingers on their cheeks, soft loving stroking of their hair, soft crooning in their ears. Then that wind too was gone and all was still.

Lora pressed against Brent, her arm around his neck. "It was the mother-wind, Brent! She saved you for me—she saved you from the others and made them let us go!"

Brent's dazed mind, with a great effort, caught at the commonplace world of everyday. "It was the craziest and most freakish wind-storm I've ever seen," he said. "Come on, Lora, I think we'll make it all right now to Yurgan."

Brent got with Lora to Yurgan all right, and to the world beyond. And now that he and she are once more part of that world, that time up on the Plateau of the Winds seems to him almost some strange dream. It seems impossible now that even for a moment he should have allowed himself to fancy that the winds could be living things.

Yet even now Brent is not quite certain in his own mind. For Lora still is very sure that the winds live, and not all his rational explanations can shake what she believes. And Brent himself, remembering some things, must wonder.

Of one thing he is sure, that wherever he and his wife go there seem more winds than anywhere else. And he does not like that. He does not like to see the winds that seem to gather round her, even though to please him she no more whistles wildly to them, and even though he tells himself that it is only fancy.

Neither does Brent like to awake at night and find Lora awake beside him, listening to winds rattling the shutters and sighing in the trees and wailing pleadingly outside the windows, as though entreating her to return, luring her with trumpeted promises of the old tameless freedom. For though Brent tells himself that winds are only winds, he is still afraid that some night she will answer that call.

The Seeds from Outside

S tandifer found the seeds the morning after the meteor fell on the hill above his cottage. On that night he had been sitting in the scented darkness of his little garden when he had glimpsed the vertical flash of light and heard the whiz and crash of that falling visitor from outer space. And all that night he had lain awake, eager for morning and the chance to find and examine the meteor.

Standifer knew little of meteors, for he was not a scientist. He was a painter whose canvases hung in many impressive halls in great cities, and were appropriately admired and denounced and gabbled about by those who liked such things. Standifer had grown weary of such people and of their cities, and had come to this lonely little cottage in the hills to paint and dream.

For it was not cities or people that Standifer wished to paint, but the green growing life of Earth that he loved so deeply. There was no growing thing in wood or field that he did not know. The slim white sycamores that whispered together along the streams, and the sturdy little sumacs that were like small, jovial plant-gnomes, and the innocent wild roses that bloomed and swiftly died in their shady cover—he had toiled to transfix and preserve their subtle beauty forever in his oils and colors and cloths.

The spring had murmured by in a drifting dream as Standifer had lived and worked alone. And now suddenly into the hushed quiet of his green, blossoming world had rudely crashed this visitant from distant realms. It strangely stirred Standifer's imagination, so that through the night he lay wondering, and gazing up through his casement at the white stars from which the meteor had come.

It was hardly dawn, and a chill and drenching dew silvered the grass and bent the poplar leaves, when Standifer excitedly climbed the hill in search of the meteor. The thing was not hard to find. It had smashed savagely into the spring-green woods, and had torn a great raw gouge out of the earth as it had crashed and shattered.

For the meteor had shattered into chunks of jagged, dark metal that lay all about that new, gaping hole. Those ragged lumps were still faintly warm to the touch, and Standifer went from one to another, turning them over and examining them with marveling curiosity. It was when he was about to leave the place, that he glimpsed amid this meteoric debris the little square tan case.

It lay half imbedded still in one of the jagged metal chunks. The case was no more than two inches square, and was made of some kind of stiff tan fiber that was very tough and apparently impervious to heat. It was quite evident that the case had been inside the heart of the shattered meteor, and that it was the product of intelligence.

Standifer was vastly excited. He dug the tiny case out of the meteoric fragment, and then tried to tear it open. But neither his fingers nor sharp stones could make any impression on the tough fiber. So he hurried back down to his cottage with the case clutched in his hand, his head suddenly filled with ideas of messages sent from other worlds of stars.

But at the cottage, he was amazed to find that neither steel knives nor drills nor chisels could make the slightest impression upon this astounding material. It seemed to the eye to be just stiff tan fiber, yet he knew that it was a far different kind of material, as refractory as diamond and as flexibly tough as steel.

It was several hours before he thought of pouring water upon the enigmatic little container. When he did so, the fiber-like stuff instantly softened. It was evident that the material had been designed to withstand the tremendous heat and shock of alighting on another world, but to soften up and open when it fell upon a moist, warm world.

Standifer carefully cut open the softened case. Then he stared, puzzled, at its contents, a frown upon his sensitive face. There was nothing inside the case but two withered-looking brown seeds, each of them about an inch long.

He was disappointed, at first. He had expected writing of some kind, perhaps even a tiny model or machine. But after a while his interest rose again, for it occurred to him that these could be no ordinary seeds which the people of some far planet had tried to sow broadcast upon other worlds.

So he planted the two seeds in a carefully weeded corner of his flower garden, about ten feet apart. And in the days that followed, he scrupulously watered and watched them, and waited eagerly to see what kind of strange plants might spring from them.

His interest was so great, indeed, that he forgot all about his unfinished canvases, the work that had brought him to the seclusion of these quiet hills. Yet he did not tell anyone of his strange find, for he felt that if he did, excited scientists would come and take the seeds away to study and dissect, and he did not want that.

In two weeks he was vastly excited to see the first little shoots of dark green come up through the soil at the places where he had planted the two seeds. They were like stiff little green rods and they did not look very unusual to Standifer. Yet he continued to water them carefully, and to wait tensely for their development.

The two shoots came up fast, after that. Within a month they had become green pillars almost six feet tall, each of them covered with a tight-wrapped sheath of green sepals. They were a little thicker at the middle than at the top or bottom, and one of them was a little slenderer than the other, and its color a lighter green. Altogether, they looked like no plants ever before seen on Earth.

Standifer saw that the sheathing sepals were now beginning to unfold, to curl back from the tops of the plants. He waited almost breathlessly for their further development, and every night before he retired he looked last at the plants, and every morning when he awoke they were his first thought.

Then early one June morning he found that the sepals had curled back enough from the tips to let him see the tops of the true plants inside. And he stood for many minutes there, staring in strange wonder at that which the unfolding of the sepals was beginning to reveal.

For where they had curled back at the tips, they disclosed what looked strangely like the tops of two human heads. It was as though two people were enclosed in those sheathing sepals, two people the hair of whose heads was becoming visible as masses of fine green threads, more animal than plant in appearance.

One looked very much like the top of a girl's head, a mass of fluffy, light-green hair only the upper part of which was visible. The other head was of shorter, coarser and darker green hair, as though it was that of a man.

Standifer went through that day in a stupefied daze. He was almost tempted to unfold the sepals further by force, so intense was his curiosity, but he restrained himself and waited. And the next few days brought him further confirmation of his astounding suspicion.

The sepals of both plants had by then unfolded almost completely. And inside one was a green man-plant—and in the other a girl! Their bodies were strangely human in shape, living, breathing bodies of weird, soft, green plant-flesh, with tendril-like arms and tendril limbs too that were still rooted and hidden down in the calyxes. Their heads and faces were very human indeed, with green-pupiled eyes through which they could see.

Standifer stared and stared at the plant girl, for she was beautiful beyond the artist's dreams, her slim green body rising proudly straight from the cup of her calyx. Her shining, green-pupiled eyes saw him as he stood by her, and she raised a tendril-like arm and softly touched him. And her tendrils stirred with a soft rustling that was like a voice speaking to him.

Then Standifer heard a deeper, angry rustling behind him, and turned. It was the man-plant, his big tendril arms reaching furiously to grasp the artist, jealousy and rage in his eyes. Hastily the painter stepped away from him.

In the days that followed, Standifer was like one living in a dream. For he had fallen in love with the shining slim plant girl, and he spent almost all his waking hours sitting in his garden looking into her eyes, listening to the strange rustling that was her speech.

It seemed to his artist's soul that the beauty of no animal-descended Earth woman could match the slender grace of this plant girl. He would stand beside her and wish passionately that he could understand her rustling whisper, as her tendrils softly touched and caressed him.

The man-plant hated him, he knew, and would try to strike at him. And the man hated the girl too, in time. He would reach raging tendrils out toward her to clutch her, but was too far separated from her ever to reach her.

Standifer saw that these two strange creatures were still developing, and that their feet would soon come free of their roots. He knew that these were beings of a kind of life utterly unlike anything terrestrial, that they began their life-cycle as seeds and rooted plants, and that they developed then into free and moving plant-people such as were unknown on this world.

He knew too that on whatever far world was their home, creatures like these must have reached a great degree of civilization and science, to send out broadcast into space the seeds that would sow their race upon other planets. But of their distant origin he thought little, as he waited impatiently for the day when his shining plant-girl would be free of her roots.

He felt that that day was very near, and he did not like to leave the garden even for a minute, now. But on one morning Standifer had to leave, to go to the village for necessary supplies; since for two days there had been no food in the cottage and he felt himself growing weak with hunger.

It hurt him to part from the plant girl even for those few hours, and he stood for minutes caressing her fluffy green hair and listening to her happy rustling before he took himself off.

When he returned, he heard as soon as he entered his garden a sound that chilled the blood in his veins. It was the plant girl's voice—a mere agonized whisper that spoke dreadful things. He rushed wildly into the garden and stood a moment aghast at what he saw.

The final development had taken place in his absence. Both creatures had come free of their roots—and the man-plant had in his jealousy and hate broken and torn the shining green body of the girl. She lay, her tendrils stirring feebly, while the other looked down at her in satisfied hate.

Standifer madly seized a scythe and ran across the garden. In two terrific strokes, he cut down the man-plant into a dead thing oozing dark green blood. Then he dropped the weapon and wildly stooped over his dying plant girl.

She looked up at him through pain-filled, wide eyes as her life oozed away. A green tendril arm lifted slowly to touch his face, and he heard a last rustling whisper from this creature whom he had loved and who had loved him across the vast gulf of world-differing species. Then he knew that she was dead.

That was long ago, and the garden by the little cottage is weed-grown now and holds no memory of those two strange creatures from the great outside who grew and lived and died there. Standifer does not dwell there any more, but lives far away in the burning, barren Arizona desert. For never, since then, can he bear the sight of green growing things.

Fessenden's Worlds

I wish now that I'd never seen Fessenden's damnable experiment! I wish my cursed curiosity had never taken me into his laboratory that night, to witness the thing that destroyed my peace of mind forever and made me for the rest of my life a somber and soul-sick man.

Arnold Fessenden was the greatest scientist this planet ever produced—and the evilest. I *know!* I'd have told about it before, but I knew that I wouldn't be believed. He assured me of that himself, grinning with sardonic mirth at me, that night he showed me what I'd like to forget.

It was a dark, wet, windy night in late October when I climbed the porch of Fessenden's big stone house near the campus, and rang the bell. He lived there quite alone now, I knew. Even his housekeeper had finally declared that she couldn't stand his queer ways any longer.

He came to the door himself. His big, powerful figure bulking against the dimly lit hall inside, he stared out at me and said, "Oh, it's you, Bradley. What do you want?"

I told him, "That's a poor way to receive guests. I just came over to gab a little—haven't seen you around the campus lately."

He hesitated a moment, then said, "I'm sorry, Bradley—I haven't had many guests of late. Come on in."

I went in and sat down in the slovenly-looking living-room. Fessenden sat in a chair and looked across at me with a queer mocking light in his piercing black eyes, and a sardonic smile on his flat, strong face.

I said, "Fessenden, why haven't you shown up at any of the faculty meetings lately? They tell me you've been letting a substitute take care of all your lecture courses, too."

Fessenden looked at me with that mocking smile and said, "What I like about you, Bradley, is that you're so transparent. You've heard everyone around the campus saying that I've got a little crazy, so you've come over to see for yourself."

"No, that's not so," I protested. "It's true that a good many people have been ridiculing those radical astrophysical theories you propounded, and that some of them think you're more than a little eccentric. But that means nothing to me. I know very well that whenever a man proposes something new, everyone at first thinks he's a little crazy."

I continued earnestly, "You know I'm only a foot soldier in the ranks of science myself—a poor devil of an instructor. Nevertheless, I've always recognized you as a great pioneer. I've been wondering a lot just what you've been working on here so intensively, and I'm honestly hoping you'll tell me something about it. But whether you do or not, you have my admiration and sympathy."

Fessenden's smile deepened. He told me, "Bradley, if you expect me to be grateful for your sympathy, you're wrong. I'm not. I have been called cold and unfeeling, and that is just what I want to be. The gabbling of the fools who have been ridiculing me does not disturb me, and means no more to me than does your sympathy."

My face must have fallen a little. Fessenden laughed.

"I'm glad that is clear to you," he said. "But now that it is, let me tell you that I have decided that I *will* show you what I am doing, after all. I'll show you the greatest experiment which any scientist on Earth has ever conducted."

I said, in surprise, "If you feel no more friendliness for me than you say, I don't see why you should."

He shrugged mockingly. "Because, unfortunately, I am still an ordinary human being at bottom, Bradley. As such, I have a certain ineradicable amount of exhibitionism in me which, deplore it as I may, persists and makes me want to show at least somebody what I have done." He laughed. "Just like any small boy who has built his first kite and wants somebody to see it. I recognize the folly of this, I am amused by it, but I can't wholly eliminate it from my make-up.

"Well, why not indulge this irrational desire for applause by demonstrating to you what I've done? You do not have enough intelligence to comprehend it all, of course. Still, you will be an auditor, an audience, and I shall satisfy this itch of mine to let someone know what I've accomplished."

I said quickly, "I promise that I'll keep everything you tell me absolutely confidential."

Fessenden roared with laughter. "You needn't promise that. For all I care, you can go out and tell the whole world what you see here. Only, if you do, they'll call you a madman and very likely confine you in an institution. By all means go ahead and tell them, if you want to."

He was still chuckling as he rose to his feet. "It's back in my laboratory, Bradley."

"But what is it, anyway?" I asked doubtfully. "What have you done?"

"I've created a universe," Fessenden told me.

I said impatiently, "That's a grandiose metaphor, but just what does it mean?"

"It's not a metaphor at all," Fessenden said blandly. "I mean literally that I have created a universe in my laboratory, a universe that has millions of suns, tens of millions of worlds."

I was silent. I was trying to avoid his eyes, to hide my disappointment from him.

Fessenden chuckled. "A minute ago," he said, "you were condemning the rest of the university for thinking me insane. Now you're thinking exactly the same thing, aren't you?—wondering how you can get out of this crazy Fessenden's house with good grace?"

He added, grinning sardonically, "Come along to the laboratory, Bradley, and see for yourself."

I followed his tall, powerful figure along the corridor. I did think now that his isolation and the ridicule his radical theories had evoked must have touched his mind. But still he must have something to show me, and I was eager to see what it was.

The laboratory was a long, stone-walled room whose walls were crowded with shelves of chemical and physical apparatus, and whose corners held great electrical mechanisms. Much of the equipment I saw was strange to my eyes. Then my gaze fastened on the thing at the center of the laboratory.

It consisted of two twelve-foot metal disks with grid-like surfaces, one on the floor and one on the ceiling directly over the other. They were connected by cables to the electrical machinery, and their grid-like surfaces shone faintly with wan blue light or force.

Between the two disks, floating unsupported in the air, hung a cloud of tiny sparks of light. It looked like a swarm of minute golden bees, countless in number, and the swarm was lenticular in shape. Mounted near this weird thing were several instruments that looked a little like telescopes, though unfamiliar in design. They seemed to be trained upon that thick little cloud of shining sparks.

Fessenden walked over to the thing and motioned calmly toward the blue-glowing disks in floor and ceiling. "These disks, Bradley, neutralize all the ordinary gravitational forces of Earth in the space between them."

"What?" I cried, astonished. I stepped forward, was about to thrust my hand between the two disks to test the assertion. But Fessenden held me back.

"Don't try that," he warned. "The human body is accustomed to Earth's gravitation, and is inwardly braced against it. If you were to step between those disks, out of Earth's gravitation, your body would explode from its own inward pressure, just as a deep-sea fish will explode when it is suddenly brought up from the tremendous pressures of its usual depths to the surface."

Fessenden added, gesturing to the floating swarm of sparks between the disks, "It was necessary that this should be outside Earth's gravitational influences. For this is the universe I have created."

I stared from him to the shining swarm, and then back again to his dark, amused face. "Those little flecks of light—a universe?"

"Just that," he assured me. "Look closer at them, Bradley."

I looked closer, and I felt a weird chill creeping over me. Those points of light were so infinitesimal that I could barely distinguish them one from another, and I knew there must be millions of them in this thick swarm. Yet there were some oddly familiar features about them.

Some of the tiny sparks were blazing white in color, others smoky red, others golden yellow. The colors of suns in our own universe! Some of them were in double or triple groups, and here and there were clusters of them that contained thousands. And here and there, too, were little glowing patches that looked like tiny nebula, and crawling sparks with tails of light like Lilliputian comets, just as the floating sparks looked like tiny suns.

Those sparks were tiny suns! I knew it, beyond doubt, even while my brain fought against the knowledge and called it impossible. I knew that I was looking at a miniature universe, one on a scale many billions of times smaller than our own universe, yet one that was comparatively as large in extent as our own. A little microcosm, floating here in Fessenden's laboratory.

Fessenden's eyes had been following my stupefied change of expression. He said calmly, "Yes, Bradley, it is true. That is a tiny, self-sustaining universe, with its own suns, nebulae and worlds. Everything in it, down to the atoms which compose it, is infinitely smaller in scale than our own. But it is a real universe, like our own."

"And you say you created this?" I gasped.

Fessenden nodded. "Yes, I did. After many failures, I succeeded in bringing that universe into being only a few weeks ago. I have been experimenting with it ever since."

His black eyes flashed a little. "Didn't I tell you that it was the greatest experiment any scientist had ever conducted? Think of what I am able to do—I can conduct my astrophysical and other experiments on a *cosmic* scale. I can change or destroy suns and nebulae at will, with the instruments I devised, can observe the minutest details of that tiny universe through my super-magnifying telescopes. I can make observations with a universe itself as my subject."

I said in amazement, "But how did you make it—start it?"

Fessenden shrugged. "How did our own universe start, Bradley? As a vast cloud of glowing gas that filled all space. The mutual attraction of the cloud's particles drew them together, so that the cloud condensed into huge nebulae. The nebulae further condensed into suns, which by tidal attraction and occasional collision, threw off matter that formed into circling worlds.

"Well, I started this tiny universe just like that. I filled the non-gravitational space between these disks with a cloud of glowing gas, whose atoms were infinitely tinier than our atoms because I had contracted their electronic orbits. Then all I had to do was watch while the same inevitable natural process that eons ago formed our universe, formed this little microcosm.

"I watched as the gas condensed into tiny nebulae. I saw those little nebulae condense further into miniature suns, just as in our own cosmos long ago. And I saw those suns, as their random wanderings brought them close to one another, throw off worlds.

"Millions on millions of tiny worlds, here in this little microcosm, Bradley! Worlds that I can change and tamper with and destroy at will, worlds with every conceivable kind of conditions, worlds whose life I can develop or wither as I wish. That is my experiment, Bradley!"

"'Whose *life*,' you say?" I repeated in a whisper. "On the tiny planets of this microcosm—life?"

"Of course," said Fessenden. "Life always develops automatically on worlds where conditions are favorable, and usually in very much the same forms." He reached toward one of the bulky, unfamiliar telescopic instruments. "Wait, and I shall find such a world for you, Bradley. I shall let you watch its life develop, for yourself."

He applied his eye to one of the lenses of the bulky telescope-instrument, focusing it upon the shining cloud of sparks; turning knobs, twisting, searching—until at last he straightened.

"Now look, Bradley."

I put my eye to one of the lenses, looked into that cloud of floating sparks. There leaped into my vision, dazzling and gigantic, a huge white sun booming majestically through the darkness of space. Just one of those tiny sparks, seen through the super-magnifying instrument!

Fessenden was beside me, gazing through the other lens of the instrument. His fingers were touching the focus knobs and he said calmly, "Keep watching. You'll see the changes of ages in a few minutes of our time. For, of course, the time of this microcosm runs at an infinitely swifter rate than the time of our vaster universe."

As he shifted the focus of the instrument, my gaze seemed to leap toward that great sun. I made out two planets that circled it, at tremendous speed. A year of their time no more than a moment of ours!

One of these planets was still partly molten, but the other was cooling, its vapor-envelope condensing. My vision leaped forward, in the telescope, until I seemed almost standing on that cooling world. It was a wild, rocky planet, rain falling heavily on its surface from the cloudy sky, water collecting with unbelievable swiftness in seas.

Green life came into being on the world, first along the shores of the warm, shallow seas, then creeping out and advancing over the land. Swiftly vegetation mantled the globe. And now crawling animal life made its appearance as the ages ticked swiftly by.

The animal life developed quickly. So rapid were the changes that my gaze could hardly follow them. Warring species of unhuman monsters passed and vanished. Tiny hordes of man-like animals began to throng here and there, to multiply with each passing moment.

I saw rude villages of huts spring up on that world. The villages quickly became cities as that people developed in intelligence, age after microcosmic age. The cities towered higher each moment, great ships sailed upon the seas, ages of progress and development were run through before my eyes in tiny moments.

I was shaking as I recoiled from the telescope. I cried, "This is all impossible—it can't be real—"

Fessenden smiled. "Your expressions of stupefaction satisfy my egotistic desire for applause, Bradley. But I assure you that that tiny race and their world are quite real." He chuckled. "No doubt that little folk think that they have reached such a pinnacle of power and knowledge that nothing can threaten them. We shall see now whether or not they are able to face a real danger."

He turned to a curious needle-like instrument and carefully trained it upon that part of the microcosm which held the tiny white spark that was the great sun of the world I had been watching.

There was a tiny comet crawling through the swarm, some distance from that white sun. Fessenden touched a knob, and from the needle-like instrument a thin, almost invisible filament of force crept into the microcosmic swarm of sparks and touched the little crawling comet. It seemed to veer a tiny bit aside.

"Now watch," said Fessenden with amused interest, "and we shall see just how great is the power of that little people."

I did not understand, but I looked again with him through the telescope at the tiny world. By now, so swift its development in terms of our time, its cities had become even vaster and were roofed with glass-like shields. Huge aircraft flashed above them.

All seemed peace and progress on that world. Generation after generation ticked by as we watched. Then came a mad stir of movement, a wild scurrying about of the little folk, a swift change in the tempo of their life. A faint green light was now falling upon their planet, the baleful glow of a monster comet that was coming headlong toward it.

I knew then that it was the tiny microcosmic comet whose course Fessenden had slightly altered. But in the telescope it was colossal, a huge orb dripping green light across the heavens as it rushed toward that world. Remorselessly it came on.

Then that comet struck the planet, and I saw the doom of the little folk's cities. The meteors that were the comet's only solid substance shattered the glass-roofed cities to ruin. The poisonous gases that made up the rest of the comet veiled that whole world in a toxic cloud.

The comet passed on as we watched, but its deadly gases had wiped away all life from that planet. It was still and brown and dead, now, a lifeless world circling its sun. The ruined cities melted swiftly down into decay and disappeared as we watched.

Fessenden's laugh rang in my ears as I stared in stunned horror. "You see—their knowledge was not enough to save them from the mere slight shifting of the comet's course."

"You killed them—killed every soul on that world!" My voice throbbed with the horror that I felt.

"Nonsense! It was just an experiment," Fessenden said. "It's no more murder than when a bacteriologist casually destroys germs he experiments with. Those little folk were millions of times smaller than any germ. But they and others like them on the countless worlds of this microcosm provide me with a subject for experimentation which no scientist has ever had before. Look at another world—here are two that interest me."

My vision in the telescope leaped to another sun, for Fessenden had shifted the focus. It was a yellow sun with four planets circling it. Two of them were airless worlds, but the other two bore different forms of life, one of them quite man-like, the other verging on the reptilian, each supreme on its own world. Both races had a certain amount of civilization, as was evident from the queer cities on their worlds. There was no contact or communication between them, for the two planets were widely separated from each other.

"Now I wonder," Fessenden was saying interestedly, "just what the result would be if those two races were to come into contact with each other. Well, we'll soon see," he mused aloud, and reached again toward the needle-like instrument.

Again a ghostly little thread of force stole into the microcosm. I saw its effects, through the telescope. One of those planets, beneath the impetus, began to change its orbit. It moved closer and closer toward the other inhabited world. Soon the two were so close together that they had formed an Earth-moon system, revolving around a common center of gravity as they circled their sun.

Soon, very soon, ships began to fly from one world to the other across the narrowed gulf. Communication had been established. And almost at once came war between the two worlds, a conflict of the man-like and reptilian races. Cities were destroyed by flashes of fire in that war, great throngs went to death in battles of incredible ferocity. The tide turned in favor of the reptilian race. Their invading hordes destroyed the last members of the man-like folk. Then it was all over. The reptilian race reigned supreme over both worlds.

"I'm a little surprised—I thought the human race would have won out," Fessenden said interestedly. "Apparently they didn't have the adaptability of the reptilian race."

I cried, "That little human people would have lived for generations in peace and happiness if you hadn't brought that other world into contact with their own! Why didn't you let them alone?"

He said impatiently, "Don't be a fool, Bradley. This is just a scientific experiment—those ephemeral little races and their tiny worlds are merely a subject for study." And he added, "Why, for days I've been observing and changing and tampering with these microcosmic worlds, just to see the reactions of their peoples to different stimuli and dangers. I've learned things from them that you'd never dream. Watch—I'll show you others."

In a stupefied trance I watched as Fessenden went on, taking my vision to world after world, prodding and changing, observing the fall of empires and the crash of planets with keen, amused detachment. I saw worlds of beauty incredible and worlds of horror unthinkable—planet after planet, race after race, and all of them merely the playthings of the experimenting scientist beside me.

Fessenden showed me a planet in the microcosm that was covered with wild forests in which dwelt little communities of hunting folk who chased the beasts of the forest. Generation after generation flashed by without change in their rude society—they were content to hunt and eat and love and die, without developing any higher civilization.

Then Fessenden turned upon that little world a tiny ray that altered its chemical stability. Beneath the influence of chemical changes, the plant life of that world began to unfold in weird hypertrophy, began to develop mobility, to change into great, rootless plant-things that soon fell upon and killed the animals. The communities of hunters battled valiantly for a few generations against the moving plant hordes, but in the end they all succumbed, and that world was covered only with restlessly moving plant life.

And Fessenden brought into our observation another world, planet of a sun out near the microcosm's edge. It was a watery world, covered with oceans over all of its surface. And teeming life had developed in that planetary sea, into intelligent, seal-like people who had reared in the sea great submarine cities whose spires lifted here and there above the waters.

Fessenden's filaments of force played upon that world, and the seas began to dwindle, the water molecules to fly off into space. And as the seas rapidly shrank, for generation after generation, more and more of that world became dry land and the seal-people had to desert many of their cities and retreat back with the waters.

Very soon, as we watched, there was but one shallow sea remaining on that little world. And here were crowded the last of the seal-folk, and here they fought blindly with all manner of scientific devices to prevent the evaporation of this last refuge. But the remorseless process that Fessenden had started went on, and that last sea dried and disappeared also, and there was only a desert planet with the ruined wrecks of the dead seal-folk's cities standing here and there as memorials of the vanished race.

World after world my dazed eyes watched. I saw an icy planet that swung far out from its parent sun, and upon which was strange life adapted to the cold, bloodless little folk who had reared also a mighty civilization. Their weird palaces and cities rose amid the awful chasms of eternal ice, and it was evident that they were far advanced in scientific power.

Fessenden reached and touched their sun with a tiny thread of force. And that sun blazed suddenly hotter and brighter, casting forth a quadrupled radiance. Its increased heat began to melt the ice-sheath of that far-swinging little world, and its people began to perish from the unaccustomed warmth.

We saw them frantically laboring for the next generation at a great work upon the side of their little world. Then its purpose became clear to us, for from that spot there projected a plume of fire and force whose rocketlike push moved their little planet suddenly outward. They were moving their world farther from their sun to escape the increased warmth, and at a suitable distance they let it settle into a new orbit where it was as cold as before. And Fessenden laughed and applauded their ingenuity.

And there was a world whose crowded peoples were ruled by an oligarchy of living brains. Time after time, each generation that passed, we saw the enslaved people revolt against the tyranny of the brains, and each time the weapons of their unhuman masters subdued them.

Fessenden's probing threads of force reached deep into the bowels of that little planet, and it rocked with terrific quakes that threw up vast masses of radioactive material from the interior. And a strange glowing plague seized the bodies of the people and also seized the brains, so that they began to rot and die.

Swiftly the people were annihilated by that glowing rot, but the brains managed to contrive for themselves an antidote against the deadly infections, so that most of the brains survived. For a few generations the brains clung to existence, served now by machines of their own devising.

192

But they must have made their mechanical servants too intelligent, for in time the machines rose against the brains and destroyed them. And later still, without any directing intelligence, the machines themselves came to wreck and vanished from that world.

Dazed with horror, I watched as we viewed world after world of the microcosm, as Fessenden probed and changed and destroyed. And then there came into my view a world whose aching beauty brought tears to my eyes, a green and blossoming world whose people were human, but of a fineness and beauty far beyond our own humanity.

Not upon their world were any towering cities or huge machines or swarming vehicles. Their civilization had reached a plane above crude material progress, and their planet was like a green and surpassingly love-ly park. Here and there amid the flowering trees shimmered exquisite buildings, and through flowers and forests went white-robed noble men and beautiful women. And their knowledge had almost conquered death, since for many microcosmic generations they remained unchanged.

I watched that world through the telescope with my heart struck at the vision, and in the peace and loveliness of that planet and its people I seemed to catch a glimpse of what humanity might aspire to in some unthinkably far future. And then I suddenly woke to the fact that Fessenden, beside me, was reaching again toward the needle-like instrument that loosed his tampering forces upon the microcosmic worlds.

I broke then from my trance and cried out, horrified, "Fessenden, you can't do anything to endanger *that* world!"

He smiled sardonically. "Of course I'm going to do something. I want to see whether that people have not become decadent in their peace and plenty—whether the science that brought them up to that level can save them now when real danger threatens."

He chuckled as he sighted the needle-like thing. "A mere tiny thread of force—but it will cause their little sun to spin so fast that it will break up. Will that people have the resourcefulness to save themselves by flight to another sun? We shall soon see."

But I tore him away from the deadly instrument and sent him stagger-ing back across the laboratory with a wild thrust.

"No!" I cried. "These worlds and peoples that you experiment with and endanger and destroy—they're real! As real as ours, even though in-finitely smaller. I'll not let you calmly vivisect and torment any more of them, out of your damnable scientific curiosity."

Fessenden's black brows drew together in a cold fury and he rasped, "I see now how foolish it was to show my experiment to an unreasoning sentimentalist like you. But that microcosm is *my* experiment, *my* property, and I'll experiment with and destroy every world in it, if I please. Get away from that instrument."

"I won't do it!" I shouted. "You've wreaked horror enough on those tiny planets with your inhuman experiments, subjecting those little races to agony and toil and death just to gratify your unholy curiosity. You're not going to do it now with this little world!"

Fessenden sprang straight at me, rage burning in his black eyes. His heavy fist descended on me and knocked me away from the instrument I held.

I reeled back from that blow. And at that moment I heard a hoarse cry. Fessenden had tripped on one of the cables in his wild spring, and was toppling into the space between the two disks.

His toppling body struck the microcosm squarely and it crashed around him in a broken shower of sparks. A universe wrecked in a second. At the same time, Fessenden's body exploded—it exploded into a bloated, torn thing of flesh, just as he had warned me any human body would do if it entered the area between the disks where there was no gravitation.

The cable he had tripped over had jerked loose—and there was a flash of fire across the lower disk. In an instant, destroying blue electrical flames enveloped the disks and Fessenden's body, and danced around the electrical machinery in the laboratory with a sputtering, increasing roar.

I turned and stumbled crazily out of the laboratory, out of the house into the wet and windy night. I heard a crackling roar behind me and the flickering light of the now flaming house shot past me as I staggered on, but I did not look back....

So ended Fessenden and his great experiment. No one doubted but that the eccentric scientist had somehow set fire to the house and had perished in the blaze, and I said nothing to change that opinion. And very soon his end was no longer remembered, and Fessenden is now forgotten by everyone. By everyone, except me.

I wish that I could forget too! But I can't forget Fessenden and his microcosmic worlds, and because I can't, my soul is sick and I have a shuddering, fearful wonder in me that will endure until I die, a black question to which I'll never get an answer, and which torments me every time I look up at the night stars.

And the question that quakes in my soul whenever I look up into the starry sky is this—is our own great universe nothing but a tiny microcosm, on some vaster scale? And in that vaster cosmos, is there a super-experimenter who regards our universe as nothing but an interesting experiment, and who smites us with disasters just to study our reactions for his own amusement? Is there a Fessenden up *there?*

Easy Money

It was a dirty frame-up, that's what it was! And it was a nutty one, too—this old Doc Murtha who framed me was so nutty he tried to tell me that I'd been clean off the Earth, that I'd been on another world. Can you tie that?

Me, I'm Slugger Martin—profession, middleweight, age, thirty. Ten years ago I nearly knocked out the champion, only he knocked me out first. Well, ten years is a lifetime for a leather pusher, and that's how come on this morning I was holding down a bench in Battery Park and wondering mighty gloomy just how I was going to eat.

Then up stepped this Doc Murtha. He was a shriveled-up little cuss with a waspy look, who had been eyeing me for ten minutes. He wore an old rusty black suit and hat, and he came over to me now and fixed his beady eye on me.

"Young man," he said to me in a kind of severe voice, "how would you like a job?"

"I'd like one if there was no work connected with it, pop," I told him, figuring he was just another busybody.

"Don't call me pop," he snapped. "I'm Doctor Francis Murtha, discoverer of the Murtha electron-wave effect."

"Never heard of it," I told him. "I'm Slugger Martin, who went nine rounds with Tiger McGinty."

"Never heard of him," the little doc snapped right back at me. "You're a pugilist, eh? That's good. I'm looking for somebody with a strong body and a dim intelligence."

"Say, listen," I said, getting up to my feet. "I know when I'm insulted. You better—"

I stopped, goggling. The little doc had shoved a century note under my nose.

"How would you like ten of these?" he asked.

I looked around uneasily before I answered.

"Okay, Doc," I said. "I'm your man. Just name the party. But no cops or frails, mind you."

"What are you talking about?" he demanded.

"About this guy you want me to bump," I said. "What's his name and address? And you'll have to give me the grand first."

"You thick-skulled lummox!" roared Doc Murtha. "I don't want you to kill anybody. I simply am willing to pay you a thousand dollars if you will submit yourself to a great scientific experiment."

"The heck with you!" I cried. "You think I'm going to let you cut me open for a lousy grand?"

"No, no!" he exclaimed furiously. "You've been reading too many Sunday supplements. I'm a physicist—I've invented a method of projecting matter across vast spatial abysses, by dematerializing its atoms into vibratory force, projecting that force through extra-dimensional gulfs, and letting it materialize again at its destination. I can project matter across the whole galactic system instantaneously, and draw it back again, by retracting the undimensional revolving field—"

"Listen, Doc, are you trying to kid me?" I interrupted threateningly. "Who ever saw a field revolving?"

Doc Murtha muttered something that sounded like a curse. He glared at me, then began again, slowly and distinctly.

"I've invented a ray," he said. "A ray that shoots things a long way and drags them back again. Can you understand that?"

"Sure I can," I said. "What do you take me for—a boob?"

He muttered something else under his breath, and then went on. "I've shot rabbits off with this ray and brought them back unhurt, proving they landed somewhere with near-terrestrial conditions. Now I want to do it with a man, who can tell me about the experience."

"Kind of a new radio that sends people, eh?" I said. "How come you picked me for the first ride on it?"

"Because if I used anybody very smart, he might steal the idea of my apparatus from me," said Doc Murtha.

That sounded to me like another crack, but I passed it up, on account I was looking hard at the bill in his hand.

"All right, Doc, I'll try it," I said. "But I want the grand before you shoot me off on this radio-ride of yours."

"You'll get it," he snapped. "My apparatus is in my Long Island home. Come along with me."

The Long Island house, when we got there, was a big, white old dump set back from the road. No one else was there, and when we went inside I saw the rooms were filled with machines and lights and racks of bottles, like a big dentist's office or something.

Doc Murtha went to a thing in the middle of one room, a flat, round copper platform setting on top of a lot of tubes and coils and junk like that. He laid his hand on it proudly.

"The Murtha field-projector," he said. "It is what will hurl you forth as dematerialized force on your great journey."

"Could you send me to Poughkeepsie on that thing?" I asked. "I know a dame there I ain't seen for a long while."

"You're going a lot farther than Poughkeepsie, Martin," the doc said, laughing kind of strange.

He handed me ten century notes.

"All right," he then said, "step up on the transmitter-disk and we'll get going."

"You mean, I'll get going," I said, staring at the machine and scratching my head. "Listen, what if you send me way off to San Francisco or somewhere and then can't get me back?"

"There's no danger of that," he snapped. "Wherever you find yourself when you rematerialize, just remain in that exact spot without moving and in five minutes I'll draw you back again."

I was kind of wishing I hadn't been so quick to agree, for this thing looked like a hot seat or something. But my motto is "try anything once," so I stepped up onto the platform. Doc Murtha dashed around, jerking levers and knobs. Motors or things like that began to hum, and there was a crackling from the tubes under my platform.

"Doc," I said uneasily, "are you sure—"

"Quiet, Martin—here you go!" he yelled.

And he turned a switch. And someone hung a hard right on my chin, or it felt like it. For I went out for the count.

When I came out of it, I was plenty mad, I want to tell you. I scrambled up, shaking my head and blinking my eyes.

"Doc, who's the son that poked me from behind?" I roared. "I'll put him in the hospital when—"

Then I stopped, my jaw hanging. You see, by then I had opened my eyes and was looking around me. And Doc Murtha wasn't there. And neither was the machine nor the house I'd been in, nor Long Island. I was standing right smack in the middle of a big city I'd never seen before!

"Holy smoke!" I gasped, looking around me. "The doc's radio has shot me off to China or some place!"

I was standing in a kind of little park, beside a tree. It was a queer tree with square red leaves, and there were a lot of other trees like it, and the grass was red and even the sun was red and looked bigger than usual. Around the park were silver streets, and huge metal buildings like pyramids, taller than the Empire State Building. I figured when I saw those pyramids that I must have been shot to Egypt.

People in the street had stopped to gawk at me. These Egyptians, the men and dames both, wore nothing at all but a little skirt and shirt of woven chain metal. They stared and pointed at me and then they burst out laughing. I got mad at that, and I went out in the street and grabbed one of those guys who was laughing at me.

"Where did you get those ridiculous garments?" he asked me, pointing at my clothes.

"What do you mean, ridiculous?" I cried. "Didn't you Egyptians ever see a civilized man before?"

Suddenly it struck me as kind of queer. This guy hadn't talked English, but some language of his own. I hadn't ever heard his language before, yet I could understand it and speak it!

That surprised me. But I knew a smart guy picks up things quick in a strange burg, and I realized I was smarter than I'd thought, to pick up this Egyptian language in a flash, as I'd done.

"Never have such queer garments been seen in Calthor before," choked the man I was holding, gasping with laughter.

"Rib me, will you?" I gritted. And I let him have my good old left on the chin. He went down and out.

There was a dead silence. Everybody looked at me horrified, as though I'd hit a dame or something. They shrank from me.

"This man's out of Control!" someone cried.

"Call an Assistant!" yelled another.

Suddenly I remembered something. Doc Murtha had told me to stay right where I landed, so he could pull me back in five minutes with his radio. And I'd moved from the tree I was under first. I had to get back to it, or pay steamship fare back to New York.

But which tree was it? There was a lot of them in that little park. Then I spotted it, from a scar on its trunk. I started hastily toward it, but just then I was grabbed from behind.

Two of these guys in little metal skirts had grabbed me. A third guy, an old bird with calm blue eyes, pointed a pencil at me. And suddenly my strength was all gone—I couldn't even stand!

"What is this?" I yelled, plenty mad.

"Moderate your voice, citizen," said the old bird impressively. "I am Tarnac, Third Assistant to the Controller."

"Nuts to you and the Controller both!" I cried. "I'll break your head and his too when I get my strength back."

Tarnac gasped! A cry of horror went up from all the crowd that was watching.

"He is almost utterly out of Control!" cried someone astoundedly. "He spoke disrespectfully of the Controller!"

"Never, in all our history, has there been a case so far out of Control as you," Tarnac said, looking at me dumbfounded.

"My temper's going to get out of control if you don't let me go," I said furiously. "You Egyptians don't need to think you can rough up an American citizen and get away with it."

Tarnac's lips tightened.

"This man is obviously mad—his weird garments show that," he said decisively. "But his being so far out of Control is a matter for the Controller to handle."

"I demand to see the United States consul!" I exclaimed. "There'll be an American cruiser around if you pinch me."

They didn't pay any attention. They marched me down the street toward the biggest pyramid of all. The two cops or whatever they were had to carry me, for Tarnac's pencil was still pointed at me and I still had no strength. I'll say that pencil was some hoodoo!

There were all kinds of rooms and halls inside that big pyramid, full of queer machines and busy people. They took me into a room deep inside the place. It was big and dim, and there was only one guy in it. He was sitting on a dais, doing nothing. I knew then he was the big shot, for only a big shot can do nothing but sit and look wise.

This guy had a queer metal thing on his head, like a big diving helmet, only the front was cut away so his face showed. There were a lot of little screws or knobs on the side of this helmet, and a little ring of glowing white lights on its top.

He was the Controller, all right. He looked down at me and I saw that his square face was very brooding and heavy and thoughtful, something like an alderman worrying about his ward, only a million times more so. Tarnac made a quick, sharp report to him.

"The man is obviously almost completely out of Control," Tarnac finished. "It's an unprecedented case."

"Call the physicians," said the Controller.

"Listen, I'm not sick," I busted in. "I was simply standing there in the park, minding my own business—"

I didn't get a chance to finish, for the physicians hurried in, a half-dozen of them. Two were dames, and one of these was a darned cute little trick with black hair and eyes.

They put on some kind of spectacles that were inches thick and connected to machines. They looked at my head with these as though they were looking right into it. Then one let out a yelp.

"This man is not an inhabitant of our world at all!" he yelped. "He is apparently from a world of very similar conditions, but his brain and other organs are definitely alien in structure."

"That explains it!" Tarnac said excitedly. "He isn't completely under Control because his brain differs from ours."

"You are undoubtedly correct, Tarnac," nodded the Controller. "His primitive brain receives the simpler elements of Control, such as language-knowledge, but is deaf to the higher elements."

"Say, what is all this?" I demanded.

"How did you come to this world?" asked the Controller.

"The stork brought me, of course," I snapped.

"The man is too primitive to give us much information," the Controller said thoughtfully. "Let the physicians thoroughly examine him—they may be able to discover his origin."

I bristled up, for I didn't want that bunch of doctors pawing over me. Then I decided maybe I'd better humor these guys. I'd have a better chance to escape and get back to that tree in the park where I had to be if Doc Murtha was ever to get me back home.

"I won't have all those doctors going over me," I told them. "I wouldn't mind that one, though."

And I pointed to the cute little black-haired dame among the physicians. The Controller nodded to her.

"You make the examination, Zura," he told her. "The man's primitive intelligence has apparently formed a liking for you."

Zura led me down a hall, with two guys following and holding those pencil-things, ready to put the blast on me if I made a break. The little black-haired dame took me into a kind of office filled with queer machines. The guards took posts outside the door.

Zura sat down beside me and put on those six-inch spectacles again.

"Please do not move," she said. "I want to examine more carefully the neurone-structure of your cerebrum."

"Aw, take them cheaters off—you look terrible in them," I said, taking the spectacles off her eyes.

"You're a swell dish, babe," I told her. "Want to feel my muscles?"

"I don't understand," she said, perplexed.

Well, seeing she didn't understand, I started to demonstrate for her. But she drew back all horrified.

"You mustn't kiss me! The Controller ordered me to examine you, and you are making me neglect his order."

"I wish you people would get this Controller guy off your minds," I said bitterly. "The big cheese!"

She gasped in horror, at me razzing the big shot. "You are out of Control, aren't you?" she said.

"Say, what is all this Control business, anyway?" I demanded. "I don't get it, at all."

"You mean there's no Control where you come from?" Zura said incredulously. "That people differ in ideals and aims?"

"I'll say they differ," I told her. "When they differ real bad, we call it a war."

"There was war here on Calthor, too, many ages ago," Zura said quickly. "People fought, and rioted, and quarreled constantly with one another, because they had different mental attitudes, different ideals and religious beliefs and aspirations. So our wise forefathers saw that to have perfect peace and cooperation, everyone must have the same mental attitude, the same loyalties, beliefs and desires.

"That is why our forefathers originated Control. It is a device to make certain that everyone has the same mental attitude on important questions. The wisest of our race is always the Controller. He wears the sacred Control helmet, the supreme achievement of our science, which amplifies and broadcasts the neuro-electric currents of his brain as a powerful vibration that affects every other human brain, setting up the same currents, the same basic ideas, in them all. Thus, what the Controller thinks is good, everybody thinks is good, and works for. So we dwell always in perfect peace and cooperation."

"You mean, because the Controller wears that helmet, everyone thinks exactly what he thinks?" I said.

"No, not exactly," Zura said earnestly. "If the broadcast vibration of the sacred helmet were turned on full force, then everyone would think and feel exactly like the Controller, would become mere automatons actuated by his mind. But the vibration is never turned on full force—it is kept just strong enough to condition our minds with the Controller's mental attitude, so that we automatically possess a common language, common ideals, common loyalty to the state."

"Some racket he's got!" I said. "And whoever gets to put on the helmet is the big boss as long as he lives?"

"Yes," she nodded. "But of course the man chosen to be Controller is always our wisest, most peaceful, most benevolent citizen. For his mental attitude becomes that of the whole race."

Suddenly, just like that, a red-hot idea hit me! An inspiration how to get out of this jam, back to that tree outside.

"Listen, Zura," I said cautiously, "I've been fooling you people. I'm not as dumb as I look."

"Impossible!" she exclaimed.

"What do you mean, impossible?" I said. "The fact is, I came here as a spy, see. There's going to be an attack on you."

"An attack? From where?" cried Zura, looking aghast. She hadn't had enough experience with liars to suspect me.

"I'll tell that to the Controller," I said cagily. "You bring him here and I'll tip him off to the whole thing."

She dashed out of the room. Before long, she was back and the Controller with her, wearing that queer helmet.

He came right in, leaving the guards still outside, and was I glad! You see, this bird had never known anything but utter respect, and never figured that anyone might pull something on him.

"What have you to tell me?" he asked.

"This!" I said, and gave him one on the chin.

He went down and out, his helmet banging on the floor. Quick as a flash I jerked that big helmet off his head. Its lights were glowing a lot brighter now, as though the power had got turned on more somehow when it hit the floor. I jammed it down on my own head.

That was my smart idea, see? If whoever wore the helmet was respected and obeyed by everybody, if what he thought they all thought, it was a cinch for me to get back out to that tree now that I wore the helmet. I felt tickled to death to have pulled it off.

"By gosh, my idea worked!" I said joyfully.

"I am happy—I am so happy!" cried Zura, her eyes shining with excited gladness, jumping up and down in glee.

The door opened and the two guards came dancing into the room. Yeah, dancing—and laughing wild with happiness.

"Joy, joy, joy!" they kept shouting.

And the Controller, who had staggered up to his feet now, grinned and laughed as though overjoyed! A big roar of voices came from outside the window. I looked out and saw the crowds out there in the streets all dancing up and down, crazy glad over something.

"What's the matter with you people?" I cried puzzledly, staring at Zura and the guards and the Controller.

And as I said it, they changed. The grins left and they all looked suddenly perplexed, staring around, puzzled as anything. The crowds outside had suddenly stopped yelling, too.

I couldn't understand it, but anyway my plan was working fine, for neither the Controller nor the guards had tried to take the helmet away from me. It showed how much they respected whoever wore it, I guessed. I grinned with relief—and the others grinned too.

"Baby, how'd you like to go back to New York with me?" I asked Zura. "I've fallen for you like a ton of bricks."

It was true, too, for now that I was all relieved and felt sure about escaping, I had time to look at Zura again and realized what a sweet number she was, and how crazy I was about her. But just as I said that, the Controller and guards tried to beat my time.

"Zura, I love you!" yelled the Controller.

"So do I! And I too!" cried the guards.

There was a pounding of feet, and men in dozens came busting into the room. Every one of them went for Zura.

"Zura, I love you!" they all kept yelling.

They crowded wildly around her, and more guys by hundreds were flocking into the building, all trying to get into this room, and every one of them hollering how much he loved Zura.

"Leave her alone, you muggs!" I yelled, burned up with jealousy and trying to knock those guys away from her.

And believe it or not, every guy there suddenly got jealous at the same time and tried to beat up all the rest.

"Let her alone! Take your hands off her!" they yelled, and then sailed into each other with their fists in wild rage.

Listen, I've been in some brawls in my time but that was the worst ever. The madder I got, the madder everybody else seemed to get. We rocked back and forth in the crowded room, swapping punches, everybody taking a sock at everybody else. And through the window. I glimpsed the crowds out in the street, staging a wild Kilkenny too!

And suddenly I caught on to what was driving them all crazy. The helmet on my head—the thing they called Control! It must have got turned on stronger somehow when the helmet hit the floor. And now the Control was so strong that everybody thought and felt exactly the same as me, who wore the helmet. When I felt joyful, they all felt joyful, and when I got mad, they all got mad.

"Holy mackerel!" I said, appalled by it.

The fighting stopped dead as I said it. And everybody in the room was as appalled and scared as I was.

I got a grip on myself. I was going to get out of here, back to that tree in the park so Doc Murtha could yank me back from this nutty place. I started out of the room and down the hall.

Everybody in the room started out at the same time. They hurried along, all looking as intent and worried as I felt. I didn't understand it until I got outside the building—then I did.

Everybody in the city was making for that tree in the park! I might have expected it. As soon as I thought of the tree, and how urgent it was for me to get there, everyone else thought of exactly the same thing. Thousands of people were heading for that park.

I groaned and ran forward, for I knew I'd never be able to reach the tree once that immense mob gathered around it. Everybody in the city groaned and sprinted at the same time I did. The harder I ran, the harder they ran—it was a crazy nightmare.

I stopped. I couldn't beat this mob to the tree and couldn't get through them once they gathered around it. Everybody else stopped as I did. I tried to figure something, and I was badly worried.

Everybody was badly worried. It would have seemed kind of funny, if it hadn't been so serious for me, to see all those thousands of people standing so worried, wringing their hands and frowning and walking back and forth, every one of them as worried as me.

I thought—well, I can take off the helmet and then make a run for the tree. But that wouldn't do. For as soon as the helmet was off me and they had their own minds back, they'd grab me and likely electrocute me for what I'd done to the Controller. I had to think of something else, and in a minute I did.

I put on a scared look, and hollered real loud:

"The park is dangerous—I must stay away from the park!"

You see, I figured they'd all get that thought and would shrink away from the park, while I went toward it. So I started toward the tree again, shouting out how I mustn't go near it.

It didn't turn out right. The whole crowd looked scared, just as I did, and they all chanted, "I mustn't go near the park! It is dangerous—I mustn't go near it!"

And while they chanted, every last one of the sons was going right toward the park as I was doing. It was no go. They'd be gathered a hundred deep around the tree before I could get there. So I quit and walked back from it, and everybody else walked back.

I felt pretty bad, by now. And believe me, there were some thousands of mighty blue people around me. The more discouraged I felt, the longer their faces got. A lot of them were heaving sighs, and some of them were crying. I got impatient at their misery.

"Shut up that bawling!" I yelled angrily.

I might have known it. Everybody else suddenly got impatient with the noise, and yelled for it to be stopped.

"Quiet, there!" they yelled at the top of their voices, all of them. It nearly split my eardrums.

Then they all got blue again, as my worries came back. I didn't dare take the helmet off, and with it on, I couldn't get to the tree without thousands being ahead of me. It was an awful fix.

"Damn old Doc Murtha for getting me into this!" I muttered viciously to myself.

They all took it up, of course. They damned Doc Murtha with every kind of swear word they knew, thousands of voices making the air blue with curses. It did me good to hear it.

But how was I going to get out of this mess? I tried to sneak toward the tree without thinking about it, but everybody else hunched down and sneaked for it, too, pretending they were thinking of something else. I stopped and swore: Everybody stopped and swore with me.

By now I was plenty tired and also beginning to feel hungry, for I hadn't eaten since that morning. I decided I'd better try to dig up some chow, and then I'd feel better and could maybe dope out something. So I headed back along the street, looking for food.

Everybody in sight began to scatter. They dived into buildings, and every last one of them was hunting grub too. For a minute I thought my chance had come, and I turned and started back for the park, but of course everybody immediately dropped the search for food and started back with me. I gave it up and went on hunting eats.

All those thousands of people were after food the same as I was. Say, I didn't have a chance in that crowd—every time I looked into a building and spotted some grub, some guy was ahead of me grabbing it. And they knew where to find it and I didn't.

So I just gave up the idea of eating and wandered discouragedly along the street. They all dropped the food and began wandering aimlessly just as I was doing, all looking mighty low. I tried to grab up something to eat then, but naturally they all made a quick dive for it again, and I got nothing but a little piece of fruit.

Boy, it would have been bad for old Doc Murtha if he had showed up in that town right then. For as I wandered tiredly along I kept telling myself what I'd do to the old doc if I ever got hands on him. And of course all the thousands wandering in the city were muttering too just what they'd do to Doc Murtha when they got him.

Finally I stumbled wearily into another park, a bigger one that had a zoo in it, a lot of animals in cages. These Egyptian animals looked kind of different to me. I sat down tiredly in front of a cage that held a big ape with bright red fur. The big monk in the cage sat down too. And when I sighed wearily, the monk sighed too.

That kind of surprised me, for it showed the monk's mind was under Control of my helmet, the same as all the people. None of the other animals in the cages seemed affected, but I guessed the monk had a brain enough like a human brain to be affected by Control. And then I got a sudden inspiration.

Since that monk was affected by Control, then if I put the helmet on his head, all these people would be affected by his broadcast thoughts and feelings! And if they were under the monk's Control, they wouldn't all rush for that tree when I went there, and neither would they know enough to stop me and arrest me for what I'd done.

I went over to the cage and opened it. People from all over started for the cage too, of course, but this time I was ahead of them. Quick as thought, I took the helmet off my head and jammed it down on the head of the bright-red monk. He didn't seem to mind the helmet at first—he just sort of reverted to his natural mental life, and sat down on his hunkers and scratched.

All the people in sight sat down on their hunkers and scratched! They all felt itchy simply because the monk did. And the worst of it was that I wanted to scratch too—I felt itchy as the devil. But I fought off that feeling—I could resist it, you see, better than all the others here, because like the Controller had said, my brain was different and didn't receive the vibrations of Control so well.

So, fighting down that itchy feeling, I started hotfoot through the streets toward that park where my tree was.

As I ran through the streets, I could tell by the crowds around me just what the monk was doing. First the crowds all started to climb—up the sides of buildings and monuments and everything else. I knew the monk must be up a tree. Then they came down and scratched some more. They hunted for water and began to drink. And then they stopped drinking and began to paw angrily at their heads.

I knew what that meant! The monk was annoyed at the helmet on his head and was trying to paw it off. I sprinted, for now the park and tree were in sight. And just as I dashed for the tree with the scarred trunk, all the thousands of people in the streets stopped pawing their heads and looked dazedly around.

"Oh, Lord, the monk's got the helmet off—they're out of Control!" I groaned, and ran the last few yards.

The crowd caught sight of me running. "Stop that man!" the Controller was yelling.

I dashed up to the tree, colliding with its trunk. And nothing happened! Nothing at all.

"Doc Murtha, where the devil are you?" I yelled wildly. The crowd was coming at me furiously from all directions.

Bang! Something hit me hard, and I didn't know anything more. And when I came to I wasn't there by the tree at all.

I was on the big copper platform of the machine in Doc Murtha's home. The doc was reviving me.

"Martin, what happened to you?" he cried. "When I retracted the force-field to draw you back in five minutes as I had promised, you didn't appear! I've been trying it at intervals ever since, in the hope of catching you. What did you see?"

I got off the copper platform, and then I looked at Doc Murtha.

"Doc," I told him, "if you wasn't an old man I'd knock you into the next county. You doublecrossing so-and-so—why didn't you tell me you were going to shoot me to Egypt?"

"Egypt?" he cried. "You're crazy! You've been on another world entirely. The field was set to project you to a world across the Galaxy with conditions approximating Earth's conditions. What makes you think you've been in Egypt?"

"I saw the pyramids there myself!" I snapped. "And it is one dirty name of a place to send anyone—those Egyptians with their Control and Controller are worse than the Bowery! You're not going to shoot any more innocent fellows there, you old rascal."

And I grabbed up a big metal tool and laid into that radio-machine of his. Just three good wallops, and the works of it were smashed into a lot of ruins. I threw down the tool, feeling mighty good to have saved some other guy from going through what I had.

"You fool!" Doc Murtha screamed. "You've destroyed twenty years' work."

"Here's your grand back," I said, paying no attention to him. I headed for the door. "Me, I'm going back and get a job as sparring-partner for the champ. It's easier money!"

He That Hath Wings

Doctor Harriman paused in the corridor of the maternity ward and asked, "What about that woman in 27?"

There was pity in the eyes of the plump, crisply dressed head nurse as she answered, "She died an hour after the birth of her baby, doctor. Her heart was bad, you know."

The physician nodded, his spare, clean-shaven face thoughtful. "Yes, I remember now—she and her husband were injured in an electrical explosion in a subway a year ago, and the husband died recently. What about the baby?"

The nurse hesitated. "A fine, healthy little boy, except—"

"Except what?"

"Except that he is humpbacked, doctor."

Doctor Harriman swore in pity. "What horrible luck for the poor little devil! Born an orphan, and deformed, too." He said with sudden decision, "I'll look at the infant. Perhaps we could do something for him."

But when he and the nurse bent together over the crib in which red-faced little David Rand lay squalling lustily, the doctor shook his head. "No, we can't do anything for that back. What a shame!"

David Rand's little red body was as straight and clean-lined as that of any baby ever born—except for his back. From the back of the infant's shoulder-blades jutted two humped projections, one on each side, that curved down toward the lower ribs.

Those twin humps were so long and streamlined in their jutting curve that they hardly looked like deformities. The skillful hands of Doctor

Harriman gently probed them. Then an expression of perplexity came over his face.

"This doesn't seem any ordinary deformity," he said puzzledly. "I think we'll look at them through the X-ray. Tell Doctor Morris to get the apparatus going."

Doctor Morris was a stocky, red-headed young man who looked in pity, also, at the crying, red-faced baby lying in front of the X-ray machine, later.

He muttered, "Tough on the poor kid, that back. Ready, doctor?"

Harriman nodded. "Go ahead."

The X-rays broke into sputtering, crackling life. Doctor Harriman applied his eyes to the fluoroscope. His body stiffened. It was a long, silent minute before he straightened from his inspection. His spare face had gone dead white and the waiting nurse wondered what had so excited him.

Harriman said, a little thickly, "Morris! Take a look through this. I'm either seeing things, or else something utterly unprecedented has happened."

Morris, with a puzzled frown at his superior, gazed through the instrument. His head jerked up.

"My God!" he exclaimed.

"You see it too?" exclaimed Doctor Harriman. "Then I guess I'm not crazy after all. But this thing—why, it's without precedent in all human history!"

He babbled incoherently, "And the bones, too—hollow—the whole skeletonal structure different. His weight—"

He set the infant hastily on a scale. The beam jiggled.

"See that!" exclaimed Harriman. "He weighs only a third of what a baby his size should weigh."

Red-headed young Doctor Morris was staring in fascination at the curving humps on the infant's back. He said hoarsely, "But this just isn't possible—"

"But it's real!" Harriman flung out. His eyes were brilliant with excitement. He cried, "A change in gene-patterns—only that could have caused this. Some pre-natal influence—"

His fist smacked into his hand. "I've got it! The electrical explosion that injured this child's mother a year before his birth. That's what did it—an explosion of hard radiations that damaged, changed, her genes. You remember Muller's experiments—"

The head nurse's wonder overcame her respect. She asked, "But what is it, doctor? What's the matter with the child's back? Is it so bad as all that?"

"So bad?" repeated Doctor Harriman. He drew a long breath. He told the nurse, "This child, this David Rand, is a unique case in medical history. There has never been anyone like him—as far as we know, the thing that's going to happen to him has never happened to any other human being. And all due to that electrical explosion."

"What's going to happen to him?" demanded the nurse, dismayed.

"This child is going to have *wings!*" shouted Harriman. "Those projections growing out on his back—they're not just ordinary abnormalities—they're nascent wings, that will very soon break out and grow just as a fledgling bird's wings break out and grow."

The head nurse stared at them. "You're joking," she said finally, in flat unbelief.

"Good God, do you think I'd joke about such a matter?" cried Harriman. "I tell you, I'm as stunned as you are, even though I can see the scientific reason for the thing. This child's body is different from the body of any other human being that ever lived.

"His bones are hollow, like a bird's bones. His blood seems different and he weighs only a third what a normal human infant weighs. And his shoulder-blades jut out into bone projections to which are attached the great wing-muscles. The X-rays clearly show the rudimentary feathers and bones of the wings themselves."

"Wings!" repeated young Morris dazedly. He said after a moment, "Harriman, this child will be able to—"

"He'll be able to fly, yes!" declared Harriman. "I'm certain of it. The wings are going to be very large ones, and his body is so much lighter than normal that they'll easily bear him aloft."

"Good Lord!" ejaculated Morris incoherently.

He looked a little wildly down at the infant. It had stopped crying and now waved pudgy red arms and legs weakly.

"It just isn't possible," said the nurse, taking refuge in incredulity. "How could a baby, a man, have wings?"

Doctor Harriman said swiftly, "It's due to a deep change in the parents' genes. The genes, you know, are the tiny cells which control bodily development in every living thing that is born. Alter the gene-pattern and you alter the bodily development of the offspring, which explains the differences in color, size, and so forth, in children. But those minor differences are due to comparatively minor gene-changes.

"But the gene-pattern of this child's parents was radically changed a year ago. The electrical explosion in which they were injured must have deeply altered their gene-patterns, by a wave of sudden electrical force. Muller, of the University of Texas, has demonstrated that gene-patterns *can* be greatly altered by radiation, and that the offspring of parents so treated will differ greatly from their parents in bodily form. That accident produced an entirely new gene-pattern in the parents of this child, one which developed their child into a winged human. He's what biologists technically call a mutant."

Young Morris suddenly said, "Good Lord, what the newspapers are going to do when they get hold of this story!"

"They mustn't get hold of it," Doctor Harriman declared. "The birth of this child is one of the greatest things in the history of biological science, and it mustn't be made a cheap popular sensation. We must keep it utterly quiet."

They kept it quiet for three months, in all. During that time, little David Rand occupied a private room in the hospital and was cared for only by the head nurse and visited only by the two physicians.

During those three months, the correctness of Doctor Harriman's prediction was fulfilled. For in that time, the humped projections on the child's back grew with incredible rapidity until at last they broke through the tender skin in a pair of stubby, scrawny-looking things that were unmistakably wings.

Little David squalled violently during the days that his wings broke forth, feeling only a pain as of teething many times intensified. But the two doctors stared and stared at those little wings with their rudimentary feathers, even now hardly able to believe the witness of their eyes.

They saw that the child had as complete control of the wings as of his arms and legs, by means of the great muscles around their bases which no other human possessed. And they saw too that while David's weight was increasing, he remained still just a third of the weight of a normal child of his age, and that his heart had a tremendously high pulse-beat and that his blood was far warmer than that of any normal person.

Then it happened. The head nurse, unable any longer to contain the tremendous secret with which she was bursting, told a relative in strict confidence. That relative told another relative, also in strict confidence. And two days later the story appeared in the New York newspapers.

The hospital put guards at its doors and refused admittance to the grinning reporters who came to ask for details. All of them were frankly skeptical, and the newspaper stories were written with a tongue in the cheek. The public laughed. A child with wings! What kind of phony new story would they think up next?

But a few days later, the stories changed in tone. Others of the hospital personnel, made curious by the newspaper yarns, pried into the room where David Rand lay crowing and thrashing his arms and legs and wings. They babbled broadcast assertions that the story was true. One of them who was a candid camera enthusiast even managed to slip out a photograph of the infant. Smeary as it was, that photograph did unmistakably show a child with wings of some sort growing from its back.

The hospital became a fort, a place besieged. Reporters and photographers milled outside its doors and clamored against the special police guard that had been detailed to keep them out. The great press associations offered Doctor Harriman large sums for exclusive stories and photographs of the winged child. The public began to wonder if there was anything in the yarn.

Doctor Harriman had to give in, finally. He admitted a committee of a dozen reporters, photographers and eminent physicians to see the child.

David Rand lay and looked up at them with wise blue gaze, clutching his toe, while the eminent physicians and newspapermen stared down at him with bulging eyes.

The physicians said, "It's incredible, but it's true. This is no fake—the child really has wings."

The reporters asked Doctor Harriman wildly, "When he gets bigger, will he be able to fly?"

Harriman said shortly, "We can't tell just what his development will be like, now. But if he continues to develop as he has, undoubtedly he'll be able to fly."

"Good Lord, let me at a phone!" groaned one newshound. And they were all scrambling pell-mell for the telephones.

Doctor Harriman permitted a few pictures, and then unceremoniously shoved the visitors out. But there was no holding the newspapers, after that. David Rand's name became overnight the best known in the world. The pictures convinced even the most skeptical of the public.

Great biologists made long statements on the theories of genetics which could explain the child. Anthropologists speculated as to whether similar freak winged men had not been born a few times in the remote past, giving rise to the worldwide legends of harpies and vampires and flying people. Crazy sects saw in the child's birth an omen of the approaching end of the world.

Theatrical agents offered immense sums for the privilege of exhibiting David in a hygienic glass case. Newspapers and press services outbid each other for exclusive rights to the story Doctor Harriman could tell. A thousand firms begged to purchase the right to use little David's name on toys, infant foods, and what not.

And the cause of all this excitement lay and rolled and crowed and sometimes cried in his little bed, now and then vigorously flapping the sprouting wings that had upset the whole world. Doctor Harriman looked thoughtfully down at him.

He said, "I'll have to get him out of here. The hospital superintendent is complaining that the crowds and commotion are wrecking the place."

"But where can you take him?" Morris wanted to know. "He hasn't any parents or relatives, and you can't put a kid like this in an orphan asylum."

Doctor Harriman made a decision. "I'm going to retire from practice and devote myself entirely to observing and recording David's growth. I'll have myself made his legal guardian and I'll bring him up in some spot away from all this turmoil—an island or some place like that, if I can find one."

Harriman found such a place, an island off the Maine coast, a speck of barren sand and scrubby trees. He leased it, built a bungalow there, and took David Rand and an elderly nurse-housekeeper there. He took also a strong Norwegian watchman who was very efficient at repelling the boats of reporters who tried to land there. After a while the newspapers gave it up. They had to be content to reprint the photographs and articles which Doctor Harriman gave to scientific publications concerning David's growth.

David grew rapidly. In five years he was a sturdy little youngster with yellow hair, and his wings were larger and covered with short bronze feathers. He ran and laughed and played, like any youngster, flapping his wings vigorously.

He was ten before he flew. By then he was a little slimmer, and his glittering bronze wings came to his heels. When he walked or sat or slept, he kept the wings closely folded on his back like a bronze sheath. But when he opened them, they extended much farther than his arms could, on either side.

Doctor Harriman had meant to let David gradually try flying, to photograph and observe every step of the process. But it did not happen that way. David flew first as naturally as a bird first flies.

He himself had never thought much about his wings. He knew that Doctor John, as he called the physician, had no such wings, and that neither did Flora, the gaunt old nurse, nor Holf, the grinning watchman, have them. But he had seen no other people, and so he imagined the rest of the world was divided into people who had wings and people who didn't have them. He did not know just what the wings were for, though he knew that he liked to flap them and exercise them when he was running, and would wear no shirt over them.

Then one April morning, David found out what his wings were for. He had climbed into a tall old scrub oak to peer at a bird's nest. The child was always inordinately interested in the birds of the little island, jumping and clapping his hands as he saw then darting and circling overhead, watching their flocks stream south each fall and north each spring, prying into their ways of living because of some dim sense of kinship with these other winged things.

He had climbed nearly to the top of the old oak on this morning, toward the nest he had spied. His wings were tightly folded to keep them out of the way of branches. Then, as he reached up to pull himself the last step upward, his foot pressed on the merest rotten shell of a dead branch. Abnormally light as he was, his weight was enough to snap the branch and he fell cleanly toward the ground.

Instincts exploded in David's brain in the moment that he plummeted toward the ground. Quite without will, his wings unfolded with a bursting whir. He felt a terrific tug on them that wrenched his shoulders hard. And then suddenly, marvelously, he was no longer falling but was *gliding* downward on a long slant, with his wings unfolded and rigidly set.

There burst from his innermost being a high, ringing shout of exultation. Down—down—gliding like a swooping bird with the clean air buffeting at his face and streaming past his wings and body. A wild, sweet thrill that he had never felt before, a sudden crazy joy in living.

He shouted again, and with instant impulse flapped his great wings, beating the air with them, instinctively bending his head sharply back and keeping his arms flattened against his sides, his legs straight and close together.

He was soaring *upward* now, the ground swiftly receding beneath him, the sun blazing in his eyes, the wind screaming around him. He opened his mouth to shout again, and the cold, clean air hammered into his throat. In sheer, mad physical ecstasy he rocketed up through the blue with whirring wings.

It was thus that Doctor Harriman saw him when he chanced to come out of the bungalow a little later. The doctor heard a shrill, exultant cry from high above and looked up to see that slim winged shape swooping down toward him from the sunlit heavens.

The doctor caught his breath at the sheer beauty of the spectacle as David dived and soared and whirled above him, gone crazy with delight in his new-found wings. The boy had instinctively learned how to turn and twist and dive, even though his movements had yet a clumsiness that made him sometimes side-slip.

When David Rand finally swooped down and alighted in front of the doctor with quick-closing wings, the boy's eyes streamed electric joy.

"I can *fly!*"

Doctor Harriman nodded. "You can fly, David. I know I can't keep you from doing it now, but you must not leave the island and you must be careful."

By the time David reached the age of seventeen, there was no longer any need to caution him to be careful. He was as much at home in the air as any bird living.

He was a tall, slim, yellow-haired youth now, his arrow-straight figure still clad only in the shorts that were all the clothing his warm-blooded body required, a wild, restless energy crackling and snapping in his keen face and dancing blue eyes.

His wings had become superb, glittering, bronze-feathered pinions that extended more than ten feet from tip to tip when he spread them, and that touched his heels with their lowest feathers when he closed them on his back.

Constant flying over the island and the surrounding waters had developed the great wing-muscles behind David's shoulders to tremendous strength and endurance. He could spend a whole day gliding and soaring over the island, now climbing high with mad burst of whirring wings, then circling, planing on motionless wings, slowly descending.

He could chase and overtake almost any bird in the air. He would start up a flock of pheasants and his laughter would ring high and wild across the sky as he turned and twisted and darted after the panicky birds. He could pull out the tail-feathers of outraged hawks before they could escape, and he could swoop quicker than a hawk on rabbits and squirrels on the ground.

Sometimes when fog banked the island Doctor Harriman would hear the ringing shout from the gray mists overhead and would know that

David was somewhere up there. Or again he would be out over the sunlit waters, plummeting headlong down to them and then at the last moment swiftly spreading his wings so that he just skimmed the wave-crests with the screaming gulls before he rocketed upward again.

Never yet had David been away from the island, but the doctor knew from his own infrequent visits to the mainland that the worldwide interest in the flying youth was still strong. The photographs which the doctor gave to scientific journals no longer sufficed for the public curiosity, and launches and airplanes with moving-picture cameramen frequently circled the island to snap pictures of David Rand flying.

To one of those airplanes occurred a thing that gave its occupants much to talk about for days to come. They were a pilot and cameraman who came over the island at midday, in spite of Doctor Harriman's prohibition of such flights, and who circled brazenly about looking for the flying youth.

Had they looked up, they could have seen David as a circling speck high above them. He watched the airplane with keen interest mixed with contempt. He had seen these flying ships before and he felt only pity and scorn for their stiff, clumsy wings and noisy motors with which wingless men made shift to fly. This one, though, so directly beneath him, stimulated his curiosity so that he swooped down toward it from above and behind, his great wings urging him against the slip-stream of its propeller.

The pilot in the open rear-cockpit of that airplane nearly had heart failure when someone tapped him on the shoulder from behind. He whirled, startled, and when he saw David Rand crouching precariously on the fuselage just behind him, grinning at him, he lost his head for a moment so that the ship side-slipped and started to fall.

With a shouting laugh, David Rand leaped off the fuselage and spread his wings to soar up past it. The pilot recovered enough presence of mind to right his ship, and presently David saw it move unsteadily off toward the mainland. Its occupants had enough of the business for one day.

But the increasing number of such curious visitors stimulated in David Rand a reciprocal curiosity concerning the outside world. He wondered more and more what lay beyond the low, dim line of the mainland over there across the blue waters. He could not understand why Doctor John forbade him to fly over there, when well he knew that his wings would bear him up for a hundred times that distance.

Doctor Harriman told him, "I'll take you there soon, David. But you must wait until you understand things better—you wouldn't fit in with the rest of the world, yet."

"Why not?" demanded David puzzledly.

The doctor explained, "You have wings, and no one else in the world has. That might make things very difficult for you."

"But why?"

Harriman stroked his spare chin and said thoughtfully, "You'd be a sensation, a sort of freak, David. They'd be curious about you because you're different, but they'd look down on you for the same reason. That's why I brought you up out here, to avoid that. You must wait a little longer before you see the world."

David Rand flung a hand up to point half angrily at a streaming flock of piping wild birds, heading south, black against the autumn sunset. "*They* don't wait! Every fall I see them, everything that flies, going away. Every spring I see them returning, passing overhead again. And I have to stay on this little island!"

A wild pulse of freedom surged in his blue eyes.

"I want to go as they do, to see the land over there, and the lands beyond that."

"Soon you shall go over there," promised Doctor Harriman. "I will go with you—will look out for you there."

But through the dusk that evening, David sat with chin in hand, wings folded, staring broodingly after the straggling, southing birds. And in the days that followed, he took less and less pleasure in mere aimless flight above the island, and more and more watched wistfully the endless, merry passage of the honking wild geese and swarming ducks and whistling songbirds.

Doctor Harriman saw and understood that yearning in David's eyes, and the old physician sighed.

"He has grown up," he thought, "and wants to go like any young bird that would leave its nest. I shall not be able much longer to keep him from leaving."

But it was Harriman himself who left first, in a different way. For some time the doctor's heart had troubled him, and there came a morning when he did not awaken, and when a dazed, uncomprehending David stared down at his guardian's still white face.

Through all that day, while the old housekeeper wept softly about the place and the Norwegian was gone in the boat to the mainland to arrange the funeral, David Rand sat with folded wings and chin in hand, staring out across the blue waters.

That night, when all was dark and silent around the bungalow, he stole into the room where the doctor lay silent and peaceful. In the darkness,

David touched the thin, cold hand. Hot tears swam in his eyes and he felt a hard lump in his throat as he made that futile gesture of farewell.

Then he went softly back out of the house into the night. The moon was a red shield above the eastern waters and the autumn wind blew cold and crisp. Down through the keen air came the joyous piping and carolling and whistling of a long swarm of wild birds, like shrill bugle-calls of gay challenge.

David's knees bent, and he sprang upward with whirring wings—up and up, the icy air streaming past his body, thundering in his ears, his nostrils drinking it. And the dull sorrow in his heart receded in the bursting joy of flight and freedom. He was up among those shrilling, whistling birds now, the screaming wind tearing laughter from his lips as they scattered in alarm from him.

Then as they saw that this strange winged creature who had joined them made no move to harm them, the wild birds reformed their scattered flock. Far off across the dim, heaving plain of the waters glowed the dull red moon and the scattered lights of the mainland, the little lights of earthbound folk. The birds shrilled loud and David laughed and sang in joyous chorus as his great wings whirred in time with their own, trailing high across the night sky toward adventure and freedom, flying south.

All through that night, and with brief rests through the next day also, David flew southward, for a time over endless waters and then over the green, fertile land. His hunger he satisfied by dipping toward trees loaded with ripening fruit. When the next night came he slept in a crotch high in a tall forest oak, crouched comfortably with his wings folded about him.

It was not long before the world learned that the freak youth with wings was abroad. People in farms and villages and cities looked up incredulously at that slim figure winging high overhead. Ignorant folk who had never heard of David Rand flung themselves prostrate in panic as he passed across the sky.

Through all that winter there were reports of David from the southland, reports that made it evident he had become almost completely a creature of the wild. What greater pleasure than to soar through the long sun-drenched days over the blue tropic seas, to swoop on the silver fish that broke from the waters, to gather strange fruits and sleep at night in a high tree close against the stars, and wake with dawn to another day of unfettered freedom?

Now and again he would circle unsuspected over some city at night, soaring slowly in the darkness and peering down curiously at the vast pattern of straggling lights and the blazing streets choked with swarms of people and vehicles. He would not enter those cities and he could not see how the people in them could bear to live so, crawling over the surface of the Earth amid the rubbing and jostling of hordes like them, never knowing even for a moment the wild clean joy of soaring through blue infinities of sky. What could make life worthwhile for such earthbound, ant-like folk?

When the spring sun grew hotter and higher, and the birds began to flock together in noisy swarms, David too felt something tugging him northward. So he flew north over the spring-green land, great bronzed wings tirelessly beating the air, a slim, tanned figure arrowing unerringly north.

He came at last to his goal, the island where he had lived most of his life. It lay lonely and deserted now in the empty waters, dust gathering over the things in the abandoned bungalow, the garden weed-grown. David settled down there for a time, sleeping upon the porch, making long flights for amusement, west over the villages and dingy cities, north over the rugged, wave-dashed coast, east over the blue sea; until at last the flowers began to die and the air grew frosty, and the deep urge tugged at David until again he joined the great flocks of winged things going south.

North and south—south and north—for three years that wild freedom of unchecked migration was his. In those three years he came to know mountain and valley, sea and river, storm and calm, and hunger and thirst, as only they of the wild know them. And in those years the world became accustomed to David, almost forgot him. He was the winged man, just a freak; there would never be another like him.

Then in the third spring there came the end to David Rand's winged freedom. He was on his spring flight north, and at dusk felt hunger. He made out in the twilight a suburban mansion amid extensive orchards and gardens, and swooped down toward it with ideas of early berries. He was very near the trees in the twilight when a gun roared from the ground. David felt a blinding stab of pain through his head, and knew nothing more.

When he awoke, it was in a bed in a sunlit room. There were a kind-faced elderly man and a girl in the room, and another man who looked like a doctor. David discovered that there was a bandage around his head. These people, he saw, were all looking at him with intense interest.

The elderly, kind-looking man said, "You're David Rand, the fellow with wings? Well, you're mighty lucky to be living." He explained, "You see, my gardener has been watching for a hawk that steals our chickens.

When you swooped down in the dusk last night, he fired at you before he could recognize you. Some of the shot from his gun just grazed your head."

The girl asked gently, "Are you feeling better now? The doctor says you'll soon be as good as ever." She added, "This is my father, Wilson Hall. I'm Ruth Hall."

David stared up at her. He thought he had never seen anyone so beautiful as this shy, soft, dark girl with her curling black hair and tender, worried brown eyes.

He suddenly knew the reason for the puzzling persistence with which the birds sought each other out and clung together in pairs, each mating season. He felt the same thing in his own breast now, the urge toward this girl. He did not think of it as love, but suddenly he loved her.

He told Ruth Hall slowly, "I'm all right now."

But she said, "You must stay here until you're completely well. It's the least we can do when it was our servant who almost killed you."

David stayed, as the wound healed. He did not like the house, whose rooms seemed so dark and stiflingly close to him, but he found that he could stay outside during the day, and could sleep on a porch at night.

Neither did he like the newspaper men and cameramen who came to Wilson Hall's house to get stories about the winged man's accident; but these soon ceased coming, for David Rand was not now the sensation he had been years ago. And while visitors to the Hall home stared rather disconcertingly at him and at his wings, he got used to that.

He put up with everything, so that he might be near Ruth Hall. His love for her was a clean fire burning inside him and nothing in the world now seemed so desirable as that she should love him too. Yet because he was still mostly of the wild, and had had little experience in talking, he found it hard to tell her what he felt.

He did tell her, finally, sitting beside her in the sunlit garden. When he had finished, Ruth's gentle brown eyes were troubled.

"You want me to marry you, David?"

"Why, yes," he said, a little puzzled. "That's what they call it when people mate, isn't it? And I want you for my mate."

She said, distressed, "But David, your wings—"

He laughed. "Why, there's nothing the matter with my wings. The accident didn't hurt them. See!"

And he leaped to his feet, whipping open the great bronze wings that glittered in the sunlight, looking like a figure of fable poised for a leap into the blue, his slim tanned body clad only in the shorts which were all the clothing he would wear.

The trouble did not leave Ruth's eyes. She explained, "It's not that, David—it's that your wings make you so different from everybody else. Of course it's wonderful that you can fly, but they make you so different from everyone else that people look on you as a kind of freak."

David stared. "*You* don't look on me as that, Ruth?"

"Of course not," Ruth said. "But it does seem somehow a little abnormal, monstrous, your having wings."

"Monstrous?" he repeated. "Why, it's nothing like that. It's just—beautiful, being able to fly. See!"

And he sprang upward with great wings whirring—up and up, climbing into the blue sky, dipping and darting and turning up there like a swallow, then cometing down in a breathless swoop to land lightly on his toes beside the girl.

"Is there anything monstrous about that?" he demanded joyously. "Why, Ruth, I want you to fly with me, held in my arms, so that you'll know the beauty of it as I know it."

The girl shuddered a little. "I couldn't, David. I know it's silly, but when I see you in the air like that you don't seem so much a man as a bird, a flying animal, something unhuman."

David Rand stared at her, suddenly miserable. "Then you won't marry me—because of my wings?"

He grasped her in his strong, tanned arms, his lips seeking her soft mouth.

"Ruth, I can't live without you now that I've met you. I can't!"

It was on a night a little later that Ruth, somewhat hesitantly, made her suggestion. The moon flooded the garden with calm silver, gleamed on David Rand's folded wings as he sat with keen young face bent eagerly toward the girl.

She said, "David, there is a way in which we could marry and be happy, if you love me enough to do it."

"I'll do anything!" he cried. "You know that."

She hesitated.

"Your wings—they're what keep us apart. I can't have a husband who belongs more to the wild creatures than to the human race, a husband whom everyone would consider a freak, a deformed oddity. But if you were to have your wings taken off—"

He stared at her. "My wings taken off?"

She explained in an eager little rush of words. "It's quite practicable, David. Doctor White, who treated you for that wound and who examined you then, has told me that it would be quite easy to amputate your wings above their bases. There would be no danger at all in it, and it would leave only the slight projection of the stumps on your back. Then you'd be a normal man and not a freak," she added, her soft face earnest and appealing. "Father would give you a position in his business, and instead of an abnormal, roaming, half-human creature you would be like—like everyone else. We could be so happy then."

David Rand was stunned. "Amputate my wings?" he repeated almost uncomprehendingly. "You won't marry me unless I do that?"

"I can't," said Ruth painfully. "I love you, David, I do—but I want my husband to be like other women's husbands."

"Never to fly again," said David slowly, his face white in the moonlight. "To become earthbound, like everyone else! No!" he cried, springing to his feet in a wild revulsion. "I won't do it—I won't give up my wings! I won't become like—"

He stopped abruptly. Ruth was sobbing into her hands. All his anger gone, he stooped beside her, pulled down her hands, yearningly tilted up her soft, tear-stained face.

"Don't cry, Ruth," he begged. "It isn't that I don't love you—I do, more than anything else on earth. But I had never thought of giving up my wings—the idea stunned me." He told her, "You go on into the house. I must think it over a little."

She kissed him, her mouth quivering, and then was gone through the moonlight to the house. And David Rand remained, his brain in turmoil, pacing nervously in the silver light.

Give up his wings? Never again to dip and soar and swoop with the winged things of the sky, never again to know the mad exaltation and tameless freedom of rushing flight?

Yet—to give up Ruth—to deny this blind, irresistible yearning for her that beat in every atom of him—to know bitter loneliness and longing for her the rest of his life—how could he do that? He couldn't do it. He *wouldn't*.

So David went rapidly toward the house and met the girl waiting for him on the moonlit terrace.

"David?"

"Yes, Ruth, I'll do it. I'll do anything for you."

She sobbed happily on his breast. "I knew you really loved me, David. I knew it."

Two days later David Rand came out of the mists of anesthesia in a hospital room, feeling very strange, his back an aching soreness. Doctor White and Ruth were bending over his bed.

"Well, it was a complete success, young man," said the doctor. "You'll be out of here in a few days."

Ruth's eyes were shining. "The day you leave, David, we'll be married."

When they were gone, David slowly felt his back. Only the bandaged, projecting stumps of his wings remained. He could move the great wing-muscles, but no whirring pinions answered. He felt dazed and strange, as though some most vital part of him was gone. But he clung to the thought of Ruth—of Ruth waiting for him—

And she was waiting for him, and they were married on the day he left the hospital. And in the sweetness of her love, David lost all of that strange dazed feeling, and almost forgot that once he had possessed wings and had roamed the sky a wild, winged thing.

Wilson Hall gave his daughter and son-in-law a pretty white cottage on a wooded hill near town, and made a place for David in his business and was patient with his ignorance of commercial matters. And every day David drove his car into town and worked all day in his office and drove back homeward in the dusk to sit with Ruth before their fire, her head on his shoulder.

"David, are you sorry that you did it?" Ruth would ask anxiously at first.

And he would laugh and say, "Of course not, Ruth. Having you is worth anything."

And he told himself that that was true, that he did not regret the loss of his wings. All that past time when he had flown the sky with whirring wings seemed only a strange dream and only now had he awakened to real happiness, he assured himself.

Wilson Hall told his daughter, "David's doing well down at the office. I was afraid he would always be a little wild, but he's settled down fine."

Ruth nodded happily and said, "I knew that he would. And everyone likes him so much now."

For people who once had looked askance at Ruth's marriage now remarked that it had turned out very well after all.

"He's really quite nice. And except for the slight humps on his shoulders, you'd never think that he had been different from anyone else," they said.

So the months slipped by. In the little cottage on the wooded hill was complete happiness until there came the fall, frosting the lawn with silver each morning, stamping crazy colors on the maples.

One fall night David woke suddenly, wondering what had so abruptly awakened him. Ruth was still sleeping softly with gentle breathing beside him. He could hear no sound.

Then he heard it. A far-away, ghostly whistling trailing down from the frosty sky, a remote, challenging shrilling that throbbed with a dim, wild note of pulsing freedom.

He knew what it was, instantly. He swung open the window and peered up into the night with beating heart. And up there he saw them, long, streaming files of hurtling wild birds, winging southward beneath the stars. In an instant the wild impulse to spring from the window, to rocket up after them into the clean, cold night, clamored blindly in David's heart.

Instinctively the great wing-muscles at his back tensed. But only the stumps of his wings moved beneath his pajama jacket. And suddenly he was limp, trembling, aghast at that blind surge of feeling. Why, for a moment he had wanted to go, to leave *Ruth*. The thought appalled him, was like a treachery against himself. He crept back into bed and lay, determinedly shutting his ears to that distant, joyous whistling that fled southward through the night.

The next day he plunged determinedly into his work at the office. But all through that day he found his eyes straying to the window's blue patch of sky. And week by week thereafter, all through the long months of winter and spring, the old wild yearning grew more and more an unreasonable ache inside his heart, stronger than ever when the flying creatures came winging north in spring.

He told himself savagely, "You're a fool. You love Ruth more than anything else on earth and you have her. You don't want anything else."

And again in the sleepless night he would assure himself, "I'm a man, and I'm happy to live a normal man's life, with Ruth."

But in his brain old memories whispered slyly, "Do you remember that first time you flew, that mad thrill of soaring upward for the first time, the first giddy whirl and swoop and glide?"

And the night wind outside the window called, "Remember how you raced with me, beneath the stars and above the sleeping world, and how you laughed and sang as your wings fought me?"

And David Rand buried his face in his pillow and muttered, "I'm *not* sorry I did it. I'm not!"

Ruth awoke and asked sleepily, "Is anything the matter, David?"

"No, dear," he told her, but when she slept again he felt the hot tears stinging his eyelids, and whispered blindly, "I'm lying to myself. I want to fly again."

But from Ruth, happily occupied with his comfort and their home and their friends, he concealed all that blind, buried longing. He fought to conquer it, destroy it, but could not.

When no one else was by, he would watch with aching heart the swallows darting and diving in the sunset, or the hawk soaring high and remote in the blue, or the kingfisher's thrilling swoop. And then bitterly he would accuse himself of being a traitor to his own love for Ruth.

Then that spring Ruth shyly told him something. "David, next fall—a child of ours—"

He was startled. "Ruth, dear!" Then he asked, "You're not afraid that it might be—"

She shook her head confidently. "No. Doctor White says there is no chance that it will be born abnormal as you were. He says that the different gene-characters that caused you to be born with wings are bound to be a recessive character, not a dominant, and that there is no chance of that abnormality being inherited. Aren't you glad?"

"Of course," he said, holding her tenderly. "It's going to be wonderful."

Wilson Hall beamed at the news. "A grandchild—that's fine!" he exclaimed. "David, do you know what I'm going to do after its birth? I'm going to retire and leave you as head of the firm."

"Oh, dad!" cried Ruth, and kissed her father joyfully.

David stammered his thanks. And he told himself that this ended for good all his vague, unreasonable longings. He was going to have more than Ruth to think about now, was going to have the responsibilities of a family man.

He plunged into work with new zest. For a few weeks he did entirely forget that old blind yearning, in his planning for things to come. He was all over that now, he told himself.

Then suddenly his whole being was overturned by an amazing thing. For some time the wing-stumps on David's shoulders had felt sore and painful. Also it seemed they were much larger than they had been. He took occasion to examine them in a mirror and was astounded to discover that they had grown out in two very large hump-like projections that curved downward on each side along his back.

David Rand stared and stared into the mirror, a strange surmise in his eyes. Could it be possible that—"

He called on Doctor White the next day, on another pretext. But before he left he asked casually, "Doctor, I was wondering, is there any chance that my wings would ever start to grow out again?"

Doctor White said thoughtfully, "Why, I suppose there *is* a chance of it, at that. A newt can regenerate a lost limb, you know, and numerous animals have similar powers of regeneration. Of course an ordinary man cannot regenerate a lost arm or leg like that, but your body is not an ordinary one and your wings might possess some power of partial regeneration, for one time at least." He added. "You don't need to worry about it, though, David. If they start to grow out again, just come in and I'll remove them again without any trouble."

David Rand thanked him and left. But day after day thereafter, he closely watched and soon saw beyond doubt that the freak of genes that had given him wings in the first place had also given him at least a partial power of regenerating them.

For the wings were growing out again, day by day. The humps on his shoulders had become very much larger, though covered by his specially tailored coats the change in them was not noticed. They broke through late that summer in wings—real wings, though small as yet. Folded under his clothing, they were not apparent.

David knew that he should go in and let the doctor amputate them before they got larger. He told himself that he did not any longer want wings—Ruth and the coming child and their future together were all that meant anything to him now.

Yet still he did not say anything to anyone, kept the growing wings concealed and closed beneath his clothing. They were poor, weak wings, compared to his first ones, as though stunted by the previous amputation. It was unlikely that he would ever be able to fly with them, he thought, even if he wanted to, which he didn't.

He told himself, though, that it would be easier to have them removed after they had attained their full size. Besides, he didn't want to disturb Ruth at this time by telling her that the wings had grown again. So he reassured himself, and so the weeks passed until by early October his second wings had grown to their full size, though they were stunted and pitiful compared to his first splendid pinions.

On the first week in October, a little son was born to Ruth and David. A fine, strong-limbed little boy, without a trace of anything unusual about him. He was normal of weight, and his back was straight and smooth, and he would never have wings. And a few nights later they were all in the little cottage, admiring him.

"Isn't he beautiful?" asked Ruth, looking up with eyes shining with pride.

David nodded dumbly, his heart throbbing with emotion as he looked down at the red, sleeping mite. His son!

"He's wonderful," he said humbly. "Ruth, dear—I want to work the rest of my life for you and for him."

Wilson Hall beamed on them and chuckled, "You're going to have a chance to do that, David. What I said last spring goes. This afternoon I formally resigned as head of the firm and saw that you were named as my successor."

David tried to thank him. His heart was full with complete happiness, with love for Ruth and for their child. He felt that no one before had ever been so happy.

Then after Wilson Hall had left, and Ruth was sleeping and he was alone, David suddenly realized that there was something he must do.

He told himself sternly, "All these months you've been lying to yourself, making excuses for yourself, letting your wings grow again. In your heart, all that time, you were hoping that you would be able to fly again."

He laughed. "Well, *that's* all over, now. I only told myself before that I didn't want to fly. It wasn't true, then, but it is now. I'll never again long for wings, for flying, now that I have both Ruth and the boy."

No, never again—that was ended. He would drive into town this very night and have Doctor White remove these new-grown second wings. He would never even let Ruth know about them.

Flushed with that resolve, he hurried out of the cottage into the windy darkness of the fall night. The red moon was lifting above the treetops eastward and by its dull light he started back toward the garage. All around him the trees were bending and creaking under the brawling, jovial hammering of the hard north wind.

David stopped suddenly. Down through the frosty night had come a faint, far sound that jerked his head erect. A distant, phantom whistling borne on the rushing wind, rising, falling, growing stronger and stronger—the wild birds, southing through the noisy night, shrilling their exultant challenge as the wind bore their wings onward. That wild throb of freedom that he had thought dead clutched hard of a sudden at David's heart.

He stared up into the darkness with brilliant eyes, hair blowing in the wind. To be up there with them just once again—to fly with them just one more time—"

Why not? Why not fly this one last time and so satisfy that aching longing before he lost these last wings? He would not go far, would make but a short flight and then return to have the wings removed, to devote his life to Ruth and their son. No one would ever know.

Swiftly he stripped off his clothing in the darkness, stood erect, spreading the wings that had been so long concealed and confined. Quaking doubt assailed him. Could he fly at all, now? Would these poor, stunted, second wings even bear him aloft for a few minutes? No, they wouldn't— he knew they wouldn't!

The wild wind roared louder through the groaning trees, the silvery shrilling high overhead came louder. David stood poised, knees bent, wings spread for the leap upward, agony on his white face. He couldn't try it—he knew that he couldn't leave the ground.

But the wind was shouting in his ears, "You can do it, you can fly again! See, I am behind you, waiting to lift you, ready to race you up there under the stars!"

And the exultant, whistling voices high above were shrilling, "Upward—up with us! You belong among us, not down there! Upward—fly!"

He sprang! The stunted wings smote the air wildly, and he was soaring! The dark trees, the lighted window of the cottage, the whole hilltop, dropped behind and below him as his wings bore him upward on the bellowing wind.

Up, up—clean, hard battering of the cold air on his face once more, the crazy roaring of the wind around him, the great thrash of his wings bearing him higher and higher.

David Rand's high, ringing laughter pealed out on the screaming wind as he flew on between the stars and the nighted earth. Higher and higher, right up among the shrilling, southing birds that companioned him on either side. On and on he flew with them.

He knew suddenly that this alone was living, this alone was waking. All that other life that had been his, down there, that had been the dream, and he had awakened from it now. It was not *he* who worked in an office and had loved a woman and a child down there. It was a dream David Rand who had done that, and the dream was over now.

Southward, southward, he rushed through the night, and the wind screamed, and the moon rose higher, until at last the land passed from beneath and he flew with the flying birds over moonlit plains of ocean.

He knew that it was madness to fly on with these poor wings that already were tiring and weakening, but he had no thought in his exultant brain of turning back. To fly on, to fly this one last time, that was enough!

So that when his tired wings began at last to fail, and he began to sink lower and lower toward the silvered waters, there was no fear and no regret in his breast. It was what he had always expected and wanted, at the end, and he was drowsily glad—glad to be falling as all they with wings must finally fall, after a brief lifetime of wild, sweet flight, dropping contentedly to rest.

Exile

I wish now that we hadn't got to talking about science fiction that night! If we hadn't, I wouldn't be haunted now by that queer, impossible story which can't ever be proved or disproved.

But the four of us were all professional writers of fantastic stories, and I suppose shop talk was inevitable. Yet, we'd kept off it through dinner and the drinks afterward. Madison had outlined his hunting trip with gusto, and then Brazell started a discussion of the Dodgers' chances. And then I had to turn the conversation to fantasy.

I didn't mean to do it. But I'd had an extra Scotch, and that always makes me feel analytical. And I got to feeling amused by the perfect way in which we four resembled a quartet of normal, ordinary people.

"Protective coloration, that's what it is," I announced. "How hard we work at the business of acting like ordinary good guys!"

Brazell looked at me, somewhat annoyed by the interruption. "What are you talking about?"

"About us," I answered. "What a wonderful imitation of solid, satisfied citizens we put up! But we're not satisfied, you know—none of us. We're violently dissatisfied with the Earth, and all its works, and that's why we spend our lives dreaming up one imaginary world after another."

"I suppose the little matter of getting paid for it has nothing to do with it?" Brazell asked skeptically.

"Sure it has," I admitted. "But we all dreamed up our impossible worlds and peoples long before we ever wrote a line, didn't we? From back in childhood, even? It's because we don't feel at home here."

Madison snorted. "We'd feel a lot less at home on some of the worlds we write about."

Then Carrick, the fourth of our party, broke into the conversation. He'd been sitting over his drink in his usual silent way, brooding, paying no attention to us.

He was a queer chap, in most ways. We didn't know him very well, but we liked him and admired his stories. He'd done some wonderful tales of an imaginary planet—all carefully worked out.

He told Madison, "That happened to me."

"What happened to you?" Madison asked.

"What you were suggesting—*I* once wrote about an imaginary world and then had to live on it," Carrick answered.

Madison laughed. "I hope it was a more livable place than the lurid planets on which I set my own yarns."

But Carrick was unsmiling. He murmured, "I'd have made it a lot different—if I'd known I was ever going to live on it."

Brazell, with a significant glance at Carrick's empty glass winked at us and then asked blandly, "Let's hear about it, Carrick."

Carrick kept looking dully down at his empty glass, turning it slowly in his fingers as he talked. He paused every few words.

"It happened just after I'd moved next to the big power station. It sounds like a noisy place, but actually it was very quiet out there on the edge of the city. And I had to have quiet, if I was to produce stories.

"I got right to work on a new series I was starting, the stories of which were all to be laid on the same imaginary world. I began by working out the detailed physical appearance of that world, as well as the universe that was its background. I spent the whole day concentrating on that. And, as I finished, something in my mind went *click!*

"That queer, brief mental sensation felt oddly like a sudden *crystallization.* I stood there, wondering if I were going crazy. For I had a sudden strong conviction that it meant that the universe and world I had been dreaming up all day had suddenly crystallized into physical existence somewhere.

"Naturally, I brushed aside the eerie thought and went out and forgot about it. But the next day, the thing happened again. I had spent most of that second day working up the inhabitants of my story world. I'd made them definitely human, but had decided against making them too civilized—for that would exclude the conflict and violence that must form my story.

THE BEST OF EDMOND HAMILTON

"So, I'd made my imaginary world a world whose people were still only half-civilized. I figured out all their cruelties and superstitions. I mentally built up their colorful barbaric cities. And just as I was through—that *click!* echoed sharply in my mind.

"It startled me badly, this second time. For now I felt more strongly than before that queer conviction that my day's dreaming had crystallized into solid reality. I knew it was insane to think that, yet it was an incredible certainty in my mind. I couldn't get rid of it.

"I tried to reason the thing out so that I could dismiss that crazy conviction. If my imagining a world and universe had actually created them, where were they? Certainly not in my own cosmos. It couldn't hold two universes—each completely different from the other.

"But maybe that world and universe of my imagining had crystallized into reality in another and empty cosmos? A cosmos lying in a different dimension from my own? One which had contained only free atoms, formless matter that had not taken on shape until my concentrated thought had somehow stirred it into the forms I dreamed?

"I reasoned along like that, in the queer, dreamlike way in which you apply the rules of logic to impossibilities. How did it come that my imaginings had never crystallized into reality before, but had only just begun to do so? Well, there was a plausible explanation for that. It was the big power station nearby. Some unfathomable freak of energy radiated from it was focusing my concentrated imaginings, as super-amplified force, upon an empty cosmos where they stirred formless matter into the shapes I dreamed.

"Did I believe that? No, I didn't believe it—but I knew it. There is quite a difference between knowledge and belief, as someone said who once pointed out that all men know they will die and none of them believe it. It was like that with me. I realized it was not possible that my imaginary world had come into physical being in a different dimensional cosmos, yet at the same time I was strangely convinced that it had.

"A thought occurred to me that amused and interested me. What if I imagined *myself* in that other world? Would I, too, become physically real in it? I tried it. I sat at my desk, imagining myself as one of the millions of persons in that imaginary world, dreaming up a whole soberly realistic background and family and history for myself over there. And my mind said *click!*"

Carrick paused, still looking down at the empty glass that he twirled slowly between his fingers.

Madison prompted him. "And of course you woke up there, and a beautiful girl was leaning over you, and you asked, 'Where am I?'"

"It wasn't like that," Carrick said dully. "It wasn't like that at all. I woke up in that other world, yes. But it wasn't like a real awakening. I was just suddenly in it.

"I was still myself. But I was the myself I had imagined in that other world. That other me had always lived in it—and so had his ancestors before him. I had worked all that out, you see.

"And I was just as real to myself, in that imaginary world I had created, as I had been in my own. That was the worst part of it. Everything in that half-civilized world was so utterly, common-placely real."

He paused again. "It was queer, at first. I walked out into the streets of those barbaric cities, and looked into the people's faces, and I felt like shouting aloud, 'I imagined you all! You had no existence until I dreamed of you!'

"But I didn't do that. They wouldn't have believed me. To them, I was just an insignificant single member of their race. How could they guess that they and their traditions of long history, their world and their universe, had all been suddenly brought into being by my imagination?

"After my first excitement ebbed, I didn't like the place. I had made it too barbaric. The savage violences and cruelties that had seemed so attractive as material for a story, were ugly and repulsive at first hand. I wanted nothing but to get back to my own world.

"And I couldn't get back! There just wasn't any way. I had had a vague idea that I could imagine myself back into my own world as I had imagined myself into this other one. But it didn't work that way. The freak force that had wrought the miracle didn't work two ways.

"I had a pretty bad time when I realized that I was trapped in that ugly, squalid, barbarian world. I felt like killing myself at first. But I didn't. A man can adapt himself to anything. I adapted myself the best I could to the world I had created."

"What did you do there? What was your position, I mean?" Brazell asked.

Carrick shrugged. "I don't know the crafts or skills of that world I'd brought into being. I had only my own skill—that of story telling."

I began to grin. "You don't mean to say that you started writing fantastic stories?"

He nodded soberly. "I had to. It was all I could do. I wrote stories about my own real world. To those other people my tales were wild imagination—and they liked them."

We chuckled. But Carrick was deadly serious. Madison humored him to the end. "And how did you finally get back home from that other world you'd created?"

"I never did get back home," Carrick said with a heavy sigh.

"Oh, come now," Madison protested lightly. "It's obvious that you got back some time."

Carrick shook his head somberly as he rose to leave. "No, I never got back home," he said soberly. "I'm still here."

Day of Judgment

Hahl froze like a living statue in the moonlit forest as he heard a quick stir in the underbrush just ahead.

He raised his short, heavy spear ready for instant use, and listened. The sighing wind lazily stirred branches and made the dappled moonlight on the ground wave. Then he heard the stir again, this time a little closer.

"One of the Clawed Clan," thought Hahl, wonderingly. "Why is he this far east?"

Hahl looked manlike, but he was not a man. There were no men left on Earth to walk these woods.

He was a stocky, erect figure whose body was covered with long brown hair. His head was not anthropoid but with a curiously elongated skull in whose dark muzzle-face his bright eyes gleamed watchfully.

Long white teeth showed as he breathed quickly, his pink tongue flashing. Despite his erect posture, spear and hide girdle, there was something very doglike about him.

Nor was that strange, for Hahl's people, the Hairy Clan, had been true canine quadrupeds not many generations before.

A hissing, whining voice suddenly called to him out of the thick underbrush ahead.

"Who comes? Greeting and peace from S'San of the Clawed Clan!"

Hahl answered, "Hahl of the Hairy Clan! Greeting and peace!"

At the reassuring formula, there emerged quickly from the brush the possessor of that hissing, challenging voice.

S'San of the Clawed Clan was also erect and manlike but he was as obviously of feline ancestry as Hahl was of canine.

His smooth-furred, tawny figure, sharp-pricked ears, luminous green eyes and taloned hands and feet were eloquent of his descent from the great cats of the previous age.

These two spoke quickly together in the meager tongue used by all the forest clans, though it sounded differently in S'San's hissing voice than in Hahl's short, barking accents.

"You venture far east, brother!" Hahl was saying in surprise. "I expected to meet no one this near the great water."

"I have been far east, indeed!" exclaimed S'San. "I bring news of wonder from the place of Crying Stones!"

Hahl was dumbfounded by amazement. If there was one place in all these forests that the Clans never approached, it was the Crying Stones.

That weird place by the sea was haunted—haunted by memory of ancient horror and fear. Even Hahl had only dared look upon it from a great distance.

"You have been to the Crying Stones?" he repeated, staring wonderingly at S'San.

The cat-man's green eyes flashed. "Only to the northern ridges, but from there I could see clearly. It was earlier tonight. The stones were not crying, so I dared approach that close.

"Then, as I watched, I saw a terrible thing happen. A star fell from the sky toward the Crying Stones! It fell quite slowly, flaming very bright, until it rested amid the stones. But resting there, it still shone. I hastened to bring the news to all the Clans!"

Hahl's deep brown eyes were wide with wonder. "A star falling from the sky? What does it mean? Does it mean that the world will burn up again?"

"I do not know," muttered S'San. "But others may know. Trondor of the Hoofed Clan is wisest of us all. Let us take this news to him."

"First, I must see this fallen star for myself!" Hahl declared.

The cat-man showed reluctance. "It is a long way back to the Crying Stones. It would take us hours."

Hahl argued, "Unless another than yourself sees it, the Clans may not believe you."

That argument won over S'San. "I will go back with you. We can follow back my own trail."

Silently as shadows, the two dissimilar figures started in a run through the moonlit forest. The springy bounds of the cat-man and the shorter, loping strides of Hahl carried them forward at an even, easy pace.

The forest was stirring about them to the rising wind, the patter of checkered shade and moonlight dancing and wavering. From far away to the west, the wind brought them once the faint echoes of a deep-voiced hunting-call.

Hahl's keen senses perceived every sigh and sound as they ran, but his thoughts were wrapped in wonder. He had always been deeply, if fearfully, interested in the Crying Stones. And now this marvel—a star falling upon them from the sky!

They changed direction, moving southward now through the forest. Presently they came to an open ridge from which they could look far southward in the moonlight.

S'San halted, pointed with his taloned hand. "Look! The star still shines!"

Hahl peered frozenly. "It is true! A star shining upon the ground!"

They were looking southward along a long, narrow island enclosed by arms of the moonlit sea. The island bore scattered trees and brush, but most of it was heaped with queerly geometrical masses of blackened, blasted stone.

A long way southward there was an oblong open space amid the rectangular masses of blackened stone, and from there shone a brilliant light that was indeed like a bright star fallen from the sky.

As Hahl and S'San peered, the west wind strengthened. And as it blew through those towering masses of shattered black stone, there came through the moonlight the mournful, swelling, wailing sound that had given this place its name.

S'San crouched tensely with hair bristling, and Hahl gripped his spear more tightly as that wailing anthem smote their ears.

"The stones cry out again!" whispered the cat-man. "Let us return!"

But Hahl remained rooted. "I am going down there! I must see that star more closely."

It took all his courage to make and announce the decision. Only his intense interest in the shining wonder down there overcame his instinctive dread of this place.

"Go into the Crying Stones? Are you mad?" demanded S'San. "This place is still cursed with the evil of the Strange Ones!"

Hahl shivered slightly, and almost forsook his intention. But he summoned his courage.

"The Strange Ones have been dead a long time, and cannot harm us now. You can wait here until I return."

Instantly, pride flared into S'San's green eyes. "Shall the Hairy Clan venture where the Clawed Clan dares not? I go with you into this madness."

Madness indeed it seemed to Hahl's whirling mind as he and the cat-man began their tense journey down into the somber place.

The ancient horror of the Strange Ones had risen to grip him. Old, old in all the forest clans, was that deep horror. Even though the Strange Ones had vanished from Earth in the catastrophe of long ago, the dread of them still haunted the forest folk.

And this weird place of towering, blackened stones that cried to the wind had been the lair of the Strange Ones before they and the old age ended. Tradition of that had kept this spot shunned always.

Yet Hahl went on, driven by his eager interest, and the cat-man's pride kept him with him. They came to the narrow river that bounded the northern end of the island. Hahl plunged in and swam strongly. S'San, with all his Clan's aversion to water, followed gingerly.

They clambered ashore and now were among the Crying Stones. Gaunt, mournful in the moonlight, rose the blackened, shattered masses that wailed so heartbreakingly in the wind.

"This trail leads straight south toward the place where the star shines," Hahl murmured. "We can get very close."

The trail was straighter than any forest trail, and was intersected and paralleled by other straight trails through the stones.

Louder, louder, rose the wail of wind among the looming stone masses, deep and solemn as a requiem. Hahl felt the hair on his back lifting to the sound.

They entered the oblong clearing in which were no masses of stone. Through the trees, the star upon the ground shone very brilliantly as they stole toward it. They finally crouched in a thicket only a spear-cast from it.

"It is no star!" whispered S'San, amazedly. "But what is it?"

"I do not know," Hahl murmured, staring. "I have seen nothing like it."

The object at which they stared was clearly visible in the bright moonlight. It glinted metallically, a big thing like an elongated egg whose sides were scarred and battered. It was so large that it bulked as high as the smaller trees.

240

Hahl perceived that the brilliant, star-like light came from an opening in the side of the metal bulk. Then his keen ears caught a slight sound.

"There is someone inside the thing!" he told S'San in a tense whisper.

"There could not be!" the cat-man protested. "None in all the Clans would dare enter such a—"

"Listen!" murmured Hahl. "Whoever it is, is coming out!"

They crouched, watching. A figure appeared in the lighted opening, slowly emerging.

It was not one of the forest folk, that erect figure. It was shaped much like Hahl and S'San, but its body was covered by close-fitting garments, its head was different, its face pink, flat and hairless.

"By the Sun!" whispered S'San, quivering wildly. "It is one of the Strange Ones of long ago!"

Hahl felt frozen by horror. "The Strange Ones who burned up the world! They've returned!"

Stupefaction held the two. All their lives, the tradition of the mad Strange Ones of the past who had almost destroyed the world before they destroyed themselves, had been told by the Clans.

It had been a terror of long ago, a dim tale of ancient dread. But now, suddenly, that terror was real.

Hahl watched, shivering. The Strange One there in the moonlight was acting queerly. He stood, looking at the somber black masses of stone that rose in the moonlight, listening to the wailing wind.

Then the Strange One hid his face in hands. A low sound came from him.

"He is weeping," whispered Hahl, incredulously.

"There is another—a she!" hissed S'San.

A second Strange One, a softer female figure, had come out of the big metal object. She put an arm around the weeping man.

"Quick, we must escape from here and warn the Clans!" whispered S'San tautly.

Hahl started to back with him through the thicket. But in his stupefied state of mind, he forgot to place his feet carefully.

A twig snapped. The man out in the moonlight jerked up his head, and swiftly drew a metal tube from his belt.

"Run for it!" cried S'San instantly.

The two plunged out of the thicket. At sight of them, the man and woman in the moonlight cried out in terror and the man levelled his tube.

A flash of light darted from it and struck both the fleeing two. Hahl felt a violent shock, then darkness.

Hahl awoke with sunlight on his face. He stirred and sat up, then uttered a howling cry of surprise and dismay.

He was in a small room with metal walls, its doorway closed by heavy wire netting. S'San was just awaking also, beside him.

"We are in the big metal thing of the Strange Ones!" cried Hahl. "They stunned us, captured us!"

S'San's feline rage exploded. The cat-man hurled himself at the netting, clawing furiously. Hahl joined him.

In both of them was the violent repulsion of free forest folk who found themselves for the first time trapped and prisoned.

"I knew when we saw the Strange Ones that they had come back to bring more evil to the world!" raged S'San.

He and Hahl suddenly stopped their vain attack on the netting and crouched back. The two Strange Ones had appeared outside the barrier.

The man and woman seemed young. They stood, looking in apparent wonder at the two dissimilar captives, the hairy dog-man and his blazing-eyed companion of the Clawed Clan.

"They will kill us now!" hissed S'San. "They always brought death, wherever they went."

"They do not *look* so cruel," Hahl said uncertainly.

For Hahl, despite his dread, could not feel the hatred and rage toward their captors that the cat-man did. Something deep in Hahl tugged strangely at his spirit as he stared at the Strange Ones.

The man outside the netting spoke to the woman. Hahl could not understand. But the sound of the voice somehow soothed him.

Food was brought and put through a hole in the barrier. S'San furiously refused it at first. But after a time, he too ate of it.

The Strange Ones then began earnestly to speak to the two prisoners. They held up pictures of various objects, and asked questions.

Hahl slowly understood. "They seek to learn our language so they can talk to us."

"Have nothing to do with them!" S'San warned distrustfully. "They have evil in their minds."

"It can do no harm to teach them how we speak," Hahl defended. "Then maybe they would let us go."

He began to answer the questions of the Strange Ones, by naming for them in the language of the forest Clans the simple pictured objects and actions.

Several days of this imprisonment passed, as Hahl patiently repeated words for the two Strange Ones. By now, he had learned that the names of the man and woman were "Blaine" and "Myra." S'San still remained stubbornly silent, crouching and watching in hate.

Then came an evening on which the Strange Ones had learned the language of the Clans enough to speak it. For the man Blaine spoke to Hahl in his own tongue.

"Who are you two?" he asked the dog-man. "What has happened to Earth?"

"We are of the Clans," Hahl answered hesitantly. "But from where did *you* come? Long ago, all the Strange Ones perished from Earth."

"Strange Ones—you mean men and women?" Blaine said. Then his face paled. "You mean that all mankind is gone from Earth?"

"It happened in the days of my forefathers, many summers ago," Hahl answered. "Then, so the tale runs, the world was different. There were hosts of Strange Ones who dwelt in mighty lairs, who wielded the powers of thunder and lightning, and who ruled the world.

"*Our* forefathers, the forefathers of our Clans, were not then like us. They ran upon four feet, nor could they speak or do the other things we can do. The Strange Ones killed them, and enslaved them, and even massacred them for sport.

"But finally came the day when the world burned. The tale says that the Strange Ones loosed their lightning powers upon each other! Awful thunder-fires raged across the world! All the Strange Ones and their mighty lairs perished when the world burned thus. Our own forefathers' four-footed races mostly perished also, but a few here and there in deep forests and mountains survived.

"But the thunder-fires had somehow changed these survivors. For when they later gave birth to young, the young were new and different races. They were like us, no longer four-footed, no longer dim of mind, but able to stand erect and to learn speech and skills. And we of the forest Clans have remained thus in the generations since then."

"Good God!" whispered Blaine. "An atomic war—it finally came, and wiped out mankind and its cities!"

His face was dead white as he looked at the girl. "Myra, we two are the last humans left alive."

She pressed his hand. "At least our race is not dead yet! You and I—the race will start from us again!"

S'San, crouched behind Hahl, raised his head and his flaring green eyes blazed at them.

The girl Myra looked incredulously at Hahl and S'San. "But how could that awful disaster change four-footed animals to manlike, intelligent races?"

"We do not know," answered Hahl. "It was something in the terrible magic of the thunder-fires."

"Sudden mutation," muttered Blaine. "Atomic explosions on that scale of that holocaust, drenching all surviving animal life with hard radiation, so altered the gene-patterns as to cause a sudden evolutionary spurt."

Hahl was looking wonderingly at the man and girl. "But from where did *you* come? We believed all the Strange Ones dead."

Blaine pointed heavily upward. "We came from another world, a world far up in the sky called Venus. Generations ago, some of our human race went there to start a colony.

"But after a little time, no more ships came from Earth. Without supplies, the colony withered. Storms and other disasters had damaged the colony's own few ships beyond use, and vainly it waited for word from Earth that never came.

"Finally, Myra and I were the last born of the dwindling colonists. We grew up, knowing ourselves doomed unless we could repair one of the old ships enough to get back to Earth. And we finally succeeded, and came back. We came back to find—*this!*"

His voice shook and his hand trembled as he gestured toward the distant masses of blackened stone looming in the sunset outside.

"This, then, is why Earth never sent more ships to its dying colony! Earth's humans had perished, self-slain in atomic war!"

Hahl had only dimly followed what the man Blaine told. But somehow, the emotion of the man and girl troubled Hahl.

Myra was looking at Blaine, her face white but brave.

"It can all start again, from us," she said. "It must, since we are the last."

Hahl asked them, "Are you going to kill S'San and myself?"

"Kill you?" Blaine seemed startled. "No! When we first glimpsed you and stunned you with a force-beam, we thought you prowling wild beasts about to attack. But when we looked at you and saw you must be intelligent creatures, we wanted only to detain and question you."

He reached in his pocket and brought forth a key. "You two are free to go now."

Hahl's heart bounded as the heavy wire door opened. He stepped out, following the man and girl down the narrow corridor to the door opening out into the sunset.

S'San, eyes flaring green fire, whispered swiftly to Hahl as he stalked along the corridor with him.

"Now is our chance, Hahl! We can slay them before he can draw the weapon! Spring with me when they reach the door!"

Hahl felt a wild revulsion. "But we can't do that! We can't slay *them!*"

"They are Strange Ones!" hissed S'San. "They will start once more the evil race that will again bring terror to the world! We can save the Clans from that by slaying. Spring—*now!*"

And with the hissed word, the cat-man launched himself in a lightning leap at the man who had just emerged behind the girl into the open air.

Instincts undreamed of until this moment exploded in Hahl's brain. He did not know why, but he could not let the Strange Ones be killed. Somehow, they were *his* Strange Ones!

Hahl uttered a yelping cry as he hurled himself only a split-second after the catman. Blaine whirled, startled, as Hahl's hairy body hit S'San and sent him rolling over and over outside.

"Myra, get back!" yelled Blaine. "The creatures are—"

He had whipped out his metal weapon but he stood without using it, astounded.

Hahl stood in front of the man and girl, all his rough hair bristling, as he glared at the raging cat-man, who had regained his feet with inconceivable swiftness a few yards away.

"Clan-truce is broken if you seek to slay these Strange Ones!" cried Hahl. "You will have to slay me first!"

"You are traitor to the Clans!" hissed S'San. "But the Clans themselves shall swiftly bring death to these evil ones!"

And with a lightning bound, the cat-man was gone into the thickets, racing away northward amid the black Crying Stones.

The man and girl were looking at Hahl in wonder.

"Hahl, you saved us from your comrade. Why did you?" Blaine asked.

Hahl squirmed uncomfortably. "I do not know. I could not let him harm you."

Blaine's face strangely softened, and he put his hand on the dog-man's hairy shoulder.

"Hahl, only one race among the creatures in the old age was man's loyal friend," he said huskily. "The race from which you are descended."

Hahl's heart swelled at the touch of the hand on his shoulder, and he felt a queer, new happiness.

From far out in the darkening twilight came the echoes of a screaming call.

"Send the Clan-call through all the forests!" echoed S'San's distant cry. "Strange Ones have returned! Gather the Clans!"

Hahl whirled to the man and girl. "The Clans will gather here quickly! They will come in hosts, and you must escape or they will kill you lest you burn up the world as the other Strange Ones did long ago."

Blaine shook his head helplessly. "We cannot escape. The power of our ship is exhausted. And there is not enough power left in my weapon to stand off a horde."

The girl looked at him, white face strained in the gathering darkness. "Then this is the end of us? Of our race?"

From far out in the night, S'San's Clan-call was faintly repeated, carried across the dark forests north and south and west.

Hahl's mind was in a fever of torment as helplessly they waited. The man and girl who now stood close together, speaking in low whispers— they were *his*, and he must somehow save them. But how?

The moon rose, a full orb casting a silver effulgence on the somber dead city. And as the night wind wailed mournfully louder through the Crying Stones, Hahl's keen ears caught other sounds, his eyes glimpsed dark shapes surging southward through the ruins.

"They are coming! All the Clans of the forest come to kill you!" he warned agonizedly.

Blaine stood in the moonlight, the girl in the circle of his arm, looking heavily northward.

"You can do nothing more for us, Hahl. Get away from here, and save yourself."

Hahl sensed the gathering of the Clans around the clearing. He knew that only this dire emergency would have brought them into the shunned and accursed place of Crying Stones.

The Clawed Clan of S'San was there, cat-eyes gleaming greenly in the dark. His own Hairy Clan, hosts of dog-men, were staring at him in amazement. The Furred Clan's bear-like horde, the Fox-Folk peering sharply—all the forest folk had come.

Last, came the Hoofed Clan, ponderous, towering, manlike, but their hoofed feet and stiff, horny hands and massive maned heads betraying the equine ancestors of whom they were an evolution.

S'San's hissing voice ripped the tense silence as the cat-man bounded out into the moonlit clearing.

"Did I lie, Clan-brothers? Are they not two Strange Ones such as worked evil long ago?"

The deep, rumbling voice of Trondor, leader of the Hoofed Clan, answered from the darkness.

"You have told truth, S'San. These are indeed two of that terrible race whom we thought dead."

"Then slay them!" raged a feline voice in the shadows. "Kill, before they again burn up the world!"

There was a surging movement of the shadowy hordes out into the moonlight where Blaine stood with Myra clinging to his side.

Hahl uttered a furious howling cry, and flung himself protectively in front of the man and girl. Eyes flaring red, sharp teeth bared, Hahl cried to the advancing horde.

"Forest-folk, is this the justice of the Clans? To condemn these two without even a hearing?"

"They are Strange Ones!" hissed S'San. "They darkened the world for ages and finally almost destroyed it. Let them die!"

"Kill them thus without hearing, and you will need to kill me first!" raged Hahl.

From his own folk, from the masses of the Hairy Clan, there came a low whine of sympathy.

"Perhaps we do not need to kill these Strange Ones when there are only two?" muttered one of the dog-men.

Big Trondor spoke in his deep voice. "You say that because you of the Hairy Clan are still haunted by an old loyalty to the Strange Ones."

The Hoofed One slowly added, "But Hahl is right, when he says that we Clans condemn none without a hearing. Let the Strange One defend himself and his race from death-sentence, if he can!"

Blaine had been listening, and had understood. Now he put the girl behind him and stepped forth in front of Hahl.

In the moonlight, the white-faced man faced the crouched masses of the hordes with his head erect and voice steady.

"Clans of the forest, since in us our race is ending, I will speak for all of my race who went before us.

"We men came of the forest-folk long ago, even as you, though our pride grew so great that we forget that fact. Yes, long and long ago we sprang from soft-skinned, weak, fumbling creatures of the forest world, creatures that had no claws or strength or swiftness.

"But one thing those creatures had, and that was curiosity. And curiosity was the key that unlocked for them the hidden powers of nature, so that they grew strong. So strong we grew, so great we deemed ourselves, that we thought ourselves a different order of beings and oppressed and tyrannized the other creatures of Earth.

"Yet for all the powers our curiosity had gathered for us, we remained in mind and heart close kin to the simple forest-creatures from which we came. Is it wonderful then that we could not handle those powers wisely? Is it wonderful that when we finally thefted the fires of the sun itself, we misused them and wrecked the world?

"Yet, forest-races, are you so sure that any of *your* Clans would have handled such powers more wisely?"

Blaine paused for a moment before his heavy voice concluded.

"But I know that that is scant excuse for the evil we did. It is yours to judge. If your judgment be against us, let the stars look down tonight on the ending of our race. Let finis be written to the terrible and wonderful story of the apes who dared lay hands on the sun, and who greatly rose and fell. And let your new forest races learn from our failure and try to do better than we."

There was a long, hushed silence among the moonlit hosts of the Clans, as Blaine's voice ceased.

Then Hahl heard the deep voice of Trondor rumble from the shadows.

"Clan-brothers all, you have heard the Strange One. Now what is your judgment on him and on his race?"

No voice answered for a moment. And then a dark figure among the bearlike Furred Clan spoke.

"Judge you for us, Trondor. You are the wisest of the Clans."

The man and girl, and Hahl who still stood defiantly in front of them in the moonlight, waited tensely.

Trondor's rumbling voice came slowly. "What the Strange One has said is true, that his race were but forest-folk like ourselves long ago. We had forgotten that, as they forgot it. It may be that with their powers, we would have been no wiser.

"The world has changed now. And it seems that the Strange Ones have changed too, and have learned. If they have, there is room in the world for them and our own new races to live in friendship."

Blaine spoke huskily. "I can promise, for ourselves. The world has changed, as you say. What powers are devised in future must be handled for the good of all our races. I think the world will not burn again."

Trondor flung up his massive maned head, and his voice rang loud.

"Then it is my judgment that we give Clan-brotherhood to the Strange Ones! That an old and blind world be forgotten in new friendship and peace!"

Swiftly, from the eager hosts of the Hairy Clan, came the yelped greetings of Hahl's brothers.

"Clan of the Strange Ones, greeting and peace!"

Clan-greeting from the Furred Ones, from the Fox-Folk, from the Hoofed Ones, echoed deafeningly through the moonlight.

Last of all, a little sulkily but with the blaze of hatred gone from his green eyes, S'San spoke.

"Greeting and peace from the Clawed Clan, Strange Ones!"

"The moon sinks, now let the Clans depart," Trondor rumbled. "But we will return, Strange Ones. This place is no longer cursed."

Blaine and Myra watched as the hosts departed. But when all had gone, Hahl still remained.

"I would like to stay with you," he said slowly. And he added hopefully, "I would be your servant."

Blaine gripped his hairy arm. "No, Hahl—master and servant no longer, but friend and friend now. In this new world where all now are friends, our tie is oldest and deepest."

From far out in the darkness echoed the last Clan-call of the separating hosts. And the wailing of the Crying Stones seemed to die into peace, as the wind sank and dawn glimmered slowly across the world.

Alien Earth

CHAPTER ONE
SLOWED-DOWN LIFE

The dead man was standing in a little moonlit clearing in the jungle when Farris found him.

He was a small swart man in white cotton, a typical Laos tribesman of this Indo-China hinterland. He stood without support, eyes open, staring unwinkingly ahead, one foot slightly raised. And he was not breathing.

"But he can't be dead!" Farris exclaimed. "Dead men don't stand around in the jungle."

He was interrupted by Piang, his guide. That cocksure little Annamese had been losing his impudent self-sufficiency ever since they had wandered off the trail. And the motionless, standing dead man had completed his demoralization.

Ever since the two of them had stumbled into this grove of silk-cotton trees and almost run into the dead man, Piang had been goggling in a scared way at the still unmoving figure. Now he burst out volubly:

"The man is *hunati!* Don't touch him! We must leave here—we have strayed into a bad part of the jungle!"

Farris didn't budge. He had been a teak-hunter for too many years to be entirely skeptical of the superstitions of Southeast Asia. But, on the other hand, he felt a certain responsibility.

"If this man isn't really dead, then he's in bad shape somehow and needs help," he declared.

"No, no!" Piang insisted. "He is *hunati!* Let us leave here quickly!"

Pale with fright, he looked around the moonlit grove. They were on a low plateau where the jungle was monsoon-forest rather than rain-forest. The big silk-cotton and ficus trees were less choked with brush and creepers here, and they could see along dim forest aisles to gigantic distant banyans that loomed like dark lords of the silver silence.

Silence. There was too much of it to be quite natural. They could faintly hear the usual clatter of birds and monkeys from down in the lowland thickets, and the cough of a tiger echoed from the Laos foothills. But the thick forest here on the plateau was hushed.

Farris went to the motionless, staring tribesman and gently touched his thin brown wrist. For a few moments, he felt no pulse. Then he caught its throb—an incredibly slow beating.

"About one beat every two minutes," Farris muttered. "How the devil can he keep living?"

He watched the man's bare chest. It rose—but so slowly that his eye could hardly detect the motion. It remained expanded for minutes. Then, as slowly, it fell again.

He took his pocket-light and flashed it into the tribesman's eyes.

There was no reaction to the light, not at first. Then, slowly, the eyelids crept down and closed, and stayed closed, and finally crept open again.

"A wink—but a hundred times slower than normal!" Farris exclaimed. "Pulse, respiration, reactions—they're all a hundred times slower. The man has either suffered a shock, or been drugged."

Then he noticed something that gave him a little chill.

The tribesman's eyeball seemed to be turning with infinite slowness toward him. And the man's raised foot was a little higher now. As though he were walking—but walking at a pace a hundred times slower than normal.

The thing was eery. There came something more eery. A sound—the sound of a small stick cracking.

Piang exhaled breath in a sound of pure fright, and pointed off into the grove. In the moonlight Farris saw.

There was another tribesman standing a hundred feet away. He, too, was motionless. But his body was bent forward in the attitude of a runner suddenly frozen. And beneath his foot, the stick had cracked.

"They worship the great ones, by the Change!" said the Annamese in a hoarse undertone. "We must not interfere!"

That decided Farris. He had, apparently, stumbled on some sort of weird jungle rite. And he had had too much experience with Asiatic natives to want to blunder into their private religious mysteries.

His business here in easternmost Indo-China was teak-hunting. It would be difficult enough back in this wild hinterland without antagonizing the tribes. These strangely dead-alive men, whatever drug or compulsion they were suffering from, could not be in danger if others were near.

"We'll go on," Farris said shortly.

Piang led hastily down the slope of the forested plateau. He went through the brush like a scared deer, till they hit the trail again.

"This is it—the path to the Government station," he said, in great relief. "We must have lost it back at the ravine. I have not been this far back in Laos, many times."

Farris asked, "Piang, what is *hunati?* This Change that you were talking about?"

The guide became instantly less voluble. "It is a rite of worship." He added, with some return of his cocksureness, "These tribesmen are very ignorant. They have not been to mission school, as I have."

"Worship of what?" Farris asked. "The great ones, you said. Who are they?"

Piang shrugged and lied readily. "I do not know. In all the great forest, there are men who can become *hunati*, it is said. How, I do not know."

Farris pondered, as he tramped onward. There had been something uncanny about those tribesmen. It had been almost a suspension of animation—but not quite. Only an incredible slowing down.

What could have caused it? And what, possibly, could be the purpose of it?

"I should think," he said, "that a tiger or snake would make short work of a man in that frozen condition."

Piang shook his head vigorously. "No. A man who is *hunati* is safe—at least, from beasts. No beast would touch him."

Farris wondered. Was that because the extreme motionlessness made the beasts ignore them? He supposed that it was some kind of fear-ridden nature-worship. Such animistic beliefs were common in this part of the world. And it was small wonder, Farris thought a little grimly. Nature, here in the tropical forest, wasn't the smiling goddess of temperate lands. It was something, not to be loved, but to be feared.

He ought to know! He had had two days of the Laos jungle since leaving the upper Mekong, when he had expected that someone would take him to the French Government botanic survey station that was his goal.

He brushed stinging winged ants from his sweating neck, and wished that they had stopped at sunset. But the map had showed them but a few miles from the Station. He had not counted on Piang losing the trail. But he should have, for it was only a wretched track that wound along the forested slope of the plateau.

The hundred-foot ficus, dyewood , and silk-cotton trees smothered the moonlight. The track twisted constantly to avoid impenetrable bamboo-hells or to ford small streams, and the tangle of creepers and vines had a devilish deftness at tripping one in the dark.

Farris wondered if they had lost their way again. And he wondered not for the first time, why he had ever left America to go into teak.

"That is the Station," said Piang suddenly, in obvious relief.

Just ahead of them on the jungled slope was a flat ledge. Light shone there, from the windows of a rambling bamboo bungalow.

Farris became conscious of all his accumulated weariness, as he went the last few yards. He wondered whether he could get a decent bed here, and what kind of chap this Berreau might be who had chosen to bury himself in such a Godforsaken post of the botanical survey.

The bamboo house was surrounded by tall, graceful dyewoods. But the moonlight showed a garden around it, enclosed by a low sappan hedge.

A voice from the dark veranda reached Farris and startled him. It startled him because it was a girl's voice, speaking in French.

"Please, Andre! Don't go again! It is madness!"

A man's voice rapped harsh answer, *"Lys, tais-toi! Je reviendrai—"*

Farris coughed diplomatically and then said up to the darkness of the veranda, "Monsieur Berreau?"

There was a dead silence. Then the door of the house was swung open so that light spilled out on Ferris and his guide.

By the light, Farris saw a man of thirty, bareheaded, in whites—a thin, rigid figure. The girl was only a white blur in the gloom.

He climbed the steps. "I suppose you don't get many visitors. My name is Hugh Farris. I have a letter for you, from the Bureau at Saigon."

There was a pause. Then, "If you will come inside, M'sieu Farris—"

In the lamplit, bamboo-walled living room, Farris glanced quickly at the two.

Berreau looked to his experienced eye like a man who had stayed too long in the tropics—his blond handsomeness tarnished by a corroding climate, his eyes too feverishly restless.

"My sister, Lys," he said, as he took the letter Farris handed.

Farris' surprise increased. A wife, he had supposed until now. Why should a girl under thirty bury herself in this wilderness?

He wasn't surprised that she looked unhappy. She might have been a decently pretty girl, he thought, if she didn't have that woebegone anxious look.

"Will you have a drink?" she asked him. And then, glancing with swift anxiety at her brother. "You'll not be going now, Andre?"

Berreau looked out at the moonlit forest, and a queer, hungry tautness showed his cheekbones in a way Farris didn't like. But the Frenchman turned back.

"No, Lys. And drinks, please. Then tell Ahra to care for his guide."

He read the letter swiftly, as Farris sank with a sigh into a rattan chair. He looked up from it with troubled eyes.

"So you come for teak?"

Farris nodded. "Only to spot and girdle trees. They have to stand a few years then before cutting, you know."

Berreau said, "The Commissioner writes that I am to give you every assistance. He explains the necessity of opening up new teak cuttings."

He slowly folded the letter. It was obvious, Farris thought, that the man did not like it, but had to make the best of orders.

"I shall do everything possible to help," Berreau promised. "You'll want a native crew, I suppose. I can get one for you." Then a queer look filmed his eyes. "But there are some forests here that are impracticable for lumbering. I'll go into that later."

Farris, feeling every moment more exhausted by the long tramp, was grateful for the rum and soda Lys handed him.

"We have a small extra room—I think it will be comfortable," she murmured.

He thanked her. "I could sleep on a log, I'm so tired. My muscles are as stiff as though I were *hunati* myself."

Berreau's glass dropped with a sudden crash.

CHAPTER TWO
SORCERY OF SCIENCE

Ignoring the shattered glass, the young Frenchman strode quickly toward Farris.

"What do you know of *hunati?*" he asked harshly.

Farris saw with astonishment that the man's hands were shaking.

"I don't know anything except what we saw in the forest. We came upon a man standing in the moonlight who looked dead, and wasn't. He just seemed incredibly slowed down. Piang said he was *hunati*."

A flash crossed Berreau's eyes. He exclaimed, "I knew the Rite would be called! And the others are there—"

He checked himself. It was as though the unaccustomedness of strangers had made him for a moment forget Farris' presence.

Lys' blonde head drooped. She looked away from Farris.

"You were saying?" the American prompted.

But Berreau had tightened up. He chose his words now. "The Laos tribes have some queer beliefs, M'sieu Farris. They're a little hard to understand."

Farris shrugged. "I've seen some queer Asian witchcraft, in my time. But this is unbelievable!"

"It is science, not witchcraft," Berreau corrected. "Primitive science, born long ago and transmitted by tradition. That man you saw in the forest was under the influence of a chemical not found in our pharmacopeia, but none the less potent."

"You mean that these tribesmen have a drug that can slow the life-process to that incredibly slow tempo?" Farris asked skeptically. "One that modern science doesn't know about?"

"Is that so strange? Remember, M'sieu Farris, that a century ago an old peasant woman in England was curing heart-disease with foxglove, before a physician studied her cure and discovered digitalis."

"But why on earth would even a Laos tribesman want to live so much *slower*?" Farris demanded.

"Because," Berreau answered, "they believe that in that state they can commune with something vastly greater than themselves."

Lys interrupted. "M'sieu Farris must be very weary. And his bed is ready."

Farris saw the nervous fear in her face, and realized that she wanted to end this conversation.

He wondered about Berreau, before he dropped off to sleep. There was something odd about the chap. He had been too excited about this *hunati* business.

Yet that was weird enough to upset anyone, that incredible and uncanny slowing-down of a human being's life-tempo. "To commune with something vastly greater than themselves," Berreau had said.

What gods were so strange that a man must live a hundred times slower than normal, to commune with them?

Next morning, he breakfasted with Lys on the broad veranda. The girl told him that her brother had already gone out.

"He will take you later today to the tribal village down in the valley, to arrange for your workers," she said.

Farris noted the faint unhappiness still in her face. She looked silently at the great, green ocean of forest that stretched away below this plateau on whose slope they were.

"You don't like the forest?" he ventured.

"I hate it," she said. "It smothers one, here."

Why, he asked, didn't she leave? The girl shrugged.

"I shall, soon. It is useless to stay. Andre will not go back with me."

She explained. "He has been here five years too long. When he didn't return to France, I came out to bring him. But he won't go. He has ties here now."

Again, she became abruptly silent. Farris discreetly refrained from asking her what ties she meant. There might be an Annamese woman in the background—though Berreau didn't look that type.

The day settled down to the job of being stickily tropical, and the hot still hours of the morning wore on. Farris, sprawling in a chair and getting a welcome rest, waited for Berreau to return.

He didn't return. And as the afternoon waned, Lys looked more and more worried.

An hour before sunset, she came out onto the veranda, dressed in slacks and jacket.

"I am going down to the village—I'll be back soon," she told Farris.

She was a poor liar. Farris got to his feet. "You're going after your brother. Where is he?"

Distress and doubt struggled in her face. She remained silent.

"Believe me, I want to be a friend," Farris said quietly. "Your brother is mixed up in something here, isn't he?"

She nodded, white-faced. "It's why he wouldn't go back to France with me. He can't bring himself to leave. It's like a horrible fascinating vice."

"What is?"

She shook her head. "I can't tell you. Please wait here."

He watched her leave, and then realized she was not going down the slope but up it—up toward the top of the forested plateau.

He caught up to her in quick strides. "You can't go up into that forest alone, in a blind search for him."

"It's not a blind search. I think I know where he is," Lys whispered. "But you should not go there. The tribesmen wouldn't like it!"

Farris instantly understood. "That big grove up on top of the plateau, where we found the *hunati* natives?"

Her unhappy silence was answer enough. "Go back to the bungalow," he told her. "I'll find him."

She would not do that. Farris shrugged, and started forward. "Then we'll go together."

She hesitated, then came on. They went up the slope of the plateau, through the forest.

The westering sun sent spears and arrows of burning gold through chinks in the vast canopy of foliage under which they walked. The solid green of the forest breathed a rank, hot exhalation. Even the birds and monkeys were stifledly quiet at this hour.

"Is Berreau mixed up in that queer *hunati* rite?" Farris asked.

Lys looked up as though to utter a quick denial, but then dropped her eyes.

"Yes, in a way. His passion for botany got him interested in it. Now he's involved."

Farris was puzzled. "Why should botanical interest draw a man to that crazy drug-rite or whatever it is?"

She wouldn't answer that. She walked in silence until they reached the top of the forested plateau. Then she spoke in a whisper.

"We must be quiet now. It will be bad if we are seen here."

The grove that covered the plateau was pierced by horizontal bars of red sunset light. The great silk-cottons and ficus trees were pillars supporting a vast cathedral-nave of darkening green.

A little way ahead loomed up those huge, monster banyans he had glimpsed before in the moonlight. They dwarfed all the rest, towering bulks that were infinitely ancient and infinitely majestic.

Farris suddenly saw a Laos tribesman, a small brown figure, in the brush ten yards ahead of him. There were two others, farther in the distance. And they were all standing quite still, facing away from him.

They were *hunati*, he knew. In that queer state of slowed-down life, that incredible retardation of the vital processes.

Farris felt a chill. He muttered over his shoulder, "You had better go back down and wait."

"No," she whispered. "There is Andre."

He turned, startled. Then he too saw Berreau.

His blond head bare, his face set and white and masklike, standing frozenly beneath a big wild-fig a hundred feet to the right.

Hunati!

Farris had expected it, but that didn't make it less shocking. It wasn't that the tribesmen mattered less as human beings. It was just that he had talked with a normal Berreau only a few hours before. And now, to see him like this!

Berreau stood in a position ludicrously reminiscent of the old-time "living statues." One foot was slightly raised, his body bent a little forward, his arms raised a little.

Like the frozen tribesmen ahead, Berreau was facing toward the inner recesses of the grove, where the giant banyans loomed.

Farris touched his arm. "Berreau, you have to snap out of this."

"It's no use to speak to him," whispered the girl. "He can't hear."

No, he couldn't hear. He was living at a tempo so slow that no ordinary sound could make sense to his ears. His face was a rigid mask, lips slightly parted to breathe, eyes fixed ahead. Slowly, slowly, the lids crept down and veiled those staring eyes and then crept open again in the infinitely slow wink. Slowly, slowly, his slightly raised left foot moved down toward the ground.

Movement, pulse, breathing—all a hundred times slower than normal. Living, but not in a human way—not in a human way at all.

Lys was not so stunned as Farris was. He realized later that she must have seen her brother like this, before.

"We must take him back to the bungalow, somehow," she murmured. "I *can't* let him stay out here for many days and nights, again!"

Farris welcomed the small practical problem that took his thoughts for a moment away from this frozen, standing horror.

"We can rig a stretcher, from our jackets," he said. "I'll cut a couple of poles."

The two bamboos, through the sleeves of the two jackets, made a makeshift stretcher which they laid upon the ground.

Farris lifted Berreau. The man's body was rigid, muscles locked in an effort no less strong because it was infinitely slow.

He got the young Frenchman down on the stretcher, and then looked at the girl. "Can you help carry him? Or will you get a native?"

She shook her head. "The tribesmen mustn't know of this. Andre isn't heavy."

He wasn't. He was light as though wasted by fever, though the sickened Farris knew that it wasn't any fever that had done it.

Why should a civilized young botanist go out into the forest and partake of a filthy primitive drug of some kind that slowed him down to a frozen stupor? It didn't make sense.

Lys bore her share of their living burden through the gathering twilight, in stolid silence. Even when they put Berreau down at intervals to rest, she did not speak.

It was not until they reached the dark bungalow and had put him down on his bed, that the girl sank into a chair and buried her face in her hands.

Farris spoke with a rough encouragement he did not feel. "Don't get upset. He'll be all right now. I'll soon bring him out of this."

She shook her head. "No, you must not attempt that! He must come out of it by himself. And it will take many days."

The devil it would, Farris thought. He had teak to find, and he needed Berreau to arrange for workers.

Then the dejection of the girl's small figure got him. He patted her shoulder.

"All right, I'll help you take care of him. And together, we'll pound some sense into him and make him go back home. Now you see about dinner."

She lit a gasoline lamp, and went out. He heard her calling the servants.

He looked down at Berreau. He felt a little sick, again. The Frenchman lay, eyes staring toward the ceiling. He was living, breathing—and yet his retarded life-tempo cut him off from Farris as effectually as death would.

No, not quite. Slowly, so slowly that he could hardly detect the movement, Berreau's eyes turned toward Farris' figure.

Lys came back into the room. She was quiet, but he was getting to know her better, and he knew by her face that she was startled.

"The servants are gone! Ahra, and the girls—and your guide. They must have seen us bring Andre in."

Farris understood. "They left because we brought back a man who's *hunati*?"

She nodded. "All the tribespeople fear the rite. It's said there's only a few who belong to it, but they're dreaded."

Farris spared a moment to curse softly the vanished Annamese. "Piang would bolt like a scared rabbit, from something like this. A sweet beginning for my job here."

"Perhaps you had better leave," Lys said uncertainly. Then she added contradictorily, "No, I can't be heroic about it! Please stay!"

"That's for sure," he told her. "I can't go back down river and report that I shirked my job because of—"

He stopped, for she wasn't listening to him. She was looking past him, toward the bed.

Farris swung around. While they two had been talking, Berreau had been moving. Infinitely slowly—but moving.

His feet were on the floor now. He was getting up. His body straightened with a painful, dragging slowness, for many minutes.

Then his right foot began to rise almost imperceptibly from the floor. He was starting to walk, only a hundred times slower than normal.

He was starting to walk toward the door.

Lys' eyes had a yearning pity in them. "He is trying to go back up to the forest. He will try so long as he is *hunati*."

Farris gently lifted Berreau back to the bed. He felt a cold dampness on his forehead.

What was there up there that drew worshippers in a strange trance of slowed-down life?

CHAPTER THREE
UNHOLY LURE

He turned to the girl and asked, "How long will he stay in this condition?"

"A long time," she answered heavily. "It may take weeks for the *hunati* to wear off."

Farris didn't like the prospect, but there was nothing he could do about it.

"All right, we'll take care of him. You and I."

Lys said, "One of us will have to watch him, all the time. He will keep trying to go back to the forest."

"You've had enough for a while," Farris told her. "I'll watch him tonight."

Farris watched. Not only that night but for many nights. The days went into weeks, and the natives still shunned the house, and he saw nobody except the pale girl and the man who was living in a different way than other humans lived.

Berreau didn't change. He didn't seem to sleep, nor did he seem to need food or drink. His eyes never closed, except in that infinitely slow blinking.

He didn't sleep, and he did not quit moving. He was always moving, only it was in that weird, utterly slow-motion tempo that one could hardly see.

Lys had been right. Berreau wanted to go back to the forest. He might be living a hundred times slower than normal, but he was obviously still conscious in some weird way, and still trying to go back to the hushed, forbidden forest up there where they had found him.

Farris wearied of lifting the statue-like figure back into bed, and with the girl's permission tied Berreau's ankles. It did not make things much better. It was even more upsetting, in a way, to sit in the lamplit bedroom and watch Berreau's slow struggles for freedom.

The dragging slowness of each tiny movement made Farris' nerves twitch to see. He wished he could give Berreau some sedative to keep him asleep, but he did not dare to do that.

He had found, on Berreau's forearm, a tiny incision stained with sticky green. There were scars of other, old incisions near it. Whatever crazy drug had been injected into the man to make him *hunati* was unknown. Farris did not dare try to counteract its effect.

Finally, Farris glanced up one night from his bored perusal of an old *L'Illustration* and then jumped to his feet.

Berreau still lay on the bed, but he had just winked. Had winked with normal quickness, and not that slow, dragging blink.

"Berreau!" Farris said quickly. "Are you all right now? Can you hear me?"

Berreau looked up at him with a level, unfriendly gaze. "I can hear you. May I ask why you meddled?"

It took Farris aback. He had been playing nurse so long that he had unconsciously come to think of the other as a sick man who would be grateful to him. He realized now that Berreau was coldly angry, not grateful.

The Frenchman was untying his ankles. His movements were shaky, his hands trembling, but he stood up normally.

"Well?" he asked.

Farris shrugged. "Your sister was going up there after you. I helped her bring you back. That's all."

Berreau looked a little startled. "Lys did that? But it's a breaking of the Rite! It can mean trouble for her!"

Resentment and raw nerves made Farris suddenly brutal. "Why should you worry about Lys now, when you've made her wretched for months by your dabbling in native wizardries?"

Berreau didn't retort angrily, as he had expected. The young Frenchman answered heavily.

"It's true. I've done that to Lys."

Farris exclaimed, "Berreau, why do you do it? Why this unholy business of going *hunati*, of living a hundred times slower? What can you gain by it?"

The other man looked at him with haggard eyes. "By doing it, I've entered an alien world. A world that exists around us all our lives, but that we never live in or understand at all."

"What world?"

"The world of green leaf and root and branch," Berreau answered. "The world of plant life, which we can never comprehend because of the difference between its life-tempo and our life-tempo."

Farris began dimly to understand. "You mean, this *hunati* change makes you live at the same tempo as plants?"

Berreau nodded. "Yes. And that simple difference in life-tempo is the doorway into an unknown, incredible world."

"But how?"

The Frenchman pointed to the half-healed incision on his bare arm. "The drug does it. A native drug, that slows down metabolism, heart-action, respiration, nerve-messages, everything.

"Chlorophyll is its basis. The green blood of plant-life, the complex chemical that enables plants to take their energy direct from sunlight. The natives prepare it directly from grasses, by some method of their own."

"I shouldn't think," Farris said incredulously, "That chlorophyll could have any effect on an animal organism."

"Your saying that," Berreau retorted, "shows that your biochemical knowledge is out of date. Back in March of Nineteen Forty-Eight, two Chicago chemists engaged in mass production or extraction of chlorophyll, announced that their injection of it into dogs and rats seemed to prolong life greatly by altering the oxidation capacity of the cells.

"Prolong life greatly—yes! But it prolongs it, by slowing it down! A tree lives longer than a man, because it doesn't live so fast. You can make a man live as long—*and as slowly*—as a tree, by injecting the right chlorophyll compound into his blood."

Farris said, "That's what you meant, by saying that primitive peoples sometimes anticipate modern scientific discoveries?"

Berreau nodded. "This chlorophyll *hunati* solution may be an age-old secret. I believe it's always been known to a few among the primitive forest-folk of the world."

He looked somberly past the American. "Tree-worship is as old as the human race. The Sacred Tree of Sumeria, the groves of Dodona, the oaks of the Druids, the tree Ygdrasil of the Norse, even our own Christmas Tree—they all stem from primitive worship of that other, alien kind of life with which we share Earth.

"I think that a few secret worshippers have always known how to prepare the chlorophyll drug that enabled them to attain complete communion with that other kind of life, by living at the same slow rate for a time."

Farris stared. "But how did *you* get taken into this queer secret worship?"

The other man shrugged. "The worshippers were grateful to me, because I had saved the forests here from possible death."

He walked across to the corner of the room that was fitted as a botanical laboratory, and took down a test-tube. It was filled with dusty, tiny spores of a leprous, gray-green color.

"This is the Burmese Blight, that's withered whole great forests down south of the Mekong. A deadly thing, to tropical trees. It was starting to work up into this Laos country, but I showed the tribes how to stop it. The secret *hunati* sect made me one of them, in reward."

"But I still can't understand why an educated man like you would want to join such a crazy mumbo-jumbo," Farris said.

"*Dieu*, I'm trying to make you understand why! To show you that it was my curiosity as a botanist that made me join the Rite and take the drug!"

Berreau rushed on. "But you can't understand, any more than Lys could! You can't comprehend the wonder and strangeness and beauty of living that other kind of life!"

Something in Berreau's white, rapt face, in his haunted eyes, made Farris' skin crawl. His words seemed momentarily to lift a veil, to make the familiar vaguely strange and terrifying.

"Berreau, listen! You've got to cut this and leave here at once."

The Frenchman smiled mirthlessly. "I know. Many times, I have told myself so. But I do not go. How can I leave something that is a botanist's heaven?"

Lys had come into the room, was looking wanly at her brother's face. "Andre, won't you give it up and go home with me?" she appealed.

"Or are you too sunken in this uncanny habit to care whether your sister breaks her heart?" Farris demanded.

Berreau flared. "You're a smug pair! You treat me like a drug addict, without knowing the wonder of the experience I've had! I've gone into another world, an alien Earth that is around us every day of our lives and that we can't even see. And I'm going back again, and again."

"Use that chlorophyll drug and go *hunati* again?" Farris said grimly.

Berreau nodded defiantly.

"No," said Farris. "You're not. For if you do, we'll just go out there and bring you in again. You'll be quite helpless to prevent us, once you're *hunati*."

The other man raged. "There's a way I can stop you from doing that! Your threats are dangerous!"

"There's no way," Farris said flatly. "Once you've frozen yourself into that slower life-tempo, you're helpless against normal people. And I'm not threatening. I'm trying to save your sanity, man!"

Berreau flung out of the room without answer. Lys looked at the American, with tears glimmering in her eyes.

"Don't worry about it," he reassured her. "He'll get over it, in time."

"I fear not," the girl whispered. "It has become a madness in his brain."

Inwardly, Farris agreed. Whatever the lure of the unknown world that Berreau had entered by that change in life-tempo, it had caught him beyond all redemption.

A chill swept Farris when he thought of it—men out there, living at the same tempo as plants, stepping clear out of the plane of animal life to a strangely different kind of life and world.

The bungalow was oppressively silent that day—the servants gone, Berreau sulking in his laboratory, Lys moving about with misery in her eyes.

But Berreau didn't try to go out, though Farris had been expecting that and had been prepared for a clash. And by evening, Berreau seemed to have got over his sulks. He helped prepare dinner.

He was almost gay, at the meal—a febrile good humor that Farris didn't quite like. By common consent, none of the three spoke of what was uppermost in their minds.

Berreau retired, and Farris told Lys, "Go to bed—you've lost so much sleep lately you're half asleep now. I'll keep watch."

In his own room, Farris found drowsiness assailing him too. He sank back in a chair, fighting the heaviness that weighed down his eyelids.

Then, suddenly, he understood. "Drugged!" he exclaimed, and found his voice little more than a whisper. "Something in the dinner!"

"Yes," said a remote voice. "Yes, Farris."

Berreau had come in. He loomed gigantic to Farris' blurred eyes. He came closer, and Farris saw in his hand a needle that dripped sticky green.

"I'm sorry, Farris." He was rolling up Farris' sleeve, and Farris could not resist. "I'm sorry to do this to you and Lys. But you *would* interfere. And this is the only way I can keep you from bringing me back."

Farris felt the sting of the needle. He felt nothing more, before drugged unconsciousness claimed him.

CHAPTER FOUR
INCREDIBLE WORLD

Farris awoke, and for a dazed moment wondered what it was that so bewildered him. Then he realized.

It was the daylight. It came and went, every few minutes. There was the darkness of night in the bedroom, and then a sudden burst of dawn, a little period of brilliant sunlight, and then night again.

It came and went, as he watched numbly, like the slow, steady beating of a great pulse—a systole and diastole of light and darkness.

Days shortened to minutes? But how could that be? And then, as he awakened fully, he remembered.

"*Hunati!* He injected the chlorophyll drug into my blood-stream!

Yes. He was *hunati,* now. Living at a tempo a hundred times slower than normal.

And that was why day and night seemed a hundred times faster than normal, to him. He had, already, lived through several days!

Farris stumbled to his feet. As he did so, he knocked his pipe from the arm of the chair.

It did not fall to the floor. It just disappeared instantly, and the next instant was lying on the floor.

"It fell. But it fell so fast I couldn't see it."

Farris felt his brain reel to the impact of the unearthly. He found that he was trembling violently.

He fought to get a grip on himself. This wasn't witchcraft. It was a secret and devilish science, but it wasn't supernatural.

He, himself, felt as normal as ever. It was his surroundings, the swift rush of day and night especially, that alone told him he was changed.

He heard a scream, and stumbled out to the living-room of the bungalow. Lys came running toward him.

She still wore her jacket and slacks, having obviously been too worried about her brother to retire completely. And there was terror in her face.

"What's happened?" she cried. "The light—"

He took her by the shoulders. "Lys, don't lose your nerve. What's happened is that we're *hunati* now. Your brother did it—drugged us at dinner, then injected the chlorophyll compound into us."

"But why?" she cried.

"Don't you see? He was going *hunati* himself again, going back up to the forest. And we could easily overtake and bring him back, if we remained normal. So he changed us too, to prevent that."

Farris went into Berreau's room. It was as he had expected. The Frenchman was gone.

"I'll go after him," he said tightly. "He's got to come back, for he may have an antidote to that hellish stuff. You wait here."

Lys clung to him. "No! I'd go mad, here by myself, like this."

She was, he saw, on the brink of hysterics. He didn't wonder. The slow, pulsing beat of day and night alone was enough to unseat one's reason.

He acceded. "All right. But wait till I get something."

He went back to Berreau's room and took a big bolo-knife he had seen leaning in a corner. Then he saw something else, something glittering in the pulsing light, on the botanist's laboratory-table.

Farris stuffed that into his pocket. If force couldn't bring Berreau back, the threat of this other thing might influence him.

He and Lys hurried out onto the veranda and down the steps. And then they stopped, appalled.

The great forest that loomed before them was now a nightmare sight. It seethed and stirred with unearthly life—great branches clawing and whipping at each other as they fought for the light, vines writhing through them at incredible speed, a rustling uproar of tossing, living plant-life.

Lys shrank back. "The forest is *alive* now!"

"It's just the same as always," Farris reassured. "It's we who have changed—who are living so slowly now that the plants seem to live faster."

"And Andre is out in that!" Lys shuddered. Then courage came back into her pale face. "But I'm not afraid."

They started up through the forest toward the plateau of giant trees. And now there was an awful unreality about this incredible world.

Farris felt no difference in himself. There was no sensation of slowing down. His own motions and perceptions appeared normal. It was simply that all around him the vegetation had now a savage motility that was animal in its swiftness.

Grasses sprang up beneath his feet, tiny green spears climbing toward the light. Buds swelled, burst, spread their bright petals on the air, breathed out their fragrance—and died.

New leaves leaped joyously up from every twig, lived out their brief and vital moment, withered and fell. The forest was a constantly shifting kaleidoscope of colors, from pale green to yellowed brown, that rippled as the swift tides of growth and death washed over it.

But it was not peaceful nor serene, that life of the forest. Before, it had seemed to Farris that the plants of the earth existed in a placid inertia utterly different from the beasts, who must constantly hunt or be hunted. Now he saw how mistaken he had been.

Close by, a tropical nettle crawled up beside a giant fern. Octopus-like, its tendrils flashed around and through the plant. The fern writhed. Its fronds tossed wildly, its stalks strove to be free. But the stinging death conquered it.

Lianas crawled like great serpents among the trees, encircling the trunks, twining themselves swiftly along the branches, striking their hungry parasitic roots into the living bark.

And the trees fought them. Farris could see how the branches lashed and struck against the killer vines. It was like watching a man struggle against the crushing coils of the python.

Very likely. Because the trees, the plants, knew. In their own strange, alien fashion, they were as sentient as their swifter brothers.

Hunter and hunted. The strangling lianas, the deadly, beautiful orchid that was like a cancer eating a healthy trunk, the leprous, crawling fungi—they were the wolves and the jackals of this leafy world.

Even among the trees, Farris saw, existence was a grim and never-ending struggle. Silk-cotton and bamboo and ficus tree—they too knew pain and fear and the dread of death.

He could hear them. Now, with his aural nerves slowed to an incredible receptivity, he heard the voice of the forest, the true voice that had nothing to do with the familiar sounds of wind in the branches.

The primal voice of birth and death that spoke before ever man appeared on Earth, and would continue to speak after he was gone.

At first he had been conscious only of that vast, rustling uproar. Now he could distinguish separate sounds—the thin screams of grass blades and bamboo-shoots thrusting and surging out of the earth, the lash and groan of enmeshed and dying branches, the laughter of young leaves high in the sky, the stealthy whisper of the coiling vines.

And almost, he could hear thoughts, speaking in his mind. The age-old thoughts of the trees.

Farris felt a freezing dread. He did not want to listen to the thoughts of the trees.

And the slow, steady pulsing of darkness and light went on. Days and nights, rushing with terrible speed over the *hunati*.

Lys, stumbling along the trail beside him, uttered a little cry of terror. A snaky black vine had darted out of the brush at her with cobra swiftness, looping swiftly to encircle her body.

Farris swung his bolo, slashed though the vine. But it struck out again, growing with that appalling speed, its tip groping for him.

He slashed again with sick horror, and pulled the girl onward, on up the side of the plateau.

"I am afraid!" she gasped. "I can hear the thoughts—the thoughts of the forest!"

"It's your own imagination!" he told her. "Don't listen!"

But he too could hear them! Very faintly, like sounds just below the threshold of hearing. It seemed to him that every minute—or every minute-long day—he was able to get more clearly the telepathic impulses of these organisms that lived an undreamed-of life of their own, side by side with man, yet forever barred from him, except when man was *hunati*.

It seemed to him that the temper of the forest had changed, that his slaying of the vine had made it aware of them. Like a crowd aroused to anger, the massed trees around them grew wrathful. A tossing and moaning rose among them.

Branches struck at Farris and the girl, lianas groped with blind heads and snakelike grace toward them. Brush and bramble clawed them spitefully, reaching out thorny arms to rake their flesh. The slender saplings lashed them like leafy whips, the swift-growing bamboo spears sought to block their path, canes clattering together as if in rage.

"It's only in our own minds!" he said to the girl. "Because the forest is living at the same rate as we, we imagine it's aware of us."

He had to believe that, he knew. He had to, because when he quit believing it there was only black madness.

"No!" cried Lys. "No! The forest knows we are here."

Panic fear threatened Farris' self-control, as the mad uproar of the forest increased. He ran, dragging the girl with him, sheltering her with his body from the lashing of the raging forest.

They ran on, deeper into the mighty grove upon the plateau, under the pulsing rush of day and darkness. And now the trees about them were brawling giants, great silk-cotton and ficus that stuck crashing blows at each other as their branches fought for clear sky—contending and terrible leafy giants beneath which the two humans were pigmies.

But the lesser forest beneath them still tossed and surged with wrath, still plucked and tore at the two running humans. And still, and clearer, stronger, Farris' reeling mind caught the dim impact of unguessable telepathic impulses.

Then, drowning all those dim and raging thoughts, came vast and dominating impulses of greater majesty, thought-voices deep and strong and alien as the voice of primal Earth.

"Stop them!" they seemed to echo in Farris' mind. "Stop them! Slay them! For they are our enemies!"

Lys uttered a trembling cry. "Andre!"

Farris saw him, then. Saw Berreau ahead, standing in the shadow of the monster banyans there. His arms were upraised toward those looming colossi, as though in worship. Over him towered the leafy giants, dominating all the forest.

"Stop them! Slay them!"

They thundered, now, those majestic thought-voices that Farris' mind could barely hear. He was closer to them—closer—

He knew, then, even though his mind refused to admit the knowledge. Knew whence those mighty voices came, and why Berreau worshipped the banyans.

And surely they were godlike, these green colossi who had lived for ages, whose arms reached skyward and whose aerial roots drooped and stirred and groped like hundreds of hands!

Farris forced that thought violently away. He was a man, of the world of men, and he must not worship alien lords.

Berreau had turned toward them. The man's eyes were hot and raging, and Farris knew even before Berreau spoke that he was no longer altogether sane.

"Go, both of you!" he ordered. "You were fools, to come here after me! You killed as you came through the forest, and the forest knows!"

"Berreau, listen!" Farris appealed. "You've got to go back with us, forget this madness!"

Berreau laughed shrilly. "Is it madness that the Lords even now voice their wrath against you? You hear it in your mind, but you are afraid to listen! Be afraid, Farris! There is reason! You have slain trees for many years, as you have just slain here—and the forest knows you for a foe."

"Andre!" Lys was sobbing, her face half-buried in her hands.

Farris felt his mind cracking under the impact of the crazy scene. The ceaseless, rushing pulse of light and darkness, the rustling uproar of the seething forest around them, the vines creeping snakelike and branches whipping at them and giant banyans rocking angrily overhead.

"*This* is the world that man lives in all his life, and never sees or senses!" Berreau was shouting. "I've come into it, again and again. And each time, I've heard more clearly the voices of the Great Ones!

"The oldest and mightiest creatures on our planet! Long ago, men knew that and worshipped them for the wisdom they could teach. Yes, worshipped them as Ygdrasil and the Druid Oak and the Sacred Tree! But modern men have forgotten this other Earth. Except me, Farris—except me! I've found wisdom in this world such as you never dreamed. And your stupid blindness is not going to drag me out of it!"

Farris realized then that it was too late to reason with Berreau. The man had come too often and too far into this other Earth that was as alien to humanity as though it lay across the universe.

It was because he had feared that, that he had brought the little thing in his jacket pocket. The one thing with which he might force Berreau to obey.

Farris took it out of his pocket. He held it up so that the other could see it.

"You know what it is, Berreau! And you know what I can do with it, if you force me to!"

Wild dread leaped into Berreau's eyes as he recognized that glittering little vial from his own laboratory.

"The Burmese Blight! You wouldn't, Farris! You wouldn't turn that loose *here!*"

"I will!" Farris said hoarsely. "I will, unless you come out of here with us, now!"

Raging hate and fear were in Berreau's eyes as he stared at that innocent corked glass vial of gray-green dust.

He said thickly, "For this, I will kill!"

Lys screamed. Black lianas had crept upon her as she stood with her face hidden in her hands. They had writhed around her legs like twining serpents, they were pulling her down.

The forest seemed to roar with triumph. Vine and branch and bramble and creeper surged toward them. Dimly thunderous throbbed the strange telepathic voices.

"Slay them!" said the trees.

Farris leaped into that coiling mass of vines, his bolo slashing. He cut loose the twining lianas that held the girl, sliced fiercely at the branches that whipped wildly at them.

Then, from behind, Berreau's savage blow on his elbow knocked the bolo from his hand.

"I told you not to kill, Farris! I told you!"

"Slay them!" pulsed the alien thought.

Berreau spoke, his eyes not leaving Farris. "Run, Lys. Leave the forest. This—murderer must die."

He lunged as he spoke, and there was death in his white face and clutching hands.

Farris was knocked back, against one of the giant banyan trunks. They rolled, grappling. And already the vines were sliding around them—looping and enmeshing them, tightening upon them!

It was then that the forest shrieked.

A cry telepathic and auditory at the same time—and dreadful. An utterance of alien agony beyond anything human.

Berreau's hands fell away from Farris. The Frenchman, enmeshed with him by the coiling vines, looked up in horror.

Then Farris saw what had happened. The little vial, the vial of the blight, had smashed against the banyan trunk as Berreau charged.

And that little splash of gray-green mould was rushing through the forest faster than flame! The blight, the gray-green killer from far away, propagating itself with appalling rapidity! *"Dieu!"* screamed Berreau. *"Non—non—"*

Even normally, a blight seems to spread swiftly. And to Farris and the other two, slowed down as they were, this blight was a raging cold fire of death.

It flashed up trunks and limbs and aerial roots of the majestic banyans, eating leaf and spore and bud. It ran triumphantly across the ground, over vine and grass and shrub, bursting up other trees, leaping along the airy bridges of lianas.

And it leaped among the vines that enmeshed the two men! In mad death-agonies the creepers writhed and tightened.

Farris felt the musty mould in his mouth and nostrils, felt the construction as of steel cables crushing the life from him. The world seemed to darken—

Then a steel blade hissed and flashed, and the pressure loosened. Lys' voice was in his ears, Lys' hand trying to drag him from the dying, tightening creepers that she had partly slashed through. He wrenched free. "My brother!" she gasped.

With the bolo he sliced clumsily through the mass of dying writhing snake-vines that still enmeshed Berreau.

Berreau's face appeared, as he tore away the slashed creepers. It was dark purple, rigid, his eyes staring and dead. The tightening vines had caught him around the throat, strangling him.

Lys knelt beside him, crying wildly. But Farris dragged her to her feet. "We have to get out of here! He's dead—but I'll carry his body!"

"No, leave it," she sobbed. "Leave it here, in the forest."

Dead eyes, looking up at the death of the alien world of life into which he had now crossed, forever! Yes, it was fitting.

Farris' heart quailed as he stumbled away with Lys through the forest that was rocking and raging in its death-throes.

Far away around them, the gray-green death was leaping on. And fainter, fainter, came the strange telepathic cries that he would never be sure he had really heard.

"We die, brothers! We die!"

And then, when it seemed to Farris that sanity must give way beneath the weight of alien agony, there came a sudden change.

The pulsing rush of alternate day and night lengthened in tempo. Each period of light and darkness was longer now, and longer—

Out of a period of dizzying semi-consciousness, Farris came back to awareness. They were standing unsteadily in the blighted forest, in bright sunlight.

And they were no longer *hunati*.

The chlorophyll drug had spent its force in their bodies, and they had come back to the normal tempo of human life.

Lys looked up dazedly, at the forest that now seemed static, peaceful, immobile—and in which the gray-green blight now crept so slowly they could not see it move.

"The same forest, and it's still writhing in death!" Farris said huskily. "But now that we're living at normal speed again, we can't see it!"

"Please, let us go!" choked the girl. "Away from here, at once!"

It took but an hour to return to the bungalow and pack what they could carry, before they took the trail toward the Mekong.

Sunset saw them out of the blighted area of the forest, well on their way toward the river.

"Will it kill all the forest?" whispered the girl.

"No. The forest will fight back, come back, conquer the blight, in time. A long time, by our reckoning—years, decades. But to *them*, that fierce struggle is raging on even now."

And as they walked on, it seemed to Farris that still in his mind there pulsed faintly from far behind that alien, throbbing cry.

"We die, brothers!"

He did not look back. But he knew that he would not come back to this or any other forest, and that his profession was ended, and that he would never kill a tree again.

What's It Like Out There?

I hadn't wanted to wear my uniform when I left the hospital, but I didn't have any other clothes there and I was too glad to get out to argue about it. But as soon as I got on the local plane I was taking to Los Angeles, I was sorry I had it on.

People gawked at me and began to whisper. The stewardess gave me a special big smile. She must have spoken to the pilot, for he came back and shook hands, and said, "Well, I guess a trip like this is sort of a comedown for *you*."

A little man came in, looked around for a seat, and took the one beside me. He was a fussy, spectacled guy of fifty or sixty, and he took a few minutes to get settled. Then he looked at me, and stared at my uniform and at the little brass button on it that said TWO.

"Why," he said, "you're one of those Expedition Two men!" And then, as though he'd only just figured it out, "Why, you've been to Mars!"

"Yeah," I said. "I was there."

He beamed at me in a kind of wonder. I didn't like it, but his curiosity was so friendly that I couldn't quite resent it.

"Tell me," he said, "what's it like out there?"

The plane was lifting, and I looked out at the Arizona desert sliding by close underneath.

"Different," I said. "It's different."

The answer seemed to satisfy him completely. "I'll just bet it is," he said. "Are you going home, Mr.—"

"Haddon. Sergeant Frank Haddon."

"You going home, Sergeant?"

"My home's back in Ohio," I told him. "I'm going in to L.A. to look up some people before I go home."

"Well, that's fine. I hope you have a good time, Sergeant. You deserve it. You boys did a great job out there. Why, I read in the newspapers that after the U.N. sends out a couple more expeditions, we'll have cities out there, and regular passenger lines, and all that."

"Look," I said, "that stuff is for the birds. You might as well build cities down there in Mojave, and have them a lot closer. There's only one reason for going to Mars now, and that's uranium."

I could see he didn't quite believe me. "Oh, sure," he said, "I know that's important too, the uranium we're all using now for our power-stations—but that isn't all, is it?"

"It'll be all, for a long, long time," I said.

"But look, Sergeant, this newspaper article said—"

I didn't say anything more. By the time he'd finished telling about the newspaper article, we were coming down into L.A. He pumped my hand when we got out of the plane.

"Have yourself a time, Sergeant! You sure rate it...I hear a lot of chaps on Two didn't come back."

"Yeah," I said. "I heard that."

I was feeling shaky again by the time I got to downtown L.A. I went in a bar and had a double bourbon and it made me feel a little better.

I went out and found a cabby and asked him to drive me out to San Gabriel. He was a fat man with a broad red face.

"Hop right in, buddy," he said. "Say, you're one of those Mars guys, aren't you?"

I said, "That's right."

"Well, well," he said. "Tell me, how was it out there?"

"It was a pretty dull grind, in a way," I told him.

"I'll bet it was!" he said, as we started through traffic. "Me, I was in the army in World War Two, twenty years ago. That's just what it was, a dull grind nine-tenths of the time. I guess it hasn't changed any."

"This wasn't any army expedition," I explained. "It was a United Nations one, not an army one—but we had officers and rules of discipline like the army."

"Sure, it's the same thing," said the cabby. "You don't need to tell me what it's like, buddy. Why, back there in '42—or was it '43?—anyway, back there I remember that—"

I leaned back and watched Huntington Boulevard slide past. The sun poured in on me and seemed very hot, and the air seemed very thick and soupy. It hadn't been so bad up on the Arizona plateau, but it was a little hard to breathe down here.

The cabby wanted to know what address in San Gabriel? I got the little packet of letters out of my pocket and found the one that had 'Martin Valinez' and a street address on the back. I told the cabby, and put the letters back into my pocket.

I wished now that I'd never answered them.

But how could I keep from answering when Joe Valinez' parents wrote to me at the hospital? And it was the same with Jim's girl, and Walter's family. I'd had to write back, and the first thing I knew I'd promised to come and see them, and now if I went back to Ohio without doing it I'd feel like a heel. Right now, I wished I'd decided to be a heel.

The address was on the south side of San Gabriel, in a section that still had a faintly Mexican tinge to it. There was a little frame grocery store with a small house beside it, and a picket fence around the yard of the house; very neat, but a queerly homely place after all the slick California stucco.

I went into the little grocery, and a tall, dark man with quiet eyes took a look at me and called a woman's name in a low voice, and then came around the counter and took my hand.

"You're Sergeant Haddon," he said. "Yes. Of course. We've been hoping you'd come."

His wife came in a hurry from the back. She looked a little too old to be Joe's mother, for Joe had been just a kid; but then she didn't look so old either, but just sort of worn.

She said to Valinez, "Please, a chair. Can't you see he's tired. And just from the hospital—"

I sat down and looked between them at a case of canned peppers, and they asked me how I felt, and wouldn't I be glad to get home, and they hoped all my family were well.

They were gentlefolk. They hadn't said a word about Joe, just waited for me to say something. And I felt in a spot, for I hadn't known Joe well, not really. He'd been moved into our squad only a couple of weeks before take-off, and since he'd been our first casualty, I'd never got to know him much.

I finally had to get it over with, and all I could think to say was, "They wrote you in detail about Joe, didn't they?"

Valinez nodded gravely. "Yes—that he died from shock within twenty-four hours after take-off. The letter was very nice."

His wife nodded too. "Very nice," she murmured. She looked at me, and I guess she saw that I didn't know quite what to say, for she said, "You can tell us more about it. Yet you must not, if it pains you."

I could tell them more. Oh, yes, I could tell them a lot more, if I wanted to. It was all clear in my mind, like a movie-film you run over and over till you know it by heart.

I could tell them all about the take-off that had killed their son. The long lines of us, uniformed backs going up into Rocket Four and all the other nineteen rockets—the lights flaring up there on the plateau, the grind of machinery and blast of whistles and the inside of the big rocket as we climbed up the ladders of its center-well.

The movie was running again in my mind, clear as crystal, and I was back in Cell Fourteen of Rocket Four, with the minutes ticking away and the walls quivering every time one of the other rockets blasted off, and us ten men in our hammocks, prisoned inside that odd-shaped windowless metal room, waiting. Waiting, till that big, giant hand came and smacked us down deep into our recoil-springs, crushing the breath out of us, so that you fought to breathe, and the blood roared into your head, and your stomach heaved in spite of all the pills they'd given you, and you heard the giant laughing, *b-r-room! b-r-r-room! b-r-r-oom!*

Smash, smash, again and again, hitting us in the guts and cutting our breath, and someone being sick, and someone else sobbing, and the *b-r-r-oom! b-r-r-oom!* laughing as it killed us; and then the giant quit laughing, and quit slapping us down, and you could feel your sore and shaky body and wonder if it was still all there.

Walter Millis cursing a blue streak in the hammock underneath me, and Breck Jergen, our sergeant then, clambering painfully out of his straps to look us over, and then through the voices a thin, ragged voice saying uncertainly, "Breck, I think I'm hurt—"

Sure, that was their boy Joe, and there was blood on his lips, and he'd had it—we knew when we first looked at him that he'd had it. A handsome kid, turned waxy now as he held his hand on his middle and looked up at us. Expedition One had proved that take-off would hit a certain percentage with internal injuries every time, and in our squad, in our little windowless cell, it was Joe that had been hit.

If only he'd died right off. But he couldn't die right off, he had to lie in the hammock all those hours and hours. The medics came and put a strait-jacket around his body and doped him up, and that was that, and the hours went by. And we were so shaken and deathly sick ourselves that we didn't have the sympathy for him we should have had—not till he started moaning and begging us to take the jacket off.

Finally Walter Millis wanted to do it, and Breck wouldn't allow it, and they were arguing and we were listening when the moaning stopped, and there was no need to do anything about Joe Valinez any more. Nothing but to call the medics, who came into our little iron prison and took him away.

Sure, I could tell the Valinezes all about how their Joe died, couldn't I?

"Please," whispered Mrs. Valinez, and her husband looked at me and nodded silently.

So I told them.

I said, "You know Joe died in space. He'd been knocked out by the shock of take-off, and he was unconscious, not feeling a thing. And then he woke up, before he died. He didn't seem to be feeling any pain, not a bit. He lay there, looking out the window at the stars. They're beautiful, the stars out there in space, like angels. He looked, and then he whispered something and lay back and was gone."

Mrs. Valinez began to cry softly. "To die out there, looking at stars like angels—"

I got up to go, and she didn't look up. I went out the door of the little grocery store, and Valinez came with me.

He shook my hand. "Thank you, Sergeant Haddon. Thank you very much."

"Sure," I said.

I got into the cab. I took out my letters and tore that one into bits. I wished to God I'd never got it. I wished I didn't have any of the other letters I still had.

2

I took the early plane for Omaha. Before we got there I fell asleep in my seat, and then I began to dream, and that wasn't good.

A voice said, "We're coming down."

And we were coming down, Rocket Four was coming down, and there we were in our squad-cell, all of us strapped into our hammocks, waiting and scared, wishing there was a window so we could see out, hoping our rocket wouldn't be the one to crack up, hoping none of the rockets cracked up, but if one does, don't let it be *ours*....

"We're coming down..."

Coming down, with the blasts starting to boom again underneath us, hitting us hard, not steady like at take-off, but blast-blast-blast, and then again, blast-blast.

Breck's voice, calling to us from across the cell, but I couldn't hear for the roaring that was in my ears between blasts. No, it was *not* in my ears, that roaring came from the wall beside me: we had hit atmosphere, we were coming in.

The blasts in lightning succession without stopping, crash-crash-crash-crash-crash! Mountains fell on me, and this was it, and don't let it be ours, please, God, don't let it be ours...

Then the bump and the blackness, and finally somebody yelling hoarsely in my ears, and Breck Jergen, his face deathly white, leaning over me.

"Unstrap and get out, Frank! All men out of hammocks—all men out!"

We'd landed, and we hadn't cracked up, but we were half dead and they wanted us to turn out, right this minute, and we couldn't.

Breck yelling to us, "Breathing-masks on! Masks on! We've got to go out!"

"My God, we've just landed, we're torn to bits, we can't!"

"We've got to! Some of the other rockets cracked up in landing and we've got to save whoever's still living in them! Masks on! Hurry!"

We couldn't, but we did. They hadn't given us all those months of discipline for nothing. Jim Clymer was already on his feet, Walter was trying to unstrap underneath me, whistles were blowing like mad somewhere and voices shouted hoarsely.

My knees wobbled under me as I hit the floor. Young Lassen, beside me, tried to say something and then crumpled up. Jim bent over him, but Breck was at the door yelling, "Let him go! Come on!"

The whistles screeching at us all the way down the ladders of the well, and the mask-clip hurting my nose, and down at the bottom a dishevelled officer yelling at us to get out and join Squad Five, and the gangway reeling under us.

Cold. Freezing cold, and a wan sunshine from the shrunken little sun up there in the brassy sky, and a rolling plain of ocherous red sand stretching around us, sand that slid away under our feet as our squads followed Captain Wall toward the distant metal bulk that lay oddly canted and broken in a little shallow valley.

"Come on, men—hurry! Hurry!"

Sure, all of it a dream, the dreamlike way we walked with our lead-soled shoes dragging our feet back after each step, and the voices coming through the mask-resonators muffled and distant.

Only not a dream, but a nightmare, when we got up to the canted metal bulk and saw what had happened to Rocket Seven—the metal hull ripped like paper, and a few men crawling out of the wreck with blood on them, and a gurgling sound where shattered tanks were emptying, and voices whimpering, "First aid! First aid!"

Only it hadn't happened, it hadn't happened yet at all, for we were still back in Rocket Four coming in, we hadn't landed yet at all but we were going to any minute—

"We're coming down...."

I couldn't go through it all again. I yelled and fought my hammock-straps and woke up, and I was in my plane-seat and a scared hostess was a foot away from me, saying, "This is Omaha, Sergeant! We're coming down."

They were all looking at me, all the other passengers, and I guessed I'd been talking in the dream—I still had the sweat down my back like all those nights in the hospital when I'd keep waking up.

I sat up, and they all looked away from me quick and pretended they hadn't been staring.

We came down to the airport. It was mid-day, and the hot Nebraska sun felt good on my back when I got out. I was lucky, for when I asked at the bus depot about going to Cuffington, there was a bus all ready to roll.

A farmer sat down beside me, a big, young fellow who offered me cigarettes and told me it was only a few hours' ride to Cuffington.

"Your home there?" he asked.

"No, my home's back in Ohio," I said. "A friend of mine came from there. Name of Clymer."

He didn't know him, but he remembered that one of the town boys had gone on that Second Expedition, to Mars.

"Yeah," I said. "That was Jim."

He couldn't keep it in any longer. "What's it like out there, anyway?"

I said, "Dry. Terrible dry."

"I'll bet it is," he said. "To tell the truth, it's too dry here, this year, for good wheat weather. Last year, it was fine. Last year—"

Cuffington, Nebraska, was a wide street of stores, and other streets with trees and old houses, and yellow wheat-fields all around as far as you could see. It was pretty hot, and I was glad to sit down in the bus-depot while I went through the thin little phone-book.

There were three Graham families in the book, but the first one I called was the right one—Miss Ila Graham. She talked fast and excited, and said she'd come right over, and I said I'd wait in front of the bus-depot.

I stood underneath the awning, looking down the quiet street and thinking that it sort of explained why Jim Clymer had always been such a quiet, slow-moving sort of guy. The place was sort of relaxed, like he'd been.

A coupé pulled up, and Miss Graham opened the door. She was a brown-haired girl, not especially good-looking, but the kind you think of as a nice girl, a very nice girl.

She said, "You look so tired, that I feel guilty now about asking you to stop."

"I'm all right," I said. "And it's no trouble stopping over a couple of places on my way back to Ohio."

As we drove across the little town, I asked her if Jim hadn't had any family of his own here.

"His parents were killed in a car-crash years ago," Miss Graham said. "He lived with an uncle on a farm outside Grandview, but they didn't get along, and Jim came into town and got a job at the power station."

She added, as we turned a corner, "My mother rented him a room. That's how we got to know each other. That's how we—how we got engaged."

"Yeah, sure," I said.

It was a big square house with a deep front porch, and some trees around it. I sat down in a wicker chair, and Miss Graham brought her mother out. Her mother talked a little about Jim, how they missed him, and how she declared he'd been just like a son.

When her mother went back in, Miss Graham showed me a little bunch of blue envelopes. "These were the letters I got from Jim. There weren't very many of them, and they weren't very long."

"We were only allowed to send one thirty-word message every two weeks," I told her. "There were a couple of thousand of us out there, and they couldn't let us jam up the message-transmitter all the time."

"It was wonderful, how much Jim could put into just a few words," she said, and handed me some of them.

I read a couple. One said, "I have to pinch myself to realize that I'm one of the first Earthmen to stand on an alien world. At night, in the cold,

I look up at the green star that's Earth and can't quite realize I've helped an age-old dream come true."

Another one said, "This world's grim and lonely, and mysterious. We don't know much about it, yet. So far, nobody's seen anything living but the lichens that Expedition One reported, but there might be anything here."

Miss Graham asked me, "Was that all there was, just lichens?"

"That, and two or three kinds of queer cactus things," I said. "And rock and sand. That's all."

As I read more of those little blue letters, I found that now that Jim was gone, I knew him better than I ever had. There was something about him I'd never suspected. He was romantic, inside. We hadn't suspected it, he was always so quiet and slow, but now I saw that all the time he was more romantic about the thing we were doing than any of us.

He hadn't let on. We'd have kidded him, if he had. Our name for Mars, after we got sick of it, was The Hole. We always talked about it as The Hole. I could see now that Jim had been too shy of our kidding to ever let us know that he glamorized the thing in his mind.

"This was the last one I got from him before his sickness," Miss Graham said.

That one said, "I'm starting north tomorrow with one of the mapping expeditions. We'll travel over country no human has ever seen before."

I nodded. "I was on that party, myself. Jim and I were on the same half-trac."

"He was thrilled by it, wasn't he, Sergeant?"

I wondered. I remembered that trip, and it was hell. Our job was simply to run a preliminary topographical survey, checking with Geigers for possible uranium deposits.

It wouldn't have been so bad, if the sand hadn't started to blow.

It wasn't sand like Earth sand. It was ground to dust by billions of years of blowing around that dry world. It got inside your breathing-mask, and your goggles, and the engines of the half-tracs, in your food and water and clothes. There was nothing for three days but cold, and wind, and sand.

Thrilled? I'd have laughed at that, before. But now, I didn't know. Maybe Jim had been, at that. He had lots of patience, a lot more than I ever had. Maybe he glamorized that hellish trip into wonderful adventure on a foreign world.

"Sure, he was thrilled," I said. "We all were. Anybody would be."

Miss Graham took the letters back, and then said, "You had Martian sickness too, didn't you?"

I said, Yes, I had, just a touch, and that was why I'd had to spend a stretch in Reconditioning Hospital when I got back.

She waited for me to go on, and I knew I had to. "They don't know yet if it's some sort of virus, or just the effect of Martian conditions on Earthmen's bodies. It hit forty percent of us. It wasn't really so bad—fever and dopiness, mostly."

"When Jim got it, was he well cared for?" she asked. Her lips were quivering a little.

"Sure, he was well cared for. He got the best care there was," I lied.

The best care there was? That was a laugh. The first cases got decent care, maybe. But they'd never figured on so many coming down. There wasn't any room in our little hospital—they just had to stay in their bunks in the aluminum Quonsets when it hit them. All our doctors but one were down, and two of them died.

We'd been on Mars six months when it hit us, and the loneliness had already got us down. All but four of our rockets had gone back to Earth, and we were alone on a dead world, our little town of Quonsets huddled together under that hateful, brassy sky, and beyond it the sand and rocks that went on forever.

You go up to the North Pole and camp there, and find out how lonely that is. It was worse, out there, a lot worse. The first excitement was gone long ago, and we were tired, and homesick in a way nobody was ever homesick before—we wanted to see green grass, and real sunshine, and women's faces, and hear running water; and we wouldn't until Expedition Three came to relieve us. No wonder guys blew their tops, out there. And then came Martian sickness, on top of it.

"We did everything for him that we could," I said.

Sure we had. I could still remember Walter and me tramping through the cold night to the hospital to try to get a medic, while Breck stayed with him, and how we couldn't get one.

I remember how Walter had looked up at the blazing sky as we tramped back, and shaken his fist at the big green star of Earth.

"People up there are going to dances tonight, watching shows, sitting around in warm rooms laughing! Why should good men have to die out here to get them uranium for cheap power?"

283

"Can it," I told him tiredly. "Jim's not going to die. A lot of guys got over it."

The best care there was? That was real funny. All we could do was wash his face, and give him the pills the medic left, and watch him get weaker every day till he died.

"Nobody could have done more for him than was done," I told Miss Graham.

"I'm glad," she said. "I guess—it's just one of those things."

When I got up to go she asked me if I didn't want to see Jim's room. They'd kept it for him just the same, she said.

I didn't want to, but how are you going to say so? I went up with her and looked and said it was nice. She opened a big cupboard. It was full of neat rows of old magazines.

"They're all the old science-fiction magazines he read when he was a boy," she said. "He always saved them."

I took one out. It had a bright cover, with a spaceship on it, not like our rockets but a streamlined thing, and the rings of Saturn in the background.

When I laid it down, Miss Graham took it up and put it back carefully into its place in the row, as though somebody was coming back who wouldn't like to find things out of order.

She insisted on driving me back to Omaha, and out to the airport. She seemed sorry to let me go, and I suppose it was because I was the last real tie to Jim, and when I was gone it was all over then for good.

I wondered if she'd get over it in time, and I guessed she would. People do get over things. I supposed she'd marry some other nice guy, and I wondered what they'd do with Jim's things—with all those old magazines nobody was ever coming back to read.

3

I would never have stopped at Chicago at all if I could have got out of it, for the last person I wanted to talk to anybody about was Walter Millis. It would be too easy for me to make a slip, and let out stuff nobody was supposed to know.

But Walter's father had called me at the hospital, a couple of times. The last time he called, he said he was having Breck's parents come down from Wisconsin so they could see me too, so what could I do then but say, Yes, I'd stop. But I didn't like it at all, and I knew I'd have to be careful.

Mr. Millis was waiting at the airport and shook hands with me and said what a big favor I was doing them all, and how he appreciated my stopping when I must be anxious to get back to my own home and parents.

"That's all right," I said. "My dad and mother came out to the hospital to see me when I first got back."

He was a big, fine-looking important sort of man, with a little bit of the stuffed shirt about him, I thought. He seemed friendly enough, but I got the feeling he was looking at me and wondering why I'd come back and his son Walter hadn't. Well, I couldn't blame him for that.

His car was waiting, a big car with a driver, and we started north through the city. Mr. Millis pointed out a few things to me to make conversation, especially a big atomic power station we passed.

"It's only one of thousands, strung all over the world," he said. "They're going to transform our whole economy. This Martian uranium will be a big thing, Sergeant."

I said, Yes, I guessed it would.

I was sweating blood, waiting for him to start asking about Walter, and I didn't know yet just what I could tell him. I could get myself in dutch plenty if I opened my big mouth too wide, for that one thing that had happened to Expedition Two was supposed to be strictly secret, and we'd all been briefed on why we had to keep our mouths shut.

But he let it go for the time being, and just talked other stuff. I gathered that his wife wasn't too well, and that Walter had been their only child. I also gathered that he was a very big shot in business, and dough-heavy.

I didn't like him. Walter, I'd liked plenty, but his old man seemed a pretty pompous person, with his heavy business talk.

He wanted to know how soon I thought Martian uranium would come through in quantity, and I said I didn't think it'd be very soon.

"Expedition One only located the deposits," I said, "and Two just did mapping and setting up a preliminary base. Of course, the thing keeps expanding, and I hear Four will have a hundred rockets. But Mars is a tough set-up."

Mr. Millis said decisively that I was wrong, that the world was power-hungry, that it would be pushed a lot faster than I expected.

He suddenly quit talking business and looked at me and asked, "Who was Walter's best friend, out there?"

He asked it sort of apologetically. He was a stuffed shirt; but all my dislike of him went away, then.

"Breck Jergen," I told him. "Breck was our sergeant...he sort of held our squad together, and he and Walter cottoned to each other from the first."

Mr. Millis nodded, but didn't say anything more about it. He pointed out the window at the distant lake, and said we were almost to his home.

It wasn't a home, it was a big mansion. We went in and he introduced me to Mrs. Millis. She was a limp, pale-looking woman, who said she was glad to meet one of Walter's friends. Somehow I got the feeling that even though he was a stuffed shirt, he felt it about Walter a lot more than she did.

He took me up to a bedroom and said that Breck's parents would arrive before dinner, and that I could get a little rest before then.

I sat looking around the room. It was the plushiest one I'd ever been in, and seeing this house and the way these people lived, I began to understand why Walter had blown his top more than the rest of us.

He'd been a good guy, Walter, but high-tempered, and I could see now he'd been a little spoiled. The discipline at Training Base had been tougher on him than on most of us, and this was why.

I sat and dreaded this dinner that was coming up, and looked out the window at a swimming-pool and tennis court, and wondered if anybody ever used them now that Walter was gone. It seemed a queer thing for a fellow with a set-up like this to go out to Mars and get himself killed.

I took the satin cover off the bed so my shoes wouldn't dirty it, and lay down and closed my eyes, and wondered what I was going to tell them. The trouble was, I didn't know what story the officials had given them.

"The Commanding Officer regrets to inform you that your son was shot down like a dog—"

They'd never got any telegram like that. But just what line *had* been handed them? I wished I'd had a chance to check on that.

Damn it, why didn't all these people let me alone? They started it all going through my mind again, and the psychos had told me I ought to forget it for a while, but how could I?

It might be better just to tell them the truth. After all, Walter wasn't the only one who'd blown his top out there. In that grim last couple of months, plenty of guys had gone around sounding off.

Expedition Three isn't coming!

We're stuck, and they don't care enough about us to send help!

That was the line of talk. You heard it plenty, in those days. You couldn't blame the guys for it, either. A fourth of us down with Martian sickness, the little grave-markers clotting up the valley beyond the ridge, rations getting thin, medicine running low, everything running low, all of us watching the sky for rockets that never came.

There'd been a little hitch back on Earth, Colonel Nichols explained. (He was our CO now that General Rayen had died.) There was a little delay, but the rockets would be on their way soon, we'd get relief, we just had to hold on—

Holding on—that's what we were doing. Nights we'd sit in the Quonset, and listen to Lassen coughing in his bunk, and it seemed like wind-giants, cold-giants, were bawling and laughing around our little huddle of shelters.

"Damn it, if they're not coming, why don't we go home?" Walter said. "We've still got the four rockets—they could take us all back."

Breck's serious face got graver. "Look, Walter, there's too much of that stuff being talked around. Lay off."

"Can you blame the men for talking it? We're not story-book heroes. If they've forgotten about us back on Earth, why do we just sit and take it?"

"We have to," Breck said. "Three will come."

I've always thought that it wouldn't have happened, what did happen, if we hadn't had that false alarm. The one that set the whole camp wild that night, with guys shouting, "Three's here! The rockets landed over west of Rock Ridge!"

Only when they charged out there, they found they hadn't seen rockets landing at all, but a little shower of tiny meteors burning themselves up as they fell.

It was the disappointment that did it, I think. I can't say for sure, because that same day was the day I conked out with Martian sickness, and the floor came up and hit me and I woke up in the bunk, with somebody giving me a hypo, and my head big as a balloon.

I wasn't clear out, it was only a touch of it, but it was enough to make everything foggy, and I didn't know about the mutiny that was boiling up until I woke up once with Breck leaning over me, and saw he wore a gun and an MP brassard now.

When I asked him how come, he said there'd been so much wild talk about grabbing the four rockets and going home, that the MP force had been doubled, and Nichols had issued stern warnings.

"Walter?" I said, and Breck nodded. "He's a leader and he'll get hit with a court-martial when this is over. The blasted idiot!"

"I don't get it—he's got plenty of guts, you know that," I said.

"Yes, but he can't take discipline, he never did take it very well, and now that the squeeze is on he's blowing up. Well, see you later, Frank."

I saw him later, but not the way I expected. For that was the day we heard the faint echo of shots, and then the alarm-siren screaming, and men running, and half-tracs starting up in a hurry. And when I managed to get out of my bunk and out of the hut, they were all going toward the big rockets, and a corporal yelled to me from a jeep, "That's blown it! The damn fools swiped guns and tried to take over the rockets and make the crews fly 'em home!"

I could still remember the sickening slidings and bouncings of the jeep as it took us out there, the milling little crowd under the looming rockets, milling around and hiding something on the ground, and Major Weiler yelling himself hoarse giving orders.

When I got to see what was on the ground, it was seven or eight men and most of them dead. Walter had been shot right through the heart. They told me later it was because he'd been the leader, out in front, that he got it first of the mutineers.

One MP was dead, and one was sitting with red all over the middle of his uniform, and that one was Breck, and they were bringing a stretcher for him now.

The corporal said, "Hey, that's Jergen, your squad-leader!"

And I said, "Yes, that's him." Funny, how you can't talk when something hits you—how you just say words, like "Yes, that's him."

Breck died that night without ever regaining consciousness, and there I was, still half-sick myself, and with Lassen dying in his bunk, and five of us were all that was left of Squad Fourteen, and that was that.

How could HQ let a thing like that get known? A fine advertisement it would be for recruiting more Mars expeditions, if they told how guys on Two cracked up and did a crazy thing like that. I didn't blame them for telling us to keep it top secret. Anyway, it wasn't something we'd want to talk about.

But it sure left me in a fine spot now, a sweet spot. I was going down to talk to Breck's parents and Walter's parents, and they'd want to know how their sons died, and I could tell them, "Your sons probably killed each other, out there."

Sure, I could tell them that, couldn't I? But what *was* I going to tell them? I knew HQ had reported those casualties as "accidental deaths," but what kind of accident?

Well, it got late, and I had to go down, and when I did, Breck's parents were there. Mr. Jergen was a carpenter, a tall, bony man with level blue eyes like Breck's. He didn't say much, but his wife was a little woman who talked enough for both of them.

She told me I looked just like I did in the pictures of us Breck had sent home from Training Base. She said she had three daughters too—two of them married, and one of the married ones living in Milwaukee and one out on the Coast.

She said that she'd named Breck after a character in a book by Robert Louis Stevenson, and I said I'd read the book in high school.

"It's a nice name," I said.

She looked at me with bright eyes and said, "Yes. It was a nice name."

That was a fine dinner. They'd got everything they thought I might like, and all the best, and a maid served it, and I couldn't taste a thing I ate.

Then afterward, in the big living-room, they all just sort of sat and waited, and I knew it was up to me.

I asked them if they'd had any details about the accident, and Mr. Millis said, No, just "accidental death" was all they'd been told.

Well, that made it easier. I sat there, with all four of them watching my face, and dreamed it up.

I said, "It was one of those one-in-a-million things. You see, more little meteorites hit the ground on Mars than here, because the air's so much thinner it doesn't burn them up so fast. And one hit the edge of the fuel-dump and a bunch of little tanks started to blow. I was down with the sickness, so I didn't see it, but I heard all about it."

You could hear everybody breathing, it was so quiet as I went on with my yarn.

"A couple of guys were knocked out by the concussion, and would have been burned up if a few fellows hadn't got in there fast with foamite extinguishers. They kept it away from the big tanks, but another little tank let go, and Breck and Walter were two of the fellows who'd gone in, and they were killed instantly."

When I'd got it told, it sounded corny to me and I was afraid they'd never believe it. But nobody said anything, until Mr. Millis let out a sigh and said, "So that was it. Well—well, if it had to be, it was mercifully quick, wasn't it?"

I said, Yes, it was quick.

"Only, I can't see why they couldn't have let us know. It doesn't seem fair—"

I had an answer for that. "It's hush-hush because they don't want people to know about the meteor danger. That's why."

Mrs. Millis got up and said she wasn't feeling so well, and would I excuse her and she'd see me in the morning. The rest of us didn't seem to have much to say to each other, and nobody objected when I went up to my bedroom a little later.

I was getting ready to turn in when there was a knock on the door. It was Breck's father, and he came in and looked at me, steadily.

"It was just a story, wasn't it?" he said.

I said, "Yes. It was just a story."

His eyes bored into me and he said, "I guess you've got your reasons. Just tell me one thing. Whatever it was, did Breck behave right?"

"He behaved like a man, all the way," I said. "He was the best man of us, first to last."

He looked at me, and I guess something made him believe me. He shook hands and said, "All right, son. We'll let it go."

I'd had enough. I wasn't going to face them again in the morning. I wrote a note, thanking them all and making excuses, and then went down and slipped quietly out of the house.

It was late, but a truck coming along picked me up, and the driver said he was going near the airport. He asked me what it was like on Mars and I told him it was lonesome. I slept in a chair at the airport, and I felt better, for next day I'd be home, and it would be over.

That's what I thought.

4

It was getting toward evening when we reached the village, for my father and mother hadn't known I was coming on an earlier plane, and I'd had to wait for them up at Cleveland airport. When we drove into Market Street, I saw there was a big painted banner stretching across:

"HARMONVILLE WELCOMES HOME ITS SPACEMAN!"

Spaceman—that was me. The newspapers had started calling us that, I guess, because it was a short word good for headlines. Everybody called us that now. We'd sat cooped up in a prison-cell that flew, that was all—but now we were "spacemen."

There were bright uniforms clustered under the banner, and I saw that it was the high school band. I didn't say anything, but my father saw my face.

"Now, Frank, I know you're tired but these people are your friends and they want to show you a real welcome."

That was fine. Only it was all gone again, the relaxed feeling I'd been beginning to get as we drove down from Cleveland.

This was my home-country, this old Ohio country with its neat little white villages and fat, rolling farms. It looked good, in June. It looked very good, and I'd been feeling better all the time. And now I didn't feel so good, for I saw that I was going to have to talk some more about Mars.

Dad stopped the car under the banner, and the high school band started to play, and Mr. Robinson, who was the Chevrolet dealer and also the mayor of Harmonville, got into the car with us.

He shook hands with me and said, "Welcome home, Frank! What was it like out on Mars?"

I said, "It was cold, Mr. Robinson. Awful cold."

"You should have been here last February!" he said. "Eighteen below— nearly a record."

He leaned out and gave a signal, and dad started driving again, with the band marching along in front of us and playing. We didn't have far to go, just down Market Street under the big old maples, past the churches and the old white houses to the square white Grange Hall.

There was a little crowd in front of it, and they made a sound like a cheer—not a real loud one, you know how people can be self-conscious about really cheering—when we drove up. I got out and shook hands with people I didn't really see, and then Mr. Robinson took my elbow and took me on inside.

The seats were all filled and people standing up, and over the little stage at the far end they'd fixed up a big floral decoration—there was a globe all of red roses with a sign above it that said "Mars," and beside it a globe all of white roses that said "Earth," and a little rocket-ship made out of flowers was hung between them.

"The Garden Club fixed it up," said Mr. Robinson. "Nearly everybody in Harmonville contributed flowers."

"It sure is pretty," I said.

Mr. Robinson took me by the arm, up onto the little stage, and everyone clapped. They were all people I knew—people from the farms near ours, my high school teachers, and all that.

I sat down in a chair and Mr. Robinson made a little speech, about how Harmonville boys had always gone out when anything big was doing, how they'd gone to the War of 1812 and the Civil War and the two World Wars, and how now one of them had gone to Mars.

291

He said, "Folks have always wondered what it's like out there on Mars, and now here's one of our own Harmonville boys come back to tell us all about it."

And he motioned me to get up, and I did, and they clapped some more, and I stood wondering what I could tell them.

And all of a sudden, as I stood there wondering, I got the answer to something that had always puzzled us out there. We'd never been able to understand why the fellows who had come back from Expedition One hadn't tipped us off how tough it was going to be. And now I knew why. They hadn't, because it would have sounded as if they were whining about all they'd been through. And now I couldn't, for the same reason.

I looked down at the bright, interested faces, the faces I'd known almost all my life, and I knew that what I could tell them was no good anyway. For they'd all read those newspaper stories, about "the exotic red planet" and "heroic spacemen," and if anyone tried to give them a different picture now, it would just upset them.

I said, "It was a long way out there. But flying space is a wonderful thing—flying right off the Earth, into the stars—there's nothing quite like it."

Flying space, I called it. It sounded good, and thrilling. How could they know that flying space meant lying strapped in that blind stokehold, listening to Joe Valinez dying, and praying and praying that it wouldn't be our rocket that cracked up?

"And it's a wonderful thrill to come out of a rocket and step on a brand-new world, to look up at a different-looking Sun, to look around at a whole new horizon—"

Yes, it was wonderful. Especially for the guys in Rockets Seven and Nine who got squashed like flies and lay around there on the sand, moaning "First aid!" Sure, it was a big thrill, for them and for us who had to try to help them.

"There were hardships out there, but we all knew that a big job had to be done—"

That's a nice word too, "hardships." It's not coarse and ugly like fellows coughing their hearts out from too much dust; it's not like having your best friend die of Martian sickness right in the room you sleep in. It's a nice, cheerful word, "hardships."

"—and the only way we could get the job done, away out there so far from Earth, was by team-work."

Well, that was true enough in its way, and what was the use of spoiling it by telling them how Walter and Breck had died?

"The job's going on, and Expedition Three is building a bigger base out there right now, and Four will start soon. And it'll mean plenty of uranium, plenty of cheap atomic power, for all Earth."

That's what I said, and I stopped there. But I wanted to go on and add, "And it wasn't worth it! It wasn't worth all those guys, all the hell we went through, just to get cheap atomic power so you people can run more electric washers and television sets and toasters!"

But how are you going to stand up and say things like that to people you know, people who like you? And who was I to decide? Maybe I was wrong, anyway. Maybe lots of things I'd had and never thought about had been squeezed out of other good guys, back in the past.

I wouldn't know.

Anyway, that was all I could tell them, and I sat down, and there was a big lot of applause, and I realized then that I'd done right, I'd told them just what they wanted to hear, and everyone was all happy about it.

Then things broke up, and people came up to me, and I shook a lot more hands. And finally, when I got outside, it was dark—soft, summery dark, the way I hadn't seen it for a long time. And my father said we ought to be getting on home, so I could rest.

I told him, "You folks drive on ahead, and I'll walk. I'll take the short cut. I'd sort of like to walk through town."

Our farm was only a couple of miles out of the village, and the short-cut across Heller's farm I'd always taken when I was a kid was only a mile. Dad didn't think maybe I ought to walk so far, but I guess he saw I wanted to, so they went on ahead.

I walked on down Market Street, and around the little square, and the maples and elms were dark over my head, and the flowers on the lawns smelled the way they used to, but it wasn't the same either—I'd thought it would be, but it wasn't.

When I cut off past the Odd Fellows' Hall, beyond it I met Hobe Evans, the garage-hand at the Ford place, who was humming along half-tight, the same as always on a Saturday night.

"Hello, Frank, heard you were back," he said. I waited for him to ask the question they all asked, but he didn't. He said:

"Boy, you don't look so good! Want a drink?"

He brought out a bottle, and I had one out of it, and he had one, and he said he'd see me around, and went humming on his way. He was feeling too good to care much where I'd been.

I went on, in the dark, across Heller's pasture and then along the creek under the big old willows. I stopped there like I'd always stopped when I was a kid, to hear the frog-noises, and there they were, and all the June-noises, the night-noises, and the night-smells.

I did something I hadn't done for a long time. I looked up at the starry sky, and there it was, the same little red dot I'd peered at when I was a kid and read those old stories, the same red dot that Breck and Jim and Walter and I had stared away at on nights at Training Base, wondering if we'd ever really get there.

Well, they'd got there, and weren't ever going to leave it now, and there'd be others to stay with them, more and more of them as time went by.

But it was the ones I knew that made the difference, as I looked up at the red dot.

I wished I could explain to them somehow why I hadn't told the truth, not the whole truth. I tried, sort of, to explain.

"I didn't want to lie," I said. "But I had to—at least, it seemed like I had to—"

I quit it. It was crazy, talking to guys who were dead and forty million miles away. They were dead, and it was over, and that was that. I quit looking up at the red dot in the sky, and started on home again.

But I felt as though something was over for me, too. It was being young. I didn't feel old. But I didn't feel young, either, and I didn't think I ever would, not ever again.

Requiem

Kellon thought sourly that he wasn't commanding a star-ship, he was running a travelling circus. He had aboard telaudio men with tons of equipment, pontifical commentators who knew the answer to anything, beautiful females who were experts on the woman's angle, pompous bureaucrats after publicity, and entertainment stars who had come along for the same reason.

He had had a good ship and crew, one of the best in the Survey. *Had* had. They weren't any more. They had been taken off their proper job of pushing astrographical knowledge ever further into the remote regions of the galaxy, and had been sent off with this cargo of costly people on a totally unnecessary mission.

He said bitterly to himself, "Damn all sentimentalists."

He said aloud, "Does its position check with your calculated orbit, Mr. Riney?"

Riney, the Second, a young and serious man who had been fussing with instruments in the astrogation room, came out and said, "Yes. Right on the nose. Shall we go in and land now?"

Kellon didn't answer for a moment, standing there in the front of the bridge, a middle-aged man, stocky, square-shouldered, and with his tanned, plain face showing none of the resentment he felt. He hated to give the order but he had to.

"All right, take her in."

He looked gloomily through the filter-windows as they went in. In this fringe-spiral of the galaxy, stars were relatively infrequent, and there were only ragged drifts of them across the darkness. Full ahead shone a small, compact sun like a diamond. It was a white dwarf and had been so for two thousand years, giving forth so little warmth that the planets which circled it had been frozen and ice-locked all that time. They still were, all except the innermost world.

Kellon stared at that planet, a tawny blob. The ice that had sheathed it ever since its primary collapsed into a white dwarf, had now melted. Months before, a dark wandering body had passed very close to this life-less system. Its passing had perturbed the planetary orbits and the inner planets had started to spiral slowly in toward their sun, and the ice had begun to go.

Viresson, one of the junior officers, came into the bridge looking harassed. He said to Kellon, "They want to see you down below, sir. Es-pecially Mr. Borrodale. He says it's urgent."

Kellon thought wearily, "Well, I might as well go down and face the pack of them. Here's where they really begin."

He nodded to Viresson, and went down below to the main cabin. The sight of it revolted him. Instead of his own men in it, relaxing or chinning, it held a small and noisy mob of overdressed, overloud men and women, all of whom seemed to be talking at once and uttering brittle, nervous laughter.

"Captain Kellon, I want to ask you—"

"Captain, if you *please*—"

He patiently nodded and smiled and plowed through them to Bor-rodale. He had been given particular instructions to cooperate with Borrodale, the most famous telaudio commentator in the Federation.

Borrodale was a slightly plump man with a round pink face and incon-gruously large and solemn black eyes. When he spoke, one recognized at once that deep, incredibly rich and meaningful voice.

"My first broadcast is set for thirty minutes from now, Captain. I shall want a view as we go in. If my men could take a mobile up to the bridge—"

Kellon nodded. "Of course. Mr. Viresson is up there and will assist them in any way."

"Thank you, Captain. Would you like to see the broadcast?"

"I would, yes, but—"

He was interrupted by Lorri Lee, whose glitteringly handsome face and figure and sophisticated drawl made her the idol of all female telau-dio reporters.

"My broadcast is to be right after landing—remember? I'd like to do it alone, with just the emptiness of that world as background. Can you keep the others from spoiling the effect? Please?"

"We'll do what we can," Kellon mumbled. And as the rest of the pack converged on him he added hastily, "I'll talk to you later. Mr. Borrodale's broadcast—"

He got through them, following after Borrodale toward the cabin that had been set up as a telaudio-transmitter room. It had, Kellon thought bitterly, once served an honest purpose, holding the racks of soil and water and other samples from far worlds. But that had been when they were doing an honest Survey job, not chaperoning chattering fools on this sentimental pilgrimage.

The broadcasting set-up was beyond Kellon. He didn't want to hear this but it was better than the mob in the main cabin. He watched as Borrodale made a signal. The monitor-screen came alive.

It showed a dun-colored globe spinning in space, growing visibly larger as they swept toward it. Now straggling seas were identifiable upon it. Moments passed and Borrodale did not speak, just letting that picture go out. Then his deep voice spoke over the picture, with dramatic simplicity.

"You are looking at the Earth," he said.

Silence again, and the spinning brownish ball was bigger now, with white clouds ragged upon it. And then Borrodale spoke again.

"You who watch from many worlds in the galaxy—this is the homeland of our race. Speak its name to yourselves. The Earth."

Kellon felt a deepening distaste. This was all true, but still it was phony. What was Earth now to him, or to Borrodale, or his billions of listeners? But it was a story, a sentimental occasion, so they had to pump it up into something big.

"Some thirty-five hundred years ago," Borrodale was saying, "our ancestors lived on this world alone. That was when they first went into space. To these other planets first—but very soon, to other stars. And so our Federation began, our community of human civilization on many stars and worlds."

Now, in the monitor, the view of Earth's dun globe had been replaced by the face of Borrodale in close-up. He paused dramatically.

"Then, over two thousand years ago, it was discovered that the sun of Earth was about to collapse into a white dwarf. So those people who still remained on Earth left it forever and when the solar change came, it and the other planets became mantled in eternal ice. And now, within months, the final end of the old planet of our origin is at hand. It is slowly spiralling toward the sun and soon it will plunge into it as Mercury and Venus have already done. And when that occurs, the world of man's origin will be gone forever."

Again the pause, for just the right length of time, and then Borrodale continued in a voice expertly pitched in a lower key.

"We on this ship—we humble reporters and servants of the vast te-laudio audience on all the worlds—have come here so that in these next weeks we can give you this last look at our ancestral world. We think—we hope—that you'll find interest in recalling a past that is almost legend."

And Kellon thought, "The bastard has no more interest in this old planet than I have, but he surely is smooth."

As soon as the broadcast ended, Kellon found himself besieged once more by the clamoring crowd in the main cabin. He held up his hand in protest.

"Please, now, now—we have a landing to make first. Will you come with me, Doctor Darnow?"

Darnow was from Historical Bureau, and was the titular head of the whole expedition, although no one paid him much attention. He was a sparrowy, elderly man who babbled excitedly as he went with Kellon to the bridge.

He at least, was sincere in his interest, Kellon thought. For that matter, so were all the dozen-odd scientists who were aboard. But they were far outnumbered by the fat cats and big brass out for publicity, the professional enthusers and sentimentalists. A real hell of a job the Survey had given him!

In the bridge, he glanced through the window at the dun-colored planet and its satellite. Then he asked Darnow, "You said something about a particular place where you wanted to land?"

The historiographer bobbed his head, and began unfolding a big, old-fashioned chart.

"See this continent here? Along its eastern coast were a lot of the biggest cities, like New York."

Kellon remembered that name, he'd learned it in school history, a long time ago.

Darnow's finger stabbed the chart. "If you could land there, right on the island—"

Kellon studied the relief features, then shook his head. "Too low. There'll be great tides as time goes on and we can't take chances. That higher ground back inland a bit should be all right, though."

Darnow looked disappointed. "Well. I suppose you're right."

Kellon told Riney to set up the landing-pattern. Then he asked Darnow skeptically, "You surely don't expect to find much in those old cities now—not after they've had all that ice on them for two thousand years?"

"They'll be badly damaged, of course," Darnow admitted. "But there should be a vast number of relics. I could study here for years—"

"We haven't got years, we've got only a few months before this planet gets too close to the sun," said Kellon. And he added mentally, "Thank God."

The ship went into its landing-pattern. Atmosphere whined outside its hull and then thick gray clouds boiled and raced around it. It went down through the cloud layer and moved above a dull brown landscape that had flecks of white in its deeper valleys. Far ahead there was the glint of a gray ocean. But the ship came down toward a rolling brown plain and settled there, and then there was the expected thunderclap of silence that always followed the shutting off of all machinery.

Kellon looked at Riney, who turned in a moment from the test-panel with a slight surprise on his face. "Pressure, oxygen, humidity, everything—all optimum." And then he said, "But of course. This place *was* optimum."

Kellon nodded. He said, "Doctor Darnow and I will have a look out first. Viresson, you keep our passengers in."

When he and Darnow went to the lower airlock he heard a buzzing clamor from the main cabin and he judged that Viresson was having his hands full. The people in there were not used to being said no to, and he could imagine their resentment.

Cold, damp air struck a chill in Kellon when they stepped down out of the airlock. They stood on muddy, gravelly ground that squashed a little under their boots as they trudged away from the ship. They stopped and looked around, shivering.

Under the low gray cloudy sky there stretched a sad, sunless brown landscape. Nothing broke the drab color of raw soil, except the shards of ice still lingering in low places. A heavy desultory wind stirred the raw air, and then was still. There was not a sound except the clinkclinking of the ship's skin cooling and contracting, behind them. Kellon thought that no amount of sentimentality could make this anything but a dreary world.

But Darnow's eyes were shining. "We'll have to make every minute of the time count," he muttered. "Every minute."

Within two hours, the heavy broadcast equipment was being trundled away from the ship on two motor-tracs that headed eastward. On one of the tracs rode Lorri Lee, resplendent in lilac-colored costume of synthesilk.

Kellon, worried about the possibility of quicksands, went along for that first broadcast from the cliffs that looked down on the ruins of New York. He wished he hadn't, when it got under way.

For Lorri Lee, her blonde head bright even in the dull light, turned loose all her practiced charming gestures for the broadcast cameras, as she gestured with pretty excitement down toward the ruins.

"It's so *unbelievable!*" she cried to a thousand worlds. "To be here on Earth, to see the old places again—it *does* something to you!"

It did something to Kellon. It made him feel sick at his stomach. He turned and went back to the ship, feeling at that moment that if Lorri Lee went into a quicksand on the way back, it would be no great loss.

But that first day was only the beginning. The big ship quickly became the center of multifarious and continuous broadcasts. It had been especially equipped to beam strongly to the nearest station in the Federation network, and its transmitters were seldom quiet.

Kellon found that Darnow, who was supposed to coordinate all this programming, was completely useless. The little historian was living in a seventh heaven on this old planet which had been uncovered to view for the first time in millennia, and he was away most of the time on field trips of his own. It fell to his assistant, an earnest and worried and harassed young man, to try to reconcile the clashing claims and demands of the highly temperamental broadcasting stars.

Kellon felt an increasing boredom at having to stand around while all this tosh went out over the ether. These people were having a field-day but he didn't think much of them and of their broadcasts. Roy Quayle, the young male fashion designer, put on a semi-humorous, semi-nostalgic display of the old Earth fashions, with the prettier girls wearing some of the ridiculous old costumes he had had duplicated. Barden, the famous teleplay producer, ran off ancient films of the old Earth dramas that had everyone in stitches. Jay Maxson, a rising politician in Federation Congress, discussed with Borrodale the governmental systems of the old days, in a way calculated to give his own Wide-Galaxy Party none the worst of it. The Arcturus Players, that brilliant group of young stage-folk, did readings of old Earth dramas and poems.

It was, Kellon thought disgustedly, just playing. Grown people, famous people, seizing the opportunity given by the accidental end of a forgotten planet to posture in the spotlight like smart-aleck children. There was real work to do in the galaxy, the work of the Survey, the endless and wearying but always-fascinating job of charting the wild systems and worlds. And instead of doing that job, he was condemned to spend weeks and months here with these phonies.

The scientists and historians he respected. They did few broadcasts and they did not fake their interest. It was one of them, Haller, the biologist, who excitedly showed Kellon a handful of damp soil a week after their arrival.

"Look at *that!*" he said proudly.

Kellon stared. "What?"

"Those seeds—they're common weed-grass seeds. Look at them."

Kellon looked, and now he saw that from each of the tiny seeds projected a new-looking hairlike tendril.

"They're sprouting?" he said unbelievingly.

Haller nodded happily. "I was hoping for it. You see, it was almost spring in the northern hemisphere, according to the records, when Sol collapsed suddenly into a white dwarf. Within hours the temperature plunged and the hydrosphere and atmosphere began to freeze."

"But surely that would kill all plant-life?"

"No," said Haller. "The larger plants, trees, perennial shrubs, and so on, yes. But the seeds of the smaller annuals just froze into suspended animation. Now the warmth that melted them is causing germination."

"Then we'll have grass—small plants?"

"Very soon, the way the warmth is increasing."

It was, indeed, getting a little warmer all the time as these first weeks went by. The clouds lifted one day and there was brilliant, thin white sunshine from the little diamond sun. And there came a morning when they found the rolling landscape flushed with a pale tint of green.

Grass grew. Weeds grew, vines grew, all of them seeming to rush their growth as though they knew that this, their last season, would not be long. Soon the raw brown mud of the hills and valleys had been replaced by a green carpet, and everywhere taller growths were shooting up, and flowers beginning to appear. Hepaticas, bluebells, dandelions, violets, bloomed once more.

Kellon took a long walk, now that he did not have to plow through mud. The chattering people around the ship, the constant tug and pull of clashing temperaments, the brittle, febrile voices, got him down. He felt better to get away by himself.

The grass and the flowers had come back but otherwise this was still an empty world. Yet there was a certain peace of mind in tramping up and down the long green rolling slopes. The sun was bright and cheerful now, and white clouds dotted the sky, and the warm wind whispered as he sat upon a ridge and looked away westward where nobody was, or would ever be again.

"Damned dull," he thought. "But at least it's better than back with the gabblers."

He sat for a long time in the slanting sunshine, feeling his bristling nerves relax. The grass stirred about him, rippling in long waves, and the taller flowers nodded.

No other movement, no other life. A pity, he thought, that there were no birds for this last spring of the old planet—not even a butterfly. Well, it made no difference, all this wouldn't last long.

As Kellon tramped back through the deepening dusk, he suddenly became aware of a shining bubble in the darkening sky. He stopped and stared up at it and then remembered. Of course, it was the old planet's moon—during the cloudy nights he had forgotten all about it. He went on, with its vague light about him.

When he stepped back into the lighted main cabin of the ship, he was abruptly jarred out of his relaxed mood. A first-class squabble was going on, and everybody was either contributing to it or commenting on it. Lorri Lee, looking like a pretty child complaining of a hurt, was maintaining that she should have broadcast time the next day for her special woman's-interest feature, and somebody else disputed her claim, and young Vallely, Darnow's assistant, looked harried and upset. Kellon got by them without being noticed, locked the door of his cabin and poured himself a long drink, and damned Survey all over again for this assignment.

He took good care to get out of the ship early in the morning, before the storm of temperament blew up again. He left Viresson in charge of the ship, there being nothing for any of them to do now anyway, and legged it away over the green slopes before anyone could call him back.

They had five more weeks of this, Kellon thought. Then, thank God, Earth would be getting so near the sun that they must take the ship back

302

into its proper element of space. Until that wished-for day arrived, he would stay out of sight as much as possible.

He walked miles each day. He stayed carefully away from the east and the ruins of old New York, where the others so often were. But he went north and west and south, over the grassy, flowering slopes of the empty world. At least it was peaceful, even though there was nothing at all to see.

But after a while, Kellon found that there were things to see if you looked for them. There was the way the sky changed, never seeming to look the same twice. Sometimes it was deep blue and white clouds sailed it like mighty ships. And then it would suddenly turn gray and miserable, and rain would drizzle on him, to be ended when a lance of sunlight shot through the clouds and slashed them to flying ribbons. And there was a time when, upon a ridge, he watched vast thunderheads boil up and darken in the west and black storm clouds marched across the land like an army with banners of lightning and drums of thunder.

The winds and the sunshine, the sweetness of the air and the look of the moonlight and the feel of the yielding grass under his feet, all seemed oddly right. Kellon had walked on many worlds under the glare of many-colored suns, and some of them he had liked much better than this one and some of them he had not liked at all, but never had he found a world that seemed so exactly attuned to his body as this outworn, empty planet.

He wondered vaguely what it had been like when there were trees and birds, and animals of many kinds, and roads and cities. He borrowed film-books from the reference library Darnow and the others had brought, and looked at them in his cabin of nights. He did not really care very much but at least it kept him out of the broils and quarrels, and it had a certain interest.

Thereafter in his wandering strolls, Kellon tried to see the place as it would have been in the long ago. There would have been robins and bluebirds, and yellow-and-black bumblebees nosing the flowers, and tall trees with names that were equally strange to him, elms and willows and sycamores. And small furred animals, and humming clouds of insects, and fish and frogs in the pools and streams, a whole vast complex symphony of life, long gone, long forgotten.

But were all the men and women and children who had lived here less forgotten? Borrodale and the others talked much on their broadcasts about the people of old Earth, but that was just a faceless name, a term that meant nothing. Not one of those millions, surely, had ever thought of himself as part of a numberless multitude. Each one had been to himself, and to those close to him or her, an individual, unique and never to be exactly repeated, and what did the glib talkers know of all those individuals, what could anyone know?

Kellon found traces of them here and there, bits of flotsam that even the crush of the ice had spared. A twisted piece of steel, a girder or rail that someone had labored to make. A quarry with the tool-marks still on the rocks, where surely men had once sweated in the sun. The broken shards of concrete that stretched away in a ragged line to make a road upon which men and women had once travelled, hurrying upon missions of love or ambition, greed or fear.

He found more than that, a startling find that he made by purest chance. He followed a brook that ran down a very narrow valley, and at one point he leaped across it and as he landed he looked up and saw that there was a house.

Kellon thought at first that it was miraculously preserved whole and unbroken, and surely that could not be. But when he went closer he saw that this was only illusion and that destruction had been at work upon it too. Still, it remained, incredibly, a recognizable house.

It was a rambling stone cottage with low walls and a slate roof, set close against the steep green wall of the valley. One gable-end was smashed in, and part of that end wall. Studying the way it was embayed in the wall, Kellon decided that a chance natural arch of ice must have preserved it from the grinding pressure that had shattered almost all other structures.

The windows and doors were only gaping openings. He went inside and looked around the cold shadows of what had once been a room. There were some wrecked pieces of rotting furniture, and dried mud banked along one wall contained unrecognizable bits of rusted junk, but there was not much else. It was chill and oppressive in there, and he went out and sat on the little terrace in the sunshine.

He looked at the house. It could have been built no later than the Twentieth Century, he thought. A good many different people must have lived in it during the hundreds of years before the evacuation of Earth.

Kellon thought that it was strange that the airphoto surveys that Darnow's men had made in quest of relics had not discovered the place. But then it was not so strange, the stone walls were so grayly inconspicuous and it was set so deeply into the sheltering bay of the valley wall.

His eye fell on eroded lettering on the cement side of the terrace, and he went and brushed the soil off that place. The words were time-eaten and faint but he could read them.

"Ross and Jennie—Their House."

Kellon smiled. Well, at least he knew now who once had lived here, who probably had built the place. He could imagine two young people happily scratching the words in the wet cement, exuberant with achievement. And who had Ross and Jennie been, and where were they now?

He walked around the place. To his surprise, there was a ragged flower-garden at one side. A half-dozen kinds of brilliant little flowers, unlike the wild ones of the slopes, grew in patchy disorder here. Seeds of an old garden had been ready to germinate when the long winter of Earth came down, and had slept in suspended animation until the ice melted and the warm blooming time came at last. He did not know what kinds of flowers these were, but there was a brave jauntiness about them that he liked.

Starting back across the green land in the soft twilight, Kellon thought that he should tell Darnow about the place. But if he did, the gabbling pack in the ship would certainly stampede toward it. He could imagine the solemn and cute and precious broadcasts that Borrodale and the Lee woman and the rest of them would stage from the old house.

"No," he thought. "The devil with them."

He didn't care anything himself about the old house, it was just that it was a refuge of quiet he had found and he didn't want to draw to it the noisy horde he was trying to escape.

Kellon was glad in the following days that he had not told. The house gave him a place to go to, to poke around and investigate, a focus for his interest in this waiting time. He spent hours there, and never told anyone at all.

Haller, the biologist, lent him a book on the flowers of Earth, and he brought it with him and used it to identify those in the ragged garden. Verbenas, pinks, morning glories, and the bold red and yellow ones called nasturtiums. Many of these, he read, did not do well on other worlds and had never been successfully transplanted. If that was so, this would be their last blooming anywhere at all.

He rooted around the interior of the house, trying to figure out how people had lived in it. It was strange, not at all like a modern metalloy house. Even the interior walls were thick beyond belief, and the windows seemed small and pokey. The biggest room was obviously where they had lived most, and its window-openings looked out on the little garden and the green valley and brook beyond.

Kellon wondered what they had been like, the Ross and Jennie who had once sat here together and looked out these windows. What things had been important to them? What had hurt them, what had made them laugh? He himself had never married, the far-ranging captains of the Survey seldom did. But he wondered about this marriage of long ago, and what had come of it. Had they had children, did their blood still run on the far worlds? But even if it did, what was that now to those two of long ago?

There had been a poem about flowers at the end of the old book on flowers Haller had lent him, and he remembered some of it.

> *"All are at one now, roses and lovers,*
> *Not known of the winds and the fields and the sea,*
> *Not a breath of the time that has been hovers*
> *In the air now soft with a summer to be."*

Well, yes, Kellon thought, they were all at one now, the Rosses and the Jennies and the things they had done and the things they had thought, all at one now in the dust of this old planet whose fiery final summer would be soon, very soon. Physically, everything that had been done, everyone who had lived, on Earth was still here in its atoms, excepting the tiny fraction of its matter that had sped to other worlds.

He thought of the names that were so famous still through all the galactic worlds, names of men and women and places. Shakespeare, Plato, Beethoven, Blake, and the splendor of Babylon and the bones of Angkor and the humble houses of his own ancestors, all here, all still here.

Kellon mentally shook himself. He didn't have enough to do, that was his trouble, to be brooding here on such shadowy things. He had seen all there was to this queer little old place, and there was no use in coming back to it.

But he came back. It was not, he told himself, as though he had any sentimental antiquarian interests in this old place. He had heard enough of that kind of gush from all the glittering phonies in the ship. He was a Survey man and all he wanted was to get back to his job, but while he was stuck here it was better to be roaming the green land or poking about this old relic than to have to listen to the endless babbling and quarrelling of those others.

They were quarrelling more and more, because they were tired of it here. It had seemed to them a fine thing to posture upon a galactic stage by helping to cover the end of Earth, but time dragged by and their flush of synthetic enthusiasm wore thin. They could not leave, the expedition must broadcast the final climax of the planet's end, but that was still weeks away. Darnow and his scholars and scientists, busy coming and going to many old sites, could have stayed here forever but the others were frankly bored.

But Kellon found in the old house enough interest to keep the waiting from being too oppressive. He had read a good bit now about the way things had been here in the old days, and he sat long hours on the little terrace in the afternoon sunshine, trying to imagine what it had been like when the man and woman named Ross and Jennie had lived here.

So strange, so circumscribed, that old life seemed now! Most people had had ground-cars in those days, he had read, and had gone back and forth in them to the cities where they worked. Did both the man and woman go, or just the man? Did the woman stay in the house, perhaps with their children if they had any, and in the afternoons did she do things in the little flower garden where a few bright, ragged survivors still bloomed? Did they ever dream that some future day when they were long gone, their house would lie empty and silent with no visitor except a stranger from far-off stars? He remembered a line in one of the old plays the Arcturus Players had read. "Come like shadows, so depart."

No, Kellon thought. Ross and Jennie were shadows now but they had not been then. To them, and to all the other people he could visualize going and coming busily about the Earth in those days, it was he, the future, the man yet to come, who was the shadow. Alone here, sitting and trying to imagine the long ago, Kellon had an eery feeling sometimes that his vivid imaginings of people and crowded cities and movement and laughter were the reality and that he himself was only a watching wraith.

Summer days came swiftly, hot and hotter. Now the white sun was larger in the heavens and pouring down such light and heat as Earth had not received for millennia. And all the green life across it seemed to respond with an exultant surge of final growth, an act of joyous affirmation that Kellon found infinitely touching. Now even the nights were warm, and the winds blew thrilling soft, and on the distant beaches the ocean leaped up in a laughter of spray and thunder, running in great solar tides.

With a shock as though awakened from dreaming, Kellon suddenly realized that only a few days were left. The spiral was closing in fast now and very quickly the heat would mount beyond all tolerance.

He would, he told himself, be very glad to leave. There would be the wait in space until it was all over, and then he could go back to his own work, his own life, and stop fussing over shadows because there was nothing else to do.

Yes. He would be glad.

Then when only a few days were left, Kellon walked out again to the old house and was musing over it when a voice spoke behind him.

"Perfect," said Borrodale's voice. "A perfect relic."

Kellon turned, feeling somehow startled and dismayed. Borrodale's eyes were alight with interest as he surveyed the house, and then he turned to Kellon.

"I was walking when I saw you, Captain, and thought I'd catch up to you. Is this where you've been going so often?"

Kellon, a little guiltily, evaded. "I've been here a few times."

"But why in the world didn't you *tell* us about this?" exclaimed Borrodale. "Why, we can do a terrific final broadcast from here. A typical ancient home of Earth. Roy can put some of the Players in the old costumes, and we'll show them living here the way people did—"

Unexpectedly to himself, a violent reaction came up in Kellon. He said roughly, "No."

Borrodale arched his eyebrows. "No? But why not?"

Why not, indeed? What difference could it possibly make to him if they swarmed all over the old house, laughing at its ancientness and its inadequacies, posing grinning for the cameras in front of it, prancing about in old-fashioned costumes and making a show of it. What could that mean to him, who cared nothing about this forgotten planet or anything on it?

And yet something in him revolted at what they would do here, and he said, "We might have to take off very suddenly, now. Having you all out here away from the ship could involve a dangerous delay."

"You said yourself we wouldn't take off for a few days yet!" exclaimed Borrodale. And he added firmly, "I don't know why you should want to obstruct us, Captain. But I can go over your head to higher authority."

He went away, and Kellon thought unhappily, He'll message back to Survey headquarters and I'll get my ears burned off, and why the devil did I do it anyway? I must be getting real planet-happy.

He went and sat down on the terrace, and watched until the sunset deepened into dusk. The moon came up white and brilliant, but the air was not quiet tonight. A hot, dry wind had begun to blow, and the stir of the tall grass made the slopes and plains seem vaguely alive. It was as though a queer pulse had come into the air and the ground, as the sun called its child homeward and Earth strained to answer. The house dreamed in the silver light, and the flowers in the garden rustled.

Borrodale came back, a dark pudgy figure in the moonlight. He said triumphantly, "I got through to your headquarters. They've ordered your full cooperation. We'll want to make our first broadcast here tomorrow."

Kellon stood up. "No."

"You can't ignore an order—"

"We won't be here tomorrow," said Kellon. "It is my responsibility to get the ship off Earth in ample time for safety. We take off in the morning."

Borrodale was silent for a moment, and when he spoke his voice had a puzzled quality.

"You're advancing things just to block our broadcast, of course. I just can't understand your attitude."

Well, Kellon thought, he couldn't quite understand it himself, so how could he explain it? He remained silent, and Borrodale looked at him and then at the old house.

"Yet maybe I do understand," Borrodale said thoughtfully, after a moment. "You've come here often, by yourself. A man can get too friendly with ghosts—"

Kellon said roughly, "Don't talk nonsense. We'd better get back to the ship, there's plenty to do before take-off."

Borrodale did not speak as they went back out of the moonlit valley. He looked back once, but Kellon did not look back.

They took the ship off twelve hours later, in a morning made dull and ominous by racing clouds. Kellon felt a sharp relief when they cleared atmosphere and were out in the depthless, starry blackness. He knew where he was, in space. It was the place where a spaceman belonged. He'd get a stiff reprimand for this later, but he was not sorry.

They put the ship into a calculated orbit, and waited. Days, many of them, must pass before the end came to Earth. It seemed quite near the white sun now, and its moon had slid away from it on a new distorted orbit, but even so it would be a while before they could broadcast to a watching galaxy the end of its ancestral world.

Kellon stayed much of that time in his cabin. The gush that was going out over the broadcasts now, as the grand finale approached, made him sick. He wished the whole thing was over. It was, he told himself, getting to be a bore—

An hour and twenty minutes to E-time, and he supposed he must go up to the bridge and watch it. The mobile camera had been set up there and Borrodale and as many others of them as could crowd in were there. Borrodale had been given the last hour's broadcast, and it seemed that the others resented this.

"Why must you have the whole last hour?" Lorri Lee was saying bitterly to Borrodale. "It's not fair."

Quayle nodded angrily. "There'll be the biggest audience in history, and we should all have a chance to speak."

Borrodale answered them, and the voices rose and bickered, and Kellon saw the broadcast technicians looking worried. Beyond them through the filter-window he could see the dark dot of the planet closing on the white star. The sun called, and it seemed that with quickened eagerness Earth moved on the last steps of its long road. And the clamoring, bickering voices in his ears suddenly brought rage to Kellon.

"Listen," he said to the broadcast men. "Shut off all sound transmission. You can keep the picture on, but no sound."

That shocked them all into silence. The Lee woman finally protested, "Captain Kellon, you can't!"

"I'm in full command when in space, and I can, and do," he said.

"But the broadcast, the commentary—"

Kellon said wearily, "Oh, for Christ's sake all of you shut up, and let the planet die in peace."

He turned his back on them. He did not hear their resentful voices, did not even hear when they fell silent and watched through the dark filter-windows as he was watching, as the camera and the galaxy was watching.

And what was there to see but a dark dot almost engulfed in the shining veils of the Sun? He thought that already the stones of the old house must be beginning to vaporize. And now the veils of light and fire almost concealed the little planet, as the star gathered in its own.

All the atoms of old Earth, Kellon thought, in this moment bursting free to mingle with the solar being, all that had been Ross and Jennie, all that had been Shakespeare and Schubert, gay flowers and running streams, oceans and rocks and the wind of the air, received into the brightness that had given them life.

They watched in silence, but there was nothing more to see, nothing at all. Silently the camera was turned off.

Kellon gave an order, and presently the ship was pulling out of orbit, starting on the long voyage back. By that time the others had gone, all but

Borrodale. He said to Borrodale, without turning, "Now go ahead and send your complaint to headquarters."

Borrodale shook his head. "Silence can be the best requiem of all. There'll be no complaint. I'm glad now, Captain."

"Glad?"

"Yes," said Borrodale. "I'm glad that Earth had one true mourner, at the last."

After a Judgment Day

Martinsen lowered his head so that he would not see the window and the Earth. He looked instead at the complex bank of telltales across the room from him. He looked at them for a long time before he really saw them, and noticed that one had changed. A tiny red star had appeared in that section.

He reached and punched a button on the desk, and then leaned and said into an intercom, "Ellam, Sixteen is coming in."

There was no answer.

"Ellam?"

He knew his voice was searching through every part of the Station, down the gleaming metal corridors, into the small laboratories and the rock supply-caverns below. He waited, but there was still no answer from Howard Ellam.

Martinsen made a tired sound, between weariness and anger, and rose to his feet. He thought he knew what had happened, though he had taken precautions against it. He walked across the room and started down a corridor, a rumpled, soiled figure in the coverall he had not changed for days, his grizzled-gray head held up, but his shoulders sagging and his feet scuffing the plastic floor.

No sound broke the silence except the gentle purr of the aerators. There was no one in the Station but Ellam and himself. Carelli had taken the two others of the staff back to Earth with him weeks before, in one of the two emergency-ferries.

"I'll be back," he had told Martinsen, "as soon as I get things untangled down there. You and Ellam stay and handle the Charlies as they come in."

Carelli hadn't come back. Martinsen felt now that he never would come back, he or anyone else. They still had the second ferry. But they also had their orders.

He walked along in the silence, remembering when he had first walked this corridor, tingling with excitement and anticipation, his first ten minutes inside Lunar Station. How he had thought of the work he would be doing here, of the importance of that work to everyone on Earth, now and in the future. The future? My God, that was a laugh.

He went on through the silent rooms and passages until he found Ellam. He was sitting. Just sitting. He looked normal, except for the fact that he hadn't shaved, but when Martinsen saw the glassiness of his fixed stare, he looted around until he found the bottle of pills, half-spilled across a table.

Martinsen sighed. There was no liquor in the Station, but there were tranquilizers. He had thought he had found and hidden them all, but apparently Ellam still had a store. Well, that was one way to take catastrophe. Wrap your mind up in cotton-wool so you can't think about it. He put the pills in his pocket. There was nothing he could do but leave Ellam to come out of it.

He went back to C Room and sat there, watching the little red star slowly change position on the board as Probe Sixteen returned toward the Moon. The other probes, all recalled at the same time, would be coming in during the next few days, until all the Charlies had returned. And then?

He found that he was staring up at Earth again. How many people were still alive there? Many? Any? He thought of calling again but there was never any answer anymore, and later would be just as good.

It was very much later when he finally went down to Communications and tried the call. He put it through three times, and waited after each time, but there was no answer. Not a flicker.

The anger rose again in Martinsen. *Everybody* on Earth couldn't be dead. Not everybody. The A-Plague might have swept the globe and wiped out hundreds of millions, but surely someone down at Main Base would have survived, and why didn't that someone answer?

But that someone still living at Main Base...would he be able to answer if he wanted to? He just might not be able to utilize the complex communications instruments. The whole little staff here in the Station had, as a matter of course, been taught how. But that certainly did not apply to all the thousands who had worked at Main Base, and if the survivors didn't know...

Martinsen shook his head. Even if that had happened, even if Carelli had found Main Base depopulated when he went back down there, still, Carelli could have called and said so. Unless...unless Carelli and Muto and Jennings had been hit by the A-Plague before they had had time to find out what conditions were, and to get back to Communications and call back. But if that had happened, it meant that the A-Plague was triumphant over Earth and all its billions.

It was funny, in a way, Martinsen thought. For decades, people had been afraid of atomic destruction. It was nuclear war they had feared most, but also they had been afraid of fallout and what it might do to their bodies. But nuclear war had never happened, and fallout had been cut to a safe level. The only trouble was that a level that did not affect human bodies might very well affect other and smaller bodies. Like the bodies of bacteria.

A series of radioactive-induced mutations had occurred in a species of hitherto not-very-harmful bacteria. The scientists had finally wakened up to what was going on. But by then it was too late, the most fearful bacteria in the world's history had appeared and were spreading, and the A-Plague was let loose. Its first incursions, with previously unheard-of high mortality rates, had been in South America. The world health organizations had taken alarm. There had been swift measures of quarantine, concentrated searches for a vaccine. But it was too late for all that, and the messages that came through to the five horrified men in Lunar Station were of cities, then countries, then whole nations, going silent. Until Main Base, too, went silent.

And five men were left marooned in Lunar Station, and then after Carelli and Jennings and Muto went back down, there were only two men, and one of them kept doping up on pills to forget a wife and kids, so you might say he was alone, with a dead or dying world down there, and...

"Knock it off," Martinsen told himself. "You can cry later."

The telltales showed more little red stars, more probes approaching the Moon. The beautiful, slim metal ships in which no human had ever ridden yet, were returning. They had quested to the nearest stars and their planets, moving in overdrive, and those in them had walked under the radiation of strange suns. But the quest had been suddenly interrupted, a hyperspace signal had flung an abrupt command, and now the probes were coming back in.

He thought it was probably all for nothing. What use was it to record carefully all the knowledge the Charlies would bring back with them, if there was nobody left alive on Earth to use it? But Carelli had left him responsible and he couldn't just sit and throw away the first rewards of the whole project.

Cybernetic-Humanoid And Related Life Study, was the project's name. CHARLS, it was more often called, and of course the cyborgs that went out in the probes were at once nicknamed Charlies. And after a time, after Probe 16 had automatically made its landing and entered the reception hangars of Lunar Station, Martinsen heard the soft footsteps of Charlie Sixteen in the passageway, going quietly toward the analysis laboratories.

Martinsen got up and went to the labs. On the spot that had his number painted on the floor, Charlie Sixteen stood silent and unmoving. Martinsen started his preliminary examination, and despite his conviction that it was all for nothing now, he was quickly caught up in the routine.

"Heart-pump, kidneys, cardio-vascular system, all look good," he muttered. "Looks like more calcium mobilization than we expected, but it'll take time to find out. Let's see how your hypothalamus reacted, Charlie."

Charlie Sixteen stood and said nothing, for he could not speak. Neither could he hear, nor think. He was not a man, but a mechanical analog of humanity used to study the effect of unusual environments on a pseudo-human body. Cyborgs, they had been called from the first one in the early 1960s...cybernetic organisms.

He looked grotesquely like a man with his skin off, for through his transparent plastic tissues you could clearly see his artificial heart-pump, the clear tubes of his arteries and veins, the alloy "bones," the cleverly simulated lung-sacs, visible for close study through an aperture in the rib-cage that gaped like a ghastly wound. People who first saw cyborgs always found them horribly lifelike, but that first impression always faded fast, and a cyborg after that was no more lifelike than a centrifuge or a television set.

The staff at Lunar Station had had toward the Charlies something of the attitude of a window-dresser handling clothes-mannequins. But these mannequins were far more than stiff wax figures. They could walk, could obey the commands programmed into their electric nerve-systems. These mannequins were not made to stand in shop windows, but to plumb the stars. In the probes, at accelerations no human frame could endure, they would be sent to the worlds of foreign suns, and would walk those worlds and breathe their air and react to their gravitation, and then the probes would bring them back again to Lunar Station and the men there would ascertain the effects of the alien environments on these human analogs.

It had taken a long time for the Station staff to get the cyborgs ready and programmed to act as humanity's scouts into the stars. And during that time the men had humorously given them the Charlie names, in the way in which one had given a car or a boat a name, and had made small jokes about Charlie Nine being brighter than the others, and Charlie Fourteen being a coward who didn't want to go to the stars, and the like. And now, to the infinitely lonely Martinsen, the joke became almost reality, and he talked to the cyborg he was examining as to a living man.

He had gone to the hangars and had got from Probe 16 the tapes that held a record of the faroff coasts which that slim metal missile had explored. He had run through the tapes, first the visual ones that showed the tawny-red desert on which Charlie Sixteen had walked beneath two shadowed moons, and then the tapes on which the sensor instruments had recorded all the physical data of that world. He pondered certain points in those records, and had returned to his examination of Charlie Sixteen, not even hearing the muted metallic sounds from the hangars that told of two more probes making their automatic return and re-entry.

"I *think*," he told Charlie Sixteen, "that you're a slightly damaged cyborg. Consider yourself lucky that that's all...if you were a man, you'd be dead."

Consider yourself lucky, Charlie! If you were a man, you'd know, and think, and remember and...

Martinsen pushed that thought out of his mind and went on with his examination. Charlies Eight and Eleven had come in by the time he finished with Sixteen, walking silently into the lab and then standing motionless on the painted numbers where their programming ended. Martinsen got the tapes from their two probes and started on them, unwilling to stop work even when the hours passed and he grew tired, unwilling to go back to the chair and sit and look at Earth.

"Now why is your temperature down six degrees?" he muttered to Charlie Eight. "You went in and out of hypothermia perfectly the first time, but the second time you didn't come quite back to normal, and..."

"Are you out of your mind, talking to a Charlie?"

Howard Ellam's voice cut across, and Martinsen turned to find Ellam standing in the doorway, his eyes red-rimmed, his body swaying a little, but looking awake enough.

"Just thinking aloud," Martinsen said.

"Thinking?" Ellam jeered. "Things have got bad, all right, when we start talking to cyborgs."

"I'd as lief talk to a Charlie as to a man coked up on sleep-pills," flared Martinsen.

Ellam stared at him and then laughed. "Want to hear a sick joke? The last two men in the world were locked up together, and what happened? They got cabin-fever."

He laughed and laughed and then he stopped laughing. He said dully, "I'm sorry, Mart."

"Oh, forget it," said Martinsen. "But forget about us being the last two men, will you? No plague, not even an A-Plague, takes everyone. There's always a few survivors."

"Sure, there's always a few survivors," said Ellam. "Kill off all the whooping-cranes, and there still turns out to be a few survivors, for a little while. But they're finished, as a species. We're finished."

"Bull," said Martinsen without conviction.

He went doggedly on with his examination of the Charlies, his notations of their reactions to specific environments. Ellam, as though regretting his outburst, helped him set up the bioinstrumentation, and the measuring of effects. Mineral dynamics was Ellam's special field, and he was quick and precise in this. More probes, more missiles homing from the shores of infinity, kept coming in. Presently all but five of the eighteen Charlies stood in the lab.

"Charlie Six hit it lucky," said Ellam, after a while. "There's a world out there at Proxima that would be just fine for humans. If there were any humans to go there."

Martinsen made no answer, but went on with his work. Presently, with a what's-the-use shrug, Ellam quit and went out of the lab.

Martinsen supposed he had gone back to his pills. But when he finally stopped working, too tired to be accurate any longer, and went back through the Station, he found Ellam sitting in C Room looking up through the window at Earth.

"Never a light," said Ellam. "It used to be we'd see the lights that were cities, through the little refractor, but it's all dark now."

"The lights may be out, but people are still alive," said Martinsen.

"Oh, sure. A few of them. Sick and dying, or afraid they'll soon be sick and dying, and all the already dead around them."

"Will you *please* knock it off?" said Martinsen.

Ellam did not answer. After a moment Martinsen turned away. He did not feel like sleeping now. He went back to the labs.

He had turned out the lights there when he left. He walked back in, dull with fatigue, and the bar of light from the passageway struck in through the dark rooms and littered off chrome flanges and bars, and showed the quiet faces, rows and rows of them, of the Charlies standing there, each on his number, not moving, not making a sound. And of a sudden, after all his long familiarity with them, a horror of them struck Martinsen and he stood shivering. What was he doing in this place upon an alien world, with these unhuman figures, all looking toward him from the shadows? He was a man, and this was not a place for men. Things had gone too fast. Once he had been a boy in a little Ohio country town, and its quiet streets and white houses and old elms and maples must be still much the same, and oh God, he wanted to go back there. But there would be nothing there but death now, man had gone too far and too fast indeed, he was trapped here with unhuman travesties who stood silently looking at him, looking and looking...

He switched on the lights with a shaking hand, and suddenly there was a change, the Charlies were just Charlies, just machines that had never lived and never would live. Nerves, he thought. It had better not happen too often, for if it did he would end up running and screaming through the Station, and that was no way for a man to end. He could take pills like Ellam, but work was a better anodyne. He worked.

For days he worked, making the routine examination of every Charlie, noting everything down and not asking himself what eyes would ever read his notes. And when all that was done, and he knew more about the worlds of foreign stars than man had ever known before, he set himself to repair those Charlies that had been damaged by radiation, poisonous atmospheres, or abnormal gravitation.

Sometimes Ellam would help him, when he was not in a state of semi-stupor from his pills. He usually worked in heavy silence, but one time when the repair of Charlies was almost completed, Ellam asked, "What's it all for, anyway? Nobody will ever be sending these Charlies out again."

"I don't know," Martinsen answered. And then, after a moment, "Maybe I will."

"You? The Station will be dead and you with it before they'd ever get back."

"I wasn't thinking of having them come back," Martinsen answered vaguely.

An unusual sound of some kind awoke him later from his sleep. He sat up and listened and then he realized its origin. It came from the hangar of the emergency ferries.

Martinsen ran all the way there. His heart was pumping and he had an icy dread on him, the fear of being altogether alone. He was in time to catch Ellam before Ellam had got the little ferry set up for its automatic launch.

"Ellam, you can't go!"

"I'm going," said Ellam stonily.

"There's nothing but death waiting on Earth!"

Ellam jeered. "What's waiting here? It may be a little longer in coming, but not much."

Martinsen gripped his arm. He had come almost to hate Ellam, during these last days, but now suddenly Ellam was infinitely precious to him as the last defense against ultimate solitude.

"Listen," he said. "Wait a little longer, till I get the Charlies all repaired. Then I'll go with you."

Ellam stared at him. "You?"

"Do you think I want to be left alone here? Anyway, it's as you say, just a matter of time if we stay here. But I have one more thing I want to do."

After a moment Ellam said, "All right, if you're going with me. I'll wait a little while."

Martinsen had no illusions about the implications of his promise. The chances were that he and Ellam would both die of the plague very soon after they reached Earth. Still, death there was only a very high probability, whereas it was a certainty here when the Station machinery stopped operating. And that being so, there was not much room for choice.

But the resolution that had been forming in him was suddenly, sharply crystallized now. Ellam would not wait too long, he knew. He would have little time to do the thing he wanted to do.

He set to work furiously in Communications, preparing master-tapes. The first one was an audio-visual vocabulary tape in which the visual picture of a thing or an action was conjoined with Martinsen's speaking the noun or verb that defined it. It would not be a very large vocabulary but it would contain the key words, and he thought that with it an intelligence of any reasonably high level could quickly advance to expanding interpretations.

He was engaged in finishing this vocabulary-tape when Ellam came into the Communications room and watched him puzzledly for a while. Then he said puzzledly, "What in the world are you doing?"

Martinsen said, "I'm going to send the probes and Charlies out, before we leave."

"Send them where?"

"Everywhere they can go. Each one will take with him a copy of the tapes I'm preparing."

Ellam said, after a moment, "I get it. Messages in bottles from a drowning person. In other words, the last will and testament of a dying species."

"I still don't think our species will die," Martinsen said. "But even if it lives, it's bound to slip back...maybe a long way and for a long time. Everything shouldn't be lost..."

"It's a good idea," said Ellam. "I'll help you. Here, give me the mike." And he spoke mockingly into it, "This is the deathbed message of a race who were such damn fools that they managed to kill themselves off. And our solemn warning is, don't ever learn too much. Stay up in the trees."

Martinsen took the microphone away from him, but he sat brooding after Ellam had left. After all, there was truth in the bitter assertion that man was responsible for his own destruction. But was it the whole truth?

He suddenly realized his inadequacy for this task. He was no philosopher or seer. He was, outside of his own specialized field of science, a thoroughly average man. How could he take it upon himself to decide what was important to tell, and what was not? Yet there was no one else to do so.

The documentary factual knowledge, the science and the history, were what he began with and they were not so terribly difficult a problem. The Station contained a large microfilm library, and it was easy enough to set up the microfilm equipment so that selected factual knowledge fed directly onto the tapes. But there were also music, art, literature, many other things, and some of all that must survive. He felt more and more overwhelmed by the task as he muddled along trying to make his selections.

How did you evaluate things? Were Newton's Laws of Motion more important than Mozart's quartets? Were the Crusades more worthy of being remembered than Plato's Dialogues? Could he throw away forever the work of long-dead master artists, just because there was no room for a picture of the Parthenon? So much had been done in the world, so many causes valiantly fought, so much beauty created, so much toil and thought and dreaming, how could one pick and choose?

Martinsen went doggedly on with it, and when the last master-tape was finished he knew how faulty and wretched a job he had done. But there was no time to try again.

He sat for a while, looking at the last tape. He felt somehow that he could not let this imperfect record end without adding his own small word.

He said, after a little while, into the microphone, "The thing that has happened to us was of our own doing. But it came not so much from evil as from fecklessness."

He brooded for a moment and then went on. "We inherited curiosity from the ape, and curiosity unlocked many doors for us. The door of power, the door of space. And finally, if all perish, the door of death. Let this be said of us, that we preferred the risk of disaster to the safety of always staying still. But whether this was good or bad, I do not know."

Wearily, he shut off the machine. There was nothing left to do but to run the master-tapes through a duplicator until there was a full set of duplicate tapes for each of the eighteen probes. Then he went to the laboratory where the Charlies were.

Ellam, because he was impatient to get this done and leave, had agreed to program the Charlies. He looked almost cheerful now as he worked with Charlie Three. The endplates of the electrical "nerves" had been removed, and a chattering instrument was feeding code into the cyborg's memory-banks, code-signals that were orders. Orders about course in space, orders covering the landing on any planet which looked habitable or inhabited, orders on delivering the tapes only if certain conditions that indicated civilization were present, orders to go on to other stars and other possible planets if they were not. The probes had an almost unlimited range in overdrive, and some would go far indeed.

"Charlie Three is going to Vega," said Ellam. "And from there, if necessary, on to Lyra 431, and maybe a lot farther. He's going to see things, is Charlie Three. They all are."

Martinsen felt a pang of regret. Once men had thought that in time they too would see those things. But it was not to be, and the cyborgs would go in their place, weird lifeless successors of man.

He thought of a poem he had read during his rummaging of the library. What was it Chesterton had written?

"For the end of the world was long ago,
And we all dwell today as children of a second birth,
Like a strange people left on Earth
After a judgment day."

The cyborgs were not people and instead of being left on Earth they were to fare into the wider universe. Yet, stillborn and lifeless though they were, they were yet in a sense the children of men, carrying out to unguessable places the story of their creators.

The programming was finished. There was a wait. Then, at the ordered moment, the cyborgs walked quietly out of the laboratory, one after another.

From the window in C Room, Martinsen and Ellam watched as the probes took off. They raced into the sky. as though eager to go, vanishing from view as they went rapidly into overdrive to cross the vast and empty spaces.

Where would be the final ends of the Charlies? Some might perish in whirlpools of strange force, in unthinkable cosmic dangers. Others might ironically become the idols or gods of savage, ignorant minds. It could be that in time some would drift to other galaxies. But sometime, somewhere, one at least might deliver his message to those who could decipher it. The music of Schubert might be heard by alien ears, the dreams of Lucretius pondered by alien minds, and the human story would not pass without leaving its imprint on the universe.

The last probe was gone. Martinsen looked up at the globe of Earth, and then he took Ellam gently by the arm.

"Come on, Howard. Let's go home."

The Pro

The rocket stood tall and splendid, held for now in the nurse-arms of its gantry, but waiting, looking up and waiting...

And why the hell, thought Burnett, do I have to think fiction phrases even when I'm looking at the real thing?

"Must give you kind of a creepy feeling, at that," Dan said.

"God, yes." Burnett moved his shoulders, half grinning. "Creepy, and proud. I invented that thing. Thirty years ago come August, in my 'Stardream' novel, I designed her and built her and launched her and landed her on Mars, and got a cent a word for her from the old Wonder Stories."

"Too bad you didn't take out a patent."

"Be glad I didn't," Burnett said. "You're going to fly her. My Stardream was prettier than this one, but only had two short paragraphs of innards." He paused, nodding slowly. "It's kind of fitting, though, at that. It was the Stardream check, all four hundred dollars of it, that gave me the brass to ask your mother to marry me."

He looked at his son, the slim kid with the young-old face and the quiet smile. He could admit to himself now that he had been disappointed that Dan took after his mother in the matter of build. Burnett was a big man himself, with a large head and large hands and heavy shoulders, and Dan had always seemed small and almost frail to him. And now here was Dan in his sun-faded khakis blooming like a rose after all the pressure tests and the vertigo tests and the altitude tests and the various tortures of steel chambers and centrifuges, tests that Burnett doubted he could have stood up to even in his best days. He was filled with an unaccustomed and embarrassing warmth.

"You won't get to Mars in her, anyway," he said.

Dan laughed. "Not this trip. We'll be happy to settle for the Moon."

They walked on across the sun-blistered apron, turning their backs on the rocket. Burnett felt strangely as though all his sensory nerve-ends had been sandpapered raw so that the slightest stimulus set them to quivering. Never had the sun been so hot, never had he been so conscious of his own prickling skin, the intimate smell of clean cotton cloth dampening with sweat, the grit of blown sand under his feet, the nearness of his son, walking close beside him...

Not close enough. Not ever close enough.

It was odd, Burnett thought, that he had never until this moment been aware of any lack in their relationship.

Why? Why not then, and why now?

They walked companionably together in the sun, and Burnett's mind worked, the writer's mind trained and sharpened by thirty-odd years of beating a typewriter for an always precarious living, the mind that could never any more be wholly engulfed in any personal situation but must stand always in some measure apart, analytical and cool, Burnett the writer looking at Burnett the man as though he were a character in a story. Motivation, man. An emotion is unreal unless it's motivated, and this is not only unmotivated, it's inconsistent. It's not in character. People often seem to be inconsistent but they're not, they always have a reason for everything even if they don't know it, even if nobody knows it, and so what's yours, Burnett? Be honest, now. If you're not honest the whole thing, man and/or character, goes down the drain.

Why this sudden aching sense of incompletion, of not having done so many things, unspecified, for, by, and with this apparently perfectly happy and contented young man?

Because, thought Burnett. Because...

The heat waves shook and shimmered and the whiteness of sand and blockhouse and distant buildings were unbearably painful to the eye.

"What's the matter, Dad?" asked Dan, sharp and far away.

"Nothing. Just the light—dazzling..."And now the sweat was cold on his big hard body and there was a cold evil inside him, and he thought, Well, hell, yes, of course. I'm scared. I'm thinking...Go ahead and drag it out, it won't be any the better for hiding away there inside in the dark. I'm thinking that this boy of mine is going to climb into that beautiful horror back there, not very many hours from now, and men are going to fasten the hatch on him and go away, and other men will push buttons and light the fires of hell in the creature's tail, and that it could be, it might be...

There's always the escape tower.

Sure there is.

Anyway, there you have it, the simplest motivation in the world. The sense of incompletion is not for the past, but for the future.

"Sun's pretty brutal here sometimes," Dan was saying. "Maybe you should have a hat on."

Burnett laughed and took off his sunglasses and wiped the sweat-damp out of his eyes. "Don't sell the old man short just yet. I can still break you in two." He put the glasses on again and strode strongly, cleanly, beside Dan. Behind them the rocket stood with its head in the sky.

In the common room of the astronauts' quarters they found some of the others, Shontz who was going with Dan, and Crider who was back-up man, and three or four more of the team. Others had already left for the global tracking stations where they would sweat out the flight with Dan and Shontz. They were all stamped out of much the same mold as Dan, and that wasn't a bad one, Burnett thought, not bad at all. Most of them had visited in his house. Three of them had even read his stories before they ever met either him or Dan. Now, of course, they all had. It seemed to delight them that they had on their team a top boy whose father was a writer of science fiction. He had no doubt that they had many a private joke about that, but all the same they greeted him with pleasure, and he was glad of them, because he needed some distraction to forget the coldness that was in him.

"Hey!" they said. "Here's the old expert himself. Hi, Jim, how goes it?"

"I came down," he told them, "to make sure you were doing everything according to the way we wrote it."

They grinned. "Well, how does it look to an old pro?" asked Crider.

Burnett pulled his mouth down and looked judicial. "Pretty good, except for one small detail."

"What's that?"

"The markings on the rocket. You ought to paint them up brighter, good strong reds and yellows so they'll show up against that deep, black, velvety, star-shot space."

Shontz said, "I had a better idea, I wanted the top brass to paint the rocket black velvet and star-shot so Them Out There couldn't see us going by. But the generals only looked at us kind of funny."

"Illiterates," said a tall solemn-faced young man named Martin. He was one of the three who had read Burnett's stories. "Cut my teeth on them," he had said, making Burnett feel more ancient than overjoyed.

"Right," said Crider. "I doubt if they ever even watched Captain Marvel."

"That's the trouble," said Fisher, "with a lot of people in Washington." Fisher was round-faced and sunburned and cheerful, and he too had cut his teeth on Burnett's stories. "When they were kids they never read anything but Captain Billy's Whiz Bang, and that's why they keep coming out with questions like, Why put a man on the Moon?"

"Oh, well," said Burnett, "that's nothing new. People said that to Columbus. Fortunately, there's always some idiot who won't listen to reason."

Crider held up his right hand. "Fellow idiots, I salute you."

Burnett laughed. He felt better now. Because they were so relaxed and unworried he could loosen up too.

"Don't get smart with me," he said. "I wrote the lot of you. When you were drooling in your cribs I was making you up out of ink and sweat and the necessity to pay the bills. And what did you do, you ungrateful little bastards? You all came true."

"What are you working on now?" asked Martin. "You going to do that sequel to 'Child of a Thousand Suns'? That was a great story."

"Depends," said Burnett. "If you'll promise to keep the hell out of the Hercules Cluster just long enough for me to get the book written..." He counted on his fingers. "Serialization, hard-cover, soft-cover...Three years at a minimum. Can you do that?"

"For you, Jim," said Fisher, "we'll hold ourselves back."

"Okay, then. But I tell you, it isn't funny. These probes peering around Mars and Venus and blabbing everything they know, and some smart-assed scientist coming up every day with a new breakthrough in psionics or cryogenics or see-tee or FTL drives...it's getting tough. Nowadays I have to know what I'm talking about, instead of just elaborating on a theory or making something up out of my own head. And now my own kid going to the Moon so he can come back and tell me what it's really like, and there will go a dozen more stories I can't write."

Talking, just talking, but the talk and the hearty, grinning young faces did him good and the coldness in him was gone...

"Have faith, Dad," said Dan. "I'll find you something down in the caverns. A dead city. Or at the least an abandoned galactic outpost."

"Well, why not?" said Burnett. "Everything else has happened."

He grinned back at them. "I'll tell you one thing, science fiction is a tough living but I'm glad it all came true while I was around to see it, and to see how the people who laughed at such childish nonsense took it. The look of blank shock on their little faces when Sputnik first went up, and the lovely horror that crept over them as they gradually began to realize that Out There is a really big place..."

He was not just talking now, he felt a throb of excitement and pride that his own flesh and blood was a part of this future that had so suddenly become the present.

They talked some more and then it was time to go, and he said goodbye to Dan as casually as though the boy was taking a shuttle hop between Cleveland and Pittsburgh, and he went away. Only once, when he looked back at the rocket, very distant now like a white finger pointing skyward, did the fear wrench at his guts again.

He flew home that night to Cartersburg, in central Ohio. He sat up very late talking to his wife, telling her about Dan, how he had looked and what he had said and how he, Jim, thought Dan was really feeling.

"Happy as a clam at high tide," he told her. "You should have come with me, Sally. I told you that."

"No," she said. "I didn't want to go."

Her face was as calm and relaxed as Dan's had been, but there was a note in her voice that made him put his arms around her and kiss her.

"Quit worrying, honey. Dan's not worried, and he's the one that's doing it."

"That's just it," she said. "He's doing it."

Burnett had an extra drink or two to sleep on. Even so he did not sleep well. And in the morning there were the reporters.

Burnett was beginning to not like reporters. Some of them were friendly guys, and some were just guys doing a job, but there were others... especially those who thought it intriguing that a science fiction writer should have fathered an astronaut.

"Tell me, Mr. Burnett, when you first started to write science fiction, did you really believe it would all happen?"

"That question's a little sloppy, isn't it?" said Burnett. "If you mean, did I think space-travel would happen...yes, I did."

"I've been reading some of your early stories. Managed to get hold of some of the old magazines..."

"Good for you. Some of them are selling for nearly as much as I got for the stories. Go ahead."

"Well, Mr. Burnett, not only in your stories but in almost all the others, I was struck by the faith in space-travel they showed. Tell me, do you think the science fiction you chaps wrote helped make space-travel come true?"

Burnett snorted. "Let's be realistic. The big reason why rockets are going out now, instead of a century from now, is because two great nations are each afraid the other will get an advantage."

"But you feel that science fiction did *something* to bring it about, don't you?"

"Well," said Burnett. "You could say that it encouraged unorthodox thinking and sort of prepared the mental climate a little for what was coming."

The reporter had finally made his point and seized triumphantly upon it. "So that one might say that the stories you wrote years ago are partly responsible for the fact that your son is going to the Moon?"

The coldness came back into Burnett. He said flatly, "One might say that if one wanted some soppy human interest angle to add to the coverage of the moonflight, but there's not any truth in it."

The reporter smiled. "Come now, Mr. Burnett, your stories surely had some influence on Dan in making his choice of a career. I mean, having been exposed to these stories all his life, reading them, listening to you talk...wouldn't all that sort of urge him into it?"

"It would not and it did not," said Burnett. He opened the door. "And now if you'll excuse me, I've got a lot of work to do."

When he shut the door, he locked it. Sally had gone off somewhere to avoid the whole thing and the house was quiet. He walked through it to the back garden and stood there staring hard at some red flowers and smoking until he could hold his hand steady again.

"Oh, well," he said aloud, "forget it."

He went back into the house, to his own room, his workroom—he had never called it a study because he didn't study in it, he only worked—and shut the door and sat down in front of his typewriter. There was a half-written page in it, and six pages of copy beside it, the groping and much x-ed-out unfinished first chapter to the sequel of "Child of a Thousand Suns." He read the last page, and then the page in the typewriter, and he put his hands on the keyboard.

A very long time later he sighed and began almost mechanically to type.

Later still Sally came in and found him sitting. He had taken that page out of the typewriter but he had not put another one in, and he was just sitting there.

"Troubles?" asked Sally.

"Can't seem to get the thing going, is all."

She shook him gently by the shoulder. "Come and have a drink, and then let's get the hell out of this house for a while."

She did not often talk like that. He nodded, getting up. "Drive in the country might do us good. And maybe a movie tonight." Anything at all to get our minds off the fact that tomorrow morning is lift-off if the weather is right. Already Dan has slipped out of our grasp into the strange seclusions of the final briefing.

"Did I urge him?" he said suddenly. "Did I, Sally? Ever?"

She looked at him startled, and then she shook her head decisively. "No, Jim, you never did. He just naturally had to go and do this. So forget it."

Sure. Forget it.

But Dan did get his horizons stretched young. And who's to say what minute seed dropped so carelessly along the way, a single word perhaps, written for two cents or one cent or half a cent, and long forgotten, may by devious ways have led the boy to that little steel room atop a skyrocket?

You might as well forget it, for there's nothing you can do.

They had the drive in the country, and they ate something, and they went to the movie, and then there was nothing to do but go home and go to bed. Sally went to bed, anyway. He did not know if she slept. He himself stayed up, sitting in his workroom alone with his typewriter and a bottle.

All around him on the walls were the framed originals of cover paintings and interior illustrations from his stories. There was one from "Stardream", written long before Dan was born, showing a beautiful white rocket in space, with Mars in the background. Underneath the pictures were rows of shelves filled with the end results of more than thirty years of writing, marching battalions of yellowing pulps a little frayed at the corners, paperbacks, the respectable hardcovers with their shiny jackets. This room was himself, an outer carapace compounded from his needs and his dreams, the full times when his mind flowered ideas like a spring river and the times of drought when nothing came at all, and always the work which he loved and without which he would cease to be Jim Burnett.

He looked at the empty typewriter and the pages beside it and he thought that if he was going to sit up all night, he ought to go on with the story. What was it that Henry had said, years ago…."A professional is a writer who can tell a story when he doesn't feel like telling a story." That was true, but even for an old pro, there were times….

At some time during the dark hours Burnett fell asleep on the couch and dreamed that he was standing outside the closed hatch of the capsule, pounding on it and calling Dan's name. He couldn't get it open, and he walked angrily around until he could look in through the port and see Dan lying there in the recoil chair, a suited dummy with a glittering plastic head, his gloved hands flicking at rows of toggles and colored levers with a cool unhurried efficiency that was unpleasantly robot-like. "Dan," he shouted. "Dan, let me in, you can't go off without me." Inside the plastic helmet he saw Dan's head turn briefly, though his hands never stopped from arranging the toggles and levers. He saw Dan's face smiling at him, a fond but somehow detached smile, and he saw the head shake just a shade impatiently. And he heard Dan answer, "I'm sorry, Dad, I can't stop now, I've got a deadline." A shield or curtain, or perhaps a cloud of vapor from the liquid hydrogen moved across the port and he couldn't see Dan anymore, and when he hammered on the hatch again he was unable to strike it hard enough to make the slightest sound.

Without warning, then, he was a long distance away and the rocket was going up, and he was still shouting, "Dan, Dan, let me in!" His voice was swallowed up in thunder. He began to cry with rage and frustration and the sound of his tears was like rain falling.

He woke to find that it was morning and a small thunderstorm was moving through, one of those little indecisive ones that change nothing. He got up rustily, wondering what the hell that dream was all about, and then looked at his watch. A little less than two hours to launch.

He had one quick one to untie the knots in his stomach and then put the bottle away. Whatever happened, he would watch it sober.

Damned queer dream, though. He hadn't been worried at all, only angry.

Sally was already up and had the coffee on. There were dark smudges under her eyes and the age-lines seemed to stand out clearer this morning than they usually did, not that Sally was old but she wasn't twenty any more either, and this morning it showed.

"Cheer up," he said, kissing her. "They've done this before, you know. Like eight times, and they haven't lost anybody yet." Immediately, superstitiously, he was sorry he had said it. He began to laugh rather too loudly. "If I know Dan," he said, "if I know that kid, he's sitting in that capsule cooler than a polar bear's nose in January, the only man in the country that isn't…"

He shut up too abruptly, and the phone rang. *The* phone. They had long ago shut off the regular one, silencing the impossible number of relatives and friends and wellwishers and reporters and plain pests, and this one that rang was a private thing between them and the Cape. He picked it up and listened, watching Sally standing frozen in mid-floor with a cup in her hands, and then he said, Thank you, and put it down.

"That was Major Quidley. Everything's Go except the weather. But they think the cloud-cover will pass. Dan's fine. He sends his love."—

Sally nodded.

"We'll know right away if they call off the shot."

"I hope they don't," Sally said flatly. "I don't think I could start this all over again."

They took their coffee and went into the living room and turned on the television and there it was, alone and splendid in the midst of the deserted field, the white flanks gleaming softly, touched around with little nervous spurts of vapor, and high above, so high, so small atop that looming shaft, the capsule thrust impatiently toward the clouds.

And Dan was in there, suited, helmeted, locked away now from man and parent earth, waiting, watching the sky and listening for the word that would send him riding the thunder, bridling the lightning with sure hands, out into the still black immensity where the stars....

Oh, Christ. Word stuff, paper stuff, and that's neither words nor paper in that goddam little coffin, that's my son, my kid, my little dirty gap-toothed boy with the torn britches and the scabs on his knees, and he wasn't ever intended to ride thunder and bridle lightning, no man is. Pulp heroes were all made of wood and they could do it, but Dan's human and soft and easily broken. He hasn't any business there, no man has.

And yet in that fool dream I was mad because I couldn't go too.

T-minus forty and holding. Perhaps they'll call it off....

Announcers' faces, saying this and that, stalling, filling up time, making ponderous statements. Personages making ponderous statements. Faces of people, mobs of people with kids and lunches and bottles of pop and deck chairs and field glasses and tight capri pants and crazy hats that wanted to blow off in the wind, all watching.

"They make me sick at my stomach," he snarled. "What the hell do they think this is, a picnic?"

"They're all with us, Jim. They're pulling for him. And for Shontz."

Burnett subsided, ashamed. "Okay," he grumbled, "but do they have to drink orange soda?"

The announcer pushed his headphone closer to his ear and listened. "The count is on again, ladies and gentlemen, T-minus thirty-nine now and counting. All systems are Go, the cloud-cover is beginning to break up, and there comes the sun..."

The announcer vanished and the rocket was there again. The sun struck hard on the white flanks, the sharp uplifted nose.

Dan would feel that striking of the sun.

T-minus thirty and counting.

I wish I could write this instead of watching it, Burnett thought. I've written it a hundred, two hundred, times. The ship rising up on the hammering flames, rising steady, rising strong, a white arrow shafting on a tail of fire, and you know when you write it that it's going to do just that because you say so, and plunge on into the free wide darkness of space and go where you damned well tell her to without any trouble.

T-minus twenty and counting.

I wish, thought Burnett, I wish....

He did not know what he wished. He sat and stared at the screen, and was only dimly aware when Sally got up from beside him and left the room.

Ten. Nine. And that's science fiction too, that countdown going backwards, somebody did it in a movie or a story decades ago because he thought it would be a nice touch. And here they are doing it.

With my kid.

Three, two, one, ignition, the white smoke bursting in mushrooming clouds from beneath the rocket, but nothing happening, nothing at all happening. But it is, the whole thing's starting to rise, only why does it seem so much slower than the others I watched, what's wrong, what the hell is wrong...

Nothing. Nothing's wrong, yet. It's still going up, and maybe it only seems slower than the other times. But where are all the emotions I was sure I was going to feel, after writing it so many times? Why do I just sit here with my eyes bugging and the palms of my hands sweating, shaking a little, not very much but a little...

Through the static roar and the chatter, Dan's voice cutting in, calm and quick. All systems Go, it looks good, how does it look down there? Good, that's good...

Burnett felt an unreasonable flash of pure resentment. How can he be so calm about it when we're sweating our hearts out down here? Doesn't he give a damn?

"Separation okay...second-stage ignition okay...all okay..." the level voice went on.

And Burnett suddenly knew the answer to his resentful wonder. He's calm because he's doing the job he's trained for. Dan's the pro, not me. All we writers who daydreamed and babbled and wrote about space, we were just amateurs, but now the real pros have come, the tanned, placid young men who don't babble about space but who go up and take hold of it...

And the white arrow went on upward, and the voices talked about it, and it was out of sight.

Sally came back into the room.

"It was a perfect shot," he said. And added, for no reason he could think of, "He's gone."

Sally sat down in a chair, not saying anything, and Burnett thought, What kind of dialogue is that for a man who's just seen his son shot into space?

The voices went on, but the tension was going out of them now, it looks good, it looks very good, it *is* good, they're on their way...

Burnett reached out and snapped off the television. As though it had been waiting for the silence, the phone rang again.

"You take it, honey," he said, getting up. "Everything's okay for now, at least....I might as well get back to work."

Sally gave him a smile, the kind of a smile a wife gives her husband when she sees all through his pretenses but wants to tell him, It's all right, go on pretending, it's all right with me.

Burnett went into his workroom and closed the door. He took up the bottle in his hands and sat down in his padded chair in front of the typewriter with the empty roller and the neat stack of clean yellow sheets on one side and the thin pile of manuscript on the other. He looked at it, and he turned and looked at the shelves where thirty years of magazines and books and dreams and love and sweat and black disappointment were lined up stiff and still like paper corpses.

"Your stories surely had some influence on Dan in making the choice of his career?"

"No," said Burnett loudly, and drank.

"Wouldn't all that sort of urge him into it...your son...going to the Moon..."

He put the cork in the bottle and set it aside. He stood up and walked to the shelves and stood by them, looking, picking out one thing and then another, the bright covers with the spaceships and the men and girls in their suits and helmets, and the painted stars and planets.

He put them back neatly into their places. His shoulders sagged a little, and then he beat his fist softly against the shelves of silent paper.

"Damn you," he whispered. "Damn you, damn you..."

Castaway

It seemed to him that Broadway had never looked so depressing as in this early winter twilight, with the gas lamps yet unlit and the remnants of old poplars stirring sluggishly in a cold wind. Hoofs and wheels slapped over the cracked paving, and a tentative flake of snow drifted down.

He thought that any place would be better than this, Richmond, Charleston, even Philadelphia. But they had really been no better, he had wearied of them all. He always wearied of places, even of most people. Perhaps it was just today's disappointment, after all the other disappointments, that made him feel this way.

He reached and entered the shabby little two-room office, and the faded little man writing at a desk looked up quickly, with a dim hope.

"No. Nothing."

The hope—there had not been much—left the face of the other. He muttered, "We can't keep going much longer." Then he said, "There's a young lady to see you. She's waiting in your office."

"I am in no mood to write in young ladies' autograph albums."

"But—she is quite a wealthy-looking young lady...."

Poe smiled his white, twisted, sarcastic smile. "I see. And wealthy young ladies have wealthy papas, who might be induced to invest in a dying literary magazine."

But when he went into the inner office, he was all the courteous Virginian as he bowed to the seated girl.

"I am most honored, Miss..."

She did not raise her eyes as she murmured, "Ellen Donsel."

She was expensively dressed, from her fur-lined cloak to her blue rohan bonnet. Her face was plump, pink, and stupid-looking. Then she looked up at him, and Poe felt surprise. The eyes in that round face were blazing, vibrant with life and intelligence.

"I suppose," he said, "that you wish me to read my poems at some gathering, a thing which I have not the time to do. Or perhaps it's a copy of 'The Raven' in my own handwriting—"

"No," she said. "I have a message for you."

Poe looked polite inquiry. "Yes?"

"A message from...Aarn."

The word seemed to hang in the air, echoing like a distant bell, and for a moment neither spoke and he could hear the clip-clop of traffic out in the street.

"Aarn," he repeated, finally. "Now, that is a fine, sonorous name. Whose is it?"

"It's not a person," said Miss Donsel. "It's a place."

"Ah," said Poe. "And where may this place be?"

Her gaze stabbed him. "Don't you remember?"

He began to feel a little uneasy. Because he had written stories of the fantastic, cranks and mentally unbalanced people tended to seek him out. This girl looked normal, even commonplace. Yet the intensity of her eyes...

"I'm sorry," he said. "I have not heard the name before."

"Have you heard the name Lalu?" she said. "It's my name. Or the name Yann? It's *your* name. And we came from Aarn, though you came long before I did."

Poe smiled guardedly. "This fancy of yours is a rare one, madam. Tell me...what is it like, this place we came from?"

"It lies in the great bay of the purple mountains." Her eyes never left his. "And the river Zair flows down through the mountains, and the towers of Aarn loom above it in the sunset..."

He suddenly interrupted her with a bursting laugh. Then he declaimed, "...glittering in the red sunlight with a hundred oriels, minarets, and pinnacles; and seeming the phantom handiwork, conjointly, of the sylphs, of the fairies, of the genii, and of the gnomes."

He laughed again, shaking his head. "That is the conclusion of my tale of 'The Domain of Arnheim.' Of course...Aarn...Arnheim. And you got the name Lalu from my Ulalume, and Yann from my Yaanek...why, madam, I must congratulate you on your cleverness."

"No," she said. And again, "No. It was quite the other way around, Mr. Poe. You got *your* names from those I have just spoken."

He regarded the girl with interest. He had not had an experience quite like this one before, and was intrigued.

"So I came from Aarn, did I? Then why don't I remember it?"

"You do, a little," she murmured. "You remember the place—almost. You remembered the names—almost. You put them into your stories and poems."

His interest heightened. This girl might look like a fool—except for those intense eyes—but she obviously had an unusual imagination.

"Where, then, is Aarn? On the other side of the world? In the garden of the Hesperides?"

"Quite near here, Mr. Poe. In space, that is. But not in time. It is a long way in the future."

"Then you...and I, you say...came from the future to the present. My dear young lady, it is you who should be writing tales of fantasy, not I!"

Her level gaze did not change. "You did write it. In the tale of the Ragged Mountain, About the man who went back through time for a little while."

"Why," said Poe, "so I did, now I think of it. I had forgotten that clumsy effort. But that was just a freakish fancy."

"Was it? Was it only chance that made you write of traveling in time, a thing no one had ever seriously written of before? Or was it a suppressed memory?"

"I wish it were so," he said. "I assure you that I am not in love with this nineteenth century. But, unfortunately, I can remember my whole life quite clearly, and I have no memories of Aarn."

"That is Mr. Poe speaking," the girl said. "He remembers only his own life. But you are not only Mr. Poe, you are also Yann."

He smiled. "Two people in one body? Tell me, Miss Donsel, have you read my 'William Wilson'? It tells of a man with two personalities, an alter ego—"

"I've read it," she said. "And I know that you wrote it because you *have* two personalities, though one of them you cannot remember."

She leaned forward, and he thought that her eyes were more compelling than those of the mesmerists in whom he had been so interested. Her voice was almost a whisper.

"I want to make you remember. I will make you remember. It's why I came after you...."

"Speaking of that, how does one travel temporally?" he interrupted, trying to keep to lightness. "In a flying machine of some sort?"

Her face remained dead serious. "The body cannot move in time. No physical, material object can. But the mind is not material, it is a web of electric force locked into the physical brain. If the mind can be unlocked from the brain, it—being pure force—can be hurled back along the dimension of time and lock itself into the brain of a man of a former age."

"But to what purpose?"

"To the purpose of dominating that brain and body and investigating the historical past through the eyes of a man living in that past. It is not easy to do and there is *danger* in it—the danger of selecting a host whose mind is so powerful that it dominates its visitant. And that is what happened to Yann, Mr. Poe—he is in your brain but dominated, numbed, affecting only your subconscious and giving it half-memories that you think are dreams and fancies."

She added, "You must have a powerful mind indeed, Mr. Poe, so to dominate Yann."

"I've been called many things but not a dullard," he said, and then, with an ironical wave of his hand around the shabby office, "You see the heights to which my intellect has brought me."

"It has happened before," she murmured. "One of us was trapped in the brain of a Roman poet named Lucretius...."

"Titus Lucretius Carus? Why, madam, I've read his *De Rerum Natura*, and its strange theories of an atomic science."

"Not theories," she insisted. "Half-memories. They so tormented him that he killed himself. And there were others, in other levels of time."

Poe said, admiringly, "A bizarre idea, that. It would certainly make a tale...."

She interrupted. "I am speaking to you, Mr. Poe, but I am trying to speak to Yann. To awaken him from his numbed captivity in your brain, to make him remember Aarn."

She went on, rapidly, almost fiercely, and all the time her eyes held his. And he listened in fascination as the names and places and things of his tales came into her speech, sometimes altered, sometimes unchanged, all woven into a fabric by this girl's impassioned imagination.

"There was—or I should say, here and now, that there *will* be, an Age of Violence beyond anything the world has known. And the climax of it will be a setting loose of fiery forces that will wreak unprecedented destruction."

337

Poe thought of his own tale in which mankind had perished in a worldwide explosion of flame, and the girl seemed to catch the thought from the half-smile on his face.

"Oh, not all of humanity were—or will be—destroyed. But many, many, and when the Age of Violence passed, there were thousands where there had been millions. So our world, of centuries from now, the world in which Aarn lives, is not the crowded, bustling place that this one is.

"Yann, *remember!* Remember our beautiful, clean, uncrowded world! Remember the day that we drifted down the Zair in your boat, all the way from the mountains. Down the yellow waters with the great water lilies about us, and the forest dark and somber beyond them, all the way until above Aarn we came to the Valley of Many-Colored Grass, and walked there amid the silver trees and looked down on the fliers skimming in the sunlight above the towers of Aarn.

"Don't you remember? That was when you first told me that you had been to the Temporal Laboratory at Tsalal, and had volunteered for the going-back. You would go back to a time not long before the Age of Violence, and would see the world as it was before the great wars shattered it, would see through the eyes of another man all the things that had been lost to history in the devastation.

"Do you remember my tears? How I begged you not to go, how I reminded you of those who had never come back, how I clung to you? But your historical researches had so obsessed you that you would not listen. And so you went. And it was as I had feared, and you did not come back.

"Yann, this is Lalu speaking! Do you know what a torture it can be to wait? Until finally I could bear it no longer and won permission from the Temporal Laboratory to come back to this time and search for you. And the weeks I've been here, in another person's body, seeking in vain, until at last I found the clue, found the names that we knew in Aarn in tales that had become famous, and knew that only the writer of them could be your host. *Yann!*"

Poe had listened, half-dreaming, as the names from his own fancied worlds had floated on the air. But that final shrill cry of agonized appeal brought him to his feet.

"My dear Miss Donsel! I do greatly admire your imaginings, but you must control yourself—"

Her eyes flamed. "Control myself? What have I been doing all these weeks, in this ugly and terrible world, confined in the body of this meaty girl?"

A cold shock stabbed through him at those words. No woman, not even in jest, would think of herself or speak of herself in that way. But then it must mean...

The room, the angry face, everything, seemed to waver, as though under water. He felt a strangeness rise in him, the world seemed to fall away from him, and for a moment his old dreams seemed to rise into reality around him, changed but real.

"Yann?"

Was the girl smiling? Of course, the minx was succeeding in hoodwinking the famous Mr. Poe with moonbeams and nonsense, and would happily tell all her little friends about it! The pride and arrogance that were deep in his nature made him stiffen, and the strangeness ebbed.

"I regret," he said, "that I cannot devote more time now to your ingenious *jeu d'esprit*, Miss Donsel. I can only thank you for the assiduousness with which you have studied my little tales."

He opened the door, and bowed to her. She stood up, and her face was not smiling now, but stricken.

"No use," she whispered, finally. "No use at all."

She looked at him, and said in a low voice, "Goodbye, Yann," and closed her eyes.

Poe stepped toward her. "My dear young lady, please..."

Her eyes opened again. He stopped short. All the intense life and intelligence had gone out of those eyes, and she stared at him with a stupid, goggling gaze.

"What?" she said. "Who..."

"My dear Miss Donsel..." he began again.

She uttered a squawking scream. She backed away from him, and put her hands up to her face, and stared at him as though he were the devil.

"What happened?" she cried. "I...everything went away...I went asleep in the middle of the day...How did I...? What am I doing...here?"

So that was it, he thought. Of course! Having played the part of the imaginary Lalu, she must now mime it out that her visitant had left her.

He said, smiling acidly, "I congratulate you, not only on your imagination but on your acting abilities."

She paid no heed to him at all. She ran past him and tore open the door. It was late, and his assistant had gone home, and by the time Poe followed her into the other office, Miss Donsel had run out into the street.

He hurried after her. The gas street lamps were on, but in the passing traffic he could not at first see her. Then he heard her shrill call, and saw her climbing into a public cab that had pulled up. He started after her, and saw her face, eyes round with terror, looking back at him the moment before she disappeared into the cab. The driver spoke to his horses and the cab went on.

Poe, always short of temper, felt an angry impatience. He had let himself be made a fool of, even to listen to that chit and her clever beguilings. Probably by now she was mirthfully triumphant.

And yet...

He walked back to the office. Thin flakes of snow were drifting down in the sickly yellow of the lamps, and the dust in the street was beginning to turn to greasy mud. The raw wind brought the sound of brawling voices from further along the street.

"This ugly and terrible world..." Well, it had often seemed so to him, and tonight it grimaced more repellently than ever. He supposed it was because of all the airy fancies of the sunset towers of Aarn that the girl had picked from his own book and stuffed into his ears.

He went back into his office and sat down at the desk. As his anger cooled a little, he wondered again if there was not a tale in all that artful nonsense? But it so echoed all his other stories that they would say he was repeating himself. Yet still, the idea was intriguing—the man lost out of his time...

"I have reached these lands but newly, from an ultimate dim Thule, from a wild, weird clime that lieth sublime, out of Space, out of Time....

"Did I write those lines? Or....did Yann?"

For a moment Poe's face yearned, haggard and haunted. If it were true, if beyond tomorrow was a finer world, Thule, Aarn, Tsalal? If the phantom, lovely shape he could never quite see, Ulalume, Lenore, Morella, Ligeia, was a memory...

He wanted to believe, but he could not, he must not. He was a man of reason and a thing like this if believed could shatter reason, could kill a man.

It would not kill him.

It would *not*.

With a hand that trembled only slightly, he opened the desk and reached in for the bottle.

Afterword

W hen Leigh was asked to choose and edit a selection of my past stories, I simply opened up my files and told her, "There they are, over
three hundred of them. You can take your pick."

I then added, "Don't look so dismayed! Half or more of those stories
are novels or novelettes too long for a collection, so you don't have to read
them *all!*"

So here are her choices. And, reading over these stories of many years,
I have been surprised to find that in the case of many of them, the story
itself is not as clear in my memory as the time and place of its writing.
Some quirk of association brings the when and where and how of the
tales vividly to mind.

The old Interstellar Patrol and other star-war series I wrote in the period 1927-1930 had their genesis in the cold winter of 1927. Living in a
small Western Pennsylvania city, I hesitated to take my first car (it was
a Model-T roadster) out on the icy streets, and of nights would walk the
mile and a bit to downtown, rather than drive.

Very clear in my mind is the walk home on the dark, long, ice-sheathed
streets, with the great belt of Orion and the Pleiades burning in frosty
splendor above the roofs. Dreaming of them as huge and awesome suns,
I visualized a far-future civilization that would web the star-worlds. It
would require a long-reaching arm of law and order to deal with cosmic
menace—and there began the Patrol.

I could not get this, to me, staggering vision down on paper fast
enough. I well remember that, working on a big old flat-top desk on a

small portable typewriter, my feverish banging on the keyboard when I came to the great space-battles made the little machine "walk" all over the desk—and how I would get up from my chair and follow the type-writer, still banging away in my excitement.

In the same way, I recall with perfect clarity the circumstances of writing the first version of "What's It Like Out There?" That was in 1933, when Jack Williamson and I had rented for the winter a five-room bungalow right on South Beach, in Key West, Florida. (The rent was eight dollars a month—eat your hearts out, you vacationers of today!) At night, writing this story beside a window open to that kindly climate, I would hear a familiar rustling and turn to watch a large white milk-snake writhe his graceful way right up the screen, on his way to our roof and whatever small game he found there. I never see this story without remembering the dry, leathery rattle of the coconut-palm fronds, the sound of Jack's typewriter in another room, and the elegantly smooth gliding upward of that inoffensive and beautiful creature.

The little story "Exile" was based on the informal club of science fiction writers which, around the early 40s, used to meet weekly in Steuben's Restaurant, in midtown Manhattan. Living out of town, I was only an occasional visitor, but have never forgotten the terrific discussions we had—Manly Wade Wellman, Henry Kuttner, Otto Binder, and many others were regulars. It was there I first met Henry Kuttner, in 1940. He mentioned Catherine Moore and I cried, "C. L. Moore is one of my idols! What is she like?" Henry looked at me in his quiet fashion and murmured, "She is very nice." And a week later, Julie Schwartz wrote me that those two had just been married. Henry was the "Carrick" character of this story.

Leigh has referred to the story, "In the World's Dusk," as a science-fantasy. The fact is that it began as one, and ended as the other. I was a great admirer of the fantasies of Clark Ashton Smith, and as a change from my usual fiction, started to write a fantasy of that type. But as it progressed, it became more and more science fictional. I remember that when I told this to Smith, he laughed and said that that was the way the story had impressed him.

A writer's first story is always dear to his heart, and so is "The Monster-God of Mamurth" to mine. It was directly inspired by my great admiration for A. Merritt's classic short, "The People of the Pit." I too wanted to write a story of a man who found an alien, horror-haunted place in the wilderness. Ironically, this story was published in the same issue as the only story Merritt ever had in *Weird Tales*—the great novelette of fantasy called "The Woman of the Wood." Against such competition I was lost, but didn't mind because I did place second, in the readers' poll, to a story by one who, to me, was The Master.

Let's face it, nearly every young writer begins by a process of imitation. I can think of exceptions, among them, Ray Bradbury, whose very first efforts at fiction struck right out on his own line. But most of us do at first "play the sedulous ape," as Robert Louis Stevenson put it. It was not A. Merritt, much as I admired his work, who most influenced my own early efforts. It was an early-day writer for the Munsey magazines, Homer Eon Flint. His stories in 1918-1919, though sometimes wooden in style and heavy in conception, set my young imagination ablaze with their vaulting visions of what vast possibilities future time and space might contain. I have, through the years, often testified my debt to this now somewhat forgotten writer, and I am glad to do so again.

Sometimes the scientific extrapolation of a very old story will become a bit outdated, as in my "Conquest of Two Worlds," yet the theme may remain authentic. The space-travel and atomic-bomb anticipations in that are now obsolete. But I wonder if the central idea is. I remember that in 1932 when I dreamed it up, I had been reading a lot of stories presenting the Earthmen as always the rightful conquering heroes, and I wondered if something might not be said for an opposite view. In those days, and for many years, I did a five-mile walk every morning to get some exercise and fresh air, and I still recall how, smitten with that idea as I tramped along in the Pennsylvania hills and woods, I hurried home at such high speed that I was practically breathless when I reached my typewriter.

It seems to me that I always worked in a tearing hurry, in those days. The short story "Easy Money" (my own title for it was "The World of Psycho-Control," but that was too heavy a title for this light yarn) was written in four days which I literally stole from another job. I had agreed in 1938 to write a forty-thousand-word novel for a new magazine, *Startling Stories*. I had a bit over three weeks to do the novel, and then the idea for this short tale occurred to me and I did it first. That left me exactly twenty-one days for the novel job. And right then I joined three pals for a weekend trip from Pennsylvania to North Carolina, to see a football game. Returning weary from fun, I had eighteen days left for the novel and had to work into the small hours each night to get it done. In fact, I made it nearer fifty than forty thousand words, having so much interesting material that I felt I could not leave out. I could not work that way, these days.

And indeed, looking back upon the older of these stories, I feel that they were written by a different person. The thin, dark, wiry young Hamilton of those days seems a bit of a stranger to me, now. *He* could pound all day on the typewriter, eagerly setting down the feverish visions that filled his head—visions of wonders to come, of great dooms sweeping upon the hapless Earth, of strange and usually ominous forms of life undreamed of now, of the vast grandeur of things to come when the starry universe would be webbed by the fleets of man. I believe that that enthusiasm was what sparked me into all that work, for certainly the monetary rewards from the magazines of those days was not much incentive.

I think it was George Gissing who, recalling his youthful days of writing, said that, "On the whole, I approve of that eager, intense young man." And, in my own case, on the whole, I do too.

Edmond Hamilton, 1976

Alexei Panshin

A. A. Attanasio

Christopher Stasheff

Nancy Kress

Stephen Leigh

Carolyn Gilman

Daniel F. Galouye

Michael Flynn

& Many More

www.PhoenixPick.com

Sign up for free ebooks. New free book every month

"An instant classic."
—*The Washington Post*

Nebula Award Nominee

"RADIX is sheer pleasure to read"—*Minneapolis Tribune*

"Here stands a high talent." —*The Los Angeles Times*

Cover Art by John Bergin (award winning artist/animator)

Interior Illustrations by James O'Barr (creator of *The Crow*)

"The best, *the best*, history of science fiction I have ever read...I expect to read *The World Beyond the Hill* over and over for the rest of my life. It is an unbelievably wonderful book."—*Isaac Asimov*

Hugo Award Winner

Hardcover, 676 Pages
ISBN 978-1-60450-443-9
Index/Bibliography

The World Beyond the Hill is a unique book—a story about stories. It tells not only where science fiction came from and how it got that way, but what science fiction means.

Science fiction has been the myth of modern times. *The World Beyond the Hill* is the tale of that myth from *Frankenstein* to *Galactic Empire*.

By setting forth this evolving story, *The World Beyond the Hill* sheds light not only on what modern culture has been thinking and doing, but where we are going next and what we need to become.

"Painstaking research and wealth of fascinating detail."
—*The Washington Post*

"This **IS** the history of science fiction...My only real complaint is that it ended too soon"—*Science Fiction Chronicle*

"I learned a great deal from reading *The World Beyond the Hill*. It is an authentic history, unified by a controlling vision, rather than a simple chronicle of names, dates and events."—*Northrop Frye*

"*The World Beyond the Hill* explores the development of science fiction with an insight and cogency that, so far as my own reading goes, has never been equaled."
—*Jack Williamson*

"A tremendous job in the collection and reevaluation of material from *The Castle of Otranto* to Asimov's *The Mule*."—*Locus*

"A landmark in literary historiography."
—*L. Sprague de Camp*

CPSIA information can be obtained at www.ICGtesting.com
Printed in the USA
BVOW08s0641240915

419294BV00002B/194/P